NEWARK TO PHOENIX

A Novel by

Brian J. Rogers

This book is a work of fiction. Places, events, and situations in this story are purely fictional. Any resemblance to actual persons, living or dead, is coincidental.

First published by AuthorHouse 07/26/04

ISBN: 1-4184-5681-0 (e-book)
ISBN: 1-4184-5042-1 (Paperback)
ISBN: 1-4184-5043-X (Dust Jacket)

Library of Congress Control Number: 2003097919

Printed in the United States of America
Bloomington, Indiana

This book is printed on acid free paper.

DEDICATION

To my wife, Diana

ACKNOWLEDGEMENTS

I'd like to thank the following people for the following reasons: Anne Warren for deciphering my handwriting; Fred Regna for locating a fellow Phoenix advisor; author and newspaper columnist Mandy Bolen and Capt. Joe Weatherby, Ed Maguire and Brian Gurka for their critical input, Fran Mink for doing and re-doing my copy; authors Marjorie Soto and David Sloan for advice and comments. To Johnny and Jan Mirehiel for their initial editing, and Matthew Thornton for his review. To Brad Kennedy, author of *HEROES or Something* and Vietnam combat veteran for his insightful comments and time consuming guidance. To my wife, Diana, my children Mike and Maureen who gave me the patience, space, and understanding to complete this work.

I also want to recognize author Philip B. Davidson and his book, "Vietnam at War. The history: 1946-1975." His literary effort singularly filled in the blanks, for me, of what political and military events had occurred during our nation's life in the late 1960's. Passages taken from his book were crucial to the completion of this story.

In the end, however, it is my work and I take full responsibility for any inaccuracies, omissions and errors.

BJR

PROLOGUE

1954

The bullets cracked over the heads of the young boys and slammed into the 15-foot high cement and cinderblock wall surrounding Newark Schools Stadium on Bloomfield Ave.

They turned the corner at Roseville and 1st Avenues and started to run again. Scott grabbed Jimmy's shirt and pulled him behind a parked black Chevrolet Deluxe Sedan. They gasped hard and tried to suck air into their heaving lungs.

"Doodletown Dukes." Jimmy spit between breaths.

"Condors." Scott countered.

They couldn't agree on which local gangs fired at them.

"Zip guns."

"Yeah, zip guns."

They both agreed on the assault weapon.

"Did one of them think that we were part of the other gang?" Scott said with a hint of hopeful pride.

"Naw, we're too little. We're only nine."

"Well my mother's a teacher and she always said to stay away from the Dukes and Condors." Scott stated. "We dodged a bullet, Jimmy, so we can't tell our parents we got shot at today. They'll kill us."

"Yeah, they'll kill us for not taking the school bus and running home again instead."

Scott looked Jimmy square in the eye.

"Then we both can't tell them that we got shot at today. Ever."

"Ever." Jimmy agreed.

"Swear to God."

"I swear."

"No, swear to God."

"Swear to God."

"On your word?"

"On my word, Scott."

"You got mine, too, Jimmy."

1969

His thin black hair was as fine as corn silk. It was cut short and didn't touch the collar of the green and white shirt he wore to work every day. The shirt always flopped outside of the chino pants he got from an Australian visitor. The man with thin black hair spoke out of both sides of his mouth and his "word" wasn't worth yesterday's garbage.

It's the first week in June, near the first
quarter moon,
the summer is comin' down warm

The corn's in the ground and the vane's
goin' round,
and tells of an oncomin' storm.

David Mallett, songwriter, Maine

CHAPTER 1

"Vietnam" was a conflict that was occupying more and more
time on the nightly news, yet it still carried some alien and
temporary impression. The Captains and Lieutenant Colonels
who taught Scott Regan's ROTC classes in college only
gradually began to include this most recent hostility as part of
their curriculum. The lessons the officers imparted never
impacted on him. Aside from unquestioned religious belief,
Scott felt that if you couldn't touch, taste, smell, feel or see it
yourself, it wasn't true. He always needed a hands-on
experience. The people on his block, who composed all the
rules of right or wrong, taught this to him years ago. There was
no gray area.

In the neighborhood where Scott spent his early years the scents from the houses and the sounds from the stoops that fronted the four family dwellings were forever synonymous. On summer nights the parents formed an ad hoc safety watch. Folding aluminum chairs with plastic ribbing formed the ubiquitous thrones where the matriarchs of the families gathered to sit and watch the ritual of street activity that unfolded before them. Slim alleyways etched the boundaries between the Tobia, Vizani, Racioppi and Lepore families who had migrated from the province of Avellino in Italy. In an era when kids had to create their own amusement, the soft fading light of dusk formed the backdrop for the only form of entertainment they had. They either played on the sidewalks and street or just hung outside until it was time for them to return home and pass through the kitchens of their railroad apartments on the way to bed.

Now, years later, Scott had to decide how he was going to personally address his involvement in the *Vietnam conflict.* One of his options was to buy time by getting a deferment until a later date. In order to achieve this status his choices were like those of other potential draftees: go to graduate school, get married, become a conscientious objector, join the Peace Corps or to move north from his college campus and into Canada.

The latter option was the least probable. It would forever label him a "deserter." This term was just starting to creep into the American lexicon and was the singular reason he had never seriously entertained the thought. This alternative somehow harkened back to his days growing up whereby anybody who had squealed or ratted out another kid to an authority figure never ever got any more respect from his peers. It was that intangible commodity called your "word." If you kept it inviolate you were a stand up guy. If you didn't, nothing you said, or thought meant anything to anybody else. It was just one of the wares you carried around. You couldn't borrow it from anybody, nobody could give it to you, and nobody could take it away. In some amorphous analogy Scott felt that he would be breaking this trusted code and clearly concluded that Canada would have to function with one less U.S. citizen.

The way he saw it, he probably would wind up getting drafted unless he joined the Reserve Officers Training Corps program. This would at least afford him the chance of going into the Army as an officer plus he would get paid $40 per month for his Junior and Senior year. Either way, unless this was stopped on a dime, he was going to visit Southeast Asia. Besides as an officer he might be able to scam some cushy position in the service, do his time, and ultimately return home and carry on with his life.

CHAPTER 2

The parade of Army officers that addressed the senior year ROTC cadets were all pitching their particular branches of service.

"Bullshit, there's no way I'm going to pick any of the combat branches!" Scott exclaimed to his pal Frank.

"How are you NOT gonna' pick a combat branch?" Frank was one of those guys who knew all the rules to things nobody cared about, like cricket. However, in this instance he was familiar with Army protocol since his older brother was a Lt. Colonel in the 82nd Airborne on his second tour in 'Nam. He was also the oracle for Frank that shed some light on the Byzantine byways of Army logic, acronyms and, of course, rules.

Frank continued. "What's gonna' happen is this. The different branches in the Army will pitch us to go with them when we get commissioned. We'll hear from the combat branches first – Infantry, Armor, Artillery. Next we'll listen to the non-combat branches like the Signal Corps, Quartermaster Corp and…"

"What's the Quartermaster Corps?" Scott interrupted.

"I'm not too sure what they do."

Frank took a second to try and recollect. "I think my brother told me they wash, count and fold all the sheets, blankets, and pillows in the whole damn Army."

"Fold sheets?" Scott's voice raised a full octave. "There are sheets wherever the Army is and the Army's all over the globe. I could love folding sheets in Ft. Monmouth or Thule, Greenland. I'll tell ya' right now," he continued with self - preservational passion, "when that guy from the Quartermaster Corps comes to sell us, I'm gonna' be draped in a toga like I was born to fold."

Little did Scott know that there was an even more alluring military salesman waiting to present himself. The Quartermaster sheet- folding representative would pale in comparison to the dapper merchant who would later show up on campus.

CHAPTER 3

While the ROTC cadets were engaged in the benign exercise of choosing their branches, President Lyndon Johnson turned up the heat on air strikes into North Vietnam. The bombing campaign was aptly named ROLLING THUNDER, and with the authorization of increased attack sorties, the level of "target pain" rose substantially for the North Vietnamese people.

It was from this enfeebling and incessant pounding that the NVN Politburo in Hanoi started to lay the groundwork for a massive retaliation against U.S. troops that would be forthcoming within the next 12 months.

****

The room was full of fuzzy-haired look-alikes when Captain Rheingold stepped to the podium. His Class "A" uniform was bedecked with more ribbons than Scott had ever seen on a float in the Columbus Day Parade. Despite the garden salad of colors he wore on his chest, Scott couldn't help being distracted by the shiny black patch that covered the officer's left eye. His right eye was steel blue and focused on the audience like an off-center cyclopstic beam. It mesmerized him for a moment until Rheingold began to speak.

7

"Gentlemen," he started, "you have chosen the ROTC as the launching point for your military commitment. The Reserve Officers Training Corps enables you to select various fields of participation whereby you, as well as thousands of others, can help to ensure that democracy will always be an option for all people in all countries for all time."

He shifted his position at the podium. "As you are well aware there currently is a conflict in Southeast Asia that requires only the most motivated and dedicated personnel to participate in its inevitable successful resolution. In the vanguard of this effort is the U.S. Infantry. However, the Infantry does not serve in Southeast Asia alone."

"Bullshit," Scott thought.

"If you choose, and if you are accepted into the Infantry, you will be asked to select three geographical areas of operation where you would prefer to be stationed."

"Oh," Scott questioned to himself, "how about I pick Hawaii, which is close enough to Vietnam to be patriotic, Ireland and Italy, which are not close but would do nicely?" He would later realize that these ostensible choices were referred to as the "dream sheet," because the Army almost never gave you the locations you picked.

The one blue eye continued. "These three area preferences that you choose will be analyzed both as to your ultimate effectiveness in the U.S. Army's world wide presence and where the military schooling that you receive could best be implemented."

Scott nudged his buddy, Frank, and noted in a whisper, "This 'best be implemented' shit worries me. It sounds like it'll best be implemented where they shoot at you."

Frank grunted.

When the 45- minute dissertation finally concluded, the class was mercifully dismissed and every student bolted for the doors like they were escaping a flash flood.

Scott and Frank had a real case of Friday thirst and like lemmings to the sea headed to the Ontario House, located off campus and in a shoddy part of town, to digest what they heard and ingest the beer they served at "happy hour."

Happy hour at the O.H. started when they opened and concluded when they closed. The metal ashtrays, in order not to become weapons, were bolted to the bar. Ten 7 oz. beers cost a dollar. In order to conform to the local liquor laws that required food to be served, potato chips were available and one hot dog rotisserie spun greasy "tube steaks." One rest room without a door lock accommodated the two genders. To say it was far from posh was the quintessential compliment, but the price was right and was designed for both college kids and locals with little money.

"Hi, Josie," Frank and Scott said as they sidled onto the rickety stools in front of the worn oak bar. "Give us ten and two" – ten beers and two shots of Three Feathers whiskey. It was always smart to have a drinking buddy with you when you visited Josie. That way you had five cold beers and he had five cold beers instead of ten beers that got warm and flat. This didn't stop the locals who just liked cheap beer no matter if it got flat or warm.

"So, what did you think of Cpt. Eye Patch today?" Frank's tone sounded like he was impressed.

"I think you should let your brother be the hero in your family. He already has a headstart on you. Let him get the fuckin' medals and you just jump in the picture with your Quartermaster uniform on."

Scott turned away on his stool and noticed a silhouette in the doorway that framed the sunlight pouring in around it. He stopped in mid thought and grabbed Frank by the elbow.

"Hey, check it out. Here's Eye Patch." Cpt. Rheingold still wore his uniform and looked somewhat out of place in a bar where blue collar working men, college kids and Tuscarora Indians drank.

"Oh, man, I want to talk to this guy," Frank said.

"Why?" Scott started to ask as Frank grabbed his four beers and shot of booze and worked his way toward the captain. They both sat down almost simultaneously. Frank immediately started in.

"Captain, I'm Frank Calabrese and I was in your class today when you spoke to us about joining the Infantry."

His head turned slowly as he asked, "So what *do you think* about joining the Infantry?"

That was just the opening that Frank needed and he proceeded to recount his family's history. It included his father's participation with the 101st Airborne Division at Normandy, his brother's second tour in 'Nam, his mother constantly glued to the T.V. in an attempt to keep informed on conditions in a land billions of miles away from Douglaston, Queens.

Scott was getting bored and, as a diversion, decided to urinate. When he returned from the gender-neutral toilet, Frank was rambling on about his family's connection to the Combat Infantry. Scott stood next to them and listened.

"Shit," Scott thought. "If he was born anywhere south of the Mason-Dixon Line, he would be spewing his great-granddaddy's contribution to the battle of Shiloh. He wouldn't know a damn thing about his ethnic heritage, but would be able to recant every step his forefather had toward the "Hornet's Nest." In the middle of Frank's elaboration and in an attempt to divert the conversation, Captain Rheingold turned to Scott and asked, "So what do *you* think about joining the Infantry?" This was an opening that Scott couldn't resist.

"Well, Cap, let me answer it this way. I have absolutely no interest in joining any group where my functioning and anatomically correct body is even remotely put in harm's way. Nothing personal because that includes hooking up with the likes of the Hell's Angels, the Black Panthers or even a really dedicated group of trapeze artists."

The jocular twist of Scott's reply only served to irritate Rheingold.

"You're a wise ass ain't you, kid?"

"Hell no, Captain," Scott shot back, "I'm just trying to be practically comical."

"Then join the circus," blue-eye glared again, "and don't think for a split second that you will ever have the intestinal fortitude or the privilege of defending your country's values while serving in the Infantry."

"O.K. by me." Scott grinned.

Somebody slipped 25¢ into the jukebox for 3 picks as Janis Joplin began her raspy slide into "Me and Bobby McGee."

"Not for anything, Cap." The beer and whiskey started to take a hold on Scott's thinking. "But is that eye patch for real or—"

"You really are a wise ass aren't you, kid?" Rheingold interrupted before Scott could finish his question.

Through the mellow glow of barroom libations Scott snapped back to the realization that he might be crossing a fine line that, at best, could make things awkward. Ignoring the inner whisper that suggested silence, Scott pushed forward.

"I was only going to ask you if you got more ass because that eye patch could start a conversation with a chick that might help you get laid somehow."

"I got laid plenty before the eye patch." Rheingold said. He spoke calmly, but his tone suggested that this dialogue might be finished but not forgotten.

"Well then, I'm happy for you, I guess." Scott grinned again.

Frank poked Scott as the captain downed his last two beers, pushed the stool away from the bar and left without another word.

"Why did you have to goad him like that?"

"What's 'goad' mean?"

"It means you just busted his cubes and burnt a bridge that you might need to cross over someday."

"Fuck you, Frank. I was just looking for a few laughs and he wasn't buying it. Fuck him, too."

The Tuscaroras started to filter into the bar as the glow of sunset smoked through the nicotine- coated front window on First Street. "I think we better drink up." Scott told Frank, "they're starting to bolt down the stools." This expression among the students simply meant that you now had the moment of opportunity to book out and say goodbye before the Tuscaroras and the booze made for one ugly combination.

CHAPTER 4

For the next three weeks the recruiting officers continued their litany of reasons everybody should select *their* military branch. All the candidates were required to make three choices and Scott finally accepted the fact that one of them had to be a combat branch. Frank was right again. It had to be either Infantry, Armor or Artillery. He couldn't remember if the Combat Engineer Corps counted also, but it didn't matter since he had already made a decision.

"Here's my picks, hero." Scott informed Frank in front of the chapel that was across a small road from the ROTC offices. "Number one, I want to fold sheets, number two, I like Signal because it sounds benign and, as a mandatory accommodation to the combat arms, I'm gonna pick Armor. The way I figure it," Scott continued," folding sheets has got to be safe, Signal sounds cool, and as far as Armor goes, I haven't read where there are a whole lot of tanks in Vietnam."

"My brother told us that we deploy things called ACAV over there. It stands for Armored Calvary Assault Vehicle. It's armored to protect the guys in the thing until they pour out of it to mix it up with the gooks."

"Well, then, what are my other options?"

"I guess none, coward."

"What coward!? Just because I'm not smart enough to be a Rhodes scholar and hide out at Oxford for the next few years and just because my parents don't know any politician "du jour" that could find a way for me to skip this shit— and all I want to do is find a fuckin' branch that I could deal with— and you call me a coward?   —Why don't you just follow in your brother's footsteps, Frank, and stop bustin' my balls."

The class was told that the last officer to address them would be from Military Intelligence and that they were expected to make their branch choices the following week. Since Scott had already decided what selections he wanted, he didn't pay much attention to the final guest who walked slowly toward the podium. It didn't immediately dawn on him as he looked up from his desk that the last speaker wasn't wearing a uniform. No medals. No ribbons. No spit-shined shoes. He just wore a dark blue business suit with a white buttoned-down oxford shirt and a blue and red diagonally striped tie.

"He looks like our flag," Scott whispered to nobody in particular.

"Gentlemen, my name is Captain Conlon. I will be speaking to you today about U.S. Military Intelligence and its overall mission. I recognize that you have heard from all the other branches of service and I will therefore attempt to keep this presentation brief and to the point. I wish to do this, also, for two other reasons. Number one: I don't care to expound on the numerous tasks worldwide that fall under the command of

Military Intelligence. Number two: I am not at liberty to expound on all the numerous tasks that fall under its command."

His reddish- blond hair was cut stylishly short, but didn't look military. He could have passed for a stockbroker, accountant, or an Ivy League-schooled attorney. The neck muscles above his starched shirt collar were the only contra-indication to this apparent lifestyle. They were thick and clearly hinted that the man was regularly involved in a daily physical regimen that belied the staid business image he projected. He continued sternly and without hesitation. "The mission of this branch is to gather information from all reliable sources concerning any hostile entity that threatens or can potentially threaten the security of our military personnel or installations."

As Scott continued to listen and observe the speaker, he became more and more drawn to the "real world" civilian approach this guy presented. He envisioned himself meeting his military obligation and at the same time wearing a sports jacket and not a flak jacket.

"This seems too good to be true," Scott murmured.

Captain Conlon continued his presentation. "If, however, you wish to choose Military Intelligence, it *must be* your first choice."

"Pompous bastard," Scott mused, but continued to be overpowered by the lack of military presence and the Ozzie Nelson - Main Street America look.

Scott met Frank in the lower level of the Student Center that afternoon and yanked Frank aside. "I think I changed my mind about picking my branch. I spoke with Willy Payne and he confirmed what I was thinking."

Frank was stuffing his mouth with the remains of a salami sandwich given to him by a thin nurse on the way to her next class. Scott did a double-take.

"Oofa, Frank, I thought that I ate fast, but you're a total *cavone*. You've got peppers stuck to your chin."

Without missing a beat, Frank swiped his chin with his free hand and took two more dinosaur bites.

"Done," he said.

"I was just walking over to tell you something. You looked like I wanted to take the last salami sandwich in the Northern Hemisphere."

"I know you," Frank burped.

"Did you hear what I just said?"

"Yeah, I heard you."

"I changed my mind about Quartermaster. I want a branch that wears no uniform at all. Now that's my kind of military commitment."

"Hey, Scott," Frank said as he rifled through the remnants of a potato chip bag. "Anything, and I mean anything, that has the word 'intelligence' in it is definitely not made for you. I'm in four of your classes and you can't bullshit me."

Scott bent down to where Frank was sitting and whispered. "This is what I really want." He said this with an alien and almost haunting tone. It made Frank stop chewing and stare at him. It was as if he had heard some stranger speak. Scott's eyes held a far away look and predestined stare.

"This is what I really want, Frank."

CHAPTER 5

Graduation day, June 4, 1967, liberated a slew of anxious celebrants from their academic cocoon. Most males were either headed for military service or a deferment. Vietnam was the 500 lb. gorilla this compressed peer group had to wrestle with or run away from. One thing was for sure, nobody could ignore it; not wives, girlfriends, siblings, parents or friends.

One by one the graduates walked up to the stage, where a canopy in the school's colors, purple and white, shaded the professors and guest speakers from the unusually hot sun that glared from a cloudless sky. A monotone of shuffling black robes edged its way to the central set. Peace signs and clenched fists together with passive acceptance of diplomas marked the exact moment that rolled sheepskin diplomas were slapped into waiting hands. Pictures flashed repeatedly as loved ones captured the graduate that mattered.

Perry Como received an honorary degree that day and, in his typically laconic fashion, nearly put the entire assemblage to sleep with his acceptance speech.

The commencement address was given by William F. Buckley Jr., a noted columnist, conservative politician, and editor of the *National Review.* His deliberate elocution was accented by a flicking tongue that Scott believed could have swatted flies if it only had been longer. The address, characterized with the use of multi-syllabic words, left the majority of non- Ivy League students in a state of amused confusion.

When the traditional ceremony concluded, the ROTC cadets were then summoned to the same stage to be awarded their commission as 2nd Lieutenants in the U.S. Army.

Nearly all of the new officers wore their bars with a newfound sense of superiority. Scott couldn't wait to dispense with the formal pomp and circumstance, wear the business suit of the Military Intelligence Officer, do his time and get out. As the ceremony concluded, he shot a broad smile to his mother as his sister, Kathy, and their father worked their way through the crowd of newly minted graduates.

"Hey, Ma, did I tell you that my active duty date was pushed back until next January?"

"No," his mother said happily. She looked at Scott in a split second of blind optimism. "Maybe this whole Vietnam mess will be over by then."

To the contrary, ten thousand miles away, the NVN Politburo, in the same month of June, summoned all of the North Vietnamese ambassadors to Hanoi. Allied intelligence sources deemed this a sure sign that a decision of major importance had been made. This interpretation of the supplied data proved accurate. The North Vietnamese Communists were pushing for the Politburo to approve a spontaneous and bloody uprising that would surprise the U.S. forces and cripple them where they stood. The North Vietnamese labeled this military push Tong Cong Kich, Tong Khai Nghia – "General Offensive, General Uprising." The North Vietnamese gave it their acronym, "TCK-TKN." To the rest of the world it would become later known as the large- scale assault that occurred during Vietnam's most celebrated holiday – TET.

"It doesn't matter if it's over or not," Scott responded to his mother's wishful thinking. "I told you I was picked for Military Intelligence. The guy who talked to us was wearing a suit. Now, how many pictures have you seen on TV with guys all suited up and toting an M-16? Huh?"

"None. That's true," his mother said flatly. "But nothing in life is ever that cut and dried."

Scott fully believed that the suit- and- tie world of a counterintelligence agent would require him to be stationed in an area where that daily business dress was the norm. The United States and Europe were two perfect examples.

Little did he know that a clandestine program was being formulated by military and CIA officials and it would soon be launched in an area thousands of miles away from the geographic locations that Scott would later list on his "dream sheet." This forthcoming effort would require the expertise of civilian personnel trained in the esoteric techniques of Intelligence gathering. In addition the military types who would be selected to participate in this program would be required to have both intelligence expertise and combat training.

The ranks were being combed for candidates.

CHAPTER 6

The summer following graduation, Scott decided instead of getting a full-time seasonal job, which he had done since he was 14, he would find part-time work. He had enough money put away from occasional odd jobs at college to allow him to spend more time at the Jersey shore.

"This schedule suits me just fine," he said to Stang.

Stang's father died when he was a baby and left him some mutual funds the kid couldn't touch until he turned 21. When he did the first thing he bought was a fire engine red 1967 Mustang convertible and his nickname quickly became a chopped version of his car model.

For the second summer season they both shared a room on a floor above a popular shore bar owned by a playboy state senator. As a result of this ownership, the hours of operation were flexible. The bartenders and waitresses comprised the majority of the tenants who lived upstairs and they took frequent liberty to party well past the mandatory closing hour of 2:00 A.M.

The events at the shore that last season passed like any other previous summer. Things seemed normal until autumn rolled around and Scott didn't return to school. The time approaching his active duty date seemed to turn faster than a calendar in the wind and a subtle uneasiness shrouded each succeeding day. The conflict in Southeast Asia wasn't going away like his mother had hoped but, in fact, was escalating.

The enemy could be anywhere and every Vietnamese, regardless of age or sex, could be Viet Cong. The rules of battle were rapidly changing.

"Scott, please be careful in the Army." His mother whispered this to him as she prepared Thanksgiving dinner for her Irish in-laws. This and St. Patrick's Day were their semi-annual reunions.

"Ma, you know I'm always careful."

She rolled her eyes knowing that her son's self perception didn't jive with her knowledge of her offspring.

"Your sister's careful; you're impulsive."

"Ma," Scott said with a slight tone of annoyance, "in the Army you can't be impulsive. You gotta' follow rules. They've got rules I probably never even heard of yet. Besides, if you want careful then we'll volunteer Kathy to take my place. That way I can go down the shore again next year and she'll save a ton of money on wardrobes for the next two years. It's a win-win. Whaddya' think?"

"You can make me crazy, Scott."

"Do you think Dad worries as much as you do?"

"No. Your father has always had the ability to be at the heaving edge of an earthquake and calmly step over the cracks. I'm responsible for worrying for both of my kids."

"Ma, nobody worries about anything these days. Look at me, I'm a 60's kid. Live and let live. So what if there's a bunch of kids up at Columbia who call themselves Students for a Democratic Society and occupy the administration offices and protest the war. So what? You would probably say they must be worried about something, right? Well, I'll tell ya' what their real agenda is. First of all they ain't worried about anything. All they're doing is instigating these demonstrations, getting the kids all on the same ideological page and, after several hours of holding placards, they'll all go back to their dorms and have sex. That's it, Ma. They ain't looking to change foreign policy. All they want to do is get naked. These orchestrations are just gigantic group foreplay."

Scott stopped gesticulating and preaching for a second to look at his mother.

"Ma, will you please stop making the sign of the cross when I'm trying to explain things to you."

"Hey, Scotty." Kathy diverted her brother's attention to the clique of Irish relatives that were sitting in the living room and talking quietly.

"Give me a hand with the drinks."

"Everybody's still doing Jameson with a side of water?"

"Yea, except for Aunt Peg."

"Oh, that's right. She likes Schaeffer."

"No. Piel's. Schaeffer was last year. She says that Piel's makes their beer with better water. She's also not smoking

27

Chesterfields anymore. It's Kents now. Something about a micronite filter."

"Wow," Scott exclaimed. "She was always on the cutting edge of health fads."

They brought the drinks and all seemed to settle in their chairs just a little bit more comfortably.

Scott smiled to his aunts and uncles and was getting ready to sit down and watch the second half of the Detroit-Cleveland game when Kathy grabbed his arm.

"Come outside, I want to mention something to you."

Out of earshot of the family, Kathy turned to her brother.

"You know mommy's worried stiff about you. Don't kid with her anymore. This is beyond a joking matter to her. Please just say something to her before you leave for Ft. Benning that makes her feel..." Kathy groped for the appropriate word "...calm."

He gave her a kiss and slapped her on the butt and said, "Bring another round of booze to the living room so that I can think of something to say to Mom."

Scott managed to assuage his mother's concerns that night by reminding her he had chosen Military Intelligence and not some high risk branch. It seemed to work for the next several weeks until the holidays rolled around.

Every religious culture has its most sacred day of the year. For Scott's family it was Christmas Eve. As a kid, the late evening of December 24th represented the hours of unbridled anticipation before Santa Claus arrived and deposited gifts in a kaleidoscope of colors, smells and sounds. Even though they knew Santa couldn't come down a chimney they didn't have, as children, they still believed that Santa's reindeer perched on the top of their house. Christmas Eve, above all else, heralded the most sacred hours of joy that led to the celebration of the birth of Jesus Christ almost 2,000 years ago.

The tables in their neighborhood on this night always seemed to be set by the same matriarch. The menus varied little from house to house and fish was always the centerpiece. The order was placed two weeks previous and the fish was expected to be fresh on December 23rd. The only exception to this date was the salted filets of cod which were stiff as an ironing board and had to be soaked and repeatedly rinsed for three days until the salt was washed off and the baccala softened enough in order to be served in a marinara sauce or enjoyed with the measured doses of olive oil, lemon, parsley and garlic.

Kathy and Scott liked to clean the snails. They were live and had to be flushed in the kitchen sink as they tried to inch their way up the sides only to be brushed back down for another bath. When they were fully rinsed they were immersed in a fra diavolo sauce and simmered. They were served piled high in a bowl and eaten much like escargot, except that they were never called that.

The last Christmas Day that Scott had spent at home before reporting for active duty found everyone, except his mother, eating, laughing, and acting pretty much normally. Annamaria Regan was uncharacteristically pensive and sad. She claimed that it was the new Frank Sinatra and Bing Crosby Christmas albums that had made her cry.

CHAPTER 7

The next week Scott greeted the New Year, 1968, with his longtime best friend, Chan, in the ribaldry of a local bar in West Orange, N.J.

Scott had met Chan when they were both 12 years old, after the Regans moved from the Newark neighborhood that had embraced two generations before him. The move was exactly one mile to East Orange but it represented a culture chasm that seemed as wide as the Grand Canyon. No longer did the kids play on black top or cement. No brick walls stood as backdrops for stick ball or "Johnny-on-the-pony." Alleyways were named driveways, ash cans were garbage cans, and bushes were called shrubs. The smells in the candy stores and delicatessens were different, and most of the kid's names didn't end in a vowel. The closest community playground was named "Columbian" and had trees, three grass baseball diamonds and clay tennis courts. It had a cinder running track where guys used to run without being chased.

Cameron Chandler "Chan" Ferine was co-captain of the football team and voted "best looking" in his high school class at Clifford Scott. His mother had been born and raised in Myrtle Beach, South Carolina and met his father as a young war widow with two small children. His stepfather who survived

WWII as an Army Pilot adopted the youngsters as his own and would forever be considered their father.

"You'll never make it as a Marine pilot," he chided his son years later as Scott prepared ham and Swiss sandwiches in their spacious kitchen overlooking Rock Spring County Club.

"I'll bet you anything that I get my wings" Chan volleyed. "If you flew fixed wing, I can fly choppers!"

"A hundred bucks says you'll wash out," he countered.

"You're on, Pop."

Chan had already completed the Marine Platoon Leader Class program at St. Lawrence University and had received his orders to report to The Basic School at Quantico, Virginia on the exact day that Scott was to start Infantry training at Ft. Benning.

As Scott brought the ham and cheese sandwiches to the fire-lit den he couldn't know that this would be the second to last time he would see his best friend and the brother he never had.

CHAPTER 8

In June of 1967 the Vietnamese Communists were furiously preparing for a spontaneous uprising expected to annihilate U.S. forces in South Vietnam and fuel anti-war sentiment in the U.S.

Gen. Nguyen Chi Thanh and Gen. Vo Nguyen Giap were the senior strategists responsible for structuring the large scale offensive. This could have been an advantage to U.S. forces since these men were noted rivals. The military posturing and the "one upmanship" that could have ensued between these two leaders in preparing the battle plan might have delayed the assault long enough so that more intelligence could have been gathered to counter the countrywide offensive.

However, on or about July 4, 1967 Thanh died at his headquarters near Hanoi. Reports varied from a fatal heart attack to fragments delivered through his chest by B-52 bombers. Regardless of the cause there was now only one man in charge— Giap. He was a historian and a brilliant strategist. He also was in sole command. This made for a deadly combination that would be evidenced some 7 months later.

Scott reported to the Infantry Officer's Basic Course on January 15, 1968. Within two weeks the large scale and well coordinated TET offensive would finally be launched against U.S. troops in targeted cities throughout Vietnam.

****

"Hey Mike," Scott asked his bunkmate in their Bachelor Officer Quarters at Benning. "Did you hear last night at the "O" club about some balls to the wall attack the gooks launched on us two nights ago?"

"Yeah, I heard something about it. But from what I understand it's a lot of shit because it's now one of their holidays when Charlie just lights fireworks and gets high. They don't fight during this time of year."

"That's not what I heard, man." Scott added emphatically. "One of the returnees told me face-to- face last night that they're using this holiday -Tip, Tit, Tet -whatever as a smokescreen to blow our nuts off. They expected us to lower our guard like the Hessian Troops did on Christmas Eve when George Washington crossed the Delaware and shocked the hell out of them."

"Scott, we're the best trained troops in the world," Mike said. "We've got the best fuckin' equipment and we pay people to tell us what's going to happen before it does. Now tell me how we're ever going to be surprised by a raggedy ass bunch of rice suckers?"

Thousands of miles away and between the hours of midnight and 3:00 a.m. on January 30, 1968 six cities in II Corps—Qui Nhon, An Khe, Kontum, Nha Trang, Dalat and Ban Me Thout came under a coordinated attack by Viet Cong forces. The assaults were originally scheduled for the nights of January 29th and 30th. Shortly before, however, Giap delayed the schedule until the following nights of the 30th and 31st. A number of the units did not receive the message and attacked prematurely. This eliminated the key advantage of any military offensive: the element of surprise. The miscommunication enabled General Westmoreland to alert his senior commanders to prepare for heavy attacks on all cities and especially on American installations. The entire command was put on maximum alert. The South Vietnamese people themselves did not believe that the Viet Cong would violate the sanctity of Tet, thus making it difficult to recall the South Vietnamese military personnel to their combat units. Nevertheless, the breach of surprise gave the U.S. and allied forces hours of defensive preparation that they otherwise never would have had.

On the nights of January 30th and 31st, the second wave of attacks were launched against thirty- four major U.S. bases, provincial capitals, and military sites from as far north as Quang Tri and Phu Bai in I Corps to the southernmost attack of Ca Mau in IV Corps' Delta region.

Fighting continued for two more weeks in Saigon and in embattled Hue for close to thirty more days, but the majority of the VC forces were beaten back within days of the second wave assault. Body count figures reported that the Communists lost a total of 45,000 troops. In addition the enemy forces didn't convert the general populace to their cause. In fact, the South Vietnamese people didn't rally to VC units, the ARVN soldiers did not surrender, and the populace became galvanized in support of the South Vietnamese government. Within days of the start of the Tet offensive COSVN admitted failing in its' effort to "seize a number of primary targets and destroy mobile and defensive units of the enemy." The military objective of TCK-TKN was to "achieve victory in the shortest possible time." It failed in its mission.

The Communist initiative did succeed, however, in exacerbating domestic discontent at home, and the media viewed the Tet offensive as an American defeat. The moody protests now took on the tone of abject defeatism. Walter Cronkite echoed the national impression when he exclaimed, "What the hell is going on here? I thought we were winning the war." In February he had made a whistle stop tour of Vietnam and, upon his return, implored the U.S. to negotiate its way out "not as victors but as honorable people." From this point forward the American press and a vast majority of U.S. citizens abandoned all patriotic ties to this commitment.

"Do you realize, Scotty," Mike said later that evening, "that just because we're in the military, snake shit is more attractive to the average American girl than us? The guy that's gonna' get laid is the one who can play three chords on a guitar and has a flower in his hair. Our hair isn't long enough to hold thread. Now where do we think we're going? Stop dreamin'"

"I'm not dreamin', man. Let's just say that Cronkite is right when he says the only honorable way out is through negotiations. We don't know jungle tactics as well as Charlie, and he's starting to kick our ass more than we thought he could. But I don't think the people at home think we're scum because we're still fighting there."

"Besides," Scott joked, "if they're going to hate anybody they should hate you. You volunteered for the Infantry, I chose Intelligence. I'm just passing through these nine weeks of basic until I get back to wearing a shirt and tie like the officer who recruited me. His name was Conlon and if it wasn't for him in a few more months I'd probably be sloshing around in rice paddies and buffalo shit right along side you."

"Hey, dreamer," Mike looked out the window into a moonless pitch tar night. "The Army works according to their own needs, not yours. If they didn't have bigger plans for you why did they send you to Infantry Training? I think you got sucker punched but haven't felt it yet."

"Me," Mike said as he turned back to Scott. "I'm goin' in with my eyes wide open."

****

Scott cruised through the remainder of basic training with the nonchalance of a civilian patriot but he couldn't stop listening to the rapidly evolving events in Vietnam. He wondered if he would ever be put in a position to instantly decide a course of action like the lieutenant at My Lai.

In fact, when the news spread shortly after the March 16, 1968 killings Scott and his comrades at Benning couldn't really understand what the media uproar was all about. The young officer had led a platoon into the hamlet and killed civilians he believed were Viet Cong.

"Haven't we been taught not to trust anyone?" Scott interrupted several troops that were leaning against a transport during a five-minute field break.

"When did we ever hear anyone tell us to give them the benefit of the doubt? He came through here like we're doing now. Don't you think he was taught to react like we're being taught? Where's the Drill Instructor in charge of moral action? All we know from the returnees is don't trust any gooks. Period."

The break was almost finished but the chorus of agreement could have gone on for hours.

A wiry southern boy with freckles that made him look about 15 years old added: "I heard that just a few days before they entered the place 30 of their guys were wasted by some common folk. Plain 'ole everyday people. The next hamlet they came upon was My Lai. Now wouldn't that put you on edge?"

"You know what?" Scott jumped in. "By the time we get out of here *we'll* be of the mind set to think about doin' the same thing he did."

"Philosophy class is over gentlemen. Fall in." A burly veteran drill sergeant barked the orders that brought everyone back to the moment. Their five- minute break had lasted four minutes. It was typical Army time.

****

When Graduation day finally arrived it took place under an overcast late March sky. The reviewing stand for the military dignitaries lent the only color the day provided. Red, white, and blue banners decked the front of the grandstand and encircled the huge replica of the silver rifle and laurel wreath of the Combat Infantryman's Badge. The soldiers formed symmetrical patterns of battalions that lined the field. Hundreds of men stood at military attention with the stocks of their M-1 rifles barely touching the outside shoe leather on their right foot.

When the time came for all graduates to pass before the reviewing stand each commander braced for a second before relaying the order passed on to them.

The brigade commander saluted the commanding general of Ft. Benning who stood ramrod straight front and center in the crowd of high- ranking officers. When the salute was returned he did an about face in a two- step movement. The toes of his right foot were placed directly behind his left heel as he pivoted to address the battalions that stood at attention before him. At a decibel level that could be heard through a thunderstorm he initialized the directive that would be echoed by each company and platoon commander.

The order to his battalions was elongated in pronunciation and rose a half octave on the last syllable.

"Battalyaaaaaan!"

Within a split second of that sound the company commanders who stood centered and forward of their respective charges remained at attention but turned their heads to the right so that their chins were directly over their collarbone and yelled "Companeeeey!"

In rhythmic cadence the platoon leaders bellowed to their men, "Toooooon!"

For one breath everyone was dead silent as the Brigade Commander readied his next order.

"Preeesent."

"Preeesent." The Company CO's enjoined.

"Preeesent." The Platoon leaders barked.

"Ahhms."

With the command to "Present Arms" hundreds of vintage M-1 rifles were slapped in syncopation and held vertically in front of each troop.

"Right Shouldah - Ahms!"

This movement placed the rifle grip on each man's right shoulder with the bottom of the stock resting in the palm of their right hand.

At the final command of "Fowahd Maach" the entire field of newly graduated Infantry officers stepped off in a simultaneous movement of ordered precision as hundreds of heels hit the ground at the same split second.

The reviewing stand of WWII and Korean War Colonels and Generals watched in stoic silence as the next wave of future Vietnam veterans passed before them.

****

Following graduation each officer received orders assigning him to a school that specifically taught his Military Occupational Specialty, or MOS.

The orders Scott received weren't exactly what he was expecting.

"Hey Mike," Scott said waiving a short note, "I just got assigned to jump school here at Benning. How do you figure that? What did you get?"

"I'm going to AIT and jump school. But I knew that. I figure your ass is going to 'Nam, Military Intelligence or not."

"I was told," Scott retorted, "That I've got to fill some time here before the next class opens up at Ft. Holabird. I bet it's just another way for the Army to tell me to hurry up and wait."

"And I bet," Mike added, "that you've been picked to do a job you didn't plan on. You committed two years of your life to the U.S. Army. They now have a huge piece of your ass and will "yes" you to death and then send you where they want. Scott, just stop bullshitting yourself."

For the next three weeks Scott had no time to think about anything.

He started his day doing the "airborne shuffle" at the crack of dawn. He learned every chant that accompanied this measured jog and worked the jump towers before making the three day- jumps and two night- jumps that earned him his wings. Scott always had a fear of high and open spaces. High spots were okay and open spaces were okay, too. But put them together and he would pucker. There was no worse place for him to be with this phobia than waiting for the command to walk out the open cargo door of a C-130. If the static line didn't jerk that chute out of his pack correctly he would have as much lift as an anvil.

Beautiful streamer open for me.

Blue sky above me.

But no canopy.

Sung to the tune of *Beautiful Dreamer* the opening lines to this tongue in cheek song frequently passed through the minds of young airborne types. Scott reflected on these lyrics also, but the main thought that occupied him was that he had to get to the U.S. Military Intelligence School in Baltimore and finally resolve the miscommunication between him and Uncle Sam. He just wanted to get back on track and do the stuff he had planned on doing. Period.

CHAPTER 9

Ft. Holabird was the U.S. Army's Intelligence School. The main gate was located on Holabird Avenue in Baltimore, MD not too far from a soap manufacturing plant. Proper identification had to be shown to the MP stationed at its entrance. Otherwise, there seemed to be no elaborate security measures to thwart access to the interior of the facility. Considering the sensitivity of the activities conducted inside it appeared to be an example of "hide in plain sight".

Of course, no one who ever reported for duty there knew everything that was *really* conducted inside. Not even high ranking military or civilian personnel. Scott was allowed to know only what pertained to his own training and mission. The entire operation ran deliberately on a "need to know" basis. If a general wanted to ferret out what was being taught to a group of military agents and it didn't specifically pertain to his area of responsibility he would not be told.

On Scott's first morning of class, the heavily scented spew from the soap factory was so thick it shrouded the early morning rays of sun and lent a heavy weight to the air. The olive drab military vehicles in front of the building had a patina of soap dust. He looked around and noted that all the cars he could see had acquired the same coating overnight.

"If it ever rained today," he thought, "this whole place would be ass deep in bubbles."

A captain stepped briskly past Scott and walked around the group of new arrivals milling about. When the captain reached the top of the stairs that led into a cinder block building, he turned around, looked at his watch and addressed the cluster.

"In five minutes, at exactly 0700 hours, you will report to room Alpha." Without another word he reached down and removed a key from his fatigue thigh pocket, opened the steel door to the building and walked in.

The talk given by the orientation officer in Alpha room was informative and to the point. Upon completion of their course they would all be counterintelligence agents with the more enigmatic title of Intelligence Research Officer and a numerical MOS of 9666. This number, like their serial number would follow them throughout their hitch and would be a constant addendum to their name and rank. In addition, they were informed that immediately prior to completing training they would receive orders for their next duty station. It could be state side or anywhere else in the world.

Counterintelligence training was the first instruction that Scott received in the service that didn't come with periodic waves of boredom. He was always the first to arrive at class everyday. His written assignments were always finished before the deadline and were accurate. Aside from the classroom work the agents also learned surveillance techniques, both from moving vehicles and on foot. They practiced live and on the streets of Baltimore, and the exercises often took them through the dilapidated wharfs and abandoned warehouses of the waterfront. The vigils also led them through East Baltimore St. and into an area known as "The Block." Whenever the "rabbit" led the surveillance team into this part of town, the neophyte agents were at an immediate disadvantage. If the subject headed there, it meant that he almost certainly knew he was being tailed and that he could easily ditch the crew in the labyrinth of back alleys and dead ends. In addition, on East Baltimore St. everybody knew everybody else. They were all pimps, whores, or hustlers who catered to a throng of dockside drunks. Through these fringe occupations they managed to sustain a lucrative cash economy in a minuscule area and they stuck together like their livelihood depended on it. It was the perfect seedy setting for the agents to learn the counterintelligence craft.

****

The remainder of Scott's stateside duty was completed at the Boston Army Base. Describing this as a "Base" was like comparing a thimble to a bucket. It was located on a pier that jutted into Boston Harbor, not too far from the actual site of the Boston Tea Party. Its drab exterior was complemented by the lackluster walls and barren furniture inside. But it was in the

U.S.A. and Scott finally was able to wear the suit and tie that first sparked his interest back in college. No uniform for Scott. Strictly suits when conducting background investigations and casuals when working surveillances. He used all sorts of unmarked government cars when he was on duty, and he bought a second hand '61 Chevy convertible from Willy Payne.

Willy and Scott both graduated from St. Vincent College in upstate New York. There were a number of other parallels in their lives. Willy had finished school one year before him. Both were elected to the student council, had dated girls from Nassau County, and were chosen for Military Intelligence. They both received Infantry Training at Ft. Benning and would later graduate from Holabird as Counterintelligence Officers. It was Willy who had encouraged Scott to pick Intelligence as his first choice.

The only difference between them after finishing at the "Bird" was that Willy was ordered to report immediately as a District Intelligence Operational Coordination Center (DIOCC) advisor in a program labeled Phoenix in Vietnam.

Neither Willy nor Scott knew exactly what the Phoenix program was at that time, but it sounded typically cryptic for the branch they had chosen. All Scott knew was that Willy went to Vietnam and not to Europe or somewhere domestic. In time, Scott got his orders for the Boston Army Base and lost touch with Willy.

Little did he know that their paths would once again cross.

****

With Scott apparently set to complete the balance of his military service stateside, he and Maryanne, his college sweetheart and former student nurse at St.Vincent's college, decided to marry. They both realized that, if they had married before he was commissioned, he would have been given a deferment and their lives would have taken a much different path.

Scott had no regrets about this though. In the first place, he was not ready to get married any earlier. Even though he and Maryanne shared strong common backgrounds and really liked each other's company, there was something unsettling about transitioning from "like" to "love" and then to a lifetime commitment. In addition to this hesitation Scott had qualms about gaining a deferment by getting married. Not that he was a roaring gung- ho patriot who wanted nothing more than to bear arms for his country, but rather he was simply willing to serve on active duty in any other theater of operation besides Vietnam. Scott did not want to avoid his military obligation totally. Just a little. With his acceptance into the suit- and- tie world of domestic counterintelligence, the thought of serving in Vietnam now seemed to be a remote possibility. So Scott and Maryanne were wed on August 31,1968 in little St. Mary's Church in Roslyn, N.Y.

"What a beautiful day!" exclaimed Scott's new father-in-law as he shoved his hands into his tuxedo pockets and looked skyward. It was a pristine afternoon under an azure sky with temperatures in the upper 70's.

Life was good.

****

Shortly after Lyndon Johnson's painful visit to Ft. Bragg on Feb. 17, 1968, General Westmoreland began to believe that his commander-in-chief was about to lift the 525,000 troop ceiling and adopt a more offensive strategy. This was precipitated by a message sent by General Earl "Bus" Wheeler, Chairman of the U.S. Joint Chiefs of Staff, to Gen. William Westmoreland on Feb 18th. He stated that he was coming to Vietnam to discuss the overall situation "since the administration must face up to some hard decisions in the near future".

Pumped up with the expectation that the military and civilian powers in Congress might be finally listening to his trumpet calling for more ground troops, Westmoreland eagerly prepared his presentation to "Bus" Wheeler and a sizeable Washington contingent. Included in his plans was another request for more marines and for the 82nd Airborne Division to come ashore via an amphibious landing somewhere around the DMZ. He did not want to use this manpower as reinforcing units for northern I Corps, but instead the General wanted them to be utilized as a full- blown airborne-amphibious spearhead against North Vietnam positions along the Ho Chi Minh trail above the border.

Wheeler, as chairman of the JCS, was forced to constantly wear two hats: one as a military officer, the other as a spokesman from the White House. In light of this, his purpose in visiting "Westy" was not to bring him news of support from Washington but instead to bring him promise of some "insurance" troops to support his military field strategy.

The compromise that was ultimately struck during the meeting between the two generals was a call up of 206,000 men to be implemented in three stages. There were loopholes and contingencies depending on enemy troop movement and tactics, but the first 108,000 men were to reach the RVN on May 1, '68 and the second increment was to deploy on September. 1, '68— the first day of Scott's and Maryann's honeymoon.

CHAPTER 10

Life at the Boston Army Base evolved into a predictable routine. As a CI agent, Scott passed his days conducting in depth background investigations on civilian and military personnel who were seeking security clearances. He wore no military uniform and, aside from the counterintelligence credentials he presented to the people he interviewed, was indistinguishable from any other businessman who commuted to and from work. He drove Willy Payne's fawn colored '61 Chevy Impala convertible to the Army Base every day.

Cpt. Thomas McGuiness was Scott's boss. He had recently completed his second tour in 'Nam where he had been a combat advisor in the newly formed Phoenix Program. A barrel chested veteran with a bulldog face and a personality to match, McGuiness was a "lifer" who had enlisted in the Army before volunteering for Officer's Candidate School. It was a decision that he seemingly regretted since he would often express his preference for the savvy of a platoon sergeant over any platoon leader or company commander. Now after two and a half years as an officer he seemed to have liked himself better when he wore stripes instead of two silver bars on each shoulder. They were a daily reminder of his perceived betrayal to the rank and file of Army life. In addition to this inherent prejudice against his fellow officers he especially disliked 2nd "looies". Chief among those were individuals who somehow weaseled their way into an almost civilian way of life as a stateside counterintelligence agent. And the only 2nd lieutenant that could be lower than that was one who also tried to sidestep his tour in 'Nam. Scott fit within both parameters.

McGuiness was very perceptive and had the ability to quickly make an accurate "read" on people. Scott knew it was true in his case. Scott looked to cut corners and McGuiness knew it.

"He's your boss, Scott." Maryanne counseled. "You could either make him your rabbi or your arch enemy. I know you like to play on the edge with this cat and mouse stuff, but don't think for a second that he doesn't have the final hammer if he wants to use it." Scott had always trusted her incisive opinions but remained stubborn. "Just be real careful and don't agitate or toy with him. I have a real unsettled feeling about this guy."

In the early morning of 31 January 1968, then 1st Lt. Thomas McGuiness was awakened in his third floor bed by a baritone sound and a thunderous concussion that resonated within his rib cage. The sapper who carried the satchel past the two MP's guarding the front door to the Civil Operations and Revolutionary Development Support (CORDS) headquarters in Phan Thiet was a recognized local who often fraternized with American personnel at the building. She was especially familiar to the woman who was sitting behind the switchboard of the top- secret clearance communication desk. She smiled and waved to the woman as she crossed the threshold and approached her as she had done so many times before. She would always make small talk before she started her predawn work shift at the local Nuoc Mam processing plant. Only this time she never started a conversation. Instead she lifted her tunic and unstrapped a small palm woven pack of C-4 explosive, skidded it across the small marble reception floor, and bolted back out the door with a thin wire trailing her and detonated the satchel as she hit and rolled in the powdered dust of the road. The receptionist and the two MP's were killed instantly. The 13 year old sapper, who had never been suspected of being Viet Cong, was gunned down by the pursuing MP's 50 meters from the explosion.

The second wave of the TET offensive had started and Lt. McGuiness and the rest of the Phoenix program operatives were major targets.

Now, almost a year later, the captain stood at the bar in the Boston Army Base's Officers Club. He was on his fifth Wild Turkey and spoke about Lt. Regan to a fellow officer.

"The thing that grabs me the most," he slurred, "is 'sat everyone else likes the kid. They tell me he's funny and they enjoy hanging around wish him. I see 'im as someone who just sees life as one big party and I don't think he could give a fiddler's fuck about anyone or anything that takes him out of this arena. You know goddamn well life ain't one continuous carnival, don' you?"

Many times before Captain Philip Russell had seen McGuiness in this state of alcohol induced bitterness, and just shook his head in agreement. Russell didn't know Scott personally since he was stationed in a different Intelligence group and worked out of Ft. Devins, Massachusetts. However, he knew that McGuiness, borderline drunk or not, was usually pretty accurate in his assessment of people.

"I went through his 201 file with a fine tooth comb," McGuiness continued, "and it was clean. No reprimands. No disciplinary action of any kind. In fact he has a letter of commendation from the CO down at Holabird. That's tough for me to swallow since all I see here is some kid that wants to skate through his 2 year hitch and fuck off while doing it. I won't let that happen, Russell," he drawled on. "You can mark my words on that."

The captain had built up a tolerance for booze that was almost legendary. He had occasionally compared himself to the Monhegan Island lobstermen in Maine who set out to sea on Dec 26th only to permanently return in the month of June. He always explained it using the same analogy: "It takes a lot of practice to set out in winds that blow the sleet horizontal and rack you on 8ft seas. Just like them it took me a long time to tame this Wild Turkey, and I try not to miss a single day of practice."

With his 6th drink in front of him he could still probably slur the alphabet if called upon by an officer of the law. But that was the farthest thought from his mind and he remained fixated on the young lieutenant.

"Ya' know what, Phil?" He continued planning his strategy aloud to his bar buddy. "Thish kid's gonna fuck up one day on shomthing and when he does, I'm going to be there to nail 'im. I'm washin' 'em like a hawk."

Russell was starting to get weary of the ranting, stood up slowly from the stool, tipped the sergeant, and collected his money from the bar.

"Tom, can I give you one piece of advice?" he asked.

"Yea?" McGuiness said somewhat surprised at hearing a voice other than his own.

"I would normally caution you not to let this whole matter drive you to drink. But, clearly you're doing it just fine on your own. Your blood pressure is through the roof so don't let this stuff give you a heart attack. You came home in one piece after both tours. Don't self- destruct stateside. Besides, this kid doesn't sound like he'll step on his dick. Forget about him and just worry about the rest of your command."

Russell didn't know if he heard him, but he looked into his drooping eyes as Mc Guiness shook his head from side-to-side. Russell wasn't certain whether McGuiness was disagreeing with him or if it was a physically uncontrollable head tremor fueled by the Wild Turkey. Without deciding Russell turned toward the door as McGuiness grabbed the edge of the hardwood with both hands and stared at the array of liquor bottles on the mahogany shelves that framed the beveled back-bar mirror. The more he drank the more he disdained the non-military, pop culture style of the young lieutenant.

****

"Hi Maryanne," Scott said brightly as he bounded up the stairs to their attic apartment on Kimball Road in Watertown.

"I shot a 91 today. What do you think about that?" He managed to squeeze out another round of golf on Army time.

Maryanne was browning veal cutlet in olive oil when she raised the spatula over the pan and said, "Hey, Hey, Scott is a 91 good or not?" I don't know anymore about golf then you did a couple years ago, but what I do know is that a 91 won't put food on anyone's table. Now if we plan to have a family you better score like the pros on T.V. or get a real job after the Army sets you free."

"One step at a time, babe. I won $14 today with side bets and all, plus I was still on the clock with Uncle Sam. Now that's a productive day, right?"

"Good. Then how about you pay for the veal cutlets? While you were out playing golf I had to deal with a 2 year old kid that was born with no ovaries. Do you know what she and her parents are going to face as she matures?"

"No" Scott said, "But what in hell does that have to do with whether I shoot a 91 or take us on the PGA tour someday?"

"I just thought you might just get a dose of perspective with the things that go on in other peoples lives on your way to living yours."

"Maryanne," Scott quizzed," are you pre-menstrual?"

"No, Scott I'm just cooking for us."

"Terrific, then. Can we please stop the whole bummer, counter- point shit that you throw at me when I'm proud of something I did?"

"You know that I'm not throwing water on your fire, Scott. It's just that sometimes you don't see the other side of people's feelings."

"You're definitely pre-menstrual." Scott laughed. "I don't care what calendar you have or what time of the month it might be, I can tell when you take some light and lively comment I make and give me a whole diatribe on the sad life of Calcutta. Let Joan Baez sing about it."

He took two steps across their small kitchen, approached her from behind and pulled her close to him.

"You really are a callous prick." She said.

"Is this a new name for Mr. Happy?" Scott pressed on.

"No it's just another name for you." She managed to wiggle from his grasp.

"Maryanne," He straightened himself to his maximum height and feigned mock sadness. "I think that you just again maneuvered your way out of a kitchen hump. The sauce boss is no longer at attention."

"Scott, back off," she said with a smile she couldn't conceal. "If you want to know the truth, I *am* pre-menstrual and any second I just might haul off and whack you with this spatula."

"Would your mother talk to your father like that? Learn from her. That spatula was made for flipping, frying, and serving. The 60's haven't changed us that much."

"Ohhh, really? She said. "You know what? I'm going to ignore that immigrant comment and say we make a date for next Thursday anyway. How's that sound?"

"I may be dead by Thursday, Maryanne."

"Well if you're dead on Thursday you'll really have to wait a long, long time for the sauce boss to come knocking."

"I don't have a snowball's chance in hell tonight, do I?"

"Bingo." She turned back toward the stove. Scott mumbled as he kicked off his shoes and headed to the shower.

"How about a date next Thursday?" Maryanne asked.

"I'll clear my calendar, Mair."

CHAPTER 11

The next morning came in a blink of an eye as Scott turned over in bed and noticed that Maryanne was gone. He thought she was probably waiting at the bus stop at the corner of Mt Auburn Street and Kimball Road. She always wanted to get to Mt. Auburn Hospital a half hour before her scheduled shift, which began at 7:00am. She liked to talk to the nurses coming off night duty to determine if there were any significant changes in the status of their patients. This time also allowed her to gab with her co-workers and have an extra cup of coffee and a cigarette in the nurses' lounge. Realizing that he was running late, Scott jumped into the bathroom and took an "Army Shower"— one minute to wet down, one minute to soap, one minute to rinse. He dressed hurriedly and threw his tie under his shirt collar and let it hang. He grabbed his electric razor and shaved in the car as he rode through Cambridge and on to Storrow Drive.

This was the morning when the agents would assemble for the once -a -month "status update" meeting. It was more commonly referred to as "morale check" time. The military had started to perceive that the growing civilian discontent concerning the direction of the war was beginning to seep into the ranks of the servicemen. These "status update" meetings at the Boston Army Base were designed to evaluate the contemporary thinking of the enlisted personnel and the officers stationed there.

Scott had noticed that during the meetings of the past several months more and more questions were asked about why the military was restrained from using its full power to bring this growing unpopular conflict to a conclusion.

By November, 1968 the esprit d' corps of both stateside and "in country" servicemen was slipping. In addition, field level commanders ran scared of Congressional oversight. The combat soldier no longer fought solely alongside his comrades, but was joined, uninvited, by elected members of Congress.

American troops in Vietnam did not suffer from the historically classic causes that lead to a breakdown in troop morale. They never faced a debilitating defeat, their food, equipment, and supplies were never in short supply, their living conditions were not sub par, and their military leaders, despite the fact that they had not previously fought a large scale guerilla war, were competent senior officers. However, external influences from home started to take their toll and fed the erosion of a united military effort.

In addition, the readily available supply of illegal drugs in South Vietnam contributed to the creeping demoralization of U.S. fighting forces. A large number of newer troops arriving in Vietnam were importing the stateside lifestyles of the 60's. That culture scorned authority and lauded the constitutional right of free speech.

A new breed of warrior was needed to fill the enlisted ranks in Vietnam. But instead of being better disciplined and with a determined fighting spirit, the newly arriving Americans, both draftees and volunteers, were ill used to strict military discipline and their will to fight was grossly undermined by an increasingly elusive enemy.

It appeared that the Viet Cong, in particular, were refusing direct contact with allied forces and were reverting to the guerilla tactics that they had used primarily during the early years of the war. Those tactics included mines, booby traps, and the primitive, but highly effective, pungi spikes. The major difference in the effectiveness of these tactics was the timing. At the inception of the war, when this stratagem was initiated, the collective determination of the U.S. troops was intact and solid. During the second employment of this combat style, the collective determination was fragmented and scattered. Thus the casualties sustained against this unseen enemy only served to have U.S. troops ratchet up their efforts to seek and destroy the Communists, which in turn only led to more futile missions. Even the "Pacification Program" which was carried out mainly by Military Intelligence and CIA operatives, was starting to falter. This mission together with "Vietnamization" was intended to establish a network of informants and allies within the VC infrastructure that would ultimately lead to their betrayal and subsequent collapse.

Part of the mission of the Phoenix Program was to carry out the successful conclusion of Pacification. The mission statement was to "win the hearts and minds of the people." With the onslaught of cynicism starting to be felt within the ranks, the statement soon evolved into: "Give us your hearts and minds or we'll burn down your fuckin' hootch."

****

With the attitude- check meeting concluded, Scott made his way to his military vehicle and shifted gears to the scheduled appointments. Scott breezed through the day, had only a couple of hours of paperwork to complete, and was looking forward to driving home for the Thanksgiving Holiday. But, unbeknownst to him, a military decision had been made, and, within a few weeks Scott would no longer be stationed at the Boston Army Base.

He would be leaving the area for good.

CHAPTER 12

Scott returned to the office to type his agent report and was met by Captain McGuiness.

"Lieutenant," he said curtly, "don't leave for the holiday tomorrow without seeing me first. I have to review something with you." He heard a tone in the captain's voice that gave him pause, but was unsure why.

"Lt. Regan, did you hear me?"

Scott moved to sit down in the squeaky, wooden desk chair and swiveled toward McGuiness.

"No problem, sir. I'll see you just before I leave."

"Fine. Perfect." The captain held his glare after his response.

Scott turned back to the gray metal desk where the Underwood typewriter faced him like a stoic recorder. His mind began to wander as he typed, in slow cadence, his report for the day. The arrhythmic beats of the keyboard seemed disconnected from the information he recorded about his interviews.

The emotional mix of the anticipation of going home for Thanksgiving and the unexpected summons from McGuiness, played in the back of his mind and unnerved him. He completed his assignment and phoned home to see if Maryanne wanted to meet him at the Union House for drinks.

He dialed twice and heard nothing but unanswered rings. Concluding she wasn't yet home from work, he decided that it would be better not to go to a local Boston watering hole without her. He had the knack of easily making new "friends" at bars and, on occasions, had thought it a great idea to invite them home and surprise Maryanne. She, however, had always met this gesture with varying degrees of displeasure. On *this* night, and carrying the weight of his news, he decided that discretion would be the better part of valor and drove straight home.

He parked the Chevy in front of the house on Kimball Road, looked up at the single window of their small living quarters, and saw the muted glow of the kitchen light through the drawn and yellowed shade.

Maryanne was packing the clothes for their trip and Scott casually mentioned McGuiness's order to meet with him before he left work the next day.

She looked at him with a growling uneasiness. "What do you think he wants?"

"I really have no idea. I haven't had any run-ins with him recently. Everything has been calm, actually. In fact, in hindsight, he seemed to have been very relaxed and almost casual toward me. He hasn't been bitching about his wife or kids and apparently the puppy is finally housebroken 'cause he hasn't recently moaned about it pissing on his recliner." He paused. "But whatever he wants to tell me won't be bad news

– his recent demeanor even indicates that he might just want to wish me a happy Thanksgiving and a safe trip."

Maryanne recognized Scott was rationalizing McGuiness's intentions in order to convince himself of their innocence. Also gauging Scott's tension she decided not to press the issue. Tomorrow, on the ride home, they would talk about it.

"Pick some clothes, Scott. We've got a busy day tomorrow."

He grabbed a sweater, some underwear and a shirt from his small press- board cabinet he called his storage bin. Now all he had to do was get his clothes ready for his abbreviated workday, meet with McGuiness the next morning, pick up Maryanne at the house and hit the road for the Holiday.

But as the couple prepared for the ride down to New Jersey a CIA war memorandum was being prepared in Vietnam for dissemination to the military and mercenary personnel who were assigned to the Phung Hoang/Phoenix Program. It read:

C-O-N-F-I-D-E-N-T-I-A-L
NO FOREIGN DISSEMINATION

26 November 1968

The Viet Cong Single Out the Phung Hoang/ Phoenix Program for Special Attention.

Over the past few months, we have noted an increasing awareness by the Viet Cong (VC) of the Allied anti-VC

Infrastructure effort (PHUNG HOANG/ PHOENIX PROGRAM). This cognizance of the program is testimony to its gradually improving effectiveness. Further, it also should constitute a warning to those in the program: they are prime targets of the VC, and they are likely to become even more so in the future. This too is testimony to the program's impact. Perhaps more important, it also probably reflects the VC's understanding that in the months ahead, the struggle between their *infrastructure and the Allied counter effort will be a prime determinant of which side ultimately will prevail in South Vietnam. Captured VC documents have included the PHUNG HOANG/ PHOENIX PROGRAM as one of the Allied efforts which must be countered. The Program was singled out as a target for intelligence and for military action. Based on this evidence, it appears that the VC have a reasonable conception of how the program works and who is responsible for it.*

Most recently, the Communists *appear to have embarked on a public campaign to damn the Program. A 24 November Liberation Radio broadcast vilified the Program in the following manner:*

"In their throes, the U.S. Puppets are frenziedly resorting to every shrewd, cunning scheme and maneuver to avert their total collapse. One of these schemes is to attempt frantically to set up spy cells called PHOENIX Organizations, composed of hooligans and diehard cruel agents of various types who have incurred many blood debts to our people.

The broadcast goes on to belabor this theme and to announce the Communist forces will "crush" this new scheme. Indeed, the announcement closed by listing tasks to be carried out by the Communist forces; among these is the exhortation to "constantly heighten vigilance, cooperate with the people in disclosing and exterminating the PHOENIX teams, wipe out all enemy spy organizations, and protect the compatriot's security."

-2-

C-O-N-F-I-D-E-N-T-I-A-L

NO FOREIGN DISSEMINATION

****

The next day all of the Intel agents reported to work in various stages of vacation readiness. Since nobody had any interviews scheduled, no suits and ties were in evidence, and everyone was dressed in surveillance casual. This ran the gamut from flannel shirts and work boots to crew neck sweaters and loafers. Most of the pre- holiday busy stuff required putting finishing touches on paper work, drinking coffee and eating buttered rolls.

It was mid-morning before Scott saw McGuiness. The captain usually walked around the work area from the time the agents arrived in the morning until they left for their interviews.

Today, however, and evidenced by his early morning absence, he appeared to be a little more reserved and quiet. Scott knew that his aloofness couldn't be due to another hangover. All the agents recognized that when the 'ole man was hung over he became much more of a nagging presence than a benign recluse. Whatever the reason, it abruptly ended as the captain made his way from his office to where Scott and a group of agents were lounging on the gun metal gray desks and wooden chairs that comprised their string of stations.

"Regan." McGuiness called for Scott in a flat tone. "Come into my office so I can quickly review something with you and then get my ass out of here for a few days."

Scott followed him, snaking between chairs and into the captain's spartan office. The starkness was a perfect complement to his boss' irascible nature.

"Lt. Regan." The captain started speaking even before he sat down behind his desk. He settled into his chair and Scott stood at attention in front of him.

"At ease, lieutenant," McGuiness stated, "and have a seat." He continued without introductory comment.

"I received initial orders for you from MACV Headquarters yesterday. On 13 January '69 a commercial flight will be arranged for you from JFK airport to the West Coast. Immediately after your arrival in California you will be transported to Travis Air Force Base where you will depart for the Republic of Vietnam. On or about 11 January you will receive, by courier, your final orders that will delineate your specific assignment and primary duties within MACV. A driver will meet you at Tan Son Nhut Airport, Saigon, and bring you to G-2 headquarters where you will receive further instructions. Do you have any questions, lieutenant?" Scott had always lugged the burden of their obviously cold relationship but never thought it would come to this.

"I have a lot of questions, sir, but I respectfully recognize that I probably won't get many answers from you." Scott quickly realized that this response could be interpreted as confrontational and hastened to add, "in light of my reporting date, sir, I would like to request a 30 day leave starting on or about 12 December."

"Granted." McGuiness growled.

"Thanks, Captain. Is that all?"

"That's it, Lt. Regan."

"Have a good Thanksgiving then, sir."

"I will." McGuiness said. "Dismissed."

Scott stood up, did an about face and walked out of the office. A myriad of thoughts sparked and faded in his mind as he pondered the news that he just had received. Maybe he would wait until after the holiday to tell Maryanne and his family, or maybe he would tell them right away. Maybe he shouldn't think about it for a couple of hours.

When he reached the Chevy in the parking lot, Scott cocked his head skyward and asked aloud: "But the recruiter that got me to join Military Intelligence wore a suit and tie. When did all this shit change?"

He held that pose a moment as if expecting a Divine response but then threw up his arms and shook his head. He made the ride home silently and in deep thought.

At the house, Maryanne was already waiting outside with a few bags of incidentals that hadn't already been packed in the car. Scott realized how feeble this looked in light of what they would soon be packing.

"Hi. So how's it goin'? How we doin'?" He slammed the door of the Impala and his tone made her respond with a look of slight confusion.

"Hi" she said.

"So we ready to head south, Mair?"

"I'm ready if you are." Maryanne slid these words slowly from her throat. She sensed that there was a lot more Scott had to tell her following his morning sit down with Captain McGuiness. She knew when he was preoccupied with thought overload, and his absent look and distracted movements indicated that there was more on this mind than just driving home.

As they loaded the bags into the back seat of the convertible a rain- dampened wind blew up Mt. Auburn Street past their apartment. Maryanne pulled the woolen scarf around her neck and tucked it into the hooded windbreaker that bore their college logo. Scott grabbed the rest of the stuff and piled it onto the floor behind the front seats.

"Let's get hoppin' before they raise the toll on the Tappan Zee." This was always his way of saying they were taking too long to go anywhere. Maryanne slid into the passenger seat and pulled her door shut, and Scott accelerated down Kimball Road and headed toward home.

CHAPTER 13

The wet, bare limbs of the trees silhouetted the overcast sky along Route 128 and seemed to accent the couple's quiet mood. Traffic moved in a hushed flow and mirrored their silence. To divert his mind, Scott began to look at license plates like he had as a kid. At first they were all stamped Massachusetts, carrying Massachusetts drivers to Massachusetts places. Towards Providence on 95 South the plates started to reflect a much less homogeneous group. Cars from their home states of New York, New Jersey and Connecticut funneled south like an earth bound flock of migratory birds.

Finally, when the road signs read New Haven, Maryanne could no longer contain herself.

"Well, how *did* your meeting with McGuiness go?" It seemed like minutes passed before he answered her question. "It was pretty brief and to the point."

If he had any intention of delaying his announcement until some later date, he completely blew it when he added "...and to the point." If he had just said that it was "brief" he probably would have averted her next obvious question.

"So what *was* the point?"

"Well." Scott fumbled. He knew he could create an answer and buy time or he could tell her the truth and get it over with. He went with the latter.

"Well" he repeated again. "Actually," he continued to fumble as he lowered the radio volume on Frankie Vali's falsetto voice hitting the notes to "Marlena."

. "I'm not really surprised at the news he gave me. I mean, if I really look back and not try to bullshit myself, I could clearly see the handwriting on the wall. For example, why was everyone with a 9666 MOS sent to Ft. Benning for Infantry Basic. Also, why was I ordered to go to jump school? Was it because I had a three- week lag between finishing at Benning and reporting to Ft. Holabird? Did this really sound like somebody who was going to spend his hitch wearing a suit and tie, playing golf on company time, and never being late for cocktail hour?"

He looked to his right at Maryanne who sat quietly in the passenger seat and stared at him.

"In addition," Scott carried on. "The parallels between me and Willy Payne are spooky in themselves. So far I've followed in every footstep he's taken. First of all his opinion about Military Intelligence was really instrumental in my choosing this branch. Then I followed him through Benning and the "Bird", and now we're riding in his car that I bought from him before he went to 'Nam."

Maryanne spoke for the first time since Scott started to explain his short meeting with McGuiness. She addressed her visceral suspicion.

"You're going over there aren't you, Scott?"

"Yes."

"When?" Her voice strained.

"In January."

"Oh, dear God in Heaven." She turned away from him, inhaled deeply and clutched her hands in her lap. Her mind tumbled with questions but she said nothing, slid down into the car seat, and stared through the rain-streaked windshield at the dashes of white lane markings that raced by in a liquid blur.

****

Unbeknownst to Scott another parallel was forming between Willy Payne and himself. Payne was stationed in Binh Thuan Province, Republic of Vietnam; an area that would soon become very familiar to Scott.

Phan Thiet was the largest town in Binh Thuan, the southernmost province in II Corps along the South China Sea. Depending on the weather the main street could be either a dusty red, sun baked dirt road or a gooey mess of thick red glue. In the dry season whole fish were placed on raised platforms of bamboo slats. They were allowed to rot in the sun and the putrefied liquid was collected in containers below and rendered into a sauce called nuoc mam. This clear golden liquid was the basis for marinate and food dressing for local cooking.   It originated from rotting fish and, in its final presentation in clear glass bottles, still smelled like rotting fish. The town emanated this pungent aroma that was exacerbated during the rainy season when the waters washed nuoc mam residue into every cranny and blended with human waste that wafted up in rolls of fetid humidity. The town had the distinction of being labeled "the nuoc mam capital of the world." The rats loved it.

Aside from the TET offensive in 1968, Phan Thiet held no real military or strategic importance to the VC or NVA. It was equidistant from Saigon to the Southwest and Cam Ranh Bay to the Northeast but was situated in an area where the Viet Cong could regroup and plot their next offensive. For this reason alone the Phoenix personnel deemed it a hot area that had to be neutralized.

Lt. Payne was sent to Binh Thuan Province as a 2nd Lieutenant and was assigned to the CIA/ MACV clandestine attempt to win the war at the grass roots level. Nobody assigned to the Province or District level was privy to the larger circle of action happening above their command. The job was gritty and fractured and each advisor had his own combat knothole to look through. The daily routine consisted of gathering a convincing amount of intelligence information on VC suspects, their movements and their intent. Once enough information was accumulated on a specific target the Phoenix teams moved in and snatched the suspect for further questioning. The number of allies involved in this attempt depended on who the target was and how tight the perceived security was. In most instances the individual who was snatched for questioning was a high- ranking male official. At other times it could be a teenager or an old woman. Nobody was immune from suspicion.

During the TET Offensive of 1968 this province was a focus of Viet Cong activity. The Communists felt that the area should be harassed in order to demonstrate terrorist control of major highways that ran along the sea and to the north. Route 1 enabled American convoys to move men and materials rapidly up country from its southernmost point in My Tho in III Corps. Phan Thiet just happened to be along the way.

For this geographic reason in '68, the area where Payne was stationed became a crucial psychological swingpoint to both the VC and the Allies. It was a struggle for a little piece of land that could become an example of who was running the war. Both sides wanted to make their point and Willy was one of the players.

CHAPTER 14

Once Scott had told Maryanne about his assignment to Vietnam, he found that it was relatively easy to explain it to the rest of his family—except for his mother. She'd always shouldered an emotional Doomsday personality, and this news threw her over the edge. Scott's father had to work overtime to console her during her frequent, and spontaneous, crying jags. Yet, despite all hopes, it was pretty simple and direct. He was going to 'Nam and all the previous maneuvers and manipulations on his part amounted to nothing.

In late 1968 the Viet Cong's effort was shifting from an all out offensive to one of "protracted assault." The tactic had the additional benefit to the VC hierarchy of allowing them to see how Lyndon Johnson's war would be embraced by the new American president, Richard Nixon. In the beginning of the new administration no strategic differences were perceived by the enemy. General Creighton Abrams, who took control of MACV in June of 1968, wanted to look for the "big battle." But Abram's adversary, Gen. Giap, knew that he needed to buy some time to rebuild the numerical strength and morale of the VC and NVA. To this end, the war now became a game of cat and mouse.

Vietnam had been occupied by both Occidental and Oriental people during the 20th century. The Japanese and the French had been the most recent intruders, the former during WWII and the latter before and after them. The Vietnamese people waited with ultimate patience and cunning guerilla tactics until they simply wore the foreign forces into submission. There was no classic battle plan, nor planned tactical use of force. It was always known that the local militia best understood their own land and the people. If their neighborhood needed protection, they were the ones who could best accomplish that mission. This singular belief extended vertically from the rice paddies to the Politburo.

Coordination and control of grassroots guerilla activities fell to Truong Chinh. Gen. Giap enlisted Gen. Chinh, his former adversary, as a director of diversions and allowed him to call the day-to-day shots.

Still, VC were being successfully identified and neutralized by the Phoenix Program. Their ranks were being infiltrated by paid agents. Their exposure and elimination were becoming more and more of a daily threat. In late 1968 Giap ordered Chinh to go underground. The Viet Cong and their civilian sympathizers were once again reverting to stratagems of jungle warfare. They were masters at this tactic. And they were aware that the American and allied forces hated fighting an unseen enemy.

As the day for Scott's departure approached he, Maryanne, and their families managed to maintain a relatively upbeat tone. On New Year's Eve they went to a party at the home of one of Chan's fraternity brothers and football teammates from St. Lawrence University, Tory Bratton. The host had never met Scott or Maryanne, but it didn't matter. In fact, Chan had forgotten to mention he had invited them to the party. When they finally found the address in Cold Spring Harbor, Long Island, Chan had not yet arrived. Scott fumbled a little with his explanation of how they came to be there, but once he mentioned Chan's name they were welcomed with open arms and an open bar.

Sipping his first Johnny Walker Black Label, Scott was scanning the crowd when he spotted Chan and his latest girlfriend making their way toward him from the cavernous entrance foyer. He put his drink down on an antique burled walnut serving table and headed toward his best friend.

"Hey, man!" they both said simultaneously, and embraced in a warm bear hug. "Happy New Year."

"Likewise, brother." As Chan turned to introduce his current romantic interest, Maryanne hustled up to greet him and say hello to the natural blonde beauty on his arm.

"Hey, Maryanne!" Chan said as he threw his arms behind her and lifted her off the floor. "How are ya' baby?"

"Good, Chan. And, how have you been?" she parried, shifting her glance to his girlfriend. Chan put Maryanne back down.

"Bonnie," he said, "I'd like you to meet two of my closest friends. This is Scott and his wife Maryanne. Guys, this is Bonnie."

"I've heard a lot about you, Scott," she smiled.

"Only believe the good stories"

"But they were *all* good stories," she winked. Her green eyes were stunning and they accented her flawless complexion and Pepsodent smile. Chan has finally gotten himself a keeper, Scott thought.

Bonnie turned to Maryanne. They greeted each other warmly and immediately began to girl chat as their men drifted toward the bar.

"Where's your drink?" Chan asked.

"Over there on that expensive looking table. When did you start to travel in circles with friends who live in mansions?"

Chan chuckled, "Tory's old man owns a metal fabricating business or something like that. But he's a good guy. Not spoiled, I mean. He's really pretty much down to earth. He was just born rich."

"With a first name like Tory he sounds like a rich kid who should live in a house like this. But I just can't see a white boy with a name like that playing college football. I mean, your name is weird enough. Chandler and Tory. You guys sound like, co-captains of a badminton team. But football?" Scott shook his head incredulously.

Chan smiled, flashing his infectious trademark grin. He always appeared to have a half smile, due to a bout with polio he had as a child that left him with an upper lip that he couldn't fully raise. He had come to realize, however, that it was a small price to pay in comparison to his biological father who was killed by the disease when Chan was five. His facial oddity was, nonetheless, actually viewed as sexy by many young women - and he had learned to play it up big.

Scott retrieved his drink from the walnut table and attempted, with a swipe of his hand, to wipe the wet circle his glass had left on the polished wood. This, however, only served to smear the water across a larger portion of the surface. When he turned around to continue talking to Chan he was gone. Maryanne and Bonnie were standing by the tall French doors at the other end of the huge living room. When Maryanne caught his eye, she disengaged from her conversation and made her way through the guests and across the thickly padded Tabriz rug that covered what looked to be a hand laid parquet floor.

"Scott," Maryanne gushed, "Bonnie really seems to like Chan a lot!"

"So does that one." Scott pointed to the entranceway of the softly lit dark paneled library where Chan was engaged in an animated discussion with a petite blonde in a pixie haircut.

"Oh C'mon," Maryanne replied. "I've seen a few of Chan's girlfriends and this one seems to have a lot in common with him. Don't you think?"

"How can I tell, Mair? They all seem to have a lot in common with him. It's whether or not he has a lot in common with them. You know Chan. He always runs hot in the beginning."

"Yeah, that could be true, but Bonnie told me that they have been seeing each other regularly for 3 months now. She either flies down from Atlanta to Pensacola every weekend or Chan logs some flight time and hops up to see her. I'm really excited for them."

"Maryanne…relax, will you please? That still leaves five days during the week where he can cat around. Besides, he's never mentioned her to me. But I do have to admit that she's sure a looker."

"She *is* so cute!" Maryanne bubbled.

"Mair, Chan doesn't give a shit about cute. He's a lot shallower than that. He's as easy to read as a cereal box. That's why I like him. Anyway, I'm going to make my way over there." Scott gestured to where Chan was talking with the blonde pixie. "Do you want me to get you a drink first?"

"No thanks," she said "I'm going to find Tory and talk to him for a bit."

Scott began to sidle toward Chan and Miss Petite just as Tory's father joined the conversation. Mr. Bratton seemed to address the young blonde exclusively. Chan took the cue and excused himself as Scott caught Chan's eye and they nodded simultaneously toward the bar.

"This takes the cake. Check this shit out." Chan said in quick succession.

"What's up?" Scott asked.

"I called Tory the day after Christmas to find out the details for tonight; what time to come over and shit like that. He proceeds to tell me that he has a surprise for all of us when we get here and we'd find out what it was on our own."

"So?" Scott quizzed.

"See that chick talking to Tory's ole' man?"

"No I didn't notice her." Scott kidded.

"Well, that's the surprise."

"The only surprise about her is that she's not sitting in your lap already."

"No, she's Tory's squeeze for the week, compliments of the 'ole man."

"What?" Scott squinted.

"Apparently his father had some business in Martinique just before Christmas. He got home as planned on the day of Christmas Eve. But, what wasn't planned was what he brought home with him. Her. She's from France, but she travels around the world going wherever her services are both fully appreciated *and* fully paid. The 'ole man thought it would be a great idea to give her to Tory for a Christmas present."

"You mean to tell me that this guy brought this chick back from vacation to his house with his wife at home?" Scott squinted more tensely.

"You got it brother."

Scott leaned back into a heavy drape that almost supported his weight and asked again, "With his wife at home?"

"You got it, man."

"Now does this make any sense to you? I mean if there's some unwritten rule about shittin' where you eat, then this guy just rewrote the book."

"These people aren't like your mother and father, Scott. They have more money than they need. They have to struggle somewhere else. It can't be for everyday bill paying. So they've got to create some other kind of uncertainty. It makes them feel like there's a challenge in their lives."

Scott looked at Chan with open eyes now. He felt a sense of naiveté realizing that his friend from Clifford Scott High School had become so easily accepting of this upper crust behavior.

"So," Chan continued, "the 'ole man brought her home Christmas Eve when Tory was getting loaded at the Chop House in Garden City."

"Where was his wife?" Scott asked.

"Asleep in bed."

Chan elaborated. "On Christmas morning his father called the wife and kid to come downstairs. But not before he had placed the gifts under the tree. One of these gifts was her, stretched out in a French bikini and all wrapped up in cellophane with a big red ribbon."

"You mean to tell me," Scott stammered, "that the knockout standing over there was laid out like a basket of fruit?" He didn't wait for an answer. "I mean, one of the cardinal rules of fucking around is that you never bring them into your home. Never mind on Christmas Eve! Your home is where your wife and kids are. That's it."

"Well, I really don't think the 'ole man was porkin' her. He just imported her for Tory."

"And the mother was O.K. with this Christmas gift?" Scott asked.

"Well, take a look." Chan gestured. "She's been here a week already so how mad could the 'ole lady be?"

"You know," Scott exasperated, "I just don't understand how Protestants think. I mean if a relative of mine is going to find a piece of ass on some Caribbean island you can bet your balls he's not going to bring her home to show his wife and family. He may bring her around town and set her up in a nice place to live for a while, but he'd never bring her into his kitchen. There *are* limits." Scott started to laugh at the self-righteous tone in his own voice. "Besides, buddy, I think that all of this weird shit starts with the food you guys eat." Chan cracked his crooked smile as he realized that Scott was about to draw some wacky analogy.

"I think that any guy with his head screwed on straight prefers a wedge of cheese and a beer over caviar and a dry martini. Don't you remember how you always came to my house and slept upstairs in my bed when I was out late? Now think clearly about this. Would you have ever done that if you knew that our refrigerator was stocked with cream cheese and Silvercup bread?"

"Well, …maybe." Chan said slowly.

"Horseshit!" Scott added. "You only stopped at our house because you knew that we had a fridge stocked with *real* food".

"Yeah. Your mother always treated me right."

"Right? Right ain't the word. Her food kept our whole world in balance. Remember all the times when I came home to *my own house* and you had already found the last slice of salami or anything else I tried to hide under lettuce leaves in the Frigidaire?"

"Yeah, so what?"

"So, there wasn't anything to eat. How did you think *I* felt about that?"

"Probably hungry." Chan dead- panned.

"Yeah, and tired. And I didn't have any place to sleep except the living room couch that was covered with plastic, and you *know* how that shit sticks to your skin."

"Yea, but don't you remember how many times I had to sleep on the same couch because I got to your house too late and *you* were already asleep in *your* bed?"

"So, I should apologize for that?"

"No, but you know what?"

"What?" Scott said.

"We've been through this 100 times."

"Yeah, screw it." Scott said. "Let's mingle."

"You mingle," Chan replied. "I want to find out more about Le Pixie."

The blonde was still talking with Tory's father when Chan made his way toward them. He was interrupted in mid-quest by Bonnie's touch at his elbow.

"I really liked talking to Maryanne and Scott. They both are sweet people."

"Well, you're half accurate," Chan joked. "Maryanne might be sweet but Scott's more like arugula."

"What's arugula?" Bonnie asked.

"Italian people eat it like lettuce. It might catch on some day." Chan crooked his smile and avoided the explanation of the bitter taste of the leafy vegetable.

"How about some cream cheese and caviar instead?" He laughed.

****

Groups now gathered for the New Year's countdown in front of several TV screens that were simultaneously broadcasting pictures of the rowdy throngs in Times Square. The Allied Chemical building stood as the backdrop that started "The Ball" to drop precisely at 10 seconds before 12:00 midnight.

Chan, Bonnie, Maryanne, and Scott stood together in front of a 25" RCA cabinet television that represented the epitome of big screen color TV. The butlers, clad in white shirts and black bow ties, moved stealthily among the guests with trays of bubbling flutes of Dom Perignon. Scott rested his third snifter of Macallan 1951 single highland malt Scotch, on the tray and reached gingerly for a glass of champagne. He had discovered the single malt after he already had two Johnny Blacks on the rocks.

"Hey Mair," he poked his wife gently, "did you know that they were serving this single malt treat from the butler trays?"

"Not really, but I know that if they had it here you'd find it."

"But how come at the bar I only get Johnny Black?"

"I think that they wanted the real Scotch drinkers to mingle and not cluster at the bar. Get the point?"

He didn't answer.

Chan and Bonnie grabbed the last two flutes on a passing server's tray, as the countdown commenced.

Ten, nine, eight, seven, six, five, four, three, two, one - Happy New Year!! With the passing of yet another 12 months, the crowd cheered and turned, kissing each other as if they were all the best of friends.

Maryanne and Scott hugged warmly and did the same with Bonnie and Chan.

The four of them looked at each other and in that moment they were gripped with the knowledge that the coming year was certain to be one of transition. Chan knew he would be getting his orders to fly choppers somewhere in I Corps and Scott had already gotten his ground assignment somewhere within MACV. Bonnie was struck with a pang of loneliness, already missing a young man she hardly knew and Maryanne saw a long year ahead filled with daily apprehension and uncertainty.

These realizations flashed through their thoughts for only a moment until they snapped back to the present revels. The crowd of celebrants completed their round of well wishes to each other and the night became just a party. The New Year of 1969 had begun.

Scott turned to his left and met a tray of crepes tied like little baskets with green ribbons, filled with some kind of creamy something. Without asking what it was he attempted to pluck one and eat it, but missed his mouth completely. The little bundle landed softly on the Tabriz. Before he could bend over and retrieve it someone with a big foot walked by and flattened it into the plush pile.

"Whoopsie daisy," Scott muttered, hazily. No one noticed, except Maryanne.

"Can't you please put a napkin under your chin before you go for the next one?"

"Why would I want another one when I don't even know what the first one tasted like?"

"Regardless of what you eat, try to do it neatly. OK?"

"Oh, sure." Scott said absently.

The Christmas gift was slithering through the crowd toward the oak and brass bar across the room.

"Excuse me for a second, Mair, I'm going to powder my nose."

Instead of relieving himself in the bathroom, located to his right, he stepped directly ahead and weaved his way to the bar where the Gift had her right foot propped on the bar rail. This posture served to lift her spaghetti strap mini dress a few inches higher up her tanned leg. The bartender glided professionally toward her and placed a napkin on the hardwood bar top.

"Bon soir madame, sil vous plais?"

"Oui, oui, vin blanc, merci"

Scott heard the verbal exchange, but assuming she must also speak English, attempted his most debbonnaire introduction.

"Hi. My…name…is…Scott." He always thought any foreigner could understand English if it was spoken loud enough and slow enough.

"Why are you yelling?" she said clearly with a schooled accent. She didn't really want a response and turned to the bartender as he placed a fume blanc on the napkin. He modulated his next question, attempting to keep the awkward conversational ball rolling.

"So how do you like coming to America?" Feeble question, Scott thought.

"I always like coming to America." She stifled a yawn.

Scott paused and thought that she would probably like going anywhere, if the price was right.

"That's certainly nice to hear. I'm from America and I like to hear you Europeans say nice things about my country. How has the family treated you so far?"

"I really like Tory. He's a nice boy."

"That's the reason you're here anyway, isn't it?"

"Well no, because I could be anywhere else, too!"

"For example, mon chere?"

"Oh, do you speak French?"

"Well, I failed French at St. Benedict's high school but I can still remember a few words, and even some idioms," he gloated.

"I just prefer to be where I'm most appreciated." She glanced at him a little more intently. Perhaps another date with opportunity would present itself here. Maybe his father had money too.

Scott caught a change in her attitude and decided to have some fun with it.

"I'm sure that most men appreciate you," he smiled warmly.

"Yes they do, but I'm very busy."

"Busy doing what?"

"I'm just busy being myself."

Pixie was quickly becoming tired of this pointless dialogue. She studied him. He wore neither a Patek Philippe nor Rolex. There was no evidence of jewelry that could have been passed down to him through some legacy. His clothing wasn't expensive and he displayed no other symbols of status. He was probably exactly what he appeared to be: an international nothing.

Scott didn't recognize she was checking out this type of stuff. He had always thought his conversational skills would transcend emblems of status. She turned to the left and faced him a bit more frontally. Scott's eyes drifted slowly down her clavicles and around her sculptured shoulders.

"So where are you going after you finish entertaining Tory and his father?"

"We haven't discussed how long we'll enjoy each other yet, but I have another appointment at the end of the month."

"Excuse me for prying," Scott asked, "but I'm just a naive kid from Jersey and I don't understand a couple of things."

"Oh? Like what?"

"Well, first of all, it seems that Tory's mother has accepted you like you were a long lost cousin. Right?"

"I don't know about that. I don't know any of her cousins," she said.

"It's just a figure of speech. What I mean to say is that her husband brought you home as a Christmas gift for his son. Right?"

"*He* can label me whatever he wants."

"So you're a global date?" She touched the side of her neck with a manicured fingernail and paused before answering.

"I never thought of myself in that way, but I must say, I do like the image."

"So I bet you can say 'how fat is your wallet' in different languages."

She ignored the jocular jab.

"Of course. All Europeans speak more than one language."

"I never knew that," Scott exclaimed.

"You should have traveled more, no?" she added.

"I'm going to the Orient in three weeks," he bragged.

"Where?"

"Vietnam."

"So am I," she exclaimed.

"I know why *I'm* going there, but why are *you* going?"

"I have a date."

"You have a date in 'Nam? With whom?"

"A general."

"An American general?"

"Yes. A well known general."

With this last admission she realized that she might have already said too much and turned away from him.

But the intoxication from the fine single malt, coupled with the provocative conversation, led Scott to push the dialogue.

"Where about are you going in Vietnam?"

"To Saigon," she answered over her bare shoulder.

"So am I. When will you be arriving?"

"Sometime in the middle of the month," she returned her glance toward him and Scott saw this as an opening to pry more.

"Wouldn't it be a coincidence if we ran into each other in Saigon?"

Her ego, fueled by a consistent pattern of intimations from men, led her to read into his comment.

"You're innocent and cute, but neither of those qualities could afford me."

Scott smiled at her bravado and shot back, "Shit, I can't even afford your right shoe and..." She turned before he was finished speaking, brushed his face with the softness of her right palm, and patted him on the head like a smug superior might do to a student. Without another word she moved briskly around him, waved to an unseen guest in the next room, and was gone.

CHAPTER 15

Scott received his final orders two days before he was due to leave on Pan Am's non-stop flight 724, from Kennedy International to San Francisco. This was the initial leg of the journey that would take him to Travis Air Force Base to board a World Airways charter jet to Okinawa and ultimately Tan Son Nhut Airport.

The military envelope arrived via courier to his in-laws house in Port Washington. Scott had to sign for it personally. He opened the letter casually and read it in the light of the bay window that faced the backyard.

Headquarters

United States Military Assistance Command, Vietnam

APO San Francisco 96222

Special Orders

10 January 1969

Number 10 Extract

83, TC220, Fol. rsq. dir. WP TON

REGAN, SCOTT J. 05248160 (148-24-2854) 2LT MI USA 9666

Proc. Det. MACV

Asg to: USA ADGRY II Corps (W-08V-03-D) APO 96318

Dy asg: NA

Maj. Comd/agcy: US Mil Asst Comd (SD5891) Vietnam, APO San Francisco 96222 C55A/01-011

Rept. date: 13 Jan 69

Aloc: CORDS/PHOENIX CBBDC BPED 4Jan67

DEROS: 2 Jan 70	ETS: 12 Jan 70	BASD: NA
ADC: 2 years	DOR: 13 Jan 68	PCS (MDC) 3MO9
Scty clne: TS		EDCSA 16 Jan 69

Emerg. data: Mrs. Maryanne Regan (w), 92 Valley Wood Rd., Pt. Washington, NY 11050

He reread the front page of the SPECIAL ORDERS NUMBER 10 so that he could try and decipher the cryptic acronyms that typified military communications. He understood his reporting date, active duty commitment, emergency data and the notation of his Top Secret clearance, but his eyes kept returning to what followed the colon after ALOC: **CORDS/ PHOENIX**. That's where Willy Payne was assigned. His life seemed to again be following in the wake of his college upperclassman friend. He placed the orders on the kitchen table and stared blankly out the bay window into a gray January sky. When he reached for the papers again he noticed that there were three other officers listed on the same page. Two officers had additional orders, and Scott was one of them. The directive read:

Indv. Asignd. to II Corps will proceed to Vung Tau, RVN for briefing prior to reporting to new duty station. Primary duties include performance of duties as tactical advisor to ARVN/GVN Infantry type military or paramilitary units in the district area of responsibility to include frequent participation in ground combat operations. (2LT Regan) (2LT Stuckard)

FOR THE COMMANDER:

OFFICIAL:

Charles A. Corcoran, General, USA

R.F. Tuckey, Major USA, Asst. AG

Scott folded his orders into quarters and shoved them into the back pocket of his Levis. He had absolutely no intention of sharing their contents with any of his family. In fact, he was just damned tired of waiting and wondering. He just wanted to get going, get it done and get back.

Maryanne and Scott drove to the Holiday Inn at JFK the day before his 8:00 am flight to San Francisco. They planned to stay overnight at the motel and avoid all the early Monday morning traffic that clogged every artery on Long Island. Neither of them viewed this as a romantic prelude to his departure. It was just a perfunctory arrangement that enabled them to begin the six-month separation before they would be allowed to reunite for his week of R&R. They had narrowed their choices to Hawaii, Australia or Japan.

Hope was in sight and the pain of separation would later be ameliorated in some distant location. The reality of what *could* happen to their lives during that six months wasn't discussed, and confidence was the pillar of their plans on their last night together in the United States.

Morning broke ringingly clear but cold. Scott, dressed in his Class A uniform and spit shined shoes, looked every inch the solider. At the airport they were directed to an outdoor gate from which they walked to the edge of the tarmac where all non-passengers had to turn back. The Pan American jet, some 50 yards away, roared to life and spewed opaque fumes from its engines. Maryanne grabbed his shoulders and made him look into her clear hazel eyes.

"The whole family will be praying to St. Jude for you to be back by May for Kathy's wedding."

"Hey, Mair, this is a one year gig. I don't think I'll make it. May is only four months away."

"Yea, Scotty, but St. Jude *is* the patron saint of all helpless causes."

"Catholics do have a knack of finding a patron saint for everything."

"Maybe that's true, but we don't bother them with trivial stuff either, do we?"

"Depends on someone's definition of trivial," he said. "I remember trying to find out who was the patron saint of basketball at St. Vincent's. If my prayers had been answered and I had played varsity when you were a cheerleader, then I would have been banging you a lot sooner." She laughed and tried to tickle his ribs through the thick uniform.

"I always did have my eye on you, even though you only played on the freshman team."

"Well, still, keep your eye on me because we're gonna' boogie again when we meet on R&R."

Their lips met again, but her eyes were open. Unspoken fears dominated Maryanne's final thoughts as she hugged him and tried to transfer her strength to him. Then it was time to go. The stream of civilians and military types had finished saying their goodbyes, were moving toward the stair lift of the waiting jet as Scott turned, walked to the back of the line, and joined the file of passengers boarding the aircraft.

Scott's window seat enabled him to watch Maryanne wave vacantly at all the portals on the plane in attempt to find his face. She was standing near the runway in a foam green raincoat with a fake fur collar. She could not have seen him as the nose of the airplane slowly pivoted away from her to the northwest. He craned his neck until he saw only the toes of her black boots. Turning back into his seat, he placed his hands on his thighs and stared straight ahead. He felt no emotion about leaving and harbored only thoughts of confident anticipation. He just wanted to get it done. He patted his final orders in his breast pocket as the jet accelerated down the long runaway and took to the air.

CHAPTER 16

San Francisco airport was as busy as any other major airport, but unlike any he had seen back east, both women and men had long hair and appeared to have no place in particular to go. Every other person was fondling a guitar, or somebody else. In the more private nooks of the baggage claim area young girls in long gingham dresses were sleeping, draped over guys in jeans and leather vests, looking like one big puppy littler with no mama.

Scott made his way to the men's room and changed from his Class A's into fatigues. He had just finished stuffing the dress uniform into his olive green duffle bag when he heard the final boarding call for the short hop to Travis Air Force Base north of San Francisco. It was a quick flight followed by a quicker turn around at Travis, where he boarded a World Airways flight for what would be the last, and longest, leg of his trek to Southeast Asia.

The cavernous plane smelled of stale air and Old Spice shaving lotion. The stewardesses were thickly built with large shoulders, heavy hands and looked like they were specifically chosen for their ability to withstand a grueling eighteen-hour flight with a minimum of creature comforts. Scott stuffed the duffel into the oversized compartment above his seat and headed for one of the bathrooms. Looking into the mirror, he washed his hands noticing for the first time the black embroidered military insignia near the points of his collar. Instead of the Military Intelligence logo, he saw the Infantry insignia of crossed rifles. He immediately looked down at the name that was stitched on the right front side of his fatigues. It said REGAN.

"Well at least they got that right," he thought.

He made his way back to his seat just as the cabin lights flickered. The roar of the revving engines made the shell of the plane creak and groan. With the longest flight of his life ahead of him, he decided to shut his eyes and try for sleep, but when he tried to recline his seat, it barely moved. With a sigh of annoyed resignation he reached under the seat in front of him and pulled out a book from his small carry on bag.

The science fiction book was titled *1984.* He began to read where he had left off. The scene opened to describe George Orwell's vision of the disciplining of non-conformists in the distant year of 1984. A small cage was placed securely over the dissenter's head and his face exposed at the front of the unit. Trapped at the other end of the cage was a starving rat. The choice was clear: either agree to conform to the dictates of Big Brother, or have one's face eaten by a frenzied feeding rodent. Scott shut the book at this passage and slammed it on his knee.

"Goddamit, I hate rats! I hate everything about rats. Even Mickey Mouse gives me the creeps."

The hours droned by, interrupted only by a brief refueling stop on Okinawa, where the passengers were allowed to disembark for a 45-minute break. Both military and civilian personnel filed out through cyclone fence pathways topped with barbed wire leading to a large, bright, whitewashed mess hall that was also enclosed with cyclone fencing. The available foodstuffs and drinks were typical for this military stopover point: Coke, milk, water, juices, piles of lukewarm hamburgers, soggy French fries, no salads and definitely no beer. Since Scott never met a food he didn't like, this was no great culinary setback. He crammed down three hamburgers with cold cheese, some rubbery fries bathed in ketchup, and washed it all down with a watery coke. He stood, stretched his shoulders, burped and headed back through the fenced enclosure, past the MP's and onto the plane. Maybe now he could get some sleep.

Hours later, the final descent woke him when both ears clogged from the effects of the decompression. He swallowed to clear his canals and looked out across the vast blackness framed by the window. Bursts of brightness flashed like fireflies and were quickly extinguished in the darkness below. He wasn't quite sure whether he was witnessing some surreal military skirmish or a celebration complete with fireworks. The only thing he knew for sure was that he arrived. The plane touched down and shook to a stop. Four Orientals pushed a rolling staircase toward the craft and opened the cargo door.

He stopped at the head of the stairway and looked at the cinder block building topped with the letters TAN SON NHUT. His face was smacked with dusty heat and his nose drew the smell of some flowery scent mixed with raw gasoline and rotting garbage. Before his senses could regroup a jeep pulled within 5 feet of him. He heard a voice.

"Lt. Regan." The driver of the vehicle wasn't asking for confirmation. He knew exactly who the officer was and he had his orders to collect him. Scott looked at the corporal without answering. The enlisted man scooped up his duffel bag and threw it into the backseat.

"Sir, I'm Cpl. Count and I'm assigned to bring you to MACV Headquarters tonight. Please jump in, sir."

Scott was in no mood to move anywhere after the long confined trip.

"Hey, corporal, can we stand here a few minutes until my blood starts to circulate vertically again. My ass feels like a pancake. What time is it anyway?"

"0300, sir."

"Isn't it past your bedtime?"

"I'm on night duty, sir."

"Well, you certainly seem perky enough to convince me of that. "So," he went on, "what's going on at Pentagon East at this hour that you have to hustle me there."

"I'm not privy to that, sir."

"Well, that makes two of us."

Scott shuffled to the passenger side of the vehicle, threw his left leg over the low side-wall of the Jeep and settled in.

"All right. Lets go, Corporal."

During the twenty-minute open air ride Scott got his first look at his new world. The dark cityscape that passed before him was serene and silent. The soft clouds of dirt kicked up by the tires and the occasional whiff of bougainvillea combined to make him sneeze.

"Hey, man could I get a different assignment cause I can't breathe here?" Scott kidded.

The driver, maintaining military posture, found no humor in Scott's quip.

"I'm not too sure, sir. You'll have to ask your commanding officer, sir."

"Will you please stop being so formal? What's you're first name?"

"Rigby, Sir. Corporal Rigby Count"

"Well, how about you make me feel right at home and address me as Scott? Ok?"

"Yes, sir."

"Hey, Rigby where are you from?"

"Bluefield, West Virginia, Scott, sir."

"Now ain't that a coincidence. I grew near a town that sounds like yours: Bloomfield, New Jersey. Have you ever heard of Bloomfield, New Jersey, Rigby?

"No, Scott. sir"

Now Scott's adrenalin was kicking in and he couldn't stop talking.

"Rigby, do you have any good Italian restaurants in your town?"

"Yes, sir, Scott, we have a great Eye-talian restaurant. It has been owned by the same family forever. They have the best spaghetti and meatballs, sir."

"Spaghetti and meatballs? Very Italian and a great house specialty. I bet you can play stickball with those meatballs, too, huh?"

"Stickball, sir?"

"Never mind, Rigby."

****

The jeep rolled up to the front of an enormous white building that seemed to border a golf course. Rigby downshifted and pulled within a few feet of an MP post. The entranceway to the building was heavily guarded as the jeep came to a full stop and three MP's briskly approached and checked Corporal Count's ID. Then, before Scott knew what was happening, he was whisked away and escorted to a locked door that opened onto an inner hallway.

"Lt. Regan, I'm Sgt. Caulfield. I'm assigned to bring you to your billet for the night."

"Hi, Sarge. Thank you for your help. I think. I just met Cpl. Count. Do you know him?"

No, sir, I don't but I was told that he was bringing you here at about 0325 this morning."

"Hey, Sgt. Caulfield," Scott hesitated, "I feel like some kind of celebrity. Are you sure someone over here doesn't think I'm Bob Hope?"

"No, lieutenant, we know who you are," the sergeant said without expression.

"Well, then if you think you know who I am, then you must also know that I'm hungry and dirty. Is there any hot water and food in my room? Also, maybe you can tell me why I was rushed here in the middle of the night."

"You weren't rushed here, sir. Your plane was scheduled to land early in the day, and we were just prepared to meet you."

Scott was trying to elicit a smile or at least some sign that the sergeant had a sense of humor. Neither happened and suddenly he started to feel dead on his feet.

"Ok, where do I bunk down?"

"Follow me, sir. Your duffel bag has been already sent up to the room."

Scott opened the door to the small quarters, and saw a tiny tray of snacks and water placed on the foot of his single bed. He grabbed the bag of Wise potato chips and pulled the sides apart with a familiar crackling sound that caused three salamanders to scurry up the walls and seek refuge. At the corners of the ceiling they uniformly turned themselves around to stare at the new arrival. Scott blinked at the unexpected roommates and slowly picked at the chips with his right hand.

Two long neck bottles of Coke sat on a small table next to his single bed and were as warm as room temperature. He reached for the first one and realized that he didn't have his p-38 opener. He had harbored the prized utensil from Ft. Benning, and through his time at Boston Army Base, keeping it attached to his car keys. It took a bit of practice to work this small tool, but it could open Campbell's soup cans as well as bottles. He couldn't believe he had forgotten it.

He grabbed the bottle and, remembering his old college trick, placed the cap between his upper and lower back teeth. He had opened Genesee and Utica Club beer bottles like this when he was at school. Just for the fun it, of course, just for the show. But this time the cap wouldn't budge. Maybe because he was tired, or maybe because there was nobody else around to take note of his talent. In any event, he thought it would be wiser just to edge the top of the bottle on the corner of the side table next to the bed and give it a downward crack with his hand. It worked as the liquid fizzed out in a gush of cream and brown bubbles. The salamanders didn't move at the sound, remaining stoically in place along the higher reaches of the walls. He raised the Coke in a toast to his lime colored roommates.

His feet felt as if they were going to well up out of his high cotton socks. He sat on the edge of the bunk and felt the awkward springs push through the thin mattress. He pursed his lips, bent forward and unwrapped his bootlaces and then laid back and lugged his legs onto the bed. Alien sounds wafted into the room through its one opened window. He wanted to close the shutters but his body was heavy and he stared at the single light bulb in the ceiling. His last thought as he drifted into sleep was how much it reminded him of the bright mid-morning sun at the Jersey shore— except it was devoid of heat.

CHAPTER 17

Morning came quickly with a persistent rapping sound. Scott stumbled his way to the door and pulled it open. Daylight poured in and backlit the form of Cpl. Count.

"Don't you ever sleep?" He squinted.

"I will, sir. I'm going off duty in ten minutes. It's now 0750 and Captain Hamm will be briefing you at 0830, right here in your quarters."

"In other words, the good captain makes house calls like an old fashioned family doctor?"

"He'll be here at 0830, sir," Count said, without a hint that there might be a personality behind his words.

"Is that everything I should know?"

"Yes, sir. It is."

"No offense, corporal, but you seem to have the sense of humor of a door knob. Can you please lighten up a little? After all, I just spent my first night in a strange place. I fully understand that it's not a picnic over here but, a fuckin' tomb would be more uplifting than you."

"I'm just following orders, sir."

"Aren't we all, Count?"

The corporal stiffened to attention for a salute and Scott managed one in return. Finally, he was gone.

Scott turned to the room, surveying it quickly, looking for anything he might've missed the night before. The only marked difference, now that light streamed in through the open window, was a view of the street below. Propping his palms on the cool stone sill he leaned forward and out the window. Vespa scooters puffed fumes as they motored along the hard packed road, girls and young women uniformly dressed in white Ao dais shuffled about in sandals, and, across the street, children gathered at a corner vending stand, buying soft breads, jars of water and stuffing both into cloth sacks that doubled as book bags.

It didn't remind Scott of anything he had ever seen before. All the faces looked the same. And curiously, the flow suggested a progression of everyday people doing routine things. No war. No worry. Just another day in River City.

Mindful Cpt. Hamm would be knocking on the door shortly, he made his way from the window to the shower hoping to make a good first impression. He towel dried quickly, jumped into his clothes and tucked the bottom of his pants into the tops of his stateside all leather combat boots. He just finished lacing the top eyelets when a knock sounded again on the door.

"Lt. Regan?" The voice asked.

"Yes, sir."

"Cpt. Hamm here. You're expecting me."

"Yes, sir, I am."

Scott didn't have time to check in the small mirror over the bathroom sink. He felt along his hips and made sure that his shirt was tucked in tight. It took only a second for him to reach the door and open it.

"Sir. I'm Lt. Regan."

"I know who you are. That's why I'm here, lieutenant. I'm Captain Hamm."

"C'mon in sir." Scott backed stiffly away and opened the door fully.

The captain didn't even look for a chair. He moved mechanically to the foot of the single bed and sat down. He appeared to have done this before.

"You can either stand up and listen to me or sit over there." He motioned to the light gray metal folding chair by the desk.

Scott grabbed it and sat on it backwards. He realized that the shave and shower didn't mean anything. The captain had an agenda that was to be recited to him regardless of how he looked, and the only thing that mattered was that he was present, conscious and listening. Proper military appearance was not required. The captain began his mechanical spiel.

"As you already know from your orders, you have been assigned to MACV. The Military Assistance Command in Vietnam is the successor to MAAG, or the Military Assistance and Advisory Group. You will be responsible for both assisting and advising the ARVN in combat and intelligence gathering operations. That, in turn, will enable them to regain their independence from communist influences in the Republic of Vietnam. You will function, initially, at the grass roots level of this effort. You will be assigned to a designated district in II Corps. Without significant input from the area to which you will be assigned the overall mission of MACV could be negatively impacted."

Scott shifted his chair as he studied the man before him. Hamm was trim from the shoulders down, but had jowls despite his otherwise youthful appearance. A pair of small eyeglasses was pressed deeply into the bridge of his nose, the thin frames almost invisible, stretching around his puffy head and back against his shaved temples.

"You must be acutely aware that from the moment of your arrival here you are a known target. The VC have compromised our intelligence sources and the Phoenix program has been designated as a focus of their concentrated efforts. They already know that you have arrived in country and there is now a price on your head. Personnel involved in the Phoenix effort have been marked for elimination. You must be aware of it and conduct yourself accordingly.

"U.S. officers and civilian mercenary types involved in this endeavor are of acute interest to the enemy. This is not so much different than our acute interest in the whereabouts and local impact of any high-ranking Viet Cong. Both sides know that the other must be neutralized. This is a high stakes game, lieutenant, and you *are* one of the chips. I'm sure you have already noticed that you are wearing Infantry insignia on your fatigues. If you were to have worn the true emblems of your branch, Military Intelligence, you probably would be dead by now; Intelligence officers and pilots are highly prized. The VC have more information about you then you can believe, so we don't want to advertise your *real* MOS."

Scott didn't particularly like the feeling he was getting about his situation and interrupted Hamm's monologue. "You just mentioned the involvement of civilian mercenary types, sir. I thought this was a military duty. Who are these civilians?"

"Right now you do not have a need to know who is involved in this particular mission. Suffice it to say that the Phung Hoang program to which you have been assigned is only one spoke in a larger wheel of an overall military goal. That goal is to win the support of the locals for the democratic Government of South Vietnam. Phoenix/Phung Hoang is an offshoot of an effort commissioned by General Johnson in 1965. It was comprised then of young officers who, unlike yourself, had previous experience as tactical advisors at the province, district or village levels. This program ultimately disbanded and was supplanted by military and civilian CIA types who are now an active arm of Phoenix. Have I answered your question?"

"Yes, sir," he felt compelled to answer, although he still didn't have a clear understanding of what this all meant to him.

"Very well, then." Hamm paused and pushed the upper frame of his glasses tighter onto the bridge of his nose, and continued. "Based on the action of last year's TET offensive, you will be working in an area that requires diligent combat intelligence gathering. There is an increased imperative for you to target and interrogate VC suspects. *You* will be instrumental in accumulating this information. Both allied and civilian forces will be available to assist you in accomplishing this mission. At the end of your tour you will be awarded the Combat Infantryman's Badge and, in all probability, the Bronze Star."

"How long will I be in this assignment, sir?"

"For six months. Your remaining time in the Phoenix Program will be spent at MACV Headquarters in Saigon. You will be granted a three day in- country R&R in about 90 days. After 180 days you will be eligible for your out- of- country R&R."

On that note, Captain Hamm concluded his rote dissertation and said, with an air of confidentiality, "You know, sometimes instead of Rest and Recuperation we call it I & I; Intoxication and Intercourse."

"I'll be sure to pass that along to my wife, sir."

"Ah, yes. I'm married, too." Hamm sighed.

"Do you have any further questions or comments?"

"No, sir."

"Very well then. You will grab your gear and report directly in front of this building at 0945 hours today. A driver will be waiting."

"That's all, Lt. Regan." Hamm returned his demeanor to Military cadence.

"OK, then. Have a good day, sir." Scott concluded.

****

Scott now had about an hour to kill before his driver was scheduled to pick him up. He emerged from the building and stood at the top of the marble steps that fronted the military hotel. The red hard pack street coughed up dust as the bicycles and motorbikes made their way left and right in front of him. The gentle aroma of bougainvillea and lemon trees conflicted with the pungent smell of durian fruit carried to him on a warm morning breeze.

He carefully made his way through the throng and across the main road to the wooden vending stand. Scott smiled at the youngsters as he walked toward the makeshift hut where Coca-Cola bottles were displayed on flat boards. He stared at the long necks with the red and white swirls and his thoughts drifted back to July heat, iced buckets and softball games. He pointed to one and motioned to the diminutive old lady. As he groped into the right pocket of his fatigue pants, he realized that he only had single U.S. dollar bills. He pulled one out and showed it to the woman. She glanced at the paper and her eyes lit up. Before he could blink, she plucked the currency from his hand and gave him two bottles. Then, just as quickly, she frantically waved him away with her hands.

"Didi mau! Didi mau!" she squeaked.

She had just scored some premier- and illegal- currency and wanted him immediately away from the scene of the crime. It was the first and last time he would hand a Vietnamese civilian a greenback. Possession of U.S. dollars was forbidden for all military personnel. The means of exchange was Military Payment Certificates, except for the use of local piastres that would be hand delivered, as inconspicuously as possible, to influence key or potential informants. This system of payoffs was effectively implemented by select Phoenix operatives.

CHAPTER 18

The Department of the Army's Phoenix School, National Training Center, Vung Tau, APO 96291 was the official address of the complex of small and inconspicuous cinder block buildings to which Scott reported. Inside its walls only those with a top-secret clearance took part in the orientation program.

The subject matter was all encompassing, ranging from the history and government of Vietnam, the current Viet Cong infrastructure and modus operandi, the effective use of interrogation techniques, to accepted forms of Vietnamese social etiquette.

The captain addressing the group wore camouflage fatigues and the toes of his canvas- sided boots were not buffed bright. That and the Combat Infantryman's Badge on his chest suggested that his regular day job hadn't always been lecturing.

The class was in progress.

"At no time should you motion to any allied Vietnamese to come quickly by waving to them with the back of your hand facing them and your fingers upright. This is a movement that is reserved for calling animals such as dogs." He continued. "The accepted form of signaling to a local is with the back of your hand facing them and your fingers pointing down." He demonstrated the move.

"Is this clear?" He shifted his gaze around the room. Most of the attendees nodded their heads slowly, except for Rodolfo Buono, who sat next to Scott in the windowless room. Rudy raised his hand.

"What about whistling?" he asked.

The instructor was caught off guard and stared at him.

"What about whistling what?" he asked.

"Like whistling for someone to come to you, sir."

The instructor noticed Rudy's rank insignia and addressed him accordingly.

"Lieutenant, we do not cover whistling in this brief course. However," he continued, "this does not mean that the Vietnamese locals don't use this as a form of communication."

Rudy squirmed in his seat and pushed forward with the query.

"So then, if someone is far away, can I crack out a whistle or not?"

This question was obviously not covered in the well-organized script that the instructor had memorized.

"Let's just say, lieutenant, that we can't."

"Roger that, sir. Thank you."

The captain gave the questioner a half glance of confusion and returned to his notebook. Scott looked at the inquisitive junior officer and smiled, thinking, "This guy is either too smart or too simple for the job."

After the 90- minute lesson in protocol ended, the class was given a 15- minute break. Scott wanted to talk to the guy who asked the only question of the day.

"Hey," he said, stopping the other lieutenant. "You woke everybody up with your question.   Why weren't you daydreaming or sleeping like the rest of us?"

"Well, I really just want to get to know all these customs. You never know – Regan." He nodded to the nametag stitched in black above the pocket on Scott's fatigues.

"The name's Scott."

"Hi. I'm Rudy."

The inevitable next question followed.

"So, where are you from?" It was so automatic it seldom had to be asked.

"I'm from Jersey." Scott offered.

"New Haven," Rudy smiled as they shook hands.

"So where's your DIOCC?" Scott asked.

"Mui Ne." Rudy grinned.   "I understand that station is a beach, man."

"So you're excited about having your ass backed up against the South China Sea?"

"Yeah, wouldn't you be?"

"No way," Scott answered.

"Why? Don't like scenic water views?"

"Hey, Rudy, if you're from New Haven, you gotta' know that there's an amazing difference between having a view of the

Sound and being pushed into it. I'd never want to be backed up against water."

"This ain't Korea, buddy." Rudy added, "You can actually swim and get a tan here."

"Fuck that, I'll get tan in Beach Haven when I get home."

When the 15-minute break was over, the two new acquaintances made their way back to the classroom. The captain took his position behind the podium and resumed their orientation lecture.

"Female Vietnamese have many ways of attempting to work themselves into the personal support system of the GI. This is not too different from what one might find back home. The crucial factor here is that their attention towards you could make all the difference between them living or dying.

"To this end their main objective is to be sponsored by you through marriage, which would enable them to expatriate themselves to the USA. They do not stop to consider that you might already be married. If you are, it becomes just another obstacle in the struggle to which they have become accustomed. They don't necessarily think of it as insurmountable.

"Be aware, also, that they will have the full support of their family and community in their efforts to win an American husband. The perception, when one of their own is sponsored by an American through marriage, is that the rest of the local populace will then have established a beachhead in the United

States. They believe that with a modicum of patience they, too, will eventually be able to work their way into our country."

The captain paused and walked around to the front of the podium.

"I don't know how many of you are married. However, I must emphasize again that the ladies **don't care.** You are seen as a meal ticket and their objective is to capture one of you.

"They work on the most basic levels of human psychology. You are in a foreign land, separated from family and friends, serving in a combat environment and waiting for a letter from home. They can offer you immediate gratification and comfort and will attack you at your most vulnerable moment and offer to make it all better. They are the vultures in our midst, just another unpleasant side of this undeclared war.

"In addition to the damage that this seduction may cause in your personal lives, you must also think about the damage it can inflict on our overall mission here in Vietnam. You all have a minimum clearance of Top Secret. Some of you have a Top Secret Crypto Clearance. The knowledge that you will possess will be of extreme interest to the VC and NVA. If, for any reason, you divulge even the most minute aspect of your daily orders to a 'local,' you could be responsible for the death of your comrades and your Vietnamese allies."

Students who had previously been bored with the dissertation now sat up straight in their plastic chairs. The captain returned to the podium and shut off the gooseneck light that illuminated his notes, closed his notebook and continued in a less formal tone. "I mentioned a minute ago that the efforts of the young ladies - girls - have full support of their families. I can't emphasize this enough. Here are their goals and in this order:

One: marry a GI and eventually get to the US.

Two: extract strategic info from you and sell it to the VC or NVA.

Three: just fuck you for your money.

"No matter how lonely or horny you get, gentlemen, always remember this: there just ain't no love in Nam!" He paused for effect, scanning the eyes of each of the men before him.

"I just want to conclude this segment by telling you about a down home local custom that you will inevitably face, that is unless you are dog- meat ugly - and even then it wouldn't matter. If you ever happen to be successfully seduced, and she invites you to her hootch to meet her family and share a meal, the first bowl of food you will probably be offered will be a rice and fish- based soup. However, your bowl will contain an additional ingredient prepared especially for you: your sweetheart's menstrual blood." He had their undivided attention again and swaggered to the conclusion of the story. "You see Vietnamese superstition believes if an American G.I. drinks this potion, in the home of the female and in the presence of her family, that she will ultimately be bound to him in a marital union.

"The cards are stacked against us on two fronts. Number one, we are fighting a guerilla war with no clear lines of demarcation. Number two, the ladies know this and play on our confusion. The girl on the barstool next to you who's looking to get into your pants could just take your money and fuck you, *or*," he emphasized with a broad stroke of his arm, "fuck you and the entire US war effort. It's simply a matter of what she's looking to extract from you. If she wants money **and** information then she could potentially fuck us all." He paced slowly in front of the classroom, his arms folded. He turned and faced the group.

"What it boils down to is this: all of you were born with two heads, the pecker head in your diapers and the one on your shoulders. Just don't let the head in your 1969 pair of diapers rule your decisions. We're fighting a guerilla war with the enemy taking on many different looks and hiding among us. I cannot repeat this enough." He paused, and once again ran his eyes over theirs.

"Questions?"

Scott looked over to Rudy who was squirming around in his seat, his hand in the air.

"Oh, boy." Scott thought.

The instructor motioned to him.

"Yes?"

"Sir, is the menstrual blood always served the same way?"

"Say again, lieutenant."

"What I mean, sir, is that if they always serve it with fish and rice then I'll be ok because I don't like most fish, and probably wouldn't eat it anyway."

"Lieutenant, you seem to be thinking of this as if it were some formal recipe out of a cookbook. It's not. Think of it this way: just like Charlie comes in a variety of shapes, sizes, and ages—so does the goddamn blood! Got it?"

"Yes, sir." Rudy said.

The captain huffed and brushed the left sleeve of his uniform as if to emphatically brush away any further questions. He looked at the group and asked again: "Are there any additional questions?"

Nobody responded.

"Dismissed." he said.

The Phoenix personnel filtered out from the classroom and onto the lime green linoleum in the hallway. Scott looked for Rudy. When he finally found him in the sea of olive fatigues, he tapped him on the shoulder.

"We have a few hours to kill before curfew. Wanna' recon the area?"

CHAPTER 19

They walked along a stretch of road that led out of the compound and past open-air bars that smelled of food on the verge of spoiling. To their right stretched the wide beach that slid into the slate gray waters of the South China Sea.

Rudy glanced across this area and said aloud to himself, "Che bella spiaggia."

"Say what?" Scott asked.

"What a beautiful beach." Rudy stated, this time more audibly.

"Was Italian that you just spoke?"

"With a name like Rodolfo, did you expect to hear Norwegian?"

"It just caught me off guard a little. With all the regional American accents in this Army I just didn't expect to hear anything from Italy. Were you born in the states or Italy?"

"Neither, I was born in Switzerland."

"Switzerland sounds as foreign to me as Iceland. Do you speak it fluently?

"Italian, you mean?"

"Yeah, Italian." Scott said.

"Of course. I also speak German, French and, obviously, English."

"Where did you learn all of those other languages?" Scott asked flatly, not wanting to show his awe.

"In school, in the area where I was born."

"So where were you born?"

"In the Ticino section of the country...a town called Belinzona, at the northern end of Lago Maggiore. It's a beautiful lake that stretches from Northern Italy into Southern Switzerland. Did you ever go there?"

"I never even heard of it," Scott answered.

"Well, looking back, I probably wouldn't have heard of it either if I hadn't spent my early years there."

"So how did you learn to speak the other languages?"

"In school we learned to speak four languages. German, French, Italian, and English. And there are other languages spoken in Switzerland also, like Walser, Lombard and Allemannisch, but I'm not too familiar with them."

"So what are you doing in 'Nam instead of teaching at one of the Army's language schools, like the one in Germany or the Presidio?"

"Me and the Army decided that my time would be best served 'killing commies for Christ.' Besides this is one of the areas of the world that I haven't seen."

"Well, why not wait until you're discharged and go see the Orient as a civilian? You could experience the culture without the distinct possibility of having your dick blown off."

Rudy's smile narrowed to a line of crooked teeth. "The reason I wanted to come here, as opposed to some other duty station in the states or Europe, where I've been before, is because I like the idea of exploring life on the edge of uncertainty. Now doesn't this place fit the bill?"

"I guess." Scott slowly added, "Are you telling me that you volunteered for the Phoenix program?"

"You know nobody volunteers for this. We were selected because of our psychological profiles. We, somehow, fit their mold. Lots of Intelligence types don't get plucked to be advisors."

"You know what, Rudy, I think that you actually believe this crap. If they could see inside *my* head they'd pass by me like a dose of malaria. I got sent to this gig by a returnee captain who had a real Boston- Irish hard on for me. I know the prick hopes that history will repeat itself, and that I'll get fucked."

"But," Rudy hastened, "you must also have somehow fit the Phoenix profile or this guy could never have pushed you through. He must have studied you real hard before he dropped a dime on you. Believe me."

"I don't know what to believe, man. All I know is that I'm anxious to get these first six months over with, see my wife on R & R, spend my next six kissing brass ass at Pentagon East, and then get back to the real world." Scott paused, drew a breath and got a grip on the present. "But all of that lays ahead, right, Rudy? What we are seriously failing to do is address the immediate."

Rudy caught on. "Yeah, it's beer time in paradise."

Scott looked at his watch. "We've got 3 hours and 15 minutes before curfew. Let's go."

They came to an open-air bar teeming with American soldiers sitting either at lopsided tables or crowded at the rickety makeshift bar. Pictures of Joe Namath and Bart Starr were nailed to bamboo beams and team photos of the New York Jets, Green Bay Packers and Oakland Raiders hung from the bamboo rafters in suspended frames. Allied soldiers had only a vague knowledge of these players and teams, but they spent their money there anyway. They, too, were on brief sabbaticals from combat duty and, like the Americans, were lusty and socially hungry. The ladies who approached them to say "hello" would give them all the sports talk they needed.

Rudy and Scott nudged their way to the dilapidated, palm-front bar where Scott ordered two Heinekens. The bartender in the Don Ho flowered shirt smiled and gave them two "Beer 33s".

"What the hell is this?" Scott asked, raising the bottle to the fading sunlight. "The damn label is reversed." The number 33 was visible on the inside of the bottle and rippled through the golden liquid.

"Who cares," Rudy said. "Everybody else is drinking it. They don't seem to be spitting it out."

"Well, I'm too thirsty to bitch, and I definitely won't ask for water."

"Did I hear you say water, mite?"

Scott turned to his right where a blonde, gap-toothed soldier was standing. His first impression was that someone could probably drive a jeep between the guy's upper front teeth. The stranger continued.

"Don't ever think of drinking water in this country. You got better tasting water coming out of your dick. How long have you been ear, mite?"

Scott, who had just been instructed not to give information like this to anyone, changed the subject.

"Why are you calling me 'mite'?" he asked.

"What's a 'mite'?" the stranger asked.

"That's what I'm asking you."

"No, no. Not mite. Mate. M-A-T-E."

Scott laughed at his misunderstanding. "Oh, that's better. Now I get it. You're an Aussie!"

"And I'm damn well proud of it, too."

"Oh, I bet you must be." Scott was tempted to make a humorous comment but instead looked skyward to the thick jaw and gapped teeth of his new acquaintance and decided against it.

The Aussie seemed friendly, with a dry sense of humor, and Scott ventured to introduce himself. He thrust his hand out and the stranger reached for it and shook it heartily.

"Sgt. Maury Jackson - 1st Australian Task Force. Phuoc Tuy."

"Hi, Maury," Scott said. He hesitated again to offer any more information about himself. "My name is Scott, U.S. Infantry."

"Welcome to Vung Tau, mite," the Aussie said, "This is the Riviera of 'Nam. It just doesn't get any better in this hell-hole of a country."

"How's your gig in Phuoc Tuy?" Scott asked.

"Not bad. It's about 30 miles southeast of Saigon near the coast. Lots of VC activity but nothing we can't handle. We work well with the locals and Phoenix personnel in the area."

"Oh really?" Scott's eyebrows rose. He was tempted not to pry but couldn't help asking one question.

"So what are those Phoenix types like?"

The Aussie turned and looked directly into Scott's eyes.

"In my opinion they're cold, secretive and they keep to themselves. Now that's not bad in itself, but they ain't no barrel of laughs either and *that's* where I draw the line." His thin lips betrayed a slight smile.

"But," he continued, "they're the best at pulling info from any VC they drag in. They're goddamn good at it. They can make a bloody boot talk. And they do their homework before they go in for a raid."

Rudy, who was listening to the Aussie over Scott's shoulder, now chimed in. "So how do you think that they learned to be so effective? Was it their training or are these guys naturals at it?"

Maury Jackson raised an oilcan -sized Foster's to his lips and drained its last drops. He looked from side to side, up and down at the other drinkers at the bar and half- whispered his response. "I think that these guys are somehow selected from birth. Who knows, they may never have found a true expression of their inner selves if this bullshit skirmish hadn't erupted."

Scott squinted into the fast fading sun. He wasn't sure whether he winced because he had no idea what this soldier was talking about or because he needed sunglasses.

"I'm really curious now about what the fuck you're saying. So in simple terms what do you think about the Phoenix operatives?"

Sgt. Jackson leaned closer and bent down into Scott's ear. The smell of the warm beer coupled with the aroma of the Aussie's cigarette breath made him cough.

"I believe they're versatile and cunning enough to move around the docks of Marseilles, the bowels of Calcutta or corporate offices in New York City. Yeah, between the Americans on the district level and the ROKS, you know, the South Koreans, there's no intelligence information they can't get."

Scott nodded. "You seem to know a lot about these guys. Could you pick them out in a crowd?"

"No way, mite. They all have some common thread but come from all walks of life and have different ways about them. They all don't match."

The Aussie had no clue that his new beer buddies were freshly arrived Phoenix counterintelligence officers, but he was right about one thing for sure: the two of them didn't match. Rudy spoke with a slight European accent and Scott sounded like a Jersey guy. Nevertheless, they would soon share the common mission of "neutralizing" the VC infrastructure in their area of responsibility while simultaneously winning the hearts and minds of the people. Scott would later jokingly think of it as "detonation diplomacy."

Rudy nudged Scott in the ribs, suggesting that they move out. He was getting uncomfortable with all of the Phoenix talk. So, when Maury Jackson slammed his beer on the reinforced bamboo bar and headed to the urinal, they took the opportunity to slip out.

Out on the street again, they now ambled by small shops selling wood carvings, silk shirts and sandals, but when they came to the "Last Chance Saloon" sheltering a bevy of obviously underage teens selling themselves, Rudy pulled Scott to a stop.

"Hey, Scott, I'll see you a little bit later. I want to see if they have Beer "33" here, too." His grin told another story.

"Yeah, right." Scott said, and turned to continue on his way. Layers of paper cups, Marlboro filters and Popsicle sticks littered the uneven stone walkway, making for unsure footing. He suddenly felt tired and wondered how he'd fallen out of prime partying shape so quickly. Before he could answer himself, he was distracted by a burst of laughter behind him. Turning, he saw three young girls engulf Rudy and escort their willing prey into a shabbily constructed street hut.

"Hey, Rudy! Remember you only have about a billion sperm in your love sack. Distribute them wisely."

CHAPTER 20

Most of the slowly shuffling parade of olive drab attendees funneling into the final day of class looked the same. A handful of them dressed in civilian garb, stood out. Rudy stood out, too, not because of his dress but rather due to a red-eye look from having been awake all night.

"Hey, Rodolfo," Scott ribbed him beneath his breath, "you must have spent a lot of money on those teenagers last night."

"Scotty, I don't remember too much. These young bitches were pros. I was buying them something called Saigon tea and they were groping and fondling the living shit out of me. But that groping part bothered me."

"Why?"

"Cause they picked me clean."

"You didn't tell them anything about why you were in Vung Tau, did you?"

Rudy quickly added, "I don't remember too much more except that I got back through the gate and into my room just a snatch hair before curfew."

"Aw, shit, Rudy, man you can't be laying our dick on the line like that. What were you drinking?"

"It wasn't Beer "33," I know that! I asked for it but instead the little sluts poured me some stuff they called Scotch into a paper cup. No ice and no glass. Just a paper cup, and I instantly fell in love with all of them."

..."I'm sure they loved you, too." Scott said, slapping Rudy on the back and suppressing a guffaw.

****

The first 50 minutes of class was comprised of the introduction and administrative announcements. From then until lunch break at 1200, the subject matter focused on the history and government of Vietnam. A Captain Ryker was the lone lecturer for those three hours. Dressed in combat fatigues with the insignia of black crossed rifles on collar, he too wore the stitched CIB over his left breast pocket. His flawless ebony complexion framed a set of perfectly formed white teeth but his serious demeanor gave him an aura of someone older than his mid-twenties.

Strolling up and down the aisles of the military and civilian personnel, he made eye contact with each of them as he began to speak.

"The history of Vietnam is a long and violent one. Their written history of this area goes back to the second century before Christ, with the conquest of the Red River Delta Area of what is now North Vietnam by the Chinese under the Han Dynasty.

"From its beginnings to the present, these people have been in a virtually constant struggle for freedom against foreign oppressors: The Chinese, the Mongols, the Japanese, and finally, the French. The national heroes of the Vietnamese, from the Trung sisters through Tran Hung Dao and Le Loi, including Ho Chi Minh, have been people prominent in this struggle for independence.

"When not fighting against foreign conquerors, the Vietnamese fought among themselves or against their neighbors, notably Cambodia and Champa."

Capt. Ryker's cadence was even, except for the occasional emphasis on verbs like "fought" or "struggle." He almost barked those words and at a higher decibel level.

"The first contact between Europeans and Vietnamese came in the 16th Century. Of course, the priests who came with the explorers and traders saw a fertile field for their missionary work. The religious conversion effort expanded greatly and exerted a profound influence on the subsequent history of Vietnam. Missionary support took political turns and was influential in the overthrow of the first Nguyen dynasty. This missionary action caused the persecution of these clergy and provided the French with an excuse to mount a campaign of conquest against Vietnam in the mid-nineteenth century."

The drone of the history lesson began to lull more than one student into nodding. Capt. Ryker, when noting this, clapped his hands sharply, causing several heads to bounce up, bug-eyed and with an artificial appearance of intent concentration. The formal indoctrination period finally ended on schedule, and the troops were given their next immediate orders. The rest of their education would come, up close and personal, from on the job training.

Scott received his orders to report to a small, secured hotel situated inland and away from the beach where he was to wait for transportation the next morning. The narrow lobby of the hotel had a front desk of marble and dark mahogany that almost looked regal. At one time it had probably served the upper class of the French colonialists. The charm and former opulence of the floor to ceiling windows behind the counter was diminished, however, by the chicken wire nailed to the heavy wooden window frame. The windows could be pushed out with a flanged pole to let in air, but the wire mesh would repel any attempt to lob an explosive into the vestibule.

Scott approached the counter and the young Vietnamese girl smiled and asked him to sign in with just his name. No rank. No address. Nothing but his printed name. She then asked for his M-16 and Colt .45 side arm. Scott started to balk at this request when an overweight American civilian appeared through a heavy stone archway that framed the entrance of a darkened side room, left of the reception desk. The man addressed him by name.

"Lt. Regan, it's standard procedure. You can't carry your weapons to your quarters. They will be locked here." He pointed to a thick metal cabinet with a combination lock and steel bar.

"Who are you?" Scott questioned.

"I'm Mr. Flagler, lieutenant. I am responsible for overseeing your safe stay in this hotel tonight. Tomorrow you will be choppered to Advisory Team 27 in Ham Thuan. My assignment is to make sure that you get there. In the meantime you are my charge."

Scott looked at the man as he spoke and felt all the more uneasy about handing over his weapons.

"With all due respect, Mr. Flagler, I have a twinge of reluctance to pass these weapons to a little Vietnamese secretary. What do you think about that?"

"As far as I'm concerned you have exactly 31 minutes to vacate the streets and adhere to curfew. If you are caught carrying weapons outside this hotel after 2300 hours, you may do some time in the brig. In the meantime, if you choose the right option, you will go to your assigned room and leave your weapons here. I'm not looking to bust your nuts about this. Just don't break mine. We'll part company at 0630 tomorrow. Got it?"

"What other choices do I have besides staying here unarmed, trusting you and this underage gookette to enforce security?"

Without blinking at Scott's attempt to create an altercation, Mr. Flagler answered, "You have none."

Scott pushed a little further. "How the hell am I supposed to sleep here without my .45, at least?"

"No one said you have to sleep, lieutenant. I am responsible for getting you to your permanent assignment tomorrow. Period. I take this responsibility seriously. As far as I'm concerned you can stand up all night and stay wide awake."

****

Scott tossed about on the thin mattress of the single bed. A week's worth of indoctrination ran through his head: Be courteous. Speak slowly. Use the Vietnamese language. Show respect for age. Respect tradition. The dream continued as he saw the black, bald headed captain walking slowly among the desks.

"You must try to have as much contact with your Vietnamese counterpart as possible." The words echoed in a chamber.

Remember he is your right arm to the ARVN. Share food, bivouac, and the dangers of battle with him. Let him know that you need him. He needs our assignment and numbers. We need to know the culture and thinking from which he comes.

"As a Phoenix combat advisor, you are both salesman and combatant. Opt for being the former. Gather information from all sources. Any potential informant is valuable. A dead

informant is useless.   It is simple.   Use your skills wisely. Extract, Extract, Extract."

Scott rolled over onto his stomach for the last time that night and, finally, dreamt no more.

CHAPTER 21

The sound of a motor scooter woke Scott. The time was 0530, giving him one hour to prepare for his ride to his DIOCC. He instinctively reached across to the heavy cardboard table, groped for his holster, and groaned as he remembered it was locked in the cabinet three floors below. He forced his legs over the side of the bed, stood and stretched to pull the cord dangling from the overhead light.

In the bathroom, the open stall shower had a single knob that he pulled out and turned. Needles of hot water sputtered out of the rusted shower head, and reaching for his small bottle of Prell and withered bar of Ivory soap, he stepped into the stream. He placed his hands against the tile shower stall like a suspect being frisked, letting the hot water run down his shoulders and back.

Realizing he had spent too much time showering and still had to reclaim his weapons, he dressed quickly and checked his belongings. He slapped his right fatigue thigh pocket. Got the Marlboro hard pack. Got the duffel bag.

"O.K.," he murmured.

Hoisting his stuffed bag onto his left shoulder, he walked to the marble stairway, his boots resonating thick rubber thumps. At the third step, he heard someone walking up the staircase from below.

"Stop, look, and listen." he thought. He reviewed the lessons that he had been taught, which included his own set of precautions carried over from youth.

"Strange people, strange actions. Be careful."

He fumbled for the box in his thigh pocket. Opening the flip-top, he noticed that he had only four remaining. His index finger groped for one as he heard shuffling feet ascending the stairs. Realizing he didn't have a match, he tucked the cigarette behind his right ear and bent over the unpolished brass handrail parallel to the stairway. A teenage Vietnamese boy continued to climb the stone stairs toward Scott.

His mind began to race.

"Who is this guy? How did he get through security at the front door? Is the Vietnamese girl the only obstacle between Charlie and me?"

Capt. Hamm's words ran through his thoughts. *"Remember they know who you are, and there's a price on your head."*

They met on the landing that separated the second floor from the lobby. They stopped simultaneously and looked at each other. No words were exchanged and the kid didn't move. Scott pulled the Marlboro from behind his ear, held it forward, and returned it to his lips asking for a light.

Devoid of expression, the adolescent slowly reached under his white tunic and groped the front and side of his beltline until he found what he wanted. He pulled out a silver pistol from his back pocket and pointed it at Scott.

Scott's mind flashed back to a conversation with a Green Beret veteran at a cavernous dirt floor Alabama nightclub across the Chatahoochee River from Ft. Benning. His eyes were dark as coal and he spoke in a deep Southern accent.

"Ya'll better know theeis. Charlie comes in all shapes and sahzes. Kids'll kill ya' just laak a wrinkly ass mama-san'll kill ya. They all ovah, and you cain't pick 'em out. So, when in doubt - drop 'em."

The young man's right index finger moved from the handle into the trigger housing. Scott dropped his duffel bag and reached for the teenager's throat in one motion. He lifted him off his feet and with a thrust of his right arm, slammed his head against the heavy plaster wall, dropping him to the floor.

The metallic sound of the pistol bouncing down the stairs echoed to the landing below. The boy pleaded, tumbling down the stairwell like a rag doll. Scott caught him on the platform separating the first floor from the lobby. The boy dove toward a corner where the pistol lay but Scott glanced a swift kick off his chin. The youth recovered quickly, enough to grab the pistol in hand and with a quick movement hold it over his head and pull the trigger. A flame shot out from the hammer, and he pulled the trigger again before Scott had time to kick him flush in the face. Another flame rose from the hammer and stayed lit as Scott recoiled from his pivot.

"Jeezus Christ" Scott hollered. "I'm ready to drop kick your head into eternity and you flash this at me?"

The deep brown eyes were filled with tears as the kid pulled the trigger again and again. Each time a harmless flame shot out. It was a lighter. It was only a lighter.

The kid's eyes were blinking rapidly as Scott grabbed him tightly by the arm and walked him down the remaining set of stairs to the reception desk. The young girl behind the stone counter held a wide-eyed stare as the lieutenant pushed the kid toward her.

"Who is this stupid mother fuckin' kid that you allowed upstairs?"

The young lady shuffled around the front of the desk and positioned herself between Scott and the kid. She tried to release the grip he had on the skinny bicep as Scott arched over the young girl's shoulder and held on fast.

"I want my M-16 and my .45 now!" he barked, "I'm not going to let go of this stupid fuck until you hand me both of those weapons. Got it?"

The girl began to speak.

"Boy numbah 1 boy. Boy numbah 1 boy. Troung uy. No worry."

"Yeah, he's number one boy, but I don't even trust you. Hand me my weapons. Both of them. And with the clips." Scott shoved the kid's chest down against the floor and flattened his boot in the small of the Viet's back.

The guy thought he was going to be hurt and pleaded over his shoulder, looking into Scott's eyes.

"You numbah 1 G.I., You numbah 1."

Scott kept his left foot planted firmly on the kid's lower spine as he pulled the silver lighter pistol from his pocket and slammed it on the counter.

"Now open that cabinet and give me my weapons."

She moved back behind the desk taking her eyes from him only to turn to the wall safe behind her, spin the combination lock, and crack its handle downward. She handed Scott his weapons and motioned for him to sign the release form that she slid towards him. He dated it and recorded the time next to his signature. Only then did he lift his foot from the boy's back.

He moved the lighter across the counter and toward the woman. "Get rid of this before somebody dies a stupid death." he glared.

Scott holstered his .45, slung the M-16 over his shoulder and walked upstairs to retrieve his bag. As if angry at the floor, he snatched the duffel bag roughly from the marble stairwell, turned around and walked back down and out the front door without saying another word.

Cpl. Rigby Count was waiting right outside the door.

"Mornin', sir" he said brightly. "Jump in, sir. You're chopper's waitin'."

"Morning, Rigby. How you doin' today?" Scott smiled for the first time since waking up.

"On a beautiful day like today, Lieutenant Regan, it would be real hard to complain. Wouldn't it?"

Scott was tempted, but decided to skip it. "You're right, Rigby. It *is* a beautiful day. A beautiful day to fly."

The jeep made its way to the airport where an outdated CH-21C helicopter was ready to airlift him to his DIOCC in the Ham Thuan district of Binh Thuan Province. The bustle of the crowd reminded Scott of a mini Port Authority Terminal in New York.

There was an assemblage of personnel gathered close to the banana shaped helicopter. The aircraft's blades spun in perfect syncopation as the crew chief directed the group through the swirling dust, up a small stepladder and into the cargo door. The helicopter was designed to carry 18 -20 passengers, or 12 stretchers. There were no casualties in sight, so this run had to be just for ambulatory soldiers and civilians. Some civilians carried baskets and small livestock on board. Scott winced at the thought that any of them might have Viet Cong ties, yet were given transportation courtesy of the U.S. Government.

He followed a middle age woman up the stepladder. The two live chickens she was carrying didn't make a sound or flutter as she walked into the bay of the chopper and squirmed sideways along the crowded bench inside.

Scott's mind began to race for the second time that morning.

"*Are they real chickens?*" he thought.   "*Or are they camouflaged explosives?*'

Another Viet pushed a piglet up the stairs and made his way into the passenger area. He squeezed his way into a seat between Scott and the chicken lady.

The crew chief slid the door partially shut and yelled to the pilot in the cockpit. The chopper was full and ready for liftoff. The din of the rotating blades increased as the single door gunner took his position and maneuvered his 12.7 mm door gun out through the open slit.

The aircraft lifted up and gently banked northeast toward Phan Thiet. Scott felt like he was in some latter day Noah's Ark. People and animals filled the flight but he continued to look suspiciously at the woman with the two chickens sitting near him. He waited to see if the little bastards clucked or fluttered, but they both seemed as still as the women who cradled them.

The dust swirling inside the chopper was drier than talcum powder as he simultaneously coughed and patted the holster nestling his sidearm. He held his rifle vertically between his legs and tucked into his crotch. He continued to shift his eyes to the chicken lady, but the monotonous syncopated whooping sound of the Shawnee blades soon overcame his vigilance, and he was lulled into a state of semi-sleep.

He snapped back to full consciousness when he heard a defiant cluck from the chicken that was roosting near him. As if some distant homing bell sounded in the hen's mind, it fluttered wildly and released itself from the grasp of the wrinkled woman and flew toward the gunner's door.

The lady chased the stub- winged bird as if it was her last meal. The chicken didn't hesitate as it headed for the light of the partially open door.   Before anyone could grab it, the powerful force of the outside air currents sucked the flapping bird out over the gunner's head.

Scott relaxed. He was now convinced that the poultry the woman clutched was nothing more than a living chicken. No disguised satchels of dynamite. Nothing more than a bird. He finally accepted the fact that the other clucker tucked tightly under her right arm was also benign and so too, probably, was the mama-san.

CHAPTER 22

The light whooping sound of the chopper's engines grew to a louder thump as it approached the Landing Zone. The skids nestled into the light orange grit as the blades released their grip on the air and wound down to silence. The crew chief motioned to the passengers to move slowly out of the craft. The gunner swiveled the door gun inward to make room for the exodus.

When Scott jumped several feet to the ground his boots barely touched the dirt before an open jeep rolled to within inches of him.

"Lieutenant Regan. Jump in."

"Jesus Christ. Every time I move right or left somebody's up my ass." he exclaimed. "Can't you just give me a 5- minute break to catch my breath and fire up a butt?"

"With all due respect, sir, isn't that a contradiction in terms?"

"Hey, what's-your-name…if you're offended by cigarette smoke, then get out of this open- air vehicle and wait for me by the left bumper or whatever."

Scott held the burning match in front of his mouth and blew it out with a long exhale, cradling the cigarette in the corner of his mouth a la Humphrey Bogart.

"I'm not rushing anywhere," he added. "Besides, the war effort won't be altered if you and me just poke around this town for a few hours, will it?"

"You're probably correct, sir, but there's not too much to see here in Phan Thiet."

Scott took a quick view of his surroundings. The guy may have been right. It wasn't exactly Shangri La.

"Well, I'm finally here," he said aloud. "If that captain hated my attitude in Boston then he just got even. Why didn't I just keep my mouth shut?" The driver didn't answer.

Scott finished his smoke, field stripped the Marlboro and put the filter into his pocket. "O.K., Buddy, let's get me to my DIOCC."

The driver jumped from the hood of the jeep. "Yes, sir, I'm ready."

"I finally am, too."

Dropping and rising through dried out gullies, the five - kilometer trip seemed like a thrill ride at Disneyland. Scott dispensed with conversation. He just didn't care about making a new acquaintance at this moment in time.

The driver finally introduced himself. "Sir, I'm E-6 Maldonado." The young man spoke with a thick Spanish accent.

"Good morning, Maldonado. What's your first name?"

"Heysuus," he pronounced.

"Like Jesus," Scott said. "I can't tell you how safe that makes me feel." Maldonado either didn't hear him or just didn't think the irreverent attempt at humor was funny.

"Well, I'm pleased to meet you. You already know who I am, right?"

"Yes, sir, I do."

"OK then you can just call me Scott. It's just this thing that I have about all the Army formality and shit."

"I believe that it all has its place. It does demonstrate respect, sir."

"Respect is good, but neither you nor anybody else is going to respect me just because you are required to address me a certain way. Are you?"

"You sure are an unusual lieutenant, sir."

"Well, let's just say that I can't feel too formal in these surroundings. I just want to do my job and get the hell home in one piece. How long have you been in country?"

"This is my second tour, sir."

"Why?" Scott questioned.

"They offered me a re-up bonus."

"Where were you stationed on your first gig?"

"Oh, I was in Saigon at MACV Headquarters."

"Doing what?"

"Mostly admin type work."

"Were you in the field at all?"

"No, sir, not until my second tour."

"Well," Scott pointed to Maldonado's black badge, "you didn't get that CIB by typing, did you?"

"No, lieutenant. They paid me $2,500 and then re-assigned me to the Program."

"So, how do you like being out of Headquarters?"

"There is no comparison."

"In what way?"

Maldanado turned his gaze and met Scott's eyes for the first time since he picked him up at the LZ.

"It's the difference between day and night, sir."

"Like how?"

"Out where you're going, sir, Charlie rules your thoughts. There's nothing between you and him except rice paddies and concertina wire. Maybe."

Jesus's eyes held fast to Scott's and then slowly disengaged. He re-focused on the rutted road ahead.

"Have you had much activity lately?"

"Sporadic, sir. Our sources inform us that there is no large offensive planned like last year, but that doesn't seem to calm anyone down. Charlie appears to be going back to basics. You know, ambushes, sappers, and land mines. Stuff like that."

"Wonderful." Scott sighed and continued. "Yeah, that's what we heard at orientation in Vung Tau. So, I guess it's true."

"It is. They're also pushing to develop informants from within our PRU and ARVN counterparts. You just never know who you can trust outside of the Aussies, the ROKs and us."

"So, what else is new?" Scott tried to smile and change the subject. It didn't work.

Jesus continued. "I guess we should be able to trust the ARVN also. I mean wouldn't you think that *everyone* in the South Vietnamese military would want to save their own country from communism?"

"You would think," Scott answered, "but, then again, they may think the North Vietnamese and the Communist Chinese are knocking on their door and it's only a matter of time before they kick it in. Maybe they're just tired of fighting. Or maybe communism looks OK to them compared to how the French and Japanese left them. Even we seem to be chopping up their land pretty good. They got to be getting weary of this shit, too."

Scott paused and glanced across the rice fields. Water buffalo plodded slowly in the muck and the pulsing sun baked their muscled backs. The jeep was now on a firm road and the ride was smooth. It was almost peaceful.

"But who knows how they think." Scott snapped back to the moment.

"Who knows who is right, sir?"

As Scott and Jesus approached the DIOCC, the lieutenant's synapses were firing overtime. This was his final destination.

All the combat drills and mock set-ups during Infantry Training at Benning had had only one purpose: to prepare him for this assignment. The final salutes were presented a long time ago. Each military snap of conclusion ushered him one step forward.

"Carry on, lieutenant." "Very well, lieutenant." "Good day, lieutenant." "Good luck, lieutenant." These seemingly innocuous dismissals represented the continuity of purpose that ultimately directed him onto a strand of the Phoenix web.

The jeep tires bumped through the final 300 meters to the barbed wire post gate that opened into the District Intelligence Operational Coordination Center. It was housed in a larger military district compound and stood in the middle of a square of baked earth. Between the outer rolls of razor sharp wire and the inner rectangle of security was an open area littered with claymore mines and trip flares. An interior barbed wire wall surrounded huts made of corrugated steel, four watchtowers manned 24 hours a day, numerous sand bag bunkers, and one plywood latrine with a see through screened top section. A shower fed by an overhead 55-gallon drum completed the sanitary accouterments. This compound held a permanent contingent of one American platoon with PRU and ARVN support, at the disposal of the Phoenix advisors, whenever the need arose. The officer roster included one major, one captain and one lieutenant. Scott was the new lieutenant, and a Vietnamese counterpart, equal to him in rank, was responsible for overseeing the ARVN platoon.

The compound had an interpreter who was relied on to give a quick, yet exact, translation in any circumstance in which he was called upon. Consequently, whatever the interpreter translated was accepted as gospel. A reliable interpreter was invaluable to the accumulation of accurate intelligence information; and the mouthpiece knew without him, communication between the ARVN and American officers would be seriously crippled.

The jeep grounded to a halt outside the gate and Scott saw a few enlisted men walking toward him. He jumped out of the vehicle and almost attempted to introduce himself. He had a second thought as the four GI's continued talking among themselves and fanned out around him. They barely nodded.

"Friendly guys. What am I invisible over here?" Scott asked Jesus.

"No, lieutenant, you're not invisible. It's just that they're on their way to happy hour in town. Besides, those guys are 'short.' They've been in country for a year or more and are ready to rotate back to the world. They've seen a lot of officers jump out of a jeep and join them…depends."

"Depends on what?"

Jesus took on the tone of a hooded messenger, but with all the concern of one who had just transported another piece of raw meat to the town butcher.

"Depends on how you act. This is the real classroom. The studying's over. There ain't no report cards here, sir. But you already know that."

"Hey, Jesus, I don't want another report card. All I want is to get my ass back to Bloomfield Avenue where I can wait in line for hot bread. My mission is to get nobody fucked up along the way."

"Good luck, lieutenant."

Jesus cranked the bald handled shift knob into first gear and started to pull away.

"Yo. Sergeant," Scott yelled. "Not so fast. I gotta' get the rest of my gear." He reached into the back of the jeep and gave his duffle a yank and slung it onto the ground at his feet "Where are you going anyway? Aren't you assigned here, too?"

"No, sir. I've got to get back to Phan Rang"

"Not for nothing, man, but it makes me feel a little uneasy when a guy named Jesus abandons me in a strange location."

The jeep made a semi-circle and stopped on a dime next to Scott. The smile on Jesus' face stretched from ear to ear.

"Don't worry, sir. Only my name is Jesus. There are many guys with that name where I come from. Besides, you pronounce it wrong." He saluted and pulled away.

"Buena suerte, sir."

CHAPTER 23

Scott hitched his duffel bag and threw back his shoulders. The smells of smoldering charcoal and animal urine wafted by. A little girl with thin black hair and dark almond eyes stared at him, playing with a yo-yo she couldn't unravel. She wore a pink knitted sweater and blue shorts, her toenails were dirty and her little feet contoured into her flat rubber sandals. Scott brushed by her and stroked her arm. He was looking to report to his commanding officer, and the young one followed him.

"Troung uy, you numbah one. You numbah one."

She was no older than four but was, nevertheless, able to determine that he was now a first lieutenant, not a second, and not yet a captain.

Scott stopped, turned around, and looked at her round face: a visage of pure innocence and trust. He continued to stare at her and swore that he had seen her someplace before. More than that, he felt that he knew her. The attraction was instant.

"Now where do you live, young lady?"

"Live." She pointed to the dirt.

"Well, that spot's a pretty small place, isn't it?"

She looked at him, confused.

"Where in hell do you stay in this compound?" She continued to blink.

He looked around to figure out where he should report and glanced back down at the tiny one before him.

"Hey, I'll tell you what. Why don't you teach me better Vietnamese and I'll teach you better English, OK?"

"OK," she said clearly.

"Ok, then, young lady."

The girl turned away and skipped through the sun- dried, pulverous dirt. She gathered the string of her wooden yo-yo, trying again to make it work, and turned to see if he was still looking at her. He was. She seemed so carefree and full of joy. He surveyed their immediate surroundings and couldn't figure out why.

Scott made his way to the largest Quonset hut, thinking that his commanding officer had to be in or around there. As he approached the rippled steel structure of the largest one, a figure hunched out of the opening, silhouetting itself against the late afternoon sky. The outline walked a few steps and stretched, hands above its head, bending and rotating. It pulled one leg up from the knee and pressed it up toward its mid-section, slowly repeating the same exercise with the other limb.

Scott stopped and studied the soldier's exercise. He thought he recognized the outline, but couldn't remember from where and continued to walk again toward the image. As he got closer the figure turned to face him.

"I've been expecting you, Lieutenant Regan."

Scott stopped in his tracks about ten paces away from the man. He recognized the voice but the setting sun blinded him, obliterating any facial features.

Squinting, he introduced himself. "I'm Lt. Scott Regan, reporting for duty and looking for the commanding officer."

"I already know that. I'm Major Rheingold. I'll be your CO until my orders – or yours – are changed." Scott snapped a salute as his stomach rumbled.

"Oh, fuck me," he thought wishing he never antagonized this guy in an Indian bar room in upstate New York. He never thought their paths would ever cross again, and knew the officer still remembered the encounter. Scott groped for words.

"Congratulations on your promotion to Major, sir."

He knew nothing he could say would help him to skate by this meeting. At first blush, though, it seemed like his wise-ass remarks to Rheingold that day at the Ontario House might have been forgiven. Forgiven, maybe, but sure as hell not forgotten. Anticipating a question from the lieutenant, the superior officer spoke:

"I recall that the last time we saw each other you wondered whether my eye patch helped me to attract ladies. I think that your exact words were 'helped me to get laid." Scott gulped and said nothing. "It was a temporary thing and I didn't care to tell you, then, why I had to wear it, and I really don't care to tell you now."

Scott clearly remembered the appearance of Rheingold's one blue eye and how it shifted and monitored everything within its scope. Now, without the patch, there were two steel blue eyes. Both focused intently upon him.

"Welcome to Ham Thuan."

"Thank you, sir." They both stood silently for only seconds. To Scott it seemed like minutes.

"You will be bunking with Captain Bligh." Scott smirked inwardly at the name, but discreetly suppressed the chuckle that welled up inside of his throat.

"Before you comment, lieutenant, Cpt. Bligh has heard all of the jokes and I'll fill you in on a couple of things. Number one: he is not a descendant of the skipper of the *Bounty* – two, he will soon be promoted to major, which will enable him to lose the captain moniker. Besides he's a West Point graduate with an impeccable service record. His combat performance under my command has been beyond reproach. In two words...got it?" Scott reached for some commonality with Bligh.

"I know how Cpt. Bligh must feel, sir. I was born on April 1st and have heard all of the April Fool's jokes. I'm actually waiting for a funny one that I haven't heard." Rheingold didn't care.

"That's your quest. In the meantime both he and I are your superior officers. You will carry out what we command. Is that clear, Lt. Regan?"

"Yes, sir."

"Very well then, square away your gear in that hut over there."

He pointed to the nearest dwelling behind them.

"At exactly 1730 hours," he continued crisply, "I want to meet with you and Bligh in the command center. At that meeting I will familiarize you with our most immediate mission."

"Yes, sir. I'll see you at 1730." He grabbed his duffel bag, felt for his holstered .45 and slung his squeaky clean M-16 over his right shoulder like a new golf bag. Walking to the assigned shelter, Scott couldn't help thinking about the utter coincidence that just enveloped him. He muttered aloud: "How in the shittin' hell could this guy weave himself back into my life? Why didn't he just laugh at my joke?"

An inner voice tapped at his temple like a Jiminy Cricket. *"Well, Scott, you may have fucked with a guy with a long memory. And maybe things really do just go round and round. It's now your time in the barrel. How are you going to get out of this one?"*

The sun slid below the grove of rubber trees, and the sky lit up in colors of orange, crimson and gold. He glanced to his left, and the reflection of the water between the dykes looked vibrant and clean. It was as if the final wave of daylight wanted to put on its best face before ushering in the blackness of night.

****

At the hut he grabbed the metal arc that served as a door handle and pushed. His boots sounded a clump on the solid plywood floor. The thud of his entry didn't interrupt the other American who was in the process of lighting the kerosene lamps in their quarters. When the tall blond figure finished his chores, he turned to face the young arrival.

"Hello, lieutenant. I'm Steve Bligh."

Scott saluted the captain, as his senior, who quickly waved his hand away in a gesture of dismissal.

"Hey, do me a favor. Forget the salutes from now on. O.K.?"

"Hey, fine with me. I was never nuts about that anyway."

Bligh continued. "There are only three U.S. officers in this center; Major Rheingold, me, and you. If we saluted each other all the time, it could signal a potential sniper that an officer is in town. The less we point each other out the better. There's been some VC activity in our area recently and our sources feel that Charlie may be looking to fuck us around a little." Scott absorbed the entire orientation from Bligh while standing in one spot. "I guess this concludes my formal introduction to you as my new roommate."

"Well, thanks, sir. I feel informed."

"Why don't you unload your gear by that bunk across from mine and put your main stuff in the footlocker. Remove the clip from your rifle, but keep it real comfortable next to you when you sleep — day or night. Secure the safety on your sidearm, keep it holstered and tuck it where you can grab it in a heartbeat."

"Do we normally expect midnight guests?"

"Not usually."

"Nice," Scott thought.

"We are meeting with Rheingold in 35 minutes."

"Yeah, he told me 1730 hours."

"Wanna grab some quick chow or would you rather get your shit squared away?" Bligh asked.

"I'd always rather chow down, sir."

"I like new arrivals that have their priorities straight, Regan. Let's walk over to mess and seize a bench."

The mess *hall* could have been described more accurately as a mess *room*. The cast iron antique stove fueled by scrap wood, stood tucked in a small corner of the hut. It was vented by a black stove pipe chimney that looked like it was straight out of Lil' Abner. Gray oilcloths covered the three plywood table- tops that rested on wooden horses. They sat down at a table designed for six, across from each other. Scott plopped his forearms on the table- top and leaned forward toward Bligh.

"What does he want to talk to us about?"

"Probably how you and I should interact and how we should deal with our counterparts."

"Yeah, I know about the lessons. I've heard them before."

"We all know the academics, lieutenant, but this ain't just classroom shit."

"So what more can the major tell me before the reality of this pretty place sets in?" Scott said.

"I don't know exactly, but we'll probably find out when we sit down with him."

Captain Bligh turned away from the table and looked out of the open hole that doubled as a window in the rippled steel structure. His mind drifted and he thought about the two other lieutenants he met since he landed at the DIOCC. They seemed to have the same questions. He especially remembered the last one, Lt. Payne.

Bligh rotated back to the table and rejoined the moment.

"So, how about we eat quick and then meet with Major Rheingold?"

"Yes, sir, sounds real good." Scott glanced down at the rice laden flat dish that was placed before him by a Vietnamese woman.

"What, no menus?" Scott joked. The meal was speckled with thin pieces of pork...or maybe it was chicken. The ubiquitous yellow fish sauce was already set upon the table next to the salt and pepper shakers. The multicolored plastic flowers and the clunky knives and forks rounded out the ambiance. Scott shook the golden liquid juice onto the dish. It stunk.

"Why do we have this crap on the table?" He motioned to the clear narrow neck bottle that he held in his right hand.

"Because we're in their country."

"That's it?"

"Yep. Now, let's chow down and go see what Rheingold has to say. Scott was already starting to long for a pot of meatballs, but settled for the yellow infused rice and mystery meat.

"You know, captain, any meal can become acceptable if I can just have some bread to wipe my plate. What are the chances of that?"

"Not today, we're out of bread."

"What kind of country is this?" Scott asked. "I don't think we're starting off on the right foot."

"What?"

"Only kidding, sir."

As they finished their chow, the woman appeared from the corner of the hut and removed their plates.

"Coffee? Coffee?" she nodded.

"Yeah," Bligh said.

"No, thanks," Scott countered.

"No coffee? No coffee?" she asked again.

"No coffee," Scott repeated.

She shook her head as if she didn't understand. She shuffled away.

"I don't drink coffee. What's the big deal?"

The old lady plunked down a heavy mug of acrid smelling coffee in front of Cpt. Bligh. Scott recoiled at the smell and sat back.

"Did you ever drink espresso, cap?"

"No, what is it exactly?"

"Well, it's like black sour jet fuel. In addition, you gotta' mash a lemon peel in it, like that would make it any better. My grandfather used to drink it by the pot full. Every time I smell military coffee I can also smell my grandfather's di nobile."

"The what?"

"A cigar. Little tiny twisted ropes. They burnt like a pile of autumn leaves, but my grandfather loved to smoke them with espresso. I always hated that smell until he died. After that I couldn't stay in his closet long enough, just to breathe the smell that remained in his clothes." The captain was raised in Damariscotta, Maine and had difficulty identifying with di nobile cigars and espresso.

"Let me pour down this cup and we'll go see the major. OK?" Scott nodded, they pushed the benches back and simultaneously swung their legs over the seat and walked toward the doorway. Two small shaggy mutts approached them and wagged their tails. They were both looking for some food or attention. Scott bent down and scratched both of their necks.

"I hope these guys aren't our guard hounds."

"No." Bligh answered flatly. "They're our mascots."

"I would still like bigger mascots."

"The black mutt is named Ham and the gray one is called Thuan. Ham, Thuan, get it?"

"Got it."

"Actually, they do serve a purpose. They have the hearing of jackals. If anything moves around here when it's quiet, they're the first to let you know. It's like they sleep with one ear and one eye open – day or night."

"Groovy."

Ham and Thuan trailed after them as the two officers made their way to the small steel hootch that served as both command headquarters and communication center. About 15 meters behind the structure, a jeep was parked on a raised platform of sturdy 6 X 6 beams and olive green sand bags. It stood above all of the arched metal huts in the compound. A 106 MM recoilless rifle was securely mounted on the vehicle. The weapon weighed over 400 lbs. and at close range the shell it fired could penetrate 16" armor plate. Tracer rounds were fired from a .50 caliber machine gun mounted on the monster. The .50 caliber round had the exact trajectory of the 106 mm shell. Once the gunner saw the tracers hit the target he then fired the mother load. It was all over in seconds.

Captain Bligh pointed to the jeep. "We'll be firing that Lil' sweetheart again tonight. Our intell info has been telling us that we have some VC movement in our area. We'll be blowing out some antipersonnel rounds. Lets Charlie know that we all ain't asleep."

"If I recall, Cap, that rifle is really loud. So who could sleep anyway?"

"With ear plugs you can get used to it. It's amazing what you can get used to here in the countryside."

"I can't wait, sir."

****

Major Rheingold was sitting inside the command center and looked at his watch when they entered. Scott interpreted it as some time check on their punctuality, recalling Vince Lombardi, coach of the Green Bay Packers, who always reminded his players when he called a meeting: "If you're on time, you're late."

The two junior officers moved toward the table where Rheingold positioned himself so that the captain and lieutenant had to sit on either side of him. He was the point of the triangle. He was the boss. Rheingold glanced at Scott, then looked down at a "Confidential" memorandum on the table before him. He shifted the document under his forearm as if to cover it.

"As you know this district, to include Phan Thiet, has been of considerable interest to the VC. It was a prime target of activity during TET last year and has continued to be an active area. In the last several weeks we've learned that Charlie is going back to basics. No head to head contact. Mines, snipers and even pungi spikes. Lethal harassment stuff. I hate losing *any* soldier, but I really hate losing my troops to a backwater booby trap. What's really infuriating is to be blown up by a trap that was set three days before, and Charlie ain't around when it blows. That sucks, doesn't it gentlemen?"

"Yes, sir." Bligh responded.

"Yes, sir, it does." Scott followed.

"Our mission here is to pinpoint VC suspects and bring them back for a chat. Nice and peaceful. That's the ideal situation. In reality, they tend to kick and moan on the occasional times they get word that we're comin'. Because of this we are constantly concerned with identifying security leaks.

"Bottom line is this: We trust us first. The ARVN, PRU's and our counterparts are second. Your interpreters are a distant third. Tell them very little. They are valuable only when they are called upon to communicate for you - on the spot. When you move out with them on patrol they will not know where you're going, why you're going, or how long you'll be gone. They're a tool for you and nothing more. In light of their language proficiency and possible access to classified information, they are perfectly positioned to be a double agent. We cannot afford to facilitate this possibility."

Rheingold pushed back from the table and moved his arm away from the typewritten memo.

"To help with our intelligence gathering efforts we have been recently given the flexibility to establish a rewards system, the Chieu Hoi program, for informants. In addition there's a memo on "professionalism." He slid over copies of Confidential

Memos dated 25 November 1968 and 12 December 1968. "Read both of them now." They lifted the documents.

CONFIDENTIAL

30 Novemberpp1968

MEMORANDUM FOR:

        CORPS PHOENIX COORDINATORS

        PROVINCE PHOENIX COORDINATORS

        DIOCC COORDINATORS

SUBJECT   :   Rewards Programs

1. The attachment summarizes current rewards programs, US and GVN, applicable throughout SVN and of interest and utility to PHUNG HOANG/PHOENIX.

2. Your attention is invited especially to Page 4, MACV Directive 381-2, 19 March 1968, VOLUNTARY INFORMANT PROGRAM (CONFIDENTIAL, title UNCLASSIFIED) (VIP). This program is designed for implementation by combat and combat support units and by advisory elements at all levels. Rewards, as established by designated commanders, may be paid to Vietnamese civilians for all information about the VC and NVA, for example, location and activities of personnel or units, identity and location of individuals in the VC infrastructure

(must lead to capture alive), location of weapons and ordinance, impending attacks, etc. Rewards may be paid for information which leads to recovery or capture of US or enemy weapons and ordnance, or for actual delivery of these items by informant. Information should be verified and acted upon whenever possible. However, rewards should be paid where the information is considered accurate but reaction is impractical. Receipts are to be obtained from informants whenever possible. However, where an informant does not want to sign a receipt or other circumstances make it impractical to obtain one, a certificate of valid expenditure by the payor is sufficient.

3. MACV Dir 37-2, 25 January 1968, FINANCIAL ADMINISTRATION MILITARY SUPPORT OF PACIFICATION (U) authorizes the use of imprest funds for "rewards for weapons turned in and significant military information provided by local inhabitants and Chieu Hoi returnees" (para. 4 f. (2) subject to restrictions in the same para and in para 4 f. (3) (1)). In general, this directive gives advisory teams a source of timely financing for un-programmed projects.

4. The GVN Ministry of Interior program (Vietnamese SECRET) is included even though to the best of our knowledge it is not now funded or actively carried out. It should be noted, however, that it is included by reference in para. VII of the

decree of 8 February 1968 setting up Self Defense Groups: "Those members of Civil Defense Units who have performed outstanding acts, such as capturing enemy or seizing weapons, will be rewarded in accordance with existing regulations".

Eylan K. Barker, Jr.
Director, PHOENIX Staff

CONFIDENTIAL

3. CHIEU HOI WEAPONS AWARDS SCHEDULE (U)

   Ministry Chieu Hoi and Information No 148, 12 July 1967

   a Purpose: Increase in awards for weapons turned in by Hoi Chanh.

   b Eligibility: Hoi Chanh

   c Funding: Foreign Aid Fund for the Open Arms.

   d Amounts: (RVN currency)

   Weapons

Flare pistol of every type	500$
Pistol of every type	1,200$
Shot gun of every type	1,500$
Home made scatter gun	1,500$
Rifle of every type	3,000$

Submachine gun of every type	5,000$
Flame thrower	7,500$
Automatic rifle of every type	7,500$
7,62mm Cal 30 machine gun	17,500$
12,7mm Cal 50 heavy machine gun	20,000$
14,5mm Communist Chinese or Russian MG	30,000$
14,5mm Antitank machine gun	40,000$
60mm Mortar or barrel	50,000$
81/82mm Mortar or barrel	60,000$
120/160mm Mortar or barrel	75,000$
Anti Aircraft of every type	50,000$
57mm Recoilless rifle	40,000$
75mm Recoilless rifle	50,000$
82mm Recoilless rifle	60,000$
Bazooka of every type	20,000$

Weapons' devices

Rifle breech, SMG breech, AR breech	2,000$
Heavy machine gun's barrel of all calibers	7,500$
Heavy machine gun's breech and cocking	15,000$
57mm RR's collimating sight	10,000$
75mm RR's collimating sight	15,000$
Mortar's collimating sight of every type	10,000$

CONFIDENTAL

MACJOIR-PHOENIX   12 December 1968

MEMORANDUM FOR: PHOENIX Military Personnel
SUBJECT: Professionalism

1. We are aware of the many problems and frustrations facing those of you at province and district level. Most of you do not speak Vietnamese and few, if any, have previous advisory experience. VC attacks are a constant threat in practically every area. These things we can understand. However, we cannot understand and we consider the situation intolerable when we come in contact with a PHOENIX representative who:

   a. Does not have (or is not familiar with) a file of PHOENIX Memoranda, Operational Aids, Newsletters, and repeated policy or operational material.

   b. Does not know what GVN or military (US, ARVN or FWMAF) units are available in the area for potential use as action/reaction forces. (He should know the designation, size, location, normal mission and actual employment of forces available, as well as their current state of training, armament, and readiness.)

c. Has made no effort to acquaint other members of the district or province advisory team with the PHOENIX/PHUNG HOANG mission, organization and need for coordination and cooperation with agencies and units at all levels.

2. The question then arises, what to do to correct deficiencies and/or to improve the situation. If you need outside assistance, where do you go for help? Here are a few hints for the needy PHOENIX representative.

a. Know your program and know your infrastructure target – in detail. Only the individual himself can accomplish this – by studying directives, newsletters and reports; by reading and studying special material, such as special studies on infrastructure, background books on Vietnam and VCI by such people as Douglas Pike and Sir Robert Thompson; and by frequent discussions with knowledgeable people — both US and Vietnamese, civilian and military.

b. Know your tools and know your people. Be inquisitive, be nosy, but by whatever means necessary, ascertain and prepare for your (and your successor's) personal use a list of pertinent units, agencies, and personalities involved in any way with either the intelligence or operations aspect of PHOENIX/PHUNG HOANG. Include information such as strong points—weak points—likes—dislikes—professional capabilities, etc., of personalities, and similar information which would be especially helpful for a successor to take over your job on your departure.

c. Provide training assistance to ARVN/GVN representatives in the DIOCC or permanent center. This is of course part of your normal duties, but what if you yourself are not an "expert" in intelligence files and procedures or in the conduct of tactical operations such as raids, ambushes, calling for fire support, etc. Very simple; Scream for help. At the province capital there is probably a PAIR (Province Area Intelligence Representative) who can provide intelligence instruction and advice on source control. Experienced combat arms officers, available at almost every echelon, can help you with regards to operational planning and conduct of patrols, raids and ambushes. Your Corps PHOENIX Coordinator probably has a combined US/GVN mobile training team established specifically to assist PHOENIX/PHUNG HOANG personnel. And don't forget US Army field manuals, many of which have been translated into Vietnamese and are available through ARVN training aids channels. So you see, help is available—it is yours for the asking.

d. Visit other PHOENIX/PHUNG HOANG activities. If you have the best DIOCC in Vietnam, pass along to your colleagues the secrets of your success. If you are just starting a DIOCC, visit one that is fully operational and effective. Pick up ideas that can be used in your area to improve operational effectiveness. We in PHOENIX preach coordination and cooperation, let's practice it as well.

Raymond G. Charter

Colonel, Inf

Acting Director, PHOENIX Staff

Distribution:

4 each: Corps PHOENIX Coordinator

2 each: Province PHOENIX Coordinator

1 each: District PHOENIX Coordinator

CHAPTER 24

Scott dropped the Confidential Memo on the table. "Do we have any flexibility in what we can pay these people?"

"If you think that your intell has more value than what's officially posted, you can bump the ante."

"How high can we go?"

"Depends. We've got deep pockets. We can pay in piastres or any other currency. It all depends. You've got to know your client. They're all whores. Our job is to find out what fires their missiles. Most of the time when we target a female she has one thing on her mind." Bligh shuffled the document in front of him. He had heard this part of the orientation before. Scott was all ears.

"All she wants to get is a free ticket out of here. Singapore, Australia, USA, Europe. It doesn't matter. We're whores too. We'll promise anything. The more she tells us the more we promise."

"The men are different. They want money, women or dope. We have a flash roll that'll make 'em cum, stables of women, and enough junk to keep them high for a lifetime. All we want is to make a guy roll on his neighbor."

Scott's mouth began to get dry.

"Is there any soda around here, major?"

"How about coffee?"

"No, thanks."

"What about you, captain?"

"I'll grab a cup. Want some, major?"

"Sure."

Bligh pushed his end of the wooden bench away from the table. He stretched his legs and moved slowly toward the huge aluminum vat that held the stale, lukewarm brew. Scott took this moment to look sideways at Rheingold and ask a casually curious question. He didn't expect the answer he got.

"Does the name William Payne ring a bell, sir?"

"Why do you ask?"

"Well, among other things, I knew him from college."

"I knew him very well." Rheingold said.

Scott didn't like the past tense reference.

"Where did you know him from?"

"From here. In fact, you are replacing him. He was my junior officer." Scott's mind raced.

"What happened?"

"He was medivaced." Getting medically evacuated usually meant a direct deposit into surgery, or into a body bag.

"How's he doing? I mean, he was a friend of mine. I still own the car I bought from him. How's he doing?"

"I haven't received any word that he was KIA."

Scott's hands laid flat on the table as he stared at Rheingold.

"He was here? With advisory team 27?"

"I just said that, didn't I?" Rheingold was starting to sound annoyed.

On a nondescript day, no different from many others, Lt. Payne, his driver, and his interpreter were traveling to a checkpoint in a routine run to speak with the villagers. The reason for the short trip was because the Phoenix operatives and the VC in the area were both trying to win the support of the local populace. Money normally talked and Willy Payne had a canvas bag full of piastres in order to convince the rice farmers to keep his DIOCC informed of any suspected Viet Cong movement in the area. The checkpoints were significant because they tended to be the central locations where the VC exercised strong- arm tactics and intimidation in order to keep the locals in their camp. The Phoenix teams, on the other hand, preferred to utilize the tried and true All American technique—bribery. Money usually did the trick except for the day that Willy didn't make the delivery.

The red powder dirt kicked up dust behind the open jeep, the sun glared oppressively in early midday and all was quiet except for the soft thumping of the tires. The water buffalos plodded peacefully in the paddies that bordered the dirt road.

Neither the driver, the interpreter, nor the lieutenant heard the deafening explosion that flipped the jeep into an uncontrollable roll. The birds on the brawny backs of the water buffalos flew away in vertical ascents. The beasts broke over the dams in an attempt to distance themselves from another noise of war. The 18- year old corporal was thrown over the steering wheel and killed instantly. The front bumper and whirling hood of the jeep severed the head of the ARVN interpreter and filleted Lt. Payne from the nape of his neck to his scrotum.

Hours passed since the trio had left the compound, and the Commanding Officer thought it was time to dispatch two newly arrived fuzzy cheeked "cherries" in another jeep with a mounted M-60 to assist Payne in distributing the currency. The CO wasn't really concerned, he just thought that the lieutenant had met with a cooperative bunch of locals and it was taking a little longer to talk with them and hand out the money. He had no suspicion that one of his troops and his ARVN responsibility had been dead for hours and that his junior officer was in the process of bleeding to death.

The PRC-6 radio crackled when the follow-up vehicle came upon the scene.

"Charlie Bravo -7, Charlie Bravo-7 this is Romeo Sierra. Over."

"Romeo Sierra, this is Charlie Bravo-7. Over".

"The guy ain't got no head!" the 18 year- old shouted in a high- pitched octave.

The E-5 who was manning the communication hut pressed his ear against the receiver.

"Romeo Sierra. Say again. Over."

"We got two KIA's and the lieutenant is split wide open. We need a duster NOW. Over."

"You in contact?" the E-5 barked

"Negative. Don't see nobody. Quiet. Over."

"Roger, Romeo Sierra, chopper airborne. Hunker. Out."

LZ Betty jumped to life as the marine pilots got the call. They were attached to the combat advisory team in Ham Thuan and no moment of action was unexpected. The poker hands were laid down on the table and the soft drinks were placed strategically so that they could be sipped after they returned. Stretchers, IV's and the corpsman's bag of painkillers were at the ready on the deck of the CH-46 helicopter as the propellers whumped increasingly faster into motion.

The Claymore mines, stolen from allied forces, were partially buried below the loose silt of the road. It was the only enemy weapon used in Ham Thuan that day and, in typical terrorist fashion, there was not a single Viet Cong around when it blew. All that was needed to unleash horror was patience and a boot, or tire, to depress the nipple nose plungers and convert the benign discs into a lethal rage.

The assassination attempt of a Phoenix officer failed in its mission, but was the first leg of a journey that would take Lt. Willy Payne through six surgeries until he was finally released from St. Alban's Hospital in Queens, N.Y., 18 months later.

Rheingold regained control of the meeting as Bligh returned with two mugs of black coffee. "We've recently gathered enough info on a suspect in our district. Here's his folder." Rheingold reached below the table and produced a resume. The target was a 45-50 year old male, a member of the local VC district committee who was considered the spearhead of Viet Cong policy implementation in Ham Thuan.

"This guy is not responsible for creating policy in our area, but he *is* the main cog in seeing that things get done. He's a grunt with a grudge. Not too different from us. He's a farmer by trade but coordinates at least three other hamlet level chapters in his spare time. He is judged to have a very strong sway over the inclinations of the local populace. He has been instrumental in frustrating the Chieu Hoi efforts and has actively resisted the encroachments of the GVN. He plays hardball." Rheingold turned and looked directly at Scott.

"We also feel that he either ordered, or directly placed, the land mine that blew up Lieutenant Payne's jeep." Scott clenched his jaw and his back muscles knotted. He no longer seemed to be paralleling Willy's life but instead seemed to be in lockstep with it and wondered what destiny had in store for him.

The screen door to the hootch opened with a high- pitched squeak. A hulking black E-6 entered the meeting.

"Good evening, major." He held the salute and addressed the other two officers. "Captain, lieutenant, good evening."

"At ease, sergeant." Rheingold said. "Lieutenant Regan, meet Sergeant Morris."

Scott rose and reached out to shake hands. Morris's right hand was the size of a 16oz. boxing glove.

"How you doin', sergeant?"

"Fine, sir." He sat down next to Scott.

"Sergeant Morris here," he nodded towards the poker faced NCO, "is our Radio Telephone Operator. There's nothing he doesn't know about a PRC 25 or a PRC 6. He can communicate with radios like he was speaking directly into your ear." Morris turned slightly toward the major, showing a pleased broad smile. He brought his attention back to all three men. "This brings me to the guts of our meeting tonight. The next new moon will be in two weeks. It's the darkest night of the month and will give us the best cover for going in and yanking our target. He lives in the outer hamlet, about 10 klicks from here."

Rheingold paused and surveyed his men, wanting to ascertain if they were intent on what he was saying. Satisfied that they were indeed with him, he went on. "There are reported to be only 90 to100 inhabitants living in some twenty hootches. He stays there because the locals are considered friendly. It's a great cover for him. He farms the paddies by day, but concentrates his agitation in the villages to the northwest. But he *always* comes back to his safe house to sleep. That's where we'll grab him."

Scott spoke. "How do we know which hootch he'll be in?"

"Tomorrow morning you will meet with your ARVN counterpart. He will be with a Civil Operations and Revolutionary Development, CORDS, representative from Binh Thuan. The CORDS rep has a Top Secret clearance and the Langley stamp of approval. He is also fluent in Vietnamese. You can trust him to interpret any questions that you have. You will be given all the info that you need to pinpoint the suspect."

Bligh listened politely as Rheingold finished his address. Sergeant Morris drummed his fingers on the table and studied Scott's face.

"What about my interpreter?" Scott asked. "Won't he be with us?

"He'll be with you that night. However, he will be told absolute jack shit before you go out on your mission," the major said.

"He'll be given about a one-hour notice, following which you will not allow him to leave your sight. Captain Bligh will determine what weapons you'll carry and how many men you'll need. Unless our intelligence info changes in the next 14 days, I think two squads should work. One ARVN and one of us. But I'll entrust that call to the captain"

Without further comment, the major leaned forward. "Any questions gentlemen?"

"No, major."

"None, sir."

"No, sir.'

"Very well then, see you tomorrow."

Morris and Scott moved toward the door as Bligh and Rheingold downed their last few gulps of coffee. Morris backed away and let Scott exit first. The gesture was a combination of military courtesy and physics. Morris's bulk just wouldn't allow his body and that of a gnat to pass through the doorway at the same time.

Scott walked toward a bunker that was positioned inside the protective minefield. He leaned against it and felt its solidity. Ham & Thuan moved rapidly from the darkness and circled his legs. Scott focused his eyes on the two half pints and laughed. "You guys are like canine sirens, with no bite." Thuan lifted his leg and peed on the lower sandbags. Ham followed and released his water on the same spot.

"Boy, do you have the life. No bills, no taxes, no worry and you can piss wherever you stand. In my next life I want to come back as you." The mutts finished their security check and scampered away. A soft humming came from inside the bunker. The urchin who walked out of the sandbag fortress singing her song was the same elfin figure who had greeted him earlier. She was playing with her fingers like they were toys. She stopped and looked up at Scott.

"Was that you singing in there?"

"I sing, I sing" she smiled.

"What are you doing up so late?"

"I sing," she said again.

"You know, you have a sweet voice. I don't recognize the tune but so what?"

She stared at him like a puppy.

"Before I leave here I'm going to teach you a song that I learned when I was about your age. O.K.?"

"O.K." she said automatically.

"I know that you never heard of a singer called Claudio Villa, but he had a great voice and I'm going to teach you how to sing his favorite songs, O.K.?"

"O.K." she said again.

Scott realized that she understood nothing except "O.K."

"What's your name?"

"Name?"

"Yeah, name. Your name?"

She pointed to her little chest. "Baby girl."

"That's your name? Baby girl?"

"Baby girl" she repeated.

"I don't like that name. What mother names her daughter Baby girl?"

She stared again.

"I'm going to name you Mary. Bullshit to Baby girl." She became very agitated.

"Baby girl, no booshih, Troung uy, Baby girl, no booshih."

"No, no. That's not what I mean...look...why don't you just go to sleep. It's way past your bedtime."

196

"You sreep?" she asked.

"Eventually, I mean, not yet. Hey you don't understand enough English and I don't know enough Vietnamese. This is just a half assed conversation now isn't it?"

"You say ass, GI. You say ass."

She put her hand over her mouth, laughed and headed back into the bunker. Scott realized that this was her home. He bent over and looked into the hole. It was pitch black and he couldn't see a thing, but he was able to hear her giggle to herself.

"You say ass, hee, hee."

"Hey," he called, "if you need me I'll be in that hootch over there. O.K.?"

"O.K." Her response was faint and punctuated with a yawn.

He straightened up and slapped the sandbags. The compound was completely dark but for the soft yellow lights that shone through the small windows of the communication hut and the sleeping quarters. The moonlight added a gray filter to the irregular shapes etched in the charcoal night. Captain Bligh was about to blow out the kerosene lamp when Scott entered.

"Where does that little girl sleep at night?" Scott said.

"In the bunker."

"What if it rains?"

"It doesn't rain here this time of year."

"She doesn't look like she's all bitten up."

197

"I never really noticed, lieutenant. Blow that out when you're ready to turn in, O.K.?"

Scott unlaced his boots, patted his fatigue shirt and felt something crinkle in the breast pocket. He pulled out a picture of him and Maryanne on their honeymoon in Bermuda, and was planning to put it somewhere safe. He moved to place it between the pages of a loose- leaf binder in his locker when he heard light footsteps pitter on the plywood of the hootch.

"Hey, I thought you were asleep, young lady, I heard you yawn before." She saw the picture in his hand, running to grab it like it belonged to her.

"See? See?" she asked smiling. He showed her the photo of a couple standing in waist deep water at a hotel swimming pool. She looked back and forth between the picture and Scott's face and finally made the connection.

"Troung uy, Troung uy" She reached to grab it like it was her favorite candy.

"No way, little one, this is mine." He retracted the snapshot and she watched him, memorizing *exactly* where he placed it in his footlocker.

"O.K. lights out now. Go to your bed or bunker, wherever you sleep. See you in the morning."

Her final spurt of nocturnal energy rapidly subsided and she walked softly to her fortified sleeping quarters for another restless night of sleep. He blew out the lamp, felt for his thin pillow and rolled it into a ball that he tucked behind his head.

He thought of Mary and stared at the wavy steel wall. The light was out for only a few minutes before the rats started to squeak. Scott looked through the netting, up at the ceiling and heard the thin scratching of their feet. He punched the pillow, cursed, and wrapped the pillow around his head. The rodent noises were soon drowned out by the thunderous crack of the Recoiless Rifle unloading its armament every 120 seconds. Compared to the unnerving rat noises, the shelling sounded like a virtual lullaby.

Somewhere in the night the 106 mm stopped pounding. Scott wasn't sure when it happened, but he woke up to daylight and silence. He turned toward his roommate in the next cot; the net was thrown overhead and the captain was gone. Scott looked at his Timex, which read 6:05. He dressed quickly, eager to be outside so he could get an idea of how the rest of the compound started the day in his new home.

CHAPTER 25

The Vietnamese locals entered through the security gate and reported to their assigned areas of work. Mama- sans and male laborers shuffled through the dirt, their dried and leathery toes clutching sandals that clung to weathered feet. Except for an occasional pair of ripped sneakers, rubber thongs were the primary footwear. Scott was watching his first procession when he heard Morris' voice.

"Lieutenant Regan, good morning."

"Morning, sergeant."

"Ready for some chow?"

"Well, I was going to take a shower first and then…"

"Not yet, lieutenant." Morris interrupted. "The water in that 55-gallon drum up there is still cold from last night. Let the sun work on it. It's best about 1200 to 1300 hours. It'll feel just like home. Almost." Over a breakfast of scrambled eggs and crackers, Scott asked about his ARVN counterpart.

"What time am I supposed to meet him?"

"Whenever he shows up. We're not going out on patrol today. No formal meetings. So there's no rush for him to check in."

"Nice life."

"Yeah, they don't have a real sense of urgency, lieutenant."

"Then why do we? I mean, it's their country isn't it? We're just trying to help them out. If they don't care if they live under Commie rule, why don't we just pack up and go home?"

"Makes sense to me, sir"

"That's too logical, Morris. There's got to be more to it than that. We're just not smart enough to see the big picture."

"Then again, lieutenant, maybe we do," he looked to gauge the officer.

Scott shoveled through his eggs and continued listening.

"Well, sir, sometimes a simple picture of things is the clearest, not all clouded up with details and such. The more opinions involved, the more confusion there is, and before you know it, the shit outweighs the bull. Just like the hawks and doves ranting about this undeclared war. It keeps them in the public eye and gets them re-elected. If they all agreed on everything, they'd be out of a job. It's sort of like race relations, huh, sir? If everybody got along we wouldn't need a spokesman for each color. The Klan and the Black Panthers would both be out of business."

"Sounds too simple, sarge. There's just got to be more to it."

****

They finished breakfast and were walking to the communications center when Morris stopped him. "Hey, lieutenant. There's your interpreter."

A young man, looking to be in his mid-twenties, moved at a fast shuffle, quickly waved at the armed guard at the security post and continued past him. He was about 5'5" and 130 lbs. His fine black hair lay flat on his head and swayed in rhythmic cadence to his pace. His green and white checked shirt hung down to the middle of his khaki-covered thighs.

"Come on, I'll introduce you."

Captain Bligh saw Sergeant Morris and Scott head toward the interpreter and moved to join them.

"Scott, it's about time you met your mouthpiece," Bligh said. "This is Ruan Van Cur'o'ng. We call him Strong. It's his nickname." Scott reached out and Strong shook his hand lightly.

"Chao, Troung uy."

"Ciao?" Scott said. "He speaks Italian?"

"No, it's pronounced the same but spelled different. They both mean "hello," Bligh explained.

"Pleased to meet you, Strong."

"Happy see you too, rieutenant." Scott tried to make eye contact, but the interpreter diverted his glance, making it difficult for Scott to read his face.

"How about we take a walk around here and get acquainted?"

"Good idea." Bligh said, and Morris nodded his approval.

They headed toward the platform that supported the 106 mm recoiless rifle as Mary, who had appeared out of nowhere, trotted toward them. Ham and Thuan barked in playful yelps behind her.

"Chao, co!" Strong greeted her.

"Chao, ong." she smiled.

"Chao, Troung uy." She looked up at Scott and raised her arms.

He picked her up and cradled her in his right arm and resumed his walk with Strong. She tucked her head against his neck and giggled.

"You Numbah One GI." He bent his head down toward her. "I know, you said that before. You probably tell that to all your men."

"You Numbah One G.I." she repeated.

Strong stared straight ahead. They paced together in silence until Scott pulled up at an empty wooden ammo box shoved against the outside wall of the north bunker. He decided that this would be as good a place as any to have a first chat with his mouthpiece.

"Have a seat," Scott said, dropping down to the box. Mary squirmed to position herself on his lap. Strong squatted on his haunches next to him, his knees touching his chest.

"So how long have you been here?" Scott asked.

"Two and half year."

"Then you've been here long enough to remember Lieutenant Payne."

"Yes, yes, tiec qua."

"Yes, what?"

"It a shame. It a pity what happened."

"Do you think you know who set the mine?"

"No, I don't know."

"We'll find him someday. Don't you think so?"

"We everyday get information. Maybe someday."

"I hope so, because I'm a little superstitious. I've known Willy a long time and it seems that our lives have had some uncomfortable parallels." Scott paused. "Do you understand what I'm saying?"

"Yes, understand good. Strong interpreter."

"So where did you learn English?"

"In l'ecole Francais."

"You speak French, too?"

"Oui, Oui," Strong smiled broadly.

"Were you a rich kid or something?"

"I never rich. My grandmother teach French here. I learn from school."

"Well, let's just keep our talk to English. I failed French in high school."

Mary shifted on his lap and he nodded to her, "She's going to teach me Vietnamese. Right, honey?"

"You Numbah One G.I."

"I think your needle's stuck in the same groove." He poked his finger under her arm and tickled her. She twisted on his knee and squealed.

"Are you going to be hanging around here the rest of the day, Strong?"

"I here all day."

"O.K., then I'll catch you later."

"Catch you, too, rieutenant."

He rose from his crouch and walked around the bunker toward the latrine. Scott put Mary down and spotted Rheingold sitting at a makeshift table in the middle of the compound. He was field stripping his M-16 and cleaning the parts.

Rheingold looked up, studied him for a fleeting moment and grunted, "Good morning." He returned his attention to his chore and offered a firm suggestion. "You might want to grab your piece and break it down. The grit around here will jam a rifle in a heartbeat. If that happens, you'll wind up with a very expensive walking stick."

"Do we have something planned?" Scott asked.

"As a matter of fact, we do. I want to take a little stroll out to checkpoint Tango. We're getting some unconfirmed reports of cowboys harassing the locals, stealing their rice, grabbing the women - trying to convert them through strong-armed tactics. Shit like that. We're pouring tons of money into this Chieu Hoi program and they're trying to fuck it up."

He looked down the barrel of his piece and stood upright, continuing, "I guess we got their attention. That means what we're doing is working. I want to distribute some pamphlets out there, do a little public relations and let them know what we'll pay for captured weapons and accurate information."

"What time are we moving out?"

"Early afternoon - siesta time. We'll be back before dark."

"Is Strong coming with us?"

"Always does." The major was tiring of the small talk and turned away from Scott.

'When do you want me to tell him?"

"When I tell you to tell him," he barked stepping off towards the CP.

"Got it." Scott offered to the departing back, "I'll just go and clean my weapon. I'll be in my hootch."

****

Rheingold had decided that one squad would be sufficient for this afternoon's public relations jaunt into the jungle. Scott's ARVN counterpart had still not reported, so they planned to go without him.

"Lieutenant, are you ready to move out?"

"My troops are ready, major."

Rheingold pulled him away from the milling group. "Normally this would be your command, but since you're new here I want to walk you out this first time. This really ain't my job."

"It's your call, sir. If you want to give me the pamphlets to toss around out there, it's ok with me. I'm comfortable with it."

"Yeah, but I'm not."

"Why?"

"My gut. Besides the only way these advertisements are 'tossed around' is by chopper. If we want to blanket an area, we shovel them out of a Huey and let the wind make the delivery. Otherwise we hand them out like a mailman. O.K.?"

"OK, sir."

"OK, Let's move out."

Scott turned to the mixed squad of ARVNs and U.S. troops motioning for them to fall in. They formed a single file behind him and plodded out through the guarded front gate. Rheingold wanted to walk "point," and Scott followed 10 meters behind him. This was an unusual formation but it was only a routine visit with no cause for concern. Strong walked behind and to Scott's right, carrying an M-79 grenade launcher. The only sounds were the clicking of the rifle butts against the fragmentation grenades secured to web belts. Nobody talked.

The small hamlet at Checkpoint Tango was at the end of a narrow dirt road that led from the DIOCC. The Corps of Engineers had built the solid dirt path in 1966. It was elevated and cut through the rice paddies that pressed against it on both sides. Major Rheingold kept pace ahead of the troops. The only firearm that he carried was his Colt .45. He didn't expect trouble, surveyed the foliage on either side of him and continued briskly. Scott trotted up to him. Strong stayed behind with the ARVN and U.S. squad.

"Hey, Major, aren't we a little exposed over here?"

"I don't think so, lieutenant."

"I mean this one way street sort of makes us look like a string of ducks. Huh?"

"I *said*, 'I don't think so', lieutenant."

Scott pushed on. "Is there another way that we can return? Another path or something?"

"Nope. This is the only road out to the point, and the only road back."

"Well, if Charlie knows that, aren't we sort of setting our ass up for contact?"

"Some days that's our job, but not today."

"Well, I don't know, sir. Couldn't we take a jeep and get there quicker?"

"That's what your buddy Willy Payne thought too. That didn't work so well, did it? Besides we have no intell at this time that would discourage this type of check out. There's been some general VC movement in the area, but nothing specific to us. They're just hassling the locals in the hamlet. No big deal."

"Roger, sir."

Scott looked behind him to see if the troops were alert. They all appeared to be in varied forms of indifference. Some of the ARVNs were smoking Gauloises cigarettes, the US troops talking quietly, smoking various brands of American filters. They all flicked the remains of their butts into the chocolate brown water that hugged the dykes along side of them. Scott was trying to keep pace with the Major when he heard the unmistakable hollow metallic "pop" of an M-79 grenade launcher.

It happened in a split-second. The round hit a crusty patch between Rheingold and Scott. It was to their right and tumbled on the raised road that separated the water filled paddies. It was a perfect shot to kill both of them. The bursting radius should have taken them out, and anyone else within ten meters. The shell was designed to explode on impact, but didn't detonate. It bounced in spastic twists until Scott finally saw the silo shaped round flip into the murky water and disappear. It defied all the laws of probabilities; it was a dud.

Rheingold stopped and turned around. It was over. Nothing happened. All hell broke loose.

The major screamed. "What the fuck was that?"

"All I saw, major,..." Scott was interrupted. "Who's carrying the launcher?" Rheingold bellowed.

"Strong."

"Where's he?" Rheingold demanded.

"Uh, he was right behind me." Scott pivoted and looked around. "I, I...there." Scott stammered pointing to his interpreter who was sloshing through the water in the rear of the file. He ran toward the American officers.

"Strong trip, Strong trip."

Scott's mouth fell open. Rheingold spit. Everyone else stopped and looked around.

"What the fucking shit do you mean you tripped'?" Rheingold glared.

Scott yelled, "Keep that motha' fuckin' breech open! Don't load it and snap it shut! I'll tell you when to lock it! Christ, we're just going out to a checkpoint. What the fuck are you doin'?"

"Strong sorry, troung uy. Strong sorry."

Scott stared at his interpreter. He didn't believe him.

"Major, let me pull up the rear. I want him in front of me." Strong looked back and forth at the officers.

"Take him where you want." Rheingold allowed.

"Strong, come with me," Scott commanded. "Let them pass." The troops re-assembled and moved forward.

"How many more rounds do you have?"

"Ba."

"Give them to me." Strong pulled three shells from his pockets.

"Drop back and stay in front of me." Scott held Strong's forearm and let the troops pass. "Now keep that breech open and follow them."

****

The hamlet seemed to be fully occupied but quiet. The midday meal was done and the fading embers of the open cooking fires sent ribbons of smoke skyward. A pungent odor of burnt wood and meat mixed with the cooked scent of lemon grass and the punch of nuoc mam. Loosely woven hammocks supported several sleeping villagers. Others rested on straw mats in their hootches.

The location was considered friendly. Strategic deployment of the troops was not required. It was a perfect time to say hello, so they just walked in.

Rheingold stopped at the center of the hamlet and motioned for Scott and Strong to join him. The major then signaled several troops to fan around the three of them and the Vietnamese papa-san who had just emerged from his hootch. Another quick hand gesture and the remainder of the squad circled the hamlet's outside perimeter.

"Chao ban toi." The withered face of the old man framed a wide, near toothless smile.

"Chao ban." Rheingold replied. The interpreter moved closer to the two men.

"Ask him how everything is...how things are going here."

"Dao nay anh co khae knong?"

Strong translated. "He say other people come a lot at night. He don't know them. They ask a lot of question. Sometime they have rifle. Sometime they friendly. But always ask question."

Scott stood several feet from the conversation. His eyes moved from the elder, to Strong, to Rheingold. The old man didn't seem to be complaining about the VC harassment. He thought the information Rheingold just received from the papa-san should have been expressed in a more agitated, concerned or fearful manner. Stealing food from the village was one thing. Grabbing women and kids was another. Something was inconsistent.

They finished speaking and the major addressed Scott. "Order the troops to hand out the pamphlets. Make sure everyone gets one. Ask the villagers about any VC disturbances. Solicit a cross section of opinions from kids, women, men, and mama-sans."

Scott motioned to Strong to follow him. The others grabbed leaflets from the canvas duffel bag and started to distribute them.

The process took 45 minutes. The tiniest villagers approached the soldiers like they were handing out special gifts, grabbing the incomprehensible papers and running away smiling. Scott and Strong completed their interviews and walked over to Rheingold.

Scott spoke. "The villagers reacted a lot like the papa-san. Yes, they admit that Charlie has been a frequent visitor. But, no, they are not worried about any violence or threats. It looks to me that the whole hamlet is in agreement; and it's either the truth or they are *extremely* well rehearsed. Now what do we do?"

"Now we go home the way we came. I'm getting real thirsty. There's nothin' more we can do here today," Rheingold answered.

"I agree, sir. This road dust can only be rinsed out of my throat with a cold beer."

"You catch on quick, lieutenant."

Scott grinned.

As they walked back to the DIOCC Scott went over the details of the day's exercise in his mind. The more he thought about it the more unsettled he felt. He didn't speak during the return trek, but in order to avoid another possible fatal "mistake" Scott kept his interpreter in front of him, slung the M-79 over his left shoulder, and watched the setting sun cast Strong's long shadow across the road ahead.

CHAPTER 26

Captain Bligh greeted the group when they returned to the compound. "You're right on time."

"For what?"

"Cocktail hour."

Sgt. Morris moved from behind Bligh. "Now's the time to shower, lieutenant. You missed prime time at 13:00 hundred hours, but the water's still warm."

"OK then. How about I unload my stuff and see you at the "O" Club in an hour?"

"I'm not an officer, sir. I have to go to the NCO Club."

"Oh, yeah, I forgot. What a dumb rule; fucks up team spirit and shit. If we can go out on patrol together then why can't we drink beer together?" He Looked at Morris' face and saw a broad smile and a slight nod of affirmation.

Scott walked to his quarters and pushed open the screen door. He grabbed his soap and found his flip-flops and made his way to the shower.

"Hello, ladies," he said, surprised. Two women squatted beneath the shower- head. They were pounding their clothes against the wet wooden boardwalk like it was a washboard. Scott expected them to leave when he removed his coarse towel. They didn't, but simply moved to the edges of the floor and allowed Scott to shower between them using his running water to continue scrubbing. They squatted, looked up at him, and smiled with severely nubbed, reddish-purple teeth. Scott looked down at them and smiled, too. It was clearly unusual, but not unacceptable; it didn't make him feel the slightest bit uncomfortable.

The water was still very warm and it helped to dampen his suspicions of earlier in the day. He dried off and draped the towel around himself for the stroll back to the hooch, where he dressed quickly and commandeered a jeep.

The Officers Club in Phan Thiet was five kilometers from the DIOCC. Beers cost 25¢ and cigarettes were 15¢ a pack. It was a place to gather together and gather your thoughts. The lounge was on the second floor of a roughly hewn wooden building.

The Red Cross office downstairs had two doors. One opened from the dirt street and led upstairs; the second opened to a small courtyard where several banana trees grew. At the end of the courtyard was the whorehouse. Red Cross volunteers ignored the stream of GI's who passed by the desk on their way to a brief encounter with carnal pleasure.

Prophylactics were readily available, but the traffic was normally in a heated rush, and nobody cared. Inevitably, the participants returned to their local medic for the shots of penicillin and streptomycin that would cure most anything they caught. No one ever asked about the details. The "clap" was a trifling infection and a small price to pay for the morale boost that came with it. There was also a barbershop in a corner of the first floor building and the combined attractions of booze, boobs and a barber ensured that this was an active stop for military personnel. Scott made his way upstairs to the noisy, smoke filled club. Wooden tables dominated the floor space, and men squeezed against the small bar that had no stools.

Judging by the din in the room, Scott was a few beers late. He scanned the room and edged through tightly grouped tables toward the bar. Everyone seemed to be in homogenous cliques. The chopper pilots were obvious: most of them sported handlebar mustaches. Others dressed in short-sleeved shirts and slacks were clearly civilian employees working for the national defense agencies. These folks had the same overall mission as the military personnel, but their cover stories and activities were so well constructed that most people believed they were innocuous participants in the war effort. Even the Viet Cong didn't view them as a threat.

Scott asked for a beer. The bartender slid him a bottle of "33." He grabbed the long neck and saw Rheingold and Bligh sitting at a table toward the back of the room. They motioned to him.

Scott walked over, pulled up a metal folding chair and sat down.

"So," Bligh said, "the major briefed me on what happened today with Strong." His intonation seemed to ask for Scott's opinion. Scott didn't hesitate.

"It's tough for me to believe that a trip caused him to fire that round. But, it's tougher for me to think that he did it on purpose. Did anybody notice anything that we missed?'

"No." Rheingold answered. "Nobody even noticed him dropping to the rear of us."

"What's his reputation around here?" Scott asked.

"Competent."

"Yeah, actually competent and reliable," Bligh stated.

"So how does a competent ally mistakenly fire an M-79 round right between two American officers? I mean the odds of that being a dud are astronomical."

Both men nodded in agreement, but Rheingold added, "I don't have any argument with that, but one fact still remains: There have been no previous incidents that would cause us to be suspicious of him."

The senior officer dismissed the entire event with a virtual swipe of his hand. Scott thought that the rejection of the incident was too cavalier...almost like he didn't want to talk about it...almost like *he* was hiding something. He realized that Rheingold still harbored some harsh feelings about that day in the bar in Niagara Falls when the ROTC cadet mouthed off at him. But would he conspire to have him *killed* because of it? If the shell that Strong "mistakenly" fired today was, in fact, orchestrated by the major then he would have also died with him. He paused for a second to rein in his imagination. He couldn't believe he was even having these ultra paranoid flashes but still felt compelled to uncover any negative attitude that Rheingold harbored against him.

"Hey, major, does Captain Bligh know when and where we first met?"

"If you didn't tell him, then he doesn't have any idea." Bligh pulled his chair a little closer to the table.

"Why don't you tell him, I'd like to hear your version," Rheingold offered. Scott addressed the captain: "Well, it happened like this. I was in ROTC and trying to pick my branch of service. The Major was one of the veteran officers who spoke to our class. You know, to try and convince us to join the branch they represented." Bligh nodded. "Anyway, he wore an eye patch over his left eye on the day he talked to us. Ain't I correct on this, major?"

"Yep."

"Well, you see, this was on a Friday and normally me and my friends always went to a local gin mill after classes. So, that particular day I was there with a buddy of mine who was all gung -ho to go Infantry and eradicate Communism. Me - well I didn't have that calling. I just wanted to go in and get out with nothing personal and nothing dramatic happening.

"So, the Major here comes to this bar, still wearing this eye patch. Well, it turns out that I started to tell him how I felt about my upcoming commitment to Uncle Sam. Not only did I say that I would never pick Infantry as my branch of choice, I also asked him if he got laid a lot more because the chicks liked the mysterious look of his patch.

"He slammed his glass on the bar and told me that he did O.K. with the ladies before he had the patch, marched out of the joint, and I never saw him again until I reported to Ham Thuan. Small world, huh, major?"

"It sure is, lieutenant." Scott tried to shift the conversational gears a little.

"I'm really glad to see that everything is OK with your eyes."

"It was only a temporary thing."

"That's good, then." Regan added. A moment passed before the lieutenant spoke again. "Can I ask you a very direct question, sir?"

"Carry on," Rheingold said blankly.

"Do I still piss you off?" Rheingold took another sip from his bottle and paused. "Well - let's put it this way. If you weren't wearing that uniform we probably wouldn't be socializing. My first impression of you was that you were an annoying smart-ass. However, you told me what you felt and looked me in the eye."

Scott coughed on his beer and stifled a laugh.

"I now view you as a U.S. Army trained combat advisor. We are in this thing together and we have a common mission. For this single reason, I will stand by you and harbor no negative feelings. In a sentence, lieutenant, you *don't* still piss me off."

Despite Regan's momentary suspicion of the major, he now believed him.

Rheingold was a career soldier who bled red, white, and blue with a personality that was forthright and direct. If he carried any ill feelings from the past, Scott would have been the first to know. Now, Regan strongly sensed that Rheingold's word was solid.

No, there was no way the major played any role in the misfiring of that grenade. However, it closed one door of suspicion, but opened another.

Scott addressed the officers. "Do we ever conduct a surveillance of our ARVN troops?" Scott asked.

"AVRN troops?" the captain spoke. "Hell, we're all being tailed at one time or another. We got a price on our head and Charlie would love to nail us, so he's always snoopn'. Then our own boys watch us to make sure we're not fuckin' up the security blanket. So they're snoopin', too."

"What I mean is do we ever target an individual for a specific reason?"

"It's done when we think it's needed," Rheingold responded.

"Don't you think Strong should be tailed for a while?" Scott said. "I mean, well maybe I'm just over-reacting here, but I have a gut feeling that we should take a closer look at my interpreter."

"Look here, Regan," the major said, "you haven't been in country long enough to see how all the players interact. You've got to see how shit unfolds. You're understandably jumpy, but chill your jets. Every SOB working for us has gone through a raft of investigations. They work up close and personal with us because they cleared security – not because we drew their names out of a helmet."

"I really would like to believe," Scott retorted, "that we all have the same focus, but I feel very edgy about what happened today. Think about it. If he blew both of us up he would have earned a huge payday.

"It was a perfect setup that put you and I in one convenient blasting range. He may never see that again. It was his moment of opportunity and, thank Christ, he fucked it up."

Regan was motioning with his hands and was looking down in front of him. He looked up to see the captain and Rheingold staring at him. The major spoke: "Sometimes a naive viewpoint is a valid one. You don't know how things work here – but – nobody has a lock on instincts."

"What do we have to lose if we have him tailed?" Scott asked.

"We have a lot to lose if we put an informant on his tail and the informant turns out to be a VC sympathizer. If he informs Strong that we're on to him, then your mouthpiece *will* have to kill you sooner. Are you willing to take this chance?" Scott paused and slid the beer bottle through a wet spot on the table; one hand to another.

"Hey, major, you have the final call, but, yeah, I would take that shot." Scott thought again, "Yeah, I definitely would take that chance."

"Who would you trust to follow him?" Rheingold asked.

"Well, the guy who would arouse the least suspicion would probably be my ARVN counterpart." Rheingold nodded.

"You'll meet with him tomorrow. I'll make sure he speaks with you before 0800." Rheingold finished.

"I'll be waiting, sir."

CHAPTER 27

Scott tossed on his cot that night and couldn't separate his dreams from conscious thoughts. He drifted back to the smells of summer evenings on 13th Street when the rainstorm had passed, and the cement sidewalk by Nick's grocery store was fragrant with the ubiquitously urban aromas of Bazooka bubble gum, melted ice cream and discarded cigars.

Blackie wore gray sharkskin slacks and his long-collared, white-on-white shirt was neatly tucked; his tapered shoes shined to a gloss. He was yelling.

"Hey, Tommy, whadda' you a jerk- off? What I do with Gloria is my business."

"I didn't say nuttin', Blackie."

"You're lyin'. She told me her 'ole man smacked her causa' what you said. I didn't even get tah' second base. Go hang somewhere else...10th Street...Abington Avenue...whatever. You rat me out then your word ain't worth shit. You only got your word...your word...your word..."

Scott tossed over, his eyes shot open and he looked across at Steve Bligh. The dark shadow of his roommate emitted irregular snores. Everything else around him was silent except for an occasional yelp from Ham and Thuan. He repositioned the mosquito net around him when he heard Mary.

"Troung uy?"

"What are you doing out at this hour?"

"'S cold."

"Cold? Here in the sub-tropics?"

"'S cold."

"Here, get under this net." She had an innocence and frailty that was irresistible to the young lieutenant and she jumped at the opportunity to get warm.

"You better watch out because I might squash you." Scott turned on his side and she cuddled into the small of his back like a kitten. The luminescent dial on his watch read 2:34 AM, as he flopped his arm across his head and they fell asleep.

Hours later Mary was still nestled against him and Bligh was pushed face down into his pillow. The silver gray light of pre-dawn silhouetted the enormous rat that circled the edge of his bed.

"Aww — shit!" Scott barked.

Mary kicked her leg at his voice and sent the rodent scurrying. Bligh bolted straight up and cocked his .45. "Where!?" He barked.

"There." Scott pointed. They both gained full consciousness at the same time.

"Do you see that rat?"

"Is that what you screamed at?"

"Yeah!"

"Oh, Christ, calm down."

"Calm down? It has to be a 50 lb rat!"

"So what?"

"Are they all that big?"

"Only the first time you see them."

"Then what happens?"

"Then they shrink until you finally give them a pet name."

"What's his name, Mary?" Bligh pointed to the arrogant guest that stared at them from the edge of the footlocker.

"Chuot," she answered.

"Chuck?" Scott asked.

"Chuot," she said again.

"Chuck?"

Bligh pushed back the mosquito net and slammed his bare feet on the plywood floor. The chuot bolted into a crevice and was gone.

"And you, young lady..." Scott said in a menacing tone. She squealed when he reached out for her, pressing her hands tightly under her chin and backing away in mock horror.

"I had a lousy night's sleep because of you! You made me sleep on the very edge of that cot," he growled. She belly laughed at his expression and her tiny legs pumped in triple time as she bolted for the doorway and into the early light.

"When did she join us?" Bligh asked.

"Sometime during the night. She was cold," Scott reached for his fatigue pants and flip-flops, "she's a real pistol."

"Don't use that description."

"OK, then, she's real cute."

"That's better." Bligh said.

Regan grabbed the washbowl that they shared for both brushing their teeth and shaving. "I'll get some water. I'll be right back."

As he walked across the compound, he saw Thuan digging by the inside fence that was ringed by barbed wire. He changed direction and made his way to the mutt, but the dog ignored his approach and continued to dig. His head was buried in a hole and dirt flew out from between his hind legs. Regan scratched Thuan's rump.

"If you're trying to dig to China, keep going because you're almost there. It's not that far from here."

The mongrel continued to ignore him. Realizing that there would be no playtime with the determined canine, Regan continued his quest for warm water. Passing the communication hooch, he saw that it was unoccupied except for a corporal who was monitoring a channel.

"Morning, Lieutenant Regan."

"Good morning, corporal. Any action last night?"

"Well, it was mostly quiet all night except for two contacts."

"Casualties?"

Couldn't tell, sir, —sounded like one KIA and a number of troops were dusted off."

"ARVNs or us?"

"Couldn't copy."

"Where did they make contact?"

"In Binh Tuy on Route 1. Just over into III Corps."

"Anything around us here last night?"

"Not last night, sir."

They both were silent for several seconds.

"So, what else is new, corporal?"

"The Jets beat the Colts in the NFL-AFL Championship game."

"What!" Scott almost jumped out of his skin. "They what?"

"It's all there in the *Stars and Stripes*, sir." The newspapers were stacked on the floor next to the table that held the industrial size pots of coffee and hot water.

"The last I heard they were 18 point dogs! I mean Namath's my hero, but he can't be *that* good!" Scott put the washbowl down and grabbed a paper.

Looking around for a quiet place to read, he noticed that the latrine was empty and figured he could kill two birds with one stone. He trotted eagerly to the wood and screen open- air toilet, dropped his pants, sat down, and opened to the sports section.

"Oh, man, it's true!" He couldn't read fast enough. He closed the paper and then opened it again to make sure the numbers were still there. That's when he heard a loud explosion, feeling debris rip through the screened section above his head and peppering the wooden frame of the commode.

"*Incoming!*" he thought.

He bolted out the door barefoot, holding his fatigues up with his left hand, and running full speed to his assigned bunker, which housed his Browning automatic rifle. Noise and confusion belched from the soldiers moving quickly to their appointed areas of cover. Rheingold was standing upright in the middle of the mayhem. "At ease, at ease," he yelled. His tattooed arms waved over his shaved head. "At ease, dammit!"

Scott slowed down to a trot and looked around; people were looking and smiling. When he finally came to a stop, Scott noticed he was holding his pants just above his knees.

"The dog got into the claymores. I saw him walking in the minefield," the major shouted. "He tripped a wire."

Scott's adrenalin level dropped, but his embarrassment level rose. The smiles turned to laughs as he hustled to pull his pants up. Morris moved toward him and whispered.

"Hey, sir, I'd love to tell your kids about this some day. Your lieutenant daddy was running bare ass to a bunker with his pecker in retreat like a turtle's head. It was quite a picture, children."

"Morris, I swear to God I'll tell your kids that it happened to **you**. It'll take a long time to convince them otherwise when I get done with this story."

Morris continued to smile. "Let's get back to the world first, sir. In the meantime, try wearing your pants up around your waist, Lieutenant Regan."

They were now both laughing.

"Shut up, sergeant."

CHAPTER 28

The CORDS representative moved easily among the workers who funneled through the main gate. He was clearly familiar to the guards and needed to show no ID.

"Good morning, Mr. Miller," three soldiers walked past him and nodded.

"Morning, gentlemen." The stocky civilian picked the lieutenant out of the crowd and walked toward him.

"Hello, Lt. Regan. My name is Tom Miller."

"Good morning, Tom."

"Harry will be here in a couple of minutes."

"Harry?"

"His nickname; your ARVN counterpart. When he comes, we'll talk about your concern that Major Rheingold mentioned to me."

Twenty minutes later, a Vietnamese officer was standing next to Mr. Miller. He wore camouflage fatigues, a wide brimmed soft hat and U.S. Army boots. His holstered .45 was attached to a web belt that was pulled tight against his thin waist. Miller made the introductions in Vietnamese and began to move toward a growth of fronds that shaded a table with wooden benches. Miller walked between Scott and Nguyen

Van Hung, his ARVN counterpart. No one spoke until they all sat down.

"Ask Harry if he's familiar with the hamlet where the suspect is."

Miller turned to Harry, translated, then answered Scott. "Yes, he's familiar with it. He says some of the people there are his old friends. He went to school with them. Others recently settled there when they lost their own village to fire."

Scott reached into his pants pocket and pulled out a picture of the suspect that Rheingold had given him.

"Does he recognize him?"

"Yes, he's the father of one of his friends. He says that he was always a farmer. Always a man close to his wife and kids."

"Does he think that he has any VC ties?"

Miller asked Harry.

"He might. If the VC threatened his family he would do anything to protect them..." Miller stopped translating for a second and reflected on Harry's description of the suspect. "You know if your target is really a close family man, then he would be the more dangerous kind."

"Why's that?"

"Because his fidelity is based on survival, not politics. If the Viet Cong have the upper hand in the area - then he's pro Charlie. If we have the upper hand, then he's pro U.S. By blowing in the wind he gathers info from us and he gathers info from them– all the while playing the middle. He declares allegiance to neither side in order to save his farm and family and can, at his whim, sell the information he's gathered. This paternal protection would be a wonderful attribute, if he were running for father-of-the-year, but for us, he's the worst kind."

"So, I guess if he was a prick who didn't care about his wife and kids then he would be more our kind of guy?"

"I'm just passing along facts, not judgment, lieutenant."

Scott had more questions. "Ask him, also, what he knows about Strong." Miller turned again to Harry.

"He says that he's only known the family for about two and a half to three years. They're not from around here originally."

"Does he trust him?"

"He said he doesn't have any reason not to trust him."

"That's what I heard from Major Rheingold also. Maybe I was a little too quick to judge. Maybe."

Miller asked, "Do you have any questions for him about your upcoming patrol?"

"No, not right now."

"OK then, Scott. Any other questions for Harry can be translated by Strong. If you feel uneasy about talking in front of him, save the questions and call me at the PIOCC. I can get here in 30 minutes."

"Thanks, Miller."

For the next several days, Harry and Scott got to know each other. Strong helped with the translating when necessary and the two lieutenants observed each other's actions and attitudes as they engaged in the daily life in the DIOCC compound. Mary seemed to position herself as the juvenile ambassador between both of them and, at times, it appeared they were both vying for her attention. She adored it. Harry always addressed her as Lan and Scott continued to call her Mary. She answered and smiled to both.

During the following week the bright, half- moon was reducing its thickness nightly, soon giving way to the new moon and an indigo night sky which would allow them to approach the nearby village unseen and pull a local VC suspect off his mat and into an interrogation unit.

The days that immediately preceded the raid were devoted to reviewing the specifics of the patrol and confirming details. Do we have the right target? Are we cleared to "move in"? How much information do we need? What do we do with him after we get the information? What steps do we take if he gives us no information? At what point do we kill him?

Scott believed these detailed questions were pulled from another barrel full of Army excess and couldn't be the way things really worked. Not even here in Ham Thuan. All these preparations and planning were just another way of giving somebody something to do; it was just all theory.

Captain Bligh knew different. "Hey, lieutenant, it looks like we've got full clearance for next Tuesday. I would suggest you start to coordinate with Harry. This one will be your job. I'm not going with you, and the major will be in Phan Thiet with some

CORDS people. Your suspect appears to be a main cog in all of Southern II Corps. He's not just a local Bozo. If we have what we think we have, this guy might be a big tuna. Let me know how I can help you get ready."

As the day drew closer Scott concentrated on reviewing the layout of the hamlet and knowing where the target should be. Harry and Scott mapped their route into and out of the village. Strong knew the topographical layout of the approach and they asked him only fragmented and broad, general questions about the area. Nothing more. Scott and Sgt. Morris coordinated with LZ Betty for chopper support that might be needed.

"Do you really think we might need gun- ships?" Scott asked Clancy Morris.

"Probably not, lieutenant. These raids are based on surprise. We go in, grab 'em and leave. They'll all be asleep and nobody will realize what's happening until we're on our way out. If they put up any resistance, they risk having their kids blown up and their hooches leveled. They just don't have that much devotion to one man." He paused a long moment to let Scott absorb his assessment of the danger and then went on, "I ain't saying that it'll be a walk in the park - we'll hear all kinds of screaming, crying and stuff like that - but they won't open up on us."

"Well…" Scott started, stopped, and started again, as Morris' words began to sink in. "Well, if this zip's a real hot property I want to get him back ASAP and lateral his ass to the boys up at Province level. I'm sure their interrogation center will be anxious for a knock- down –drag-out 'chat'."

"Uh, uh, on the same page, sir. We don't have any reason to hang around and make small talk."

"I also want to meet with the squad leaders and Doc," Scott stated.

"OK. We'll have to do that sooner or later. Let's call them in now. It's as good a time as any."

Morris scanned the area and whistled. Harry called his squad leader and motioned for him to rally up. Within minutes, the medic, Harry, Strong and two squad leaders - one ARVN and one American – were huddled around Scott and Morris.

Scott began to speak. "We've got one quick assignment. Our job tomorrow morning is to go in and remove a suspected local for interrogation. We'll have three four-man rifle teams per squad and chopper relief, if we need it. We don't expect any resistance, so it should be a fast and easy, in and out."

Scott paused between sentences in order for Strong to translate to Harry and his squad leader. Heeding Rheingold's warning to divulge little tactical information to his interpreter, he deliberately didn't mention the hamlet's location.

"There will be two squads plus Doc and our RTO, Sgt. Morris. We'll carry one M-60 per squad..." Scott stopped short when he realized that he just volunteered the size and weaponry of the patrol. Strong translated and the counterpart nodded in agreement. Scott wanted to deliver more of a mission directive, but he thought it would probably be better if he kept his mouth shut.

"Alright, we'll assemble here at 0330. Make all of your preparations now. Questions?" There were none but Morris nudged him and whispered:

"Tell them to make sure they wear their pretty make-up, sir."

"Oh, yeah," Scott added. "Don't forget to grease up...the blacker the better."

Morris smiled. "I couldn't say it any better, lieutenant."

Scott concluded the muster. "Let's break. See you in a few hours. Dismissed."

The men left in silence and he and Morris walked to the communication hut.

"I know, I'm not going to get any sleep. What are you doing?" Scott asked.

"Me? I'm getting' me a few hours of shut-eye."

"Man, you're blessed. I'm going to make sure LZ Betty has the hamlet coordinates. Just in case. Then I'll break down my piece again."

Morris attempted to relieve his own anxiety by playing a little with Scott. "You can clean that weapon over and over again, but don't forget that it still needs ammo. You ain't gonna be able to fire any kinda' burst if you forget your clips, sir."

"No, no - I won't forget to load. C'mon, man."

"Funnier things *have* happened, sir."

They both laughed at the weak comic relief. Morris turned away and started towards his quarters. Scott's eyes followed the RTO and noticed his sergeant's hulking shoulders rise and fall as he let out a deep sigh.

CHAPTER 29

The hours preceding the raid flew by like minutes. The troops were all assembled at 0315, and were edgy as safecrackers before a break-in.

"Morris, are you ready?"

"Yes, sir."

"Strong, ask Harry if his guys are ready."

Harry didn't need an interpretation. He turned and gave Scott a thumbs-up.

Morris was kneeling on one knee and adjusting the weight of the PRC-6 radio he'd be carrying. Scott moved toward him.

"Hey, sergeant, how many of these snatches have you gone on?"

"Four."

"Any trouble?"

"Nope."

"Did you ever go for anybody as big as him?"

"Nope."

"Is he really that much of a heavyweight?" Scott wanted to hear it again.

"That's what we understand, sir."

Scott now stood up to address the men who were waiting for his order. Since he had arrived in Ham Thuan his cynicism had been gradually giving way to a feeling of commitment. The macroscopic war effort had begun to take on a more specific, more defined, more personal day-to-day rhythm. He could now taste, touch, and feel it; everything he ever needed to understand things, to make them real. Scott's chest began to heave, as his breathing became more rapid and a totally unexpected level of excitement rose within him.

The troops knelt on one knee, fidgeting with their weapon straps, and repositioning the frag grenades on their web belts. He looked into the eyes of their blackened faces and felt a rush of adrenalin, blood pulsing in his neck. They stared back at him with a confident hardness; he knew his men were ready, and so was he. Scott grabbed the stock of his rifle and girded.

"Alright, men," he commanded, "let's - move out!"

The combatants slapped the M-16 clips into their weapons and the sound cracked loud in the night air. The bandoliers of the M-60 machine guns clicked against the backs and shoulders of the gunners as they stood up and moved forward in silence. Scott led his squad out the gate and Harry followed to the rear. Strong walked with the young lieutenant, and the radio strapped to Morris' back was within Scott's reach.

For the next 35 minutes, the nocturnal noises of foreign insects and mammals rose and fell in multiple octaves, reminding Scott of summer nights in Shark River Hills. He was almost lulled into a distant reverie until the sound of his breathing brought him back to the present.

"How we doin', lieutenant?" Morris stopped and turned around.

"As long as we hug this grove and keep the main road to our left we should be right on target. We'll be bending in behind the hamlet instead of going straight in."

"Who plotted this route?" Morris asked.

"Me and Harry with a little help from Strong. Why?"

"Cause is seems like we're a little off course; we're getting more soggy than we should."

Scott realized that they *were* sloshing through the outer edge of a series of paddies but wasn't concerned about their direction.

"Well, that's why we have these new and improved boots, Morris. You know that Uncle Sam is always thinking about our comfort," Scott smiled. "See how easily they drain." He lifted his water logged canvas and leather boot out of the paddy and looked at his RTO. In that same instant, Morris's head was freeze- framed in Scott's mind as the man's cheekbone, left eye and nose broke away from his face in a spontaneous burst of sound and light.

The Viet Cong attack was instantaneous, ferocious, and seemed to come from all directions. The sergeant dropped like a felled oak tree into the watery muck; his huge back still supporting the radio. Scott flung himself between his splayed legs as Morris' bowels released in his face; the lieutenant burying his head in the E-6's buttocks for cover and groping for the handset. Military protocol language was abandoned.

"Lima Zulu niner, Lima Zulu niner. This is Alpha Tango two seven. Get the fuck out here! Contact! Ambush! Over!"

"Two seven, this is niner. Location. Over."

"Dunno'. Wandered off. Poppin' willie peter. Out."

Scott held his M-16 above the water line and scrambled to return fire. The gunners, bracing their M-60's, fired a stream of lead at 450 rounds per minute. The riflemen held their 16's on full automatic, aiming into the center of the communist assault and emptying their 19 round clips in seconds.

Scott hurled a canister of white phosphorous and an incendiary grenade toward the gut of the enemy fire. Twenty-five meters ahead the foliage exploded in flames as the thermate mixture turned to molten iron, burning at 4,000 degrees, and illuminating the rising smoke like a thunderous funeral pyre. They were now made visible to their imminent air support *and* to their attackers, but Charlie already knew where they were.

LZ Betty activated as the Marine pilots squeezed into the 3 feet wide Cobra gun ships and pursued their target guided by the deadly beacon illuminating the graphite jungle, their 7.62mm turret mini guns and 40mm grenades pounding into the tucked VC position. Screams, ear splitting weapons fire and the acrid smell of burning battlefield draped the ambush site, amplifying its fury. The Cobras completed their initial barrage, banked in the ink black sky and made a second pass, continuing to expend the lethal fire- power that finally reduced the assault to sporadic cracks from AK-47's and a retreating enemy.

Barely 75 meters had separated the Viet Cong strike from the Americans. It had been a well- planned set up, and members of Advisory Team 27 had walked into a hornet's nest. Scott had hardly time to think, and never was able to move more than 5 feet from where Morris laid. Doc sloshed down between them and turned the sergeant over as Scott rolled toward the medic and stared at his RTO. His face was unrecognizable and resembled a grotesquely distorted Halloween mask.   The morphine and I.V. were never administered.

CHAPTER 30

"Are you done with your report, lieutenant?"

"Yes, sir."

"What's the status?"

"Four KIA...Sgt. Morris and three ARVN, eleven wounded - seven ARVN and four of our troops. They were all dusted to Cam Ranh around 0500."

"We need to include a VC body count in that report. Have you made preparations for that?"

"Yes, I have. I'll be moving out with Harry and his men. I really want my guys to get some sleep."

The major looked at Scott. "How you doing, lieutenant?"

"Confused...tired...and, sir," Scott hesitated, "I don't' even remember exactly what I did."

"You will later on, lieutenant." Rheingold's tone drifted solemn and prophetic. "What are you confused about?" He quickly continued.

"How they knew we were coming. How did they know our route? They nailed us at the worst spot like they knew what we were thinking. Almost like they were in our huddle. I want to know how we got blown up and how our target got away. That never should've happened, major. You know that."

Rheingold grabbed a canvas chair and sat down next to Scott.

"Lieutenant - listen to me. You're going to think about that patrol over and over, and every time you do you will come up with another interpretation. One time you might feel good that you're wearing your tags, another time you might feel lousy you're still alive. You'll rehash what was and what could've been; you'll try to reenact something that can't be changed."

The set of his jaw was firm as was the tone in his voice. "That event is over. Nothing about that can be altered. It's like last night's chow. It has to be digested – no matter how long it takes, and just like last night's chow, you eventually have to shit it out and forget about it."

Scott looked straight into Rheingold's eyes while flashes of recollection played through his mind. *The M-79 round should have killed them both. The ambush should have killed a lot more troops. He did nothing to save his troops. The Cobras from the Marine detachment saved their lives. Somebody rolled over on them. Somebody close to them gave up their word.*

"Lieutenant, do you hear me?"

Scott snapped back from this one all- consuming thought. "Yes, sir. Yes, major. I hear you. Thanks for telling me this."

Hours later, the VC body count was concluded. Scott, Harry, Strong and a squad of ARVNs tagged 11 KIA. From the look of the dug-in ambush sight, it appeared that the Viet Cong dragged away a lot more dead and wounded. Bloodied shrouds of clothing hung from the palm fronds, gnarled branches and twisted roots. One of the ARVNs showed Harry and Scott a Russian made RPK automatic rifle with a cleanly severed arm resting on the barrel.

As the days passed, Scott and Cpt. Bligh assumed the task of packing the personal items of Sgt. Clancy Morris and the three other American KIAs. Despite this chore, Scott occasionally expected to see the ivory smile of his RTO or hear his laugh coming from the communications hut.

But, every time he thought about Morris, he was hurled back into the moment of the attack. The memory didn't make him feel sad or angry. It made him feel emotionally tepid and began to form a comfortable cushion of protection; a rational, soft pillow of insanity.

****

Four days after the failed mission, Scott finally grabbed a moment to talk to Major Rheingold. His thoughts were clear and he could now propose some further action. Rheingold was pouring a cup of coffee and Scott walked toward him.

"Major, can I see you for a couple of minutes?" Within the last several days they had sat at the same table but Scott couldn't say what he wanted. Now he felt that he could. Rheingold sipped his coffee and Scott opened a bottle of lukewarm Coke.

"Sir, I should have been dead twice within the last few weeks. One of those times you should have croaked with me. I just don't see these two things as chance events. I've got a gut feeling we've been set up."

"By whom?" Rheingold asked.

"By Strong."

"Lieutenant, control your imagination. It could turn out to be your worst enemy."

Scott pressed on. "I want to put Strong under surveillance. I want to have Harry call on our local operatives and I want his ass to be tailed 24 hours until we determine that he's not working against us." Scott realized that his voice was rising and he stopped talking. He took a deep breath and continued.

"Major, I really believe this guy's word ain't worth a maggot's fart. This picture ain't hard to paint." The comment was said slowly and emphatically. "We've got to have him followed, major."

Rheingold listened. Despite the initial rebuff of his lieutenant's suspicions Scott confirmed the major's reluctant and unspoken mistrust. He slowly shook his head up and down.

"I agree, lieutenant."

At 0630 the next day, Scott jumped out of his cot. The movement made the baby rodent pitter out from his boot and find another area of darkness. With the absurd living conditions becoming acceptable, Scott automatically reached for his left boot and shook it out. His olive drab socks were under his pillow and he felt them for any nocturnal visitors before turning them inside out and pulling them over his feet. He headed out to the communications hooch and grabbed the headset from the temples of the PFC who was monitoring the radio.

The soldier sat up straight. "Morning, lieutenant," he said. Nobody liked being caught dozing on duty. "Yes, sir, how can I help you?" He stammered.

"Patch me into the PIOCC. I need to speak with Mr. Miller."

"No problem, lieutenant." Fifteen seconds later he was on the line.

"Tom Miller here."

"Tom, Scott Regan. I need your help."

"When?"

"I need you to interpret for me."

"When?"

"As soon as you can get here. Twenty minutes?"

"I'm leaving now."

Scott looked for Harry. He found him near the front gate.

"Harry." Scott motioned for him to come. Palm down, fingers pulled in.

"Didi mau," Scott shouted. Harry trotted faster.

Strong was nearby and saw the exchange and walked toward Scott feeling that he should be part of the meeting, not knowing this was the last thing Scott wanted. Harry arrived within steps of Strong and looked at Scott for direction. Scott started to fidget and made up something to say.

"Strong, ask Harry if his platoon is back to full force." Strong relaxed, feeling part of the team, and asked Harry the question.

"He say no, not yet. He missing good people and he don't want to take bad soldier to fill rank. He wait for good man. Why?"

Scott didn't answer and turned away from Strong to address Harry in English. "Harry, wait here with me. We will talk to a civilian from CORDS. Maybe only another 10-15 minutes, OK?"

"OK." Harry responded automatically.

Strong understood the message and also understood that he was not included. Harry didn't understand what Scott said, but read his face and heard the inflection. Scott continued to stall and waited for Miller to arrive. He turned toward Strong. "We need more info on VC movement in Ham Thuan. Does Harry have his contacts looking and listening?" Strong interpreted. The ARVN lieutenant knew that keeping his contacts active was standard operating procedure and knew Scott was stalling.

Miller finally arrived, driving his own jeep, and moving quickly through the gate that opened in anticipation of his arrival. He braked hard, put the jeep into first gear and killed the engine. Scott didn't care to make a comfortable dismissal of Strong. "I want to speak with Harry and Miller alone," he said with no subtlety. Strong got the message and moved several steps away.

Miller understood what Scott had told him over the phone and turned to Strong.

"Didao."

Strong moved away with an expression of suspicion. The camps were forming and Ruan Van Cur'o'ong knew he wasn't in the main group.

Scott no longer cared about the proper way to interact with his interpreter. He felt it didn't matter anymore. "Mr. Miller, tell Harry I have permission to have Strong followed day and night until I determine he's not VC. In addition, tell him if we go out on patrol again before our surveillance is finished, I do not want him to be part of any tactical planning. He is to remain completely suspect until I feel OK about him. Oh, and tell him also I don't care what lies we have to tell him to keep him away from us until I feel 100% about him."

Harry's main daily mission became the overseeing of the surveillance of Ruan Van Cur'o'ng. Scott sensed that Strong was suspicious of his recent attitude toward him and, because of this, the stalking had to be even more obscure. This also meant that it would take longer to come to a conclusion, a fact that Scott didn't particularly like. If Strong was, in reality, a VC agent, the sooner they neutralized him the better.

As the days passed, Scott would often feel his thigh muscles tighten and his fingernails dig into the palms of his hands. He not only mistrusted Strong; he was starting to hate him.

Miller had recommended to Harry and Scott that while the surveillance was being conducted they both should have minimum contact with each other. Any meaningful communication between them would be in writing, sealed in an envelope and deposited at a drop spot located in the rear stone wall of a movie theater in Phan Thiet. The chiseled- out mortar was the perfect receptacle for a 4" X 8'1/2" enclosed letter. Miller would visit the location twice daily. The slit in the wall was about 3 1/2' above the ground and aligned itself with their backs so that by casually leaning against the stones, the lieutenants could deposit their correspondence and Miller could retrieve it. He would then translate the message and have it couriered to them at the DIOCC using different individuals each time.

Five days came and went. Miller made his daily stops, but each time he found no content. On the morning of the sixth day he positioned himself against the wall and his fingers groped the cool large stones. He stopped when his right index finger flicked the edge of a slightly protruding piece of paper. He moved his thumb and index finger to form a pincer and slid the letter out of the repository. He tucked it in his back beltline under his hanging shirt and brought his hands out from behind him, casually reading the time on his Seiko watch, then started a slow walk through the local traffic, two blocks west to his office.

The shutters were locked from the previous night, emitting tiny rays of daylight through their slats. Miller shut the door behind him and decided not to open the windows. The soft sound of the overhead fan circulated the stale air in the small plaster- walled room. He turned on a small battery powered lamp, sat down at his desk, and removed the envelope from his belt. He examined it carefully, holding it up to the lamp, his fingers moving across the surface of the envelope. Finding nothing unusual, he deemed it safe and carefully cut an eighth of an inch off of the narrow side, tapped the letter out and unfolded the single sheet of paper.

It was from Harry. He read the three- sentence note, dropped it on his desk and turned to his Underwood typewriter. He rolled a piece of paper into the grasp of the cylinder and typed the translation for Scott.

"Ruan Van Cur'o'ng is from Phuoc Tuy Province. Will see if he has any affiliation with the Main Force VC D-199 battalion in that area. Will report again soon."

Miller folded the letter and sealed it, but instead of having a courier deliver it as originally planned, he decided to see Lt. Regan personally. He especially wanted to deliver some additional information about D-199 and other VC units from Phuoc Tuy.

Brian J. Rogers

****

Scott looked out at the road that led from the DIOCC to Phan Thiet. A plume of dust followed a jeep that was bouncing and rocking sideways as it made its way toward the gate. He recognized Mr. Miller, and temporarily abandoned his search for Mary whom he had not seen recently. He backed away when the gates were pulled open and Miller drove into the compound.

"Good morning, lieutenant. Are Capt. Bligh and Major Rheingold available?"

"Uhh" – Scott had to stop and think. Miller seemed anxious.

"Uh - no. Well, I mean, the captain's in town, but the major's around here somewhere."

"Let's see if we can find him. I got some news from Harry and your superiors should hear it from me, too." They were walking toward the mess hut when Rheingold emerged from a cold morning shower.

"Major Rheingold," Scott called. "Mr. Miller has some info that he wants to share with us. Got a moment, sir?"

"Does it look like I'm ready to meet with anybody? Let me get dressed for Chrissake. Grab some joe and meet me over there."

He pointed to a transport truck parked 20 meters away. Miller headed for a mug while Scott walked to the deuce- and - a -half. He began to feel tense, suspicious and angry again.

256

These emotions were now infiltrating his dreams as well as consuming him during the day. His concerns had ebbed when he was distracted by his search for Mary, but came flooding back with a vengeance when Miller began to relay the message. Rheingold now joined them and he addressed the two officers.

"Your interpreter came here from Phuoc Tuy. Harry is in the process of seeing if he has, or had, any connection with a Main Force VC battalion, D-199, that was active in that Province. He will get back to you 'soon,' lieutenant, with any further details." Miller shifted the coffee mug into his left hand and leaned closer.

"Now let me tell you what we know about that particular unit." When the term "we" was used by CORDS personnel it was understood to mean The Central Intelligence Agency. Nobody asked for clarification.

Miller began. "About this time last year, 1 February to be exact, elements of D-199 hit the district capital of Long Dien with a mortar and ground attack. They were beaten back after six hours, leaving 40 enemy KIA. The town suffered only light physical damage in the shelling. However, 23 local civilians were found dead.

"This was accomplished with small arms fire and in close fighting, some hand-to-hand. On the same morning Long Tan and Long Phuoc villages were occupied by elements of the D-172 concentration company, assisted by local VC platoons.

Following the TET offensive, they moved to the northeast and conducted operations from the border of Binh Tuy - just a little south of this district. But what disturbs me *most* is that after TET, COSVN ordered the D-172 to dissolve as a unit and to rebuild their infrastructure from the bottom up by recruiting terrorists, tax collectors, sappers and goons in the immediate Provinces of Binh Tuy, Lam Dong and yours - Binh Thuan."

Miller took a sip of coffee. He continued. "All of this could have been irrelevant if Lieutenant Harry had not identified Strong as coming from Phuoc Tuy. It's only human nature to recruit people that you know personally. People from your own neighborhood, so to speak. Cur'o'ng was from their area. I don't want to jump the gun here, but based on the circumstances surrounding that M-79 incident and the well laid ambush, I think that you might have a valid concern, gentlemen."

****

No further news developed during the week that followed. Scott continued to interact very little with his counterpart, Harry, but he did pay close attention to Strong. He wanted to keep a closer eye on him, while at the same time giving him the impression that everything was O.K. He didn't want the interpreter to realize that he was under surveillance and hit the road. It was a performance that was going to take a lot of self-control as well as some effective acting. The problem was that Scott wasn't naturally very good at either and he was becoming increasingly irritable and short tempered, which he attributed to a cumulative lack of sleep.

When he *was* able to doze, he was racked with haunting images of Willy Payne lying flat on his back in the arid red clay dust of a narrow road, blood seeping into his lightweight fatigues like russet molten lava, his severed stomach muscles releasing intestines that lay gathered in a clump at his side; and Strong bent over, swatting flies away from Willy's eyes to see if they had lost all glimmer of life.

He saw the projectile from the grenade launcher skipping in slow motion across the top of the dyke. He saw, again, the unleashed hell of the ambush. And again, through it all, the face of Ruan Van Cur'o'ng.

"I wonder if he has something to do with Mary missing?" Scott spoke out loud and wobbled forward.

A Spec 4 holding a clipboard with a check- list stopped what he was doing and faced Scott. They were standing near the fortified ammo bunker at the remote end of the DIOCC. Scott had been walking around the compound all morning, had hardly slept for days, and was now swaying against the solid sandbags.

"Whaaa?" Scott asked.

"Were you addressing me, sir?"

"About whaa?" Scott's voice was a combination of a whisper, a rasp and a hiss.

"Never mind, lieutenant, my mistake."

Scott's right knee buckled when he moved away for another walk around the DIOCC. He fumbled for a Marlboro but broke it in half. He couldn't even concentrate on completing simple tasks. If he could only get some sleep.

He walked toward the shower. "Hey, you seen Mary?" Scott opened the wooden door below the 55- gallon drum. An old woman was swishing clothes in the water dripping from the shower- head.

"Chao, Troung uy"

"You seen Mary?"

"qi?"

"I said you seen Mary? Yes or no."

The woman looked at Scott's face protruding into the stall. She said nothing this time, turned back down and continued her scrubbing.

"Fuck you - you ancient bitch. I don't trust you either." He slammed the door and started to stagger away as Rheingold approached him.

"Lieutenant," he commanded. Scott stumbled two more steps before he was able to stop.

"Yes, sir. Yes, major?"

"Captain Bligh says that you've had a tough time getting some sleep this past week."

"How's he know?"

"You bunk together."

"Oh yeah, you're right, sir."

"Lieutenant, I'm ordering you to go immediately to your hooch and hit the cot. I can't make you sleep but I can get you off your feet. I don't want you wandering around here in a stupor. I should have sent you to Doc earlier in the week. If he gives you medication now, you might be out for 48 hours. I can't afford that. We've got some work to do around here in the next several days. Do you have any questions?"

"Where's Mary, Major?"

"Don't know."

"I haven't seen her for a long, long, long time. I'm worried about her."

If Rheingold didn't know better he would have bet a month's pay that the lieutenant was on qualudes. His pronunciation was thick and slow and his head hung down in a nod.

"We have enough to worry about, lieutenant, without keeping tabs on four-year olds. Now get to your bunk double time."

"Yes, sir. Am I dismissed?"

"Go. Now!"

****

Scott sat on the bunk and unlaced one boot. He pulled his foot out of it and flopped backward onto the cot. His other leg hung off the side. He heard voices outside in the compound as he stared up at the corrugated metal arch of his room. They sounded familiar, from decades ago...he heard children laughing and running through a heavy stream of water propelled from a fire hydrant on a hot August day. He heard the soft "thuck" of a broom -stick hitting a Spalding high bouncer over the roof of a three-family house. And he heard Carl Perkins singing "Blue Suede Shoes." He smelled food; hot dogs, potatoes, peppers and onions all stuffed into the hollowed out pocket of a half- moon piece of bread. On his dangling foot, the Army issued jungle boot felt like a sweat stained PF Flyer. He felt the humidity rising up from the hot asphalt playground after a rain shower. He was cocooned in the predictability of his youth. He was back in New Jersey.

****

It was late afternoon when Major Rheingold pushed open the door of the hooch and walked in without knocking. Scott's leg still hung off the edge of his cot and his eyes were open.

"Lieutenant, I need you."

Without moving his head Scott lowered his gaze from the ceiling and looked at the major.

"I'm here, sir."

"Did you get any sleep?"

"I don't know. I think - maybe."

"I want you to oversee a work detail tonight. Harry has volunteered several of his men to dig some trenches to lay some commo wire between the bunkers and the towers. I also ordered four of our own troops to work along with them. Grab your interpreter also. The ARVNS might have some questions. Go get some chow and be out front in an hour."

"I'm not hungry, sir."

"Then be outside in an hour anyway."

Scott reached for his boot and tried to put it on. He stopped when he realized he was trying to pull it over his foot that already wore one. He paused and figured it out, then stuck his unshod foot into the empty boot and laced it slowly. His eyes felt like pin cushions. He looked into a hand held mirror and saw the whites of his eyes had turned blood red.

"Maybe I *didn't* sleep," he murmured. He stood in front of the half filled table basin and splashed water on his stubbled face. He forgot to dry himself and water dripped down from his forehead as he opened the wood and screen door and stepped into the late afternoon sunlight.

"Over here, lieutenant." Rheingold called. The group assembled around the major included Ruan Van Cur'o'ng.

"I just briefed our soldiers on what I want to have done. Tell your interpreter what I want and have him translate it for the others. If you need me I'll be somewhere in the compound."

263

"Rog...no, no, I mean, sir, Wilco, sir"

Scott turned to Strong. He stared at him without saying a word. Cur'o'ng looked at the lieutenant's face and took a step backward.

"Tell these gooks to dig a trench - we want to lay some wire." Before the interpreter registered the slang expression Scott looked around and decided to start the digging by the front northeast bunker.

"Follow me," he said in a voice racked with fatigue and barely audible.

The American and Vietnamese troops worked together into the early dusk. The digging was slow in the hard packed clay and rock with WWII vintage folding entrenching tools serving as the main shovels for excavation.

Bare hands and small J-bars were all the supporting implements the troops had to finish the job. Scott sat on the small overhang of a sandbag and leaned back against the unyielding wall of the bunker, watching the activity in front of him with little interest and couldn't focus on any single thought. Darting clusters of incomplete images spun through his mind, and every sleepless minute added to his utter exhaustion and dizzying hallucinations.

Darkness settled over the crew, the chopping noise of metal and rock creating arrhythmic beats as Scott stared absently at the eight-man detail. The four ARVNS worked their way around a jeep as the Americans and Cur'o'ng labored directly in front of him. Scott plunged his knuckles into his searing eyes and tried to rub out the now crippling weariness.

He blinked several times and looked away from the activity, toward a transport vehicle some 10 meters away. That's when he saw Harry appear from around the high fender of the truck, standing in full tiger fatigues, looking well groomed and confident. He pointed to Ruan Van Cur'o'ng and shook his head affirmatively. His index finger pointed emphatically at the interpreter and he rapidly nodded his head; his lips forming the words "Viet Cong."

Scott's studied his counterpart and deemed that the surveillance was concluded; his suspicions were accurate. The verdict was in. He didn't hear his own rasping, tormented scream as he launched himself from the sandbags. "And you stole Mary, too!"

The digging stopped and the eight- man crew looked up at the twisted face of the officer in charge as Scott threw himself across the body of his interpreter. He pulled the entrenching tool from the grip of Cur'o'ng and stood up. The Viet slithered across the ground hoping for the return of oxygen to his lungs when Scott raised the shovel in a leveraged arc and brought it down solidly across the crown of the traitor's head.

"You lyin' motha' fuck!" Scott howled.

The blow knocked his face into the hard pack as Scott, again, flew at the stunned man, grabbed his head, clutched at his fine hair and rammed his temple against a rock dug up by Cur'o'ng himself.

A soft mushy crackle resulted from the impact as Scott turned him over on his back and straddled him. He held the sides of his silky hair and smashed the back of his skull against the solid earth. Blood trickled from his nose and ears, he moaned softly, his arms fluttered spasmodically in the dirt. The young Americans watched in frozen silence as Scott stood up and reached again for the digging tool. He pulled it to where Cur'o'ng layed. Scott's face was now a tornado of sweat and splattered blood; his lips slightly apart, etching a demonic grimace. Then with one last maniacal yowl he planted his foot on the top of the shovel blade, and with the sole of his boot drove it through the crackling throat of the Viet.

Voices erupted around him as he hurriedly scooped the body in his arms and carried it away from the group; Cur'o'ng's weakening heart pumping the last sanguine pints out from his severed carotid artery and onto Scott's boots.

He had to find Major Rheingold. Cur'o'ng was draped like a blood-drenched shroud, as weightless and lifeless as gauze. The ARVN and U.S. soldiers came together and watched Scott carrying the body toward the lights of the communication hut. They gathered in stunned silence realizing that no communication between them was possible. Their interpreter was dead. Cur'o'ng dangled in Scott's arms and he used the legs of the body to bang on the door of the hut.

"Major," Scott barked.

"Regan - what the hell—"

"Major, *listen* to me. He's hard core VC. Harry confirmed it. He told me so. He pointed to him and shook his head. Our surveillance of this guy panned out. He tried to blow us up. Then he ratted us out when we got waxed in that ambush. And then he probably stole Mary, too. I was right! I was right!"

Rheingold looked at the scene.

As a Korean War PFC, he had seen, firsthand, the effect of insomnia and fatigue. In the subzero weather at the Chosin reservoir he had fought with the 32nd Infantry and had seen sleepless men driven to either immobility or irrational action. What he saw before him now was another horrifying example of the latter.

'Lieutenant, Harry was not here tonight."

"I saw him here, major!"

"He and Miller called me from Phan Thiet 20 minutes ago. He told me that he has some more leads to run down and he'll fill you in tomorrow."

Scott insisted. "I saw him, major!"

"No, you didn't, lieutenant."

Cur'o'ng was now an ashen rag doll flopped across his forearms.

"Lieutenant, we've got to get you out of here."

CHAPTER 31

It was now 12 hours since Scott had carried his interpreter's body to Major Rheingold. He wore new fatigues but had no recollection of how he got that way, and the only thing familiar to him was the leather shaving kit he carried in his swollen right hand.

The 8th Field Hospital at Cam Ranh Bay was a central medical repository for both allied and US troops. Scott's admission tag read "1C Walking NP (Cooperative)." He was led to the large ward that housed cramped rows of beds, given a set of thin pants with a large shirt and gently guided onto a narrow bed. Another IV was inserted in his arm.

He looked around and saw that he was the only non-oriental. Some bed sheets were dappled with blood, and everyone was resting. He groped for his kit, but couldn't find it. It mattered for only seconds until he felt his entire body sink into the thin bedding and sleep.

****

Two flies swarmed around his face as his eyes adjusted to the early sun that streamed through the dusty plastic window beyond his feet. He tried to swoosh them aside with both hands but felt the subtle restraint of the inserted IV in his left arm. An opaque figure stood next to him and read his medical chart:

Probable allergic conjunctivitis aggravated by hyperactive conjunctivitis. 20 years previous. Strabismus surgery.

"Morning, lieutenant." Scott's eyes slowly focused on the outline next to him.

"Hel, - Hello, sir?"

Major Martin Waxmann, Medical Corps, addressed the prone figure before him. "How are you feeling this morning?"

"I guess I'm O.K. Groggy, but O.K."

"You were admitted from Bin Thuan Province yesterday and I'm here to follow up on your condition. I'd like to examine you a bit more."

"Sure, sir."

Scott remembered that he had been quickly removed from the DIOCC and, undoubtedly, some cover story had been concocted to get him flown to Cam Ranh Bay. He squirmed, and was unsettled, knowing he didn't have a clue as to what was supposed to have happened before he was medivaced. He also knew the overall mission of the Phoenix program was a lot more important than protecting one advisor. His head cleared slowly, and he realized he had been cut adrift. He remembered killing an ally and, despite his certainty that Cur'o'ng was VC, recognized what he had done could still be considered murder. The Phoenix program did not want notoriety. It operated in the shadows and wanted to conclude its mission in the shadows. He listened closely to determine what his role was to be. The Major helped Scott sit up in bed.

"Swing your legs over the side here, lieutenant." Scott pivoted and sat sideways on the bed. Waxmann held a pinpoint light to Scott's eyes.

"Look to your far left. Now look to the right. Have these scars been any source of irritation to you since you had the operation?"

The scars from his operation years ago had never been a source of irritation, but Scott started to grasp that this might be part of his cover story. "Uh - well - that eye operation was a long time ago. I was - like - two years old."

"You still have prominent scars. This has been a source of aggravation to you, hasn't it lieutenant?"

Scott felt like he was being prodded to answer in the affirmative. *"Play along,"* he thought. *"Everyone's just looking to cover their ass and move me along. They'll make the details fall into place."*

He answered the question: "Yes, recently during the summer back home. It started up again when I came in country."

Scott searched the Major's face for a reaction to his response. The doctor lowered his eyes and pursed his lips. He shook his head in slow agreement. Scott could almost read his mind and hear him think: *"Good lieutenant. This makes my part a lot easier. We're both on the same page - aren't we now?*

Your commanding officer will deal with the disappearance of your interpreter and debrief any witnesses in your DIOCC. Nice and clean. No publicity about the Phoenix program is good publicity."

The doctor spoke. "OK, then. I'll complete an Abbreviated Clinical Record report and then we'll proceed from there. Lie back down in bed and don't move. You'll be contacted tomorrow."

He removed the IV from Scott's arm and departed. Scott looked around the cavernous ward; the 8th Field Hospital seemed to be an all-purpose medical holding facility, and every collision of war appeared to be represented. A young Vietnamese soldier occupied the bed immediately next to his, one leg elevated by a series of pulleys and ropes. His chest rose and fell in shallow irregular movement. His eyes were closed. Blood oozed from wrapped bandages on his left forearm and spackles of it seeped through the loosely draped sheet that covered the lower thigh of his amputated left leg. Other patients had all their limbs, but were secured, motionless, in protective Stryker frames. Some swung slowly on crutches.

When the sedatives began to release their grip Scott smelled disinfectant wafting over an underlying odor of torn flesh healing; the battle against infection forming pus pockets that released a sickly, rotten redolence.

Hours passed while medics administered drugs to the seriously wounded, and he waited for another IV to be inserted.

After a while he recognized that no further sedatives would be forthcoming and, waiting for the next meal to be delivered, propped the single pillow behind his head and exhaled with boredom.

During the course of the day large rotary fans whirred in an attempt to parry the stifling heat which seemed to drape his bed, and he made numerous trips to the large latrine that serviced the hospital wing, just for something to do. He turned away the food that was brought to him on a metal tray. "Have you got any prescriptions to help me sleep?" The cherubic-looking nurse didn't answer immediately, but stepped to the foot of his bed and read his chart. "I don't see any further medication scheduled for you, lieutenant. Are you in pain?"

"No, no I'm not in pain, just restless."

"Only restless? You're very fortunate." She motioned to Scott's tray to determine if he'd changed his mind about eating.

"No, I'm not hungry now. Thanks."

She left the food anyway and walked past his bed and down the narrow aisle. He sat upright against the solid bars of the headboard and stared out at the ebbing daylight. The fetid smell of viscous, infected tissue returned to assault his senses, and the extended shadows of evening slowly ushered in another night.

CHAPTER 32

Scott opened his eyes abruptly when he heard a familiar voice.

"Miller?"

The American CORDS senior agent was speaking in hushed tones to Major Waxmann. They were both looking at the report the doctor had prepared the previous night. It was a little past sunrise, and the temperature in the ward was comparatively cool.

"Thank you, major. Your cooperation in this matter is appreciated."

"You're welcome, Mr. Miller. I understand the sensitivity."

Waxmann slapped Scott lightly on his shin and handed the clipboard with the attached Clinical Record Form 539 to Miller.

"Good luck, lieutenant." He turned from Scott's glance and didn't look back.

"Thanks, again, sir," Scott trailed.

Miller looked down at Scott, and dispensing with all pleasantries said, "We've made arrangements to medivac you to a hospital in Japan."

"Can I ask you a question, Miller?" He stared at Scott without answering.

"What are you doing here?"

"I'm responsible for getting you out of country under a feasible cover story and with zero notoriety. I know you understand our situation."

"Did Waxmann help - uh - us?"

"After you killed your interpreter, Major Waxmann was notified that you were being dusted to the 8th Field Hospital..."

Scott interrupted. "How much does he know about what happened?"

"He was told as much as he had to know. He knows who we are and how we must operate. He didn't ask extraneous questions."

"But who knew about my eye scars and built a story around that?"

Miller started to soften his official demeanor, becoming a little more conversational. He did so as an accommodation to Scott. Despite his brashness Miller instinctively liked the lieutenant.

"Nobody is chosen by the Company to work in the Phoenix program, or any other organization the Company sponsors, without knowing that person inside and out. We never know when the slightest event in someone's past can be used as a lever against them, or as an aid to assist them. I'm sure you understand this."

"But who concocted this story?"

"Irrelevant, lieutenant. All you need to know is that you will be airlifted to the 249th General Hospital at North Camp Drake,

Japan at 1330 hours today. In the meantime, you should read the report that Waxmann prepared on your condition. Upon your arrival all pertinent individuals will have been briefed on our situation, and why you're being admitted. Any questions?"

"Should I know anything else?"

"Not now."

Miller took several steps backward and felt free to speak louder. "Lieutenant, in due course I will see to it that your personal items are shipped to your home of record. For now they will be crated and held at Province level. As of this moment I will no longer be in direct contact with you. I wish you well, Scott."

When Miller turned to walk out of the hospital wing, Scott reached for the clipboard and read the narrative of his purported medical status.

"History of strabismus surgery o.u. in past. Now developing suture reaction. Treated with steroids no help. Rec: Evacuate to PACOM."

Major Waxmann, Ward No. 5.

At exactly 1330 hours Scott made his way up the ramp of the C-130 cargo carrier that had been converted into a flying ambulance. Stretchers were stacked against the walls of the plane like sailor's hammocks in a galleon. Ambulatory patients sat in hard seats with rough strap seatbelts. The passengers either rocked rhythmically in suspended stretchers along the walls of the plane or sat silently in the dimly lit hollow of the plane's belly.   Scott breathed in heavy waves of medicinal smelling salve as hanging IV bags swung in syncopation to the bumping plane as the rumbling wheels picked up speed and headed down the runway.

He was leaving Vietnam after only two and a half months, but, in replaying his tour, felt as though he had lived a lifetime there.

****

The monotonous drone of the four turbo-prop engines became a cacophonous rattle as the huge transport made its final descent over the U.S. military airfield in Japan.   Scott slid halfway out of his seat before he braced his feet against the bulkhead in front of him.   The stretchers all swung toward the nose of the plane and the angle seemed to be uncommonly steep but within several moments the projection changed and the craft floated upwards and leveled out. It touched down on a three- point landing as the engines screamed with reverse torque, bumped down the runway and finally taxied onto the tarmac and was guided to a stop.

The non-ambulatory patients were wheeled off first and steered in various directions away from the now motionless aircraft. Scott was part of a small contingent that was directed to follow a medical guide. Secured to a button on his hospital shirt was his DD form 602 medical tag.

"Stop and wait here." The voice addressed nobody in particular but Scott turned to look anyway. "Yes, you. Don't move." A slightly built Caucasian with an ashen face and wearing a crew neck blue sweater walked toward him. Scott didn't like the stranger's tone, nor how he looked.

"Take this report and don't lose it." The stranger extended his arm handing him a narrative summary of his clinical record that had already been written in precise detail. "For tonight, we're placing you in the psychiatric ward. You will hold the folder until tomorrow, when you will give it to the head nurse after we move you. She'll be expecting it."

Scott was tense and weary from his trials of the last hurried hours, and was also annoyed at this guy's style and approach.

"Hey, look. You know what? I want to just be left the fuck alone for a while. OK? I don't give a particular shit who you are, or what you're telling me to do. In fact, I have something to tell you. Get my ass back to Ham Thuan. Now, go arrange that. Everyone there knows what happened and why it will probably happen again to somebody else. I want to be with the people who know the score.

"Give me a fuckin' break," he pushed on, "we're neutralizing suspects there daily. If we were out on patrol and I waxed him in a firefight by 'mistake,' would that make it better?" Scott stopped speaking when he realized he had run off at the mouth. He didn't know how many of the details this guy actually knew, and waited for a response.

The lithe stranger looked at him with ice in his eyes. "It would have been a lot easier to explain."

At that moment Scott was grabbed firmly on his right bicep by a powerful hand. Another voice spoke. "Do not lose that report and walk this way with me. Do not say anything more, and do *not* raise your voice." Scott turned to see a hulking figure in a black leather jacket. He was briskly guided to a waiting sedan that sped him to a secluded section of the 249th General Hospital.

****

The double doors that led to an inner ward swung open. A gurney, with a man strapped on it, was pushed by two attendants and glided silently past Scott. A rubber stopper was shoved in his mouth and was held in place by white adhesive tape. His muffled voice emitted a deep base gurgle which quickly changed to a high pitched hellish shrill. His arms and legs were secured tightly to the metal rails and a head restraint prevented him from thrashing. He tried to free himself, but had no leverage. The sound became muted as they wheeled him around the corner of the building and into darkness.

"I'm going in _there_?" Scott pointed to the double doors. The man in the black leather jacket answered: "Just for tonight. I'm going to notify admissions that you have arrived. Just take a seat in the waiting room until your name is called."

He was still wearing the thin hospital pajamas, and the molded plastic seat felt cold. He pulled the corduroy bathrobe around him and again opened the medical report that Waxmann had prepared.

HISTORY OF PRESENT ILLNESS: This 23 year old Cau male was admitted from the 8th Field Hospital for follow-up regarding "suture reaction OU." He apparently had both medical rectus and lateral rectus surgery OU at about two years of age for congenital estropia. He has had essentially no problems with a small residual left estropia until about 4 or 5 years ago when he developed ocular irritation UP each summer. Similar symptoms have occurred and became severe in RVN. The patient has had difficulty performing his duties in the field because of the blurring vision and blepharospasm. He was evacuated for follow-up evaluation and treatment. The patient apparently has some amblyopia OC. There is a positive family history of strabismus.

Scott folded the report back into the manila envelope. "Holy Christ!" he whispered. "I thought street hookers and junkies were the best liars. These guys reinvented the art." Several feet away from Scott a male orderly opened a heavy metal door and held it open for a female attendant.

"Lt. Regan?" The nurse glanced around as if she was looking for a particular individual in a crowded waiting room. Scott was the only one there.

"Uh, right here, nurse."

"Oh, yes, lieutenant." She made a sweeping exaggerated gesture like she was on stage. Very theatrical, and Scott wondered for a second if this nurse wasn't really a patient instead.

He laughed aloud at his thought, which in turn made the nurse look at him as if he were one of those people who talked and joked with themselves. Scott felt that he should explain why he was laughing —in an empty waiting room — in the psychiatric wing of a military hospital — in Japan; but he didn't know where to begin, so he said nothing.

"Follow me, lieutenant."

"Roger, nurse. You do know that I'm only going to be in this ward temporarily. Right? Nurse?" She said nothing.

"Nurse – what's your name?"

"Kelly."

"Nurse Kelly, it's real important to me that we're on the same page over here."

"I've been fully informed, Lt. Regan." She spoke over her shoulder and continued to walk.

"I hope that you *haven't* been fully informed."

"Pardon me?"

"I said I hope that you haven't been fully informed."

"I know you're staying here for only one night."

"What else do you know?"

"Nothing other than that."

"Perfect."

She stopped at a heavy glass enclosed medical station and spoke to the attendant. Scott couldn't hear the brief dialogue, but was led to a small kitchen area.

"You'll have some chow here, lieutenant. When you're done, push this button and I'll come and bring you to your bed for the night. Whatever you do, you CANNOT leave this mess area by yourself." Her voice rose in emphasis. "This is a secure room in the hospital, because there are knives, forks and glassware in here. I will lock the door manually from the outside. I'll be back to let you out."

An attendant slid by Kelly in the doorway and placed a steaming plate of food on the table.

"No problem, Kelly."

The nurse let the attendant out, shut the gunmetal gray door, and locked it. The mess room was bright and stark with white walls, no windows, and an exhaust fan that whirred softly in the corner. It could have been a perfect interrogation room. The only things missing were stale air, cigarette smoke and body odor. Twenty minutes passed before Scott heard the rattle of keys.

Nurse Kelly opened the door with authority. "Done, lieutenant?"

She didn't wait for an answer as the attendant swooped into the room and removed the plate in front of Scott.

"Come with me now, I'll show you where you'll be sleeping tonight. Afterwards you may move around within the confines of the ward until lights out."

She ushered him into a large, dimly lit room; the walls lined with cots. She walked slowly in front of the beds, checking for availability, and stopped in front of an empty one.

"Right here," she motioned.

Night- stands separated the beds that lined the perimeter of the room, and Scott flopped his shaving kit on the stand he shared with the guy next to him.

"Hey, Hey." The stranger admonished Scott.

"The top of this night stand is for me and my paints. I was here first. You can put your stuff in the first drawer."

"Paints? What paints?"

The soldier sat upright in bed and made make- believe brush strokes on a make- believe canvas with make-believe paints.

Scott caught on. "OK, but when you're done with your painting can you let me know so I can put some of my other stuff on top?"

The soldier looked at Scott with a patronizing expression. "Oh, this picture will take a long, long time to finish. Can't you see all the detail I'm putting in it?"

Scott started to feel sorry for this emotional casualty and just wanted to end the conversation. "You know what, Trooper? Just take your time. I'll leave all of my shit down below. No big deal. You can leave your paints on top."

"Thank you for not rushing me."

"You got it."

Scott had no intention of lying down. He looked toward the far end of the ward and saw part of a ping-pong table in a well-lighted room. He got up and walked to the recreation area, where soldiers milled around in small groups or sat pensively by themselves. There were several card tables and soft stuffed chairs. No pool tables. No potentially deadly pool cues or balls. The room was much warmer than the rest of the ward, and a sweet aroma hung in the air. It smelled like someone had baked a batch of cookies in the room, and the confectionary scent still lingered in the cushy furniture and flimsy curtains that framed the windows.

Scott was hardly in the room when a guy sitting at a card table called to him.

"You wanna play some cards?"

"What are you playin'?"

"Acey-Deucey."

"Yeah, I'll play." He walked to the table and looked around the room.

"Before we start, though, I got a couple of questions."

"Shoot," said the soldier.

"First, what are we doing for money? Second, we need more people to play."

"Money? We play with IOU's, little chits with our name on it. People? Just watch this." He raised his right arm and made a circular motion with his index finger extended from his fist. Within seconds the table was full.

"Works just like it does in the bush, huh? These guys were trained well. Their DI's should be proud. What's your name?"

"Scott Regan."

"I'm Sergeant First Class Daniel Copper, 1st of the 9th First Air Cav by way of Commerce, Oklahoma."

"Home of The Mick!" Scott said. "Did you know Mickey Mantle?"

"No, he left town when I was just a kid. I do remember his father, Mutt, and his mother, Louell, though."

"I never heard of them."

"They were quiet folk. Everybody from Commerce is quiet except me. So who are you again, and where ya' from?"

"Lieutenant Regan, Combat Advisor." He started to say Phoenix program but stopped short. "Advisory team 27, Binh Thuan Province via New Jersey."

Copper shuffled the cards and looked up. "Shitty crowded little state ain't it?"

Scott, realizing that he was in a psychiatric ward, didn't know how to take this comment.

"Well – I really don't think it's shitty – or crowded, but it's getting tougher and tougher to find vacant land to bury a smart ass like you."

The exchange was shunted when one of the patients sitting at the card table pounded his hand on the wooden surface. "So are we playin' or ain't we. I'm a busy man with no time to waste—no time to waste."

Copper countered, "Sure, Ramos, you're on a tight schedule, just like the rest of us. They just spin us round and round until we're twirled into the center of their bulls-eye and then they squash us. That's the only schedule we have in this nut ward. Who you tryin' to bullshit?"

Scott pulled up a chair, sat down, and placed his forearms on the table. He smiled around at the group, pulled the deck of cards to him, and started to shuffle.

They played for 1½ hours until it was time for lights out. Nobody won any real money, but Ramos had a pocketful of IOU's.

"Hey, Regan, you gonna' pay me your IOU's tomorrow?"

"Ramos, think about it. Do you *really* believe any of us will have any more money tomorrow than we do today? But if it makes you feel any better, I'll give you a brand new IOU in the morning."

"Oh, that'll be great."

"I thought you'd like that."

The soldier was still painting his imaginary picture when Scott sat down on his bed. He thought about asking him how he was progressing, but instead stretched out, rolled over on his side and pulled the coarse woolen blanket over his head.

Scott looked out from under the covers and saw a scene that was right out of Plato's dialogues. The light from the nurse's station shone through the extra thick glass that fortified the cubicle and cast a gray light that stretched toward the back wall of the ward. Whenever the nurse rose from her seat, she pitched a moving shadow across the rows of beds and draped them in darkness.

****

He didn't even realize he had fallen asleep until a hand slapped him on his feet and it was daylight.

"Gonna' get a little chow, lieutenant?" Daniel Copper asked.

Scott forced his head from the pillow.

"What?"

"Chow?"

"Well" - Scott stuttered - "I, I really don't know what my schedule is."

"Your schedule? Your schedule is like any one of ours."

"No. No, Sarge. I'm being moved out of this ward today."

"Sure. That's what they all say."

"No, really. This was just for one night. It's a complicated story, but I'll be moving sometime today."

Scott tossed off the blanket and looked under the bunk for his hospital slippers.

"Now let me hit the latrine and wash up a little. I'll be back in a minute and we'll go eat."

Returning, Scott made his bunk before walking to the mess hall with Copper.

"So, why you here, lieutenant?"

"I told you, sergeant. This was just for the one night." Scott had no intention of explaining anything, and decided to flip the question.

"So, why are *you* here?"

Daniel Copper stopped walking, put his hand on the officer's shoulder, and spoke. "Because I left too many callin' cards."

Scott looked at him. "You know, I have no idea what you just said."

"Well, maybe I'll show you somethin' later which'll help you understand what I just said."

"I won't be here that long."

"See! There you go again with that crazy talk. You really *are* one of us. No disrespect, sir, but crazy people come in all ranks."

They sat down at a long metal table and silently ate watery scrambled eggs and pieces of bacon that had been burnt together. Scooping scrambled eggs off a cardboard plate,

289

Scott's mind was transported to a world thousands of miles away.

"You know what I really miss around here?" Scott asked.

"Yeah, the same thing we all do - pussy."

"Yeah - I mean no. I was thinking about food."

"I'll repeat again - pussy."

"No. Pepperoni. My mother used to make pepperoni and eggs. We'd have fresh crusty bread that was still warm from the bakery oven. I'd slap open the sports page and chow down. Life was good then." He looked at Dan and realized that his face was as blank as a brick. "I guess you don't eat like that in Commerce, huh?"

"Well, I know what pepperoni is."

"Good boy. Good start."

"The Cherokees mix some funny foods together, too. Is your mother Injun?"

Scott laughed. "Almost. Yeah, she's from the Avellino tribe." Scott could see the sergeant's eyes flipping through his mental rolodex. Nothing found. "Hey Dan, don't exhaust yourself. You don't understand what I just said and I didn't understand what you said before. So, we're even."

"Oh, yeah, thanks for remindin' me. C'mon. I'll show you what I mean. I have it in a book by my bed. Finish up."

Scott followed Copper back to his bunk where he reached between his mattress and the springs.

"I keep this picture here." He pulled out a thin book of short stories by Hemingway. "I stuck it between the pages of his story, 'The Killers', you know why?"

"Nope." Scott answered.

"Because this story gets right to the point. It's just about two guys talking in some backwater restaurant. Hemingway omits all the useless words. No bullshit. I like that." He flipped to the page and snapped out two pictures.

"Lookey here."

The first one was Daniel Copper and a dead body clad in black pajamas. The sergeant's foot was planted on the chest of the VC guerilla and the M-16 rested on his raised thigh with the muzzle pointing skyward.

"Just like Hemingway in Africa - ain't it? He loved huntin' big game. How do I look?"

"Unusual - I'd say."

"Well, I could almost agree with you. But, I like the term 'committed' better." He snapped the second picture in front of Scott's face like a magician. "Now here's where my problem stems. Can you believe it?" The black and white Polaroid showed Copper kneeling down on one knee, his hand supporting the neck and head of another Viet in dark clothes.

"See the patch—that's my callin' card." The large unmistakable emblem of the 1st Air Cavalry was squarely planted on the wet bloody scalp of the Viet Cong guerilla. "You gotta' lop the top," he grinned. A swipe with a machete burst the capillaries and the coagulating blood allowed the patch to stay in place. "That way Charlie knows we're in town."

"This wasn't a practice of the 1st Air Cav was it?"

"Hell, no. I invented this all on my own. No one else did this but me, 'cause I was speaking for all grunts. I was doin' fine until the 'ole man caught me. I guess I just got greedy. I wanted to plant more and more callin' cards. I was called 'Dan, Dan, the plantin' man'."

Scott looked from the picture to Copper. "Between you and me, buddy, somebody did you a huge favor by turning you in. I don't agree with ratting out people, but this is an exception to the rule." Dan didn't reply and returned the pictures back between the pages of the book. As he started to place it under his mattress, Nurse Kelly approached them.

"Morning, lieutenant, morning, sergeant. Lt. Regan, gather your belongings, you're being transferred to the EENT wing. You have a written medical report for me?"

"See I told you I was leaving, Copper." He didn't mean to sound like a taunting grammar school kid, but he did.

"Bullshit, lieutenant. For as long as I've been here nobody has left. They just take you for tests and dump you right back here again."

"Are you ready, lieutenant," Kelly asked.

"Yea, I'm ready. Take care of yourself, Dan." Scott extended his hand but Dan wouldn't shake.

"You'll be back. I ain't sayin' goodbye." Scott shot a parting glance at Sgt. Daniel Copper and thought he saw him wipe tears from his eyes.

The nurse and Scott walked toward the locked rear door of the ward that led to the Eyes, Ears, Nose, and Throat unit. It was directly across the marble hallway from the psychiatric ward, through wide swinging double doors.

"Hey, Kelly, did you notice if Sgt. Copper was crying?"

"No, but he cries every day at one time or another."

"About what?"

"That's what the doctors are trying to find out. He's another casualty with no bandages. He's banged up in a different way."

"It's a wonder we're not all crazy, huh, Kelly?"

"It's a wonder, lieutenant."

CHAPTER 33

Scott stood inside the doorway of the new ward and looked around. It had large windows that captured the sun for the entire day and differed greatly from the psychiatric ward, which was just across the hall, but seemed to be tucked into some forgotten corner of the hospital. Scott followed Nurse Kelly as she swung open the doors to his new sleeping quarters and led him down the narrow aisles between the rows of beds. She stopped in front of an empty one.

"Here you are, lieutenant." She smiled and pointed toward his new bed.

"How long will I be here?"

"I have no idea. I was only ordered to make sure that there was a bed for you in the EENT today. And that's all I know." On the bed was a pair of clean pajamas, new socks and underwear.

"You can shower over there. You'll find towels on the shelf inside to the left. The head nurse on this unit will stop by to see you shortly." She paused and watched Scott survey the bed. "Good luck, lieutenant. Take care of yourself."

"OK, Nurse Kelly, thanks." She walked away and Scott turned to the task of making his bunk, plunked himself down and tested the comfort level. Propping a pillow behind the small of his back, he stretched his legs and slapped the mattress with both hands.

"It'll do," he said to nobody.

His eyes lifted upward across the narrow aisle and focused on the human form that rested in the bed directly opposite him. Their toes were only 3 feet apart. The body of the patient was fully intact, his hands resting limply by his sides, and snaked opaque tubes allowed him to breathe. Scott strained to see what he thought he saw, and with every blink he saw the same ghastly picture.

A nurse wheeled a cart down the narrow aisle and didn't stop to administer any medications, water or juices to any of the other patients. She came directly to the foot of Scott's bed and stopped. Without acknowledging him she pulled out a chessboard from the lower shelf on the wheeling table, tapped the hand of the patient across from Scott and placed the board on his lap. All the pieces were positioned on their spots and the ongoing match continued. He reached out with both hands, felt the contours of the rooks and pawns, and was delighted to have company. The nurse did not speak; the heat of her presence spoke volumes.

Scott noted her angelic smile, how it drew him back to the memory of Mary, and how he missed the orphan's laughter. He shifted his gaze back to the patient across the aisle, realizing no matter how happy the soldier was, he could never smile. He had no lower face. His mandible was blown away when the chopper he'd flown crashed. He had no mouth. His face ended just under his nose. He was completely blind and totally deaf. The nurses came twice a day to play chess with him. He loved it.

Scott continued to watch the interaction and wondered what dauntless engine drove that pilot to fight for his next breath. What would his life be like when the doctors did all that they could to reconstruct him? Would he ever have a life that would be even remotely normal? What would he look like?

"Nurse?" Scott beckoned. She answered him without moving her eyes from the chest board.

"Yes?"

"I think I feel sick."

"OK. The pan is under your bed. Grab it."

She continued the game. This picture of the pilot and nurse before him composed a portrait he knew he would never be able to forget. He wanted to get off his bed and go somewhere else, but was immobilized by the scene playing out in front of him and smelled a frothy rot of iodine and pus. He reached under the bed and grabbed the pan. Regurgitated soft eggs poured out of his mouth and nose. He wiped his lips with the back of his hand. Nobody noticed.

When time ruled that their game be suspended, she carefully packed the board underneath her cart; everything was kept in place according to their last moves. She patted his hands again and whispered goodbye to her deaf charge. He knew she was leaving and groped for her hand to hold. She waited for as long as he needed her touch, and reached for the handle of the cart only when he relaxed his grip and let go. They never spoke a word, yet exchanged more feelings than a passionate dialogue between lovers.

Scott disengaged his look from the pilot's face and glanced around the wide- open ward. It was bathed in sunlight, and he tried to calculate if any of the rays would eventually fall across the pilot's legs so that he could at least feel the heat of the sun. The golden glow filled the ward, and Scott rooted for the beams to fall across the pilots' body. But when they did finally stretch to him, Scott realized the pilot had once again succumbed to the intravenous drugs and could no longer feel a thing. He was fast asleep.

Scott, too, drifted off but was interrupted by the sound of another cart rolling down the aisle. Behind the cart was another nurse. She stopped in front of him and stared, open-mouthed.

"Scott?" He turned toward the woman's voice.

"Roberta?"

"Yes, Scott. Oh my God, how are you – what – I mean — you look great – why – what are you doing here?"

"I was sent here from – from II Corps."

Roberta Cuteri was as pretty as he remembered her. She was no longer a young student nurse on St. Vincent's campus, but was still a real looker.

"Let me see your chart." She was anxious to determine his medical status. "You were medivaced; nothing critical here. You were in the ward next door. Psychiatric. Only one day. No meds ordered." She tried to reconcile the relatively benign diagnosis with his presence in an acute EENT wing of the hospital. She wanted to probe, but decided against it.

"You remember 'Speedy' don't you?" she asked instead.

"Of course. Why?"

"She's the head nurse on this floor. I can't wait to tell her that you're here. We'll just have to have an impromptu college reunion." Lorraine "Speedy" Ramirez had graduated from college with Roberta, Scott and Maryanne.

"If she is the head nurse then she probably knows I'm here."

"Well, if she did, she didn't tell me. Why wouldn't she tell me?"

Scott wanted to keep it light.

"Because she was always jealous of you. You always got the best- looking guys. Maybe she thought that you would grab me before she had a shot."

"Yeah, but you're not good looking."

"Well, maybe she thought I had potential."

"Potential? That's too far in the future. Either you got it today or you don't."

They bantered as though they had seen each other yesterday; crisp and honest like they were sitting in the Student Center 2½ years ago.

"So how do I look now, Roberta?"

"You look like one of my prone patients."

"I was always patient. You know I always wanted you."

"You're such a smoothie."

"Come, rub my back."

"Scott, leave me alone," she giggled, "I've got to make my rounds."

"I can't believe you're here. It's karma. I *know* you always wanted me."

"Oh, stop it, Scott."

"I can't help myself." They both laughed at this strange re-connection.

"You chose Maryanne before me. Don't you remember?"

"That's because I never thought we would meet again in some foreign land. Who ever thought that our paths would cross as romantically as this?"

"What's so romantic about you wearing hospital pajamas with your ass sticking out?"

"So – they don't sell clothes here?"

"Not the kind you would need to go out on the town."

"How far is Tokyo from here?"

"Too far to go in slippers and that flimsy outfit."

"Hey, Robbie – I don't know how long I'll be here, but we gotta' go for a couple of beers and dinner. Can you spring me out of this place? Do you have any pull?"

"Scott, no matter what pull *I* have, *you* don't have the medical clearance. Most patients here can't think about moving anywhere. In fact, most of the troops here can't think at all. Consider yourself lucky even to be having this conversation."

The levity in her voice subsided, and with it, Scott's light-hearted demeanor.

"I hear what you're saying. Believe me when I tell you that I think about this situation a lot. And I *don't* take this for granted." He laid back down into the pillow and his voice trailed off.

"I wish I were able to talk to you, talk to *anyone* - about what happened."

Roberta didn't hear this murmuring and reached for her cart. For the first time in his life Scott felt a deep, morose sadness in an empty hollow he couldn't pin- point.

"Speedy will be working the 3 to 11 shift later today. She's going to be really excited to see you again."

"I told you I think she already knows I'm here."

"So, now she's smart AND clairvoyant? Hey, if I don't see you before my shift ends, then I'll see you tomorrow."

Scott remained silent and waved. He glanced down, past the end of his bed and into the half face of the pilot. His sadness deepened and he felt a throbbing to his very core. It shook at the pillars of his soul and dislodged the cage door sequestering the pangs of guilt. He realized how weak and scared he had been. He wasn't strong enough to overcome fear and suspicion. He wasn't strong enough to react more quickly during the ambush. He wasn't strong enough NOT to kill his interpreter. He wasn't strong enough to control himself. And through these thoughts stared the visage of the pilot, the utter antithesis to Scott's self-reflection, a true hero among thousands.

The hammer of culpability pounded deeper into his psyche and the dismissal of his memories was impossible.

****

Lorraine "Speedy" Ramirez had a smooth olive complexion borne out of her Italian/Mexican heritage. Her dark brown eyes projected a brightness that was almost luminescent and her personality danced in that aura. She approached Scott's bed, but he didn't notice her until she spoke.

"Hey, Scotty." Her voice bounced.

"Hi, Speedy. Robbie told me you were working here. Talk about a small world. How're things?"

"Not bad. How are things with you?"

"As good as they could be – considering all the circumstances." He paused to see if Speedy picked up on anything. Although she didn't proffer any indication that made him feel uneasy, she was very perfunctory despite the background they shared. He was hoping for more campus nostalgia in their interaction. There wasn't much.

"You'll be moved out of this ward later today – maybe tomorrow."

"Where am I going, babe?"

She looked starkly at him. "I haven't been told yet."

"Well, I spoke with Roberta before and I'd really like to get out of this place for a while and go out to dinner." Scott shoved his guilt and sadness back into their box and continued. "Maybe the three of us could go somewhere. You know, I'd like to experience someplace local."

"The only local places outside of the 249th serve mostly raw fish. How's that sound?"

Scott's forehead wrinkled. "Raw fish?"

"Yeah, it's called sushi or sashimi. It's all raw." His mind reeled with images of bloody blue fish and eels from the Jersey docks of his youth.

"What?"

"You heard me."

"Speedy, tell it to me slowly. These people eat raw fish and still live?"

"They've been doing it for centuries. They also eat seaweed."

"What?? Raw fish and seaweed?"

"Yes."

Scott saw an opportunity to express some bravado. "Hey, I'll tell you what. If you or Roberta can get my genetic European ass out of this hospital – for just one night – to eat raw fish and seaweed – then – the treat's on me. OK?" His exuberance dismissed the fact that he had no money.

"One other thing, Scott."

"What?"

"They wash it down with rice wine."

"Rice wine?"

"Yep."

"No grapes?"

"Rice."

Scott double blinked. "No wonder those guys lined up to become Kamikaze pilots. They had nothing to live for. Who would want to come home after a hard day's work to the smell of raw fish in your kitchen?"

Speedy couldn't help but catch a glimpse of the college youth she once knew. A melancholy smile crossed her face.

"From what I can gather, Scotty, you might have bigger fish to fry. Besides, I don't think that you'll be here too much longer. It's been my experience that you're going to be assigned elsewhere. This is just between you and me. You know that I don't know all the details of this exercise, but I've seen enough patterns to make a judgment."

"I just want to go back to my DIOCC." He said as if she understood the acronyms common to MACV jargon.

"I understand that's what *you* wish, Scott."

"So?"

"You probably won't be returned. If they sent you here it's because they *want* you to be here. It's a first step away from trouble. *Their* trouble."

Scott listened to Speedy and realized how solemn she, too, had become. He hoped for a semblance of spark from her. She still had a little of it, but it seemed to have faded. "So, what do I do now?"

"I should have further orders tomorrow," she answered.

****

It was late afternoon the following day when he saw Roberta again. She held a large sealed envelope in her left hand and pushed the medication cart with her right. The omnipresent chessboard had been transferred to her and it was carefully stored on the lowest shelf.

"Here you go, Scotty. Speedy asked me to give this to you." She handed him an envelope and pulled a small duffel out from a compartment under the cart. "It feels like there's some clothes in here, also." She turned her attention toward the pilot, patted his hand, and he immediately came to life.

Scott opened the envelope and withdrew the correspondence. Money fell out; all yen – and a typewritten note on plain white bond paper with no signature. "Change into these clothes and report to Sgt. Major Sykes at the BOQ. He'll be expecting you."

Brief directions were given to the Bachelor Officer's Quarters a half-mile from the hospital. He gathered the yen that spilled out onto the sheets and looked to see if anyone noticed the unusual windfall. Roberta saw him handle the money, but quickly turned back to the chess game.

He opened the duffel and found a gray pair of pants, a navy-blue crew neck sweater, black- laced shoes and dark socks.

"Robbie?"

"Yes, Scott?"

"I guess I'm supposed to be moving out of here."

He wanted to tell her where he was going and possibly they could meet somewhere. Maybe *then* he could talk to her; get some feedback. Maybe *then* all of his thoughts wouldn't be just his own. Maybe *then* there might be another side to everything that happened. If nothing else, she could be his confessor. Get absolution and a fresh start; ten Our Fathers, ten Hail Marys, whatever it took. She turned around and faced him.

"Scotty, take care of yourself. Perhaps someday we'll see each other again in the 'world'."

Her professionalism had an undertone of compassion. She felt that Scott was taking the first step into a process that might never be totally concluded. She rose from the game and stepped toward him. The kiss on his cheek lingered just long enough to let him know that she worried for his safety. Stepping back she held him at arms length and looked him deeply in the eyes. "Take care, Scott."

They both recognized they couldn't share any more thoughts and had to stay dressed in their virtual uniforms. He wanted to hug her, but thought better of it, taking her hands instead.

"Roberta?"

She looked.

He nodded toward the bed. "Take care of that pilot."

He glanced for the last time at the image he knew he would never be able to forget. "Please, just take care of that guy."

She turned back to the chess game as Scott gathered his belongings and walked off to get dressed.

CHAPTER 34

"Sgt. Major Sykes, I'm Scott Regan."

"Good evening, Lieutenant Regan."

Scott had changed into his civilian clothes and his shoes felt tight. "Your BOQ is ready, sir. All I need is the envelope and the note that came with it." Scott offered it.

"Keep the money, lieutenant. What I need is the note and the envelope."

Scott wasn't used to having money. It all seemed to be paper. "Oh, yeah – right, Sgt. Major. How much does the money total anyway?" He laid the yen in front of the senior enlisted man like a kid with a handful of tokens at a carnival.

"Enough for your daily expenses, sir."

Scott handed him the note and the envelope. Sykes turned away, opened the heavy metal door behind his desk, and walked out into the chilly air. He held the envelope and the note at arms length, pulled a Zippo lighter from his back pocket and lit them. When the small blaze turned to black embers, he twisted them into the ground with the spit-shined toe of his leather boot. He came back inside and reached for a small key that was hooked to a plywood board.

"This is the key to your room, lieutenant. Follow the walkway up and to the right. Number 227."

Scott nodded. "What about food? Where do I eat?"

"That's what the money is for. You're now on the economy."

"Can't I go to the mess hall?"

"No, sir."

"I have to eat raw fish?"

"It's not all raw fish, sir. Do you like steak?"

"Sure."

"Well, then eat steak."

"Where?"

"Out there." The Sgt. Major leaned forward. "Lieutenant - I'm not your culinary guide - but as strange as it may sound, this sushi stuff isn't that bad. I'm telling you this, and I'm from Kansas City — meat country. Here's the key, sir."

The BOQ was a multi-level series of bantam, neat apartments, tiered into a small hill accented by pine trees and cedars. Each detachment was perched individually into the natural curvature of the rocky limestone setting. Narrow wooden walkways connected the rooms to each other in an aesthetically pleasing design that worked with the natural rhythm of the landscape.

The window in Scott's room fronted a thick, ages old conifer that undoubtedly filtered much of the late day sun through its heavy pine bows. He set his scant belongings on the bed and surveyed his new quarters. Reaching into his pants he felt the wad of paper money. He had no orders to remain anywhere, the door wasn't locked, he didn't have to report to anybody, and he felt comfortably un-tethered. He checked his look in the mirror on the wall and decided to stretch his liberty.

Although he was alone and didn't speak a word of Japanese, he wandered away from the hospital grounds and instinctively looked for a place to eat. The sun had already set behind a crusty hill, and reflections of small streetlights glistened off the cold wet pavement as he ambled past compact homes, clutched together like strung lanterns. The soft yellow light emanating from the tiny windows barely added illumination to the stone walkways, his breath venting in puffs of steam tapped out in rhythm to the clicking sound of his new shoes. Dampness crawled around his neck and he pulled the collar of his raincoat tighter against his throat.

A cluster of lights caught his attention and, approaching them he saw a small neighborhood restaurant. He peered through the large front window. People were sitting at a long bar and gathered in twos and fours around smallish tables, eating and talking, drinking and laughing. He decided to join them.

Closing the door to the dampness outside, he was greeted by a smiling, petite woman who shuffled toward him. Not many round eyes had approached her eatery and she politely gestured to his shoes and motioned to the pine closet next to her. He realized that he was overdressed from his ankles down, and the woman offered a light pair of woven slippers in their stead.

He pretended he knew what he was doing and pointed to the bar. The woman nodded gently and guided him to an empty seat directly in front of a young man with an extremely sharp knife that sliced fish with infinite precision. He was happy that a sturdy wooden counter separated them.

Scott looked left and right and behind him at the tables where others were being served. All the food looked the same. Fish. Raw fish. Some rolled in a dark wrapper; some pieces more colorfully laid out on black plates. Little globs of green paste were stuck here and there on wooden raised platforms and everyone seemed to be happy. The drink of the house was either tea or a clear liquid served from porcelain beakers. Then he saw a thick bottle of beer. He had found salvation. It read "Kirin". The hostess glided toward him and smiled again.

"Beer, please," he said and pointed to the brown bottle two tables away.

"Hai," she nodded.

"Hello," he said. They both looked confused at the verbal exchange.

In the last lucid moment Scott remembered, he was shoveling a fistful of yen onto the waitress's tray after having eaten every slice of raw fish put before him, and drinking copious amounts of Kirin and sake. He thought maybe he'd gotten the custard dessert for free. Thanking everyone profusely he bounced out the door, still wearing his newfound slippers. The waitress followed him into the damp night air, shoes in hand. They made a courteous exchange on the curb and Scott lit up with a broad, inebriated smile. The raw fish really wasn't that bad after all.

****

He was sleeping soundly when his phone rang. It was sometime in the middle of the night of his third day in the BOQ.

"Lt. Regan? This is Sgt. 1st Class Wyman, 6th MI Group, Ft. Meade, Maryland."

Scott groped for his watch. It was 3:21 AM.

The sergeant continued. "At 0800, your time today, you are to report to 500th MI Group stationed at North Camp Drake. Colonel Larson will brief you further. Do you have any questions, sir?" Scott took several seconds to clear his head and assimilate what he had just heard.

"Well, can you give me an idea what this is about?"

"I suggest you direct all questions to the Colonel, sir."

"Is that all, sergeant?"

"That's it, sir."

"OK - goodbye." His expectations rose and he hung up quickly.

Untangling the cord from around his neck, he placed the body of the phone on the floor and sat up on the edge of the bed. He groped for the table lamp on the night- stand and clicked it on, the 40-watt bulb cutting the darkness like a floodlight. He returned the handset to the cradle and was wide-awake.

"*Daaaamn. I'm going back. Hot shit!*" he thought. "*They covered my ass when they needed to,*" he murmured aloud, "*and now they're calling me back. I'm older and wiser. The trouble is over, and I'm back to square one.*"

For the first time since he was evacuated he wanted to call Maryanne. Letters from him were overdue and he worried about that absence. He wanted to tell her he was OK and that his lack of communication was really nothing to worry about. He decided that he would spare her the details of the recent events, but wanted to reassure her of his condition. A conclusion was close at hand; there was light at the end of the tunnel and he would be returning to Ham Thuan. He could explain it all in a letter once he got back to his DIOCC.

It was still jet black outside as he jumped into the small shower to get ready for his meeting with Colonel Larson. He was four hours early but was chomping at the bit to hear when he would return to duty.

CHAPTER 35

The large stone building was ringed with a ten-foot high cyclone fence. Barbed wire rolled menacingly along the top, and the MP's checked the IDs of anyone entering the area. Scott approached the gate dressed in the civilian clothes he had been issued. An MP moved forward, his M-16 at port arms, and blocked Scott's advance.

"I'm Scott Regan – Lt. Regan – I was issued a verbal order to see Col. Larson at 0800 this morning."

"Do you have any identification, Lt. Regan?"

Scott realized for the first time since he had been lifted from Vietnam that he carried no ID at all. He groped in his pockets to find something to make him a legitimate visitor.

"Actually – well no – I don't."

The MP noticed two chains hanging across Scott's upper neck.

"Are those your dog tags?"

"Yeah, - my tags and a chain with a cross."

"Would you pull them out for me, Lt. Regan."

The MP tossed the cross aside, and took the dog tags between his meaty fingers. He read the stamped imprint.

Regan, Scott J

05248160

A pos

Roman Catholic

"That's the best I can do." Scott offered.

The MP checked the roster of visitors snapped to a clipboard.

"Your name isn't on the list." He addressed him civilly, but without rank.

"Look it – I didn't call this meeting – but I think that maybe my name just got deleted. Why don't you try calling the Colonel's office. Tell him I'm here."

The MP understood that these covert types sometimes were given entry to the building for various undisclosed reasons, but all of them carried *some* form of ID, authentic or otherwise. He walked to his guard stand, reached for the phone and dialed a number. The voice on the other end was apparently stern.

"Yes, Colonel Larson. Understood, sir. He had no ID and his name wasn't...yes, sir. He'll be there double time." He returned and motioned Scott through the gate.

"Lt. Regan, Colonel Larson is waiting for you." He now wore the sheepish look of someone who had inadvertently interfered with an important schedule.

The Colonel sat behind a huge mahogany desk, the dark polished wood holding Scott's reflection as he walked into the room. They exchanged military greetings and Scott sat down in a padded leather chair facing the senior officer.

The scent of freshly ground coffee filled the room and thick drapes covered the long vertically rectangular windows etched in the back wall of the office. Thin rays of sunlight sliced through the slits of the drawn curtains and radiated across his desk. Larson sat between the beams of golden light and appeared ecclesiastical.

"Grab a cup, lieutenant." The Colonel's initial comment had the ring of an order. Scott rose from the chair as if he liked drinking coffee and walked to the small table that was pressed against the oak paneled wall. He poured half a cup.

"So, you had worked under Major Rheingold?"

"Yes, sir I do."

Colonel Larson hesitated at Scott's inference to the present tense. "He's a fine officer and a close friend of mine. We attended War College together. He's an exceptional leader with a keen sense of mission."

"I have a lot of respect for him also, Colonel."

"So do I." Larson leaned forward and continued. "He contacted me the night that – that – he determined you should be transported out of his command. He's an upstanding officer and I know that he wouldn't want to see things get blown out of proportion. The press back home is hungry for any morsel they could pick off our bones; always looking for another headline." The Colonel stared at Scott.

"Yes, sir. I clearly understand what you're saying, sir."

"In light of this possibility, it was determined that you should be permanently re-assigned elsewhere."

Scott rose slightly in his seat. He had expected an approval to return to his DIOCC. He didn't anticipate this news and felt his cheeks flush as he began to speak.

"Colonel, I got a call last night— actually this morning— from a Sgt. 1st Class Wyman from Fort Meade. He told me to see you at 0800. It was my hope that you might give me the green light to report back to Ham Thuan."

The Colonel locked on Scott's eyes and remained stoic.

"We both know what happened there – what I did there – but I think that Major Rheingold would be willing to clear channels for me to go back and finish my tour."

Scott couldn't read the deep glare of Larson and felt edgy.

"Sir, I mean – I'm sure that Major Rheingold told you that we're really starting to make inroads into the VC infrastructure in our District. I know I'm only small potatoes, but I I've got a good handle on what's happening in our AO. I really feel when my interpreter was, er, was – neutralized – that we had cracked a main component of terrorism in Binh Thuan Province. When he died we eliminated a pair of enemy eyes and ears in our midst."

The older officer listened silently. Scott saw no gestures of affirmation from him, but still carried on. "Sir, please understand something, sir. What I'm saying now comes from my heart. I know that there's no course at Benning called 'emotion,' but somewhere along the line, I developed an emotional fever about what we're trying to do for a lot of the innocent people in that country. Like, for example, there's a little girl back there named Mary; well, I named her Mary. She's about 3 ½ or 4 years old. She's an orphan who hangs around our DIOCC. I didn't see her for days before the major shipped me up to Cam Ranh. I think about her a lot. I worry about her. She's nowhere without us watching out for her.

"Sir, please hear me out. I've never been gung- ho. In fact, I chose Military Intelligence because I believed it would be the only branch that would keep me stateside. That's as honest as I can be. But, you know what, sir? When I first hit my assignment I didn't understand the big picture of our effort in 'Nam. I still don't. I just started to see little pictures of daily life and I realized that I couldn't change the big one. What I came to believe was that I might be able to help and change the little day- to-day stuff around me." He floundered to explain himself more clearly and needed desperately to make his point.

"Sir, Major Rheingold and I should have been wasted from an M-79 round—fired by my interpreter—that turned out to be a dud. We also got hammered during an ambush that, I'm convinced, was a set up by my interpreter, too. And you know what? I dodged a bullet and I'm still alive. I *owe* somebody *something*. And another thing, sir, there's a chopper pilot lying in a bed in the EENT wing right here in the 249th — he has *half of a face*, and *he's still alive*! He plays chess, sir! I know that I'll never see him again and that I'll never speak to him, but if I can go back to my DIOCC and just do my job I might be able,

somehow, to prevent some other guy from winding up like him."
Scott eased back down in his chair. "I'd like to make a request,
Colonel, that you don't assign me elsewhere."

He continued to study Scott for what seemed like an
eternity. "Lieutenant, I do believe what I'm hearing from you,
and I have no reason to doubt your sincerity. And, if I had the
unilateral ability to honor your request, I might consider it.
However, the decision to remove you from the scene was
initiated by Major Rheingold and immediately endorsed by
MACV and CORDS. The decision to change anything now is
way above my command. It's out of my hands, lieutenant. I'm
sorry."

Scott recognized there was no room for a counter proposal
and sank deeper into the heavily padded cushion. Colonel
Larson rose and moved slowly from behind the burnished desk.
He walked deliberately to a wide closet across the room,
opened the door, and reached into the darkness. He pulled out
a Class "A" uniform hung neatly on a velvet- cloaked wooden
hanger, held it up and addressed the junior officer.

"Here's the uniform that you will wear on your final leg to
New York. Your initial destination will be Travis Air Force Base,
California. Once you arrive home you will have 10 days leave,
after which you will report to the 6th MI Group, Fort Meade. You
can be housed in the BOQ until you find off-base housing for
you and your wife, if she wishes to join you. Your active duty

commitment will still terminate on your original date and you will not be allowed to re-up."

The impeccably pressed uniform hung like a tailored suit. Scott noticed the dimensions and realized that it was cut precisely for him. He wanted to ask who had known his exact measurements but paused remembering Mr. Miller's words – *"Nobody is chosen by the Company to work in the Phoenix Program, or any other organization that the Company sponsors, without knowing that person from the inside out."*

Your driver will meet you at your quarters at 0630 tomorrow and transport you to your plane. I have no further instructions, Lt. Regan. Do you have any questions?"

"Yes, I do, sir. Can I call my family and let them know that I'm coming home? And, second, how do I get from California to New Jersey?"

"You can make one call to the US. However, you must make it from here. It's a secure line. As to your second question, when you arrive at Travis, you will be transported to San Francisco Airport, from where you will board a commercial flight to New York. All the arrangements have been made, and your orders to Ft. Meade will be waiting for you at your home of record."

CHAPTER 36

Scott's flight to New York wasn't scheduled to leave until 8:31AM. He checked his watch and knew he still had 7½ hours to kill in San Francisco Airport.

He looked for a spot to drop his small duffel bag and hang his newly issued uniform. The place was relatively active for early morning. He scanned the eclectic mix of travelers, some sitting quietly in the molded plastic chairs, others on the bare marble floor. Counter- culture types huddled and, heads bent together, smoked and laughed the time away. Scott spied an empty corner and made his way toward it.

"Hey, asshole!"

The guitar music stopped as Scott walked past a small denim-clad group sitting cross-legged on the floor.

"Hey, killer, how many babies did you blow up?"

He stopped and turned; the antagonist was about Scott's age, a white kid with unwashed curly hair growing down beyond his shoulders. His friends, nodding in agreement, studied him and waited for a response.

Scott looked around then returned his gaze to the speaker. *"Do I owe him an answer?"* he thought. *"Where would I begin?"* Instead he said nothing, clutched his bag tighter and turned away.

"You baby killer. Imperialist fuckin' pig." It was one of the girls who had stopped playing her harmonica.

"I'd rather eat shit than suck *your* dick."

He heard somebody spit; convinced himself it didn't hit him, and kept walking.

Several hours passed and Scott was dozing lightly against his duffel bag in a corner of the airport's main concourse. He opened his eyes when he heard footsteps walking toward him.

"Hello, soldier." The stranger stood uncomfortably close to him. Scott sat up.

"Are you looking for someone to be your friend?" The man extended his hand as if to help him to stand up. Scott recoiled and stood on his own. He towered nearly a head over Scott, had a ruddy complexion, a soft, fat face and wore Buddy Holly-styled black horn-rimmed glasses. His baggy pants and un-tucked short sleeve shirt did nothing to hide his all too obvious corpulence.

"If you feel lonely tonight, I know a place where we can go to and have some f-u-n." He reached out again to hold Scott's hand. Without taking his eyes off the man, Scott reached down to retrieve his bag.

"Leave me alone." His voice was bland and weary. "Just - leave me alone."

There were now rows of empty spots in the cavernous area and Scott made his way to one of them, settling in a seat facing a bank of tall windows that looked out on the runways. A misty rain tapped lightly on the windows making the blacktop shine; the small marker lights reflected off the sheen of the runways, causing them to appear festive.

Scott plopped his duffel bag on his lap and watched the lethargic pre-dawn activity unfold. Reflections of his recent past and projections of what might lie ahead occupied his thoughts and he felt suspended between two countries. He hadn't accomplished anything in Vietnam but never thought he would care about that. Now he couldn't purge this singular thought from his head. What would he tell his friends back home? He knew he would have to stick to the manufactured story line, but how long could he withhold the truth from Maryanne and the rest of his family?

Rheingold's words kept coming back to him like the lyrics of a haunting song: *"Nothing about it can be altered. It's like last night's chow. It must be digested – no matter how long it takes. You must digest it. And just like last night's chow, you eventually must – must – let it out and forget about it."*

He felt his anxieties rising again. In front of him a reflection in the huge window showed a man walking quickly towards him. As the man came closer, the liquid image became more defined; the body was round and he wore black horn-rimmed eyeglasses. Scott dropped his head onto his propped up duffel bag and hoped the guy would just pass him by. It didn't happen.

"Hi, again, soldier. Have you had time to reconsider my fun invitation?" He stood behind Scott and put soft, warm hands on his shoulders. Scott raised his head, stood up, smiled, and slowly walked around the row of chairs to face him.

"Yes, I *have* reconsidered your invitation, and now I'd like to do something about it." Scott reached up and gently put his hand behind the tall man's head. He caressed his slippery hair and guided him down to eye level. "I want you to come close to me." Scott beckoned. The man's face lit up in joyous anticipation. When the tall stranger's head was in line with Scott's mouth he struck like a viper, clamping onto the man's earlobe and speaking through clenched teeth. The stranger yelped and tried to pull away, but Scott bit down harder.

"Listen, you motha' fucker, I'm gonna' rip your fuckin' ear off and spit it on the floor if you don't get the fuck away from me. You understand?"

"Yes! Yes!" He whimpered; his eyes slammed shut.

"You got one second."

The man thrashed and rolled his head, launching the thick-framed glasses across the marble floor. Scott released his bite and the stranger groped to retrieve his eyeglasses; rose awkwardly, clutched his ear with both hands, trotted toward a corner and was out of sight.

Scott stared straight ahead, wanting desperately to brush the residue of flesh from his mouth, but remained still and reviewed the events of the last few hours. After several minutes, he gathered his gear and prepared to move again. *"Welcome home, Troop,"* he thought. *"America loves you."*

A thin orange line cut the bottom darkness on the horizon. It looked like the weather was going to clear. Scott grabbed his bag, walked to the men's room to change into his uniform, and within minutes was wearing his perfectly tailored Class "A" uniform. All his ribbons were pinned in place and he wore new silver bars. No longer a price on his head, he was now allowed to wear the true insignia of his specialty: the pointed dagger and sunburst emblem of Military Intelligence. He was going home, but not without trepidation.

CHAPTER 37

Maryanne drove the fawn-colored convertible to the arrival area at LaGuardia. Knowing her husband would have little baggage to carry, she parked in the hourly spaces and jogged across the lot to the arrival gate.

When she got his call from Japan, the only message she clearly understood was that he was somehow coming home now, and he would not be waiting for his baggage to arrive. She didn't hear too many details after that and was beyond ecstatic.

"Mom, call my mother-in-law. Mom, she was right about St. Jude…he's definitely the patron saint of hopeless causes. We prayed and he answered."

Rosalie stopped her cleaning.

"What? Who?" She stammered in response to Maryanne's excitement.

"It was Scott, from somewhere in Japan. He's coming home!"

"San Antonio é tutti santi," Rosalie exclaimed. "When?"

"Wednesday afternoon. I can't believe it!"

****

Maryanne craned her neck to see the huge plane touch down on schedule. As it began to taxi toward the gate, she hurried to the reception area with dozens of other people expecting to greet that one special person. The crowd pushed forward against the low metal guardrail and scanned the faces of the disembarking throng.

"Scott- Scott, here!" She screamed at the top of her lungs as he walked through the passageway. She moved laterally behind the people pressed against the barrier; her voice seemed to echo from four directions and Scott pivoted in a 360-degree circle. He knew she was within reach, but couldn't place her.

"Scotty, here. I'm here, Scotty." He saw the wave of a hand. Those were her fingers wiggling above the crowd of heads, and then he finally saw her face.

"Mair!"

He searched for the quickest way around the barriers but the only exit was straight ahead and through a small funneled opening. When he was finally in front of her she threw her arms around him and held him as tightly as she could, trembling and laughing and crying at once.

He dropped his duffle and squeezed her until he thought he would crack her ribs. Streams of tears soaked into his collar and she didn't speak; her feelings could not yet find words.

Scott released his bear hug, put his arm around her shoulders and started to maneuver them out of the waiting area to the parking lot outside. As they walked she burst into a string of questions.

"Scotty, we were so worried. We didn't get a letter in weeks. Where were you? Why didn't you write? What happened? How did you get to Japan? Why were you there?"

He was overwhelmed. "Maryanne, let's get to the car first and get out of here."

"Did you know that after you called we received a telegram from the Red Cross saying that you were in a hospital in Japan? Thank God, they at least told us that you weren't critical – but that's all we knew. *You* didn't say that you were in a HOSPITAL!"

"Well, they were right. I wasn't critical. Mair, - I understand you need answers. But please, just let me try to figure them out."

"Figure out the answers, Scott? We were consumed with worry."

"I know, Mair. I know you must have been. But it's all over now. I'm home. Let's just concentrate on the future. I'm okay and you're okay. What the hell are we worried about?"

Maryanne looked up at the profile of her husband. His usual upturned smile was replaced with a straight line forced grin.

"Right, Mair? What are we worried about?"

****

They drove to East Orange to spend his first night home at his parents' house. When they pulled up to the curb the front door was wide open. They could see three heads peering out at them. His mother ran out the door and down the steps and let out a scream, threw her arms around him and rocked him from side to side.

"C'mon Mom. You're embarrassing me. What if my old girlfriend is looking out the window?" She paid no attention to his teasing comment.

"We were *so* worried. We hadn't heard from you in weeks. Why didn't you write? Why didn't you try to ease our torment? Why didn't you do something!?"

"Ma, first you kiss me, then you beat me up. Don't worry about anything. I'll tell you all about it soon. You'll have all the answers you need."

She grabbed his arm, pulling him toward the brick stairs, almost bowling Maryanne over. "C'mon into the kitchen. I've got a pot of gravy and meatballs and I made a nice antipasto."

"Ma, how come everybody else calls it sauce, not gravy? I never understood that."

"Marinara sauce, pizza sauce — but put meat in it and it becomes gravy. Don't ask me why." She slapped him on the back of his head.

"I know you didn't get my last letter, but I wrote that I don't eat Italian food anymore." She dismissed the comment as patently absurd and slapped him on the head again.

"You're right, Ma, I'm only kidding." Scott put his arm around her waist and gave her a squeeze. Maryanne followed them up the stairs. Kathy stood leaning against the kitchen stove and his father sat at the table.

"Hey, Dad, what's up?"

He rose and hugged his son heartily. "What do you mean 'what's up?'" he said. "You're home, right?"

"Yeah, I'm here."

Kathy, dutifully waiting her turn at him, finally pushed past their father and grabbed him around the neck.

"Mom was right. She always said you'd be home for my wedding."

"Well, it surprised the shit out of me."

"Not me, Scott. When was our mother ever wrong?"

"According to us or according to her?" They laughed as only siblings can.

Scott's father opened a bottle of Pabst Blue Ribbon and his mother poured wine into squeaky- clean glasses that had once held ounces of Welch's grape jelly.

"Grandpa always said to save his wine for a special occasion. God rest his soul." She blessed herself at the thought of her father's request.

"This - *is* a special occasion," she proclaimed, raising the bottle in a salute to them all. Scott raised his wine- filled jelly glass, his father hoisted his 12 oz. bottle of Pabst, Kathy joined the toast with a wooden gravy spoon and Maryanne draped her arm across the shoulder of her father-in-law and gave him a squeeze. It was a picture.

Maryanne conceived that night in Kathy's double bed, as his sister dutifully accepted her brother's former bachelor bedroom across the tiny hallway. As the rest of the family slept soundly in the silence of their rooms, Scott and Maryanne tried to muffle the sounds of their union until it didn't matter anymore.

CHAPTER 38

Joseph Michael Regan was born at Kimbrough Army Hospital, Ft. Meade, Maryland. Scott drove Maryanne from their apartment to the hospital sometime in the middle of the night when her contractions started to come in one-minute intervals. He wasn't allowed to be with her during the labor or the delivery. Those were the rules. Instead, he paced in the "waiting" room and watched the black and white television that provided the only diversion for expectant fathers. The programs in the wee small hours of the morning dealt with hard-core Southern Baptist themes. Scott watched the screen.

"Hi, Mom, Hi Dad — Tommy's stopping by tonight. Can I go with him for a milkshake in town?"

The pert little innocent maiden wore a loose flowing dress with a starched white bib. Bobby socks covered her ankles and fit snugly into her dark and white saddle shoes. Her mother was also modestly dressed and deferred to the father.

"So, what do you think, Herb?"

The father placed his cup of tea on the end table and re-folded the evening newspaper. "Tommy's a nice boy, Evelyn. I suppose it would be OK. After all, it is Saturday night. Youngsters will be youngsters."

He got up from his living room chair and approached his daughter. He cupped his hands on her elbows and gave her a soft directive. "Just be home by 9:30."

"Oh, thank you, Daddy. Praise the Lord and I love you, too."

Scott stared with tired eyes, questioning how much of this could possibly be real. In California, only three thousand miles to the West, a whole culture was blowing dope and fornicating in Haight-Ashbury. He wondered if Little Miss Prim wasn't really going for a milkshake, lying to her parents, and not wearing any underwear.

The ebony hours slid into dawn then grudgingly into bright daylight. At 12:30 p.m. a member of the hospital staff informed him that his wife had had a healthy baby boy and he could now come to see her in the recovery room.

"Hi, Maryanne, how're you feeling?"

"Give me a goddamn Marlboro."

"What?"

"Marlboro. A damn butt."

"But you quit nine months ago."

"That's right. Make it quick and give me a light."

Scott fumbled for his pack.

"How long were you in labor?"

"How long were you here, Scott?"

"Uh- about 14 hours, I guess."

"Figure it out, then."

"We had a boy?" Scott asked.

With this question she immediately forgot the pains and hours of labor and her entire demeanor changed.

"A boy," Maryanne smiled and put the cigarette down on the bed sheet, "a healthy, beautiful boy, Scott."

Within seconds a WAC nurse cradling a little pink person in her arms walked gingerly toward the couple, her cushioned white shoes making barely audible squeaks on the pristine tiled floor. She placed him into Maryanne's outstretched arms and asked her if she felt OK with the infant.

"I'm fine – he's fine, too. Thank you."

She brought him closer to her and adjusted her nipple to rub against the corner of his mouth. Eons of conditioning were triggered by this primal introduction and the infant's response was instant. He turned to his mother's breast and suckled until he fell asleep. Scott removed the unlit cigarette from the bed sheet and threw it in the small trash pail placed next to the gunmetal gray side table. Maryanne never smoked again.

****

Their apartment complex in Laurel, Maryland was filled to overflowing with both Army personnel from Fort Meade and collegians from Towson State College. The corporate owners collected guaranteed rent from the U.S. Government and didn't care too much about the maintenance of the property. If the college kids bellied up on the rents, it was chalked off to the "cost of doing business." Their main nut was covered by Uncle Sam. The apartments were cheaply and hastily constructed during the escalation of the Vietnam conflict, with the awareness that the throng of military personnel would sustain a steady demand for any local housing.

No conversation over the decibel level of a whisper was ever private. In fact, when the next-door neighbor was frying anything on the stove in their kitchen, Scott and Maryanne could not only smell it, but could hear it too. The flimsy drywall between their apartments acted like a tympanic membrane, resonating sounds as if it were a giant eardrum. It transmitted a curious, and clearly discernable array of coughs, sneezes, moans, groans, meows, arguments, laughter, whimpers and snores. As best they could tell, their beds abutted a common wall.

"I'm sure they hear the same thing from us, Scott."

"Yeah, but you know, I haven't been able to sleep soundly anyway. Even when I move out to the couch I can't sleep. Shit, I can't even sleep deep enough to snore."

"You know, you're right. You don't snore like you use to. You just puff and mumble. I hear it when I get up for the baby. I don't know what's worse. Probably snoring, but I don't like to hear you mumble because I can't understand what you're saying so I don't know whether you're half awake and trying to talk to me or if you're just mumbling in your sleep."

"Well, I don't know either except that in the morning I feel more agitated than rested. I think that I keep hearing sounds from next door – or from somewhere."

Maryanne looked at him, tapping her cheek with her index finger.

"Maybe I should sleep in the living room tonight with the baby. You can have the bed to yourself and maybe sleep more soundly."

Hours later, through the dim luminescence of the nightlight she was barely able to read the time: 3:35 AM. She rose from the couch and walked towards the strange sound that seemed to emanate from somewhere in the kitchen. She hit the switch and the area was instantly bathed in light. Scott stood naked in front of the small plastic garbage can and was urinating into the paper bag.

"Scott!" Maryanne yelled.

"What? Are you crazy?" Scott asserted. "Hit it!"

Maryanne wanted to scream at him again but hesitated and felt a cold chill run down her spine. She was afraid to wake him.

"Scott," she whispered, "It's okay. It's me, Maryanne. You're sleepwalking. You're dreaming." She held her breath, worried about what he might do next. The infant woke up in his bassinet and cried softly.

"Go see if she's okay." His voice sounded a little less strange but still appeared confused. "What - what's going on here? Mair, what are you doing in the kitchen with the light on? Where's Joey?"

She let out a sigh of relief, but an edge of annoyance crept back into her tone. "I'm in the kitchen because I heard you taking a leak in the garbage can."

Scott looked down and noticed what he was doing. "Aw, shit."

"Do you remember what you were dreaming?"

"I think it was about Mary."

"Who's Mary?"

"That little girl from Ham Thuan—the orphan—you know, I told you."

"Scott, you never told me anything about any orphan in Vietnam. You don't talk about your time there. Period." The cobwebs of his dream started to tear as he became more fully awake.

"So, tell me about her." Maryanne pushed.

"Mair, it's the middle of the night."

"I got time."

"Mair, I was only there two and a half months, there's nothing to tell. No big deal. Anyway, she was just a little kid that hung around where we lived."

Maryanne sensed it *was* a big deal but, for whatever reason, Scott wasn't going to elaborate.

"Dream about anything else?"

"Don't remember."

"When you do remember you *will* talk to me about it, right Scott?"

"Of course – of course I will."

An annoying ring returned to her voice. "Now please take that pail outside and put it in the dumpster. I'll buy a new one tomorrow."

"Let's wait 'till daylight. I'll do it in the morning."

"No. No take it out *now*. Do you think I want to have that lying around in the kitchen for the next several hours?"

"It won't bother me," Scott said.

"I understand this, but it will bother the hell out of me. Just take it downstairs and then try to go back to sleep."

"But, Maryanne…"

"But nothing, please do it. Now!"

Scott reluctantly grabbed the edges of the can and walked to the doorway.

"Scott."

"What now?"

"You're naked."

"Aw, shit."

He went out wearing only a plain white T-shirt, gray shorts, combat boots and no socks. The walk to the dumpster nearly gave him frost- bite. Maryanne carried Joey into the bedroom so they all could sleep together; leaving Scott alone turned out to be a bad idea.

When he returned, he plunked his boots at the side of the bed before crawling in and pulling the goose down comforter over the three of them. Maryanne lay on her side and carefully cuddled Joey against the crook of her arm. Soon she and the infant slept peacefully and the sweetness of their breathing filled the room. Scott couldn't help staring at the utter blankness of the ceiling.

He tried to remember what he had dreamed. He wanted to review the images and conclude the story. Everything seemed to be so open ended with no resolution. But the more he tried to recall it, the longer he would stare at the flat and unyielding ceiling. This emotional deficiency ground at him almost nightly until, reluctantly, he grew to accept that any attempt to work at dream recall would only uncover more loose ends.

CHAPTER 39

For the final months of his military commitment, Scott was the Supply Officer for the 6th M.I. Group at Ft. Meade, a duty completely unrelated to his Military Occupational Specialty, with daily activities benign as they were boring.

"Hey, Hughie, you know what?"

"What's that, lieutenant?"

PFC Hugh R. Colset, Scott's Company clerk, was one of those guys destined to enter the Army as a Private First Class and leave as a Private First Class. Whenever he had come eligible for promotion he was invariably passed over. Other times, when he did get bumped up to corporal, he would face disciplinary charges for various infractions and be busted back to PFC. At least, Scott had noted, he was familiar with the supply room grind.

They walked past the stacked shelves of diverse household and business products and into Scott's office. The walls and ceiling were painted a pale green and the floor was laid with a black polished linoleum. To personalize his station, he had a poster of Jimmy Hendrix wearing a cowboy hat and sitting atop a white horse, instead of the customary picture of the current President of the United States. On another wall he had a map of Ft. Meade that was required posting in every officer's work area. It was common practice to highlight strategic sites within the fort; buildings like the hospital, the MP's or the main gate. Scott had all 18 holes of the golf course outlined; nothing else.

"Doesn't Colonel Ryan get pissed when he sees, er...," PFC Colset groped for the appropriate expression, "the non-military look of your office, sir?"

"He did, until I told him the reason I have Hendrix up there and not the Secretary of Defense or the President is because Jimmy served in the Army. He was Airborne with the 101st. Melvin Laird and Lyndon Johnson weren't. That simple."

"And he bought that?"

"So far."

"So what have you got planned when you get out, lieutenant?"

"Well, my cousin's a stockbroker and he thinks that *I* would be good at it. I'll probably give it a go. What about you?"

"Well, I might re-up so that I can have another chance at makin' corporal."

Scott shot him an incredulous look. "What are you a masochist?"

Colset looked puzzled. "Maso...?" He paused. "No, sir, Lutheran."

"No, I mean – ah – why don't you just get a job and forget about the Army?"

"Because I feel like I left somethin' unfinished here. I mean, I'm still a PFC."

Scott knew just what he meant. "Yeah, well, I left something unfinished too, but I'm not going to re-up in order to get it done." PFC Colset didn't need to know that Scott would if he could but had no choice in the matter.

"What didn' *you* finish, sir?"

"I just didn't finish my job over there, and what I did do, I fucked up. I wish I could just rewind the whole reel and do it all again."

"From what I'm hearin', a lot of guys are coming back with all kinds of different thoughts. I don't know about that personally 'cause I've only been stationed in Germany but, I guess, sir, that you're another returnee with a bagful of memories to deal with. How long you there?"

"Two and a half months."

"Two months? I don't reckon nothin' bad can happen in only two months! If I was you sir, I'd just forget about it and look to the future. I'd say you're one lucky guy, lieutenant."

"*As if I need to be reminded of that,*" he thought, as his mental screen flashed through what was now a familiar sequence; the M-79 skipping across the dyke, the smell of the ambush, the limp body of Cur'o'ng, the partial face of the pilot. Yes, he knew that he had been lucky and had somehow dodged a bullet that thousands of other soldiers didn't.

"You're right, it *was* only two months, and you know what? I *am* just going to forget about all of it."

345

For the remaining months, Scott did work on forgetting it all, but that uninvited white elephant would still show up from time to time and take up space in Scott's living room. On occasions when he and Maryanne went off base for dinner, they generally did so in a mixed company of officers and enlisted men together with their wives or girlfriends. Yet, through all the dining and camaraderie, there seemed to be a box of privacy some soldiers moved within.

He could always tell whether a soldier had just returned from a tour in 'Nam or had not yet been ordered to go. It wasn't in the conversations he overheard, nor was it in the gestures of intimacy and murmurings between the couple, but there was something different about the G.I. when the female excused herself and went to the ladies room. In that quiet moment, when the soldier sat alone, was when he gave himself away. A guy who had not yet done a tour tended to look around the restaurant or continue to eat and drink. The recent returnee, however, would often fall into a look of contemplation, an involuntary moment of deep reflection that would only be broken with the lady's return.

****

Scott spent his time with the 6th M.I. Group in a state of extended ennui. Between endless poker hands and planned escapes to the golf course, he forced himself to remain focused on only three things: number one, his son, number two, his return to civilian life and, number three, putting a day-by-day distance between "the World" and Ham Thuan. He now knew that there was no way that he could ever rectify his mistakes, so he tried to make each day just another 24 hour cushion between what he could have done and what he had done. He swore to himself that he would eventually get to digest it and forget it, and one day, he would wake up and it would no longer occupy so much of his thinking. It might even go away completely, and eventually recede into the white noise of life. But in the meantime, he had to address his return to civilian life and it wasn't proceeding like Swiss clockwork.

"Scott, we don't have a place to live."

He lowered the sports page of the Baltimore Sun and looked over it at his wife.

"Don't worry. We *will* find a place. And a good place too."

"We only have a month before you're discharged."

"28 days," he rebutted with a grin.

"Worse yet," she added.

"Don't worry. If push comes to shove, we'll stay with my parents for a while. We know that we've gotta' be in Jersey. I hope to start with Sherman, Hammitt in March."

Scott's cousin, Maria Jane, was married to Ned Handlet, a stockbroker with the Wall Street firm of Sherman, Hammitt. Ned introduced Scott to Sheldon Weinglass, the manager of the Newark branch office. Sheldon interviewed Scott three times within five months and they had developed a comfortable rapport during that time.

"But you have no SALES experience," Sheldon lamented during Scott's third interview. His elbows rested on his desk and he held his head between his hands and shook it back and forth.

"Shelly, stop looking so damn distraught. Besides what's sales experience anyway? Just look around." He stood and backed up toward the office windows. "Here, come over here and look out this window." Weinglass shot him a pained look.

"Shelly, please stop with that expression. You look constipated." They stood fourteen floors above Broad Street in Newark. Scott pointed down to the mid-day crowd making their way in and out of stores and office buildings. "See those people down there? Everyone one of them has got sales experience." Shelly looked at Scott and grimaced. "You know why?" Scott asked.

"Yes, I do know why, because everybody is selling somebody something."

"That's right, Shell. Sometimes it's advice, sometimes it's an idea, sometimes it's romance, sometimes it's religion. It's only the particular commodity that's different. We're *all* selling."

"Alright, sit down now. You're giving me a headache already."

"Think about it, Shell, this is the third time we're talking about me joining Sherman, Hammitt. I've driven up from

Maryland three times to interview with you, so you know that I can sell myself, or else you wouldn't have seen me three times."

"Like you have so much to do in the Army?"

"I got a lot to do. I'm a busy guy down there. I start my day in the office before you even get out of bed."

"So on top of everything else, now you know when I get out of bed?"

"Look, I'd make a bet," Scott said.

"Never say things like that unless you already know the answer. A 50/50 chance of being right can make you look like a putz."

Scott bore straight ahead. "O.K. Shell, let's cut to the chase. I'm getting discharged in two weeks. Maryanne and I have to find a place and then I can start the first week of March. How does that fit in?"

"Fit in with what?"

"With your schedule?"

"My schedule? Here you are hocking me to work here and I haven't made a decision yet. And, in addition, you don't even know how much I'll pay you. So what kind of businessman are you? You just want to work for the love of it?"

"Of course not, but I figure that you'll be fair."

Sheldon Weinglass looked down at his desk and shook his head again. "That's the second mistake you made in 10 minutes. Nothing in business is fair. If you settle for fair – you lost."

"O.K. then. Let's say you hired me. What's my salary going to be?"

Weinglass looked at Scott and arched his eyebrows. His forehead wrinkled right up the front of his bald- head. "*If* I hire you, I will pay you $600 a month, until you finish company training and get your broker's license. After that, you'll be on a $400 a month draw versus commission."

"Shelly!" Scott exclaimed. "With everything combined, I make more than that in the Army."

"So stay in the Army."

"Is that your best offer?"

"That was not even an offer. It's just a conversation. But if it were an offer, it would be my best one."

"So, when will I know?"

"I want to talk to Ned again. He does recommend you highly. But then, he should. You're family. I'll let you know in the next several days."

They shook hands, Scott thanked him, and turned to leave the office. At the doorway he stoped for a moment, then turned back to Sheldon. "You know what? I think that I just settled for fair."

Sheldon Weinglass looked at Scott and broke into an ear-to-ear grin. Only this time he didn't shake his head in disagreement or dismay.

Five days later Scott received a three-sentence letter from Sherman, Hammitt. It was the only piece of mail that day. It read:

"O.K. You're hired. You start Monday, March 16th. Your pay will start at $150 per week. Shelly Weinglass."

Scott read the letter in the hallway of their apartment complex and bounded loudly up the stairs. Maryanne heard his heavy boots hit the steps and opened the door. She held the baby in her left arm and Scott held the letter in front of her.

"One down, one to go." He said.

"What do you mean? What's down?"

"I found a job! One down, and now all we have to do is to find a place to live."

He kissed Maryanne hello and rubbed his son's soft head.

"That's great news, Scotty. Let's call your mother and tell her, and while we have her on the phone, we can find out if she's had any luck trying to locate a place for us yet." Her words were hardly out before the phone rang.

"Hi Mom. We were just getting ready to call *you*." Scott surmised from listening to the one sided responses from Maryanne that his mother was running her usual 20 question routine about Joseph Michael.

"He's fine."

"Schedule's good."

"No, no colic."

"Good stools."

"Good stools?!" Scott raised his voice so that his mother could hear him all the way to New Jersey. "Hey, Ma, when are you going to ask about us?"

Maryanne handed him the phone. He took the handset and leaned against the kitchen sink. "Hi – yeah, I'm good. Uh, huh – I'm on a regular feeding schedule too and I thought you should know that my stools are fine also." He cupped his hand over the mouthpiece and turned to Maryanne. "It went right over her head."

He turned his attention back to the dialogue. "You did?" he said. "So, what did Albie say?" His face held a curious look. "When is it available? Wow, Ma, that is *really* weird." Maryanne tugged at the rolled up cuffs of his fatigue shirt in an effort to be part of the chat. "Yeah, yeah, that'll be fine." She held on to his shirt and looked into his eyes in an attempt to read into the context of the conversation.

"$125 bucks a month? Sure. Book it."

She watched as he finished the call, hung up, and leaned against the refrigerator, his hands clasped over his head like a boxer in victory.

"Man, how weird is this?"

"What's weird? What did your mother have to say?"

"We can have the apartment on 13th Street, the exact same one I grew up in; the same flat in the same house! My mother ran into Verna Vitale at the A&P on Ampere Parkway and she said that Albie's tenants are moving out Feb. 1st and that he's looking to rent the place again. The timing's perfect." He was ecstatic.

****

Their sparse furniture was delivered from military storage during a particularly mild day for the end of February. As the movers carried in boxes, Scott began to feel like a kid again. He tried to stay out of the way, but kept opening doors and touching moldings that flooded him with brilliant recollections.

From the kitchen, the narrow hallway where he and his sister had played on rainy days had seemed to them as long as a bowling alley. Now it led a mere several steps to the two rear bedrooms. Scott and Maryanne's bedroom would be the larger one and Joseph would sleep in the same smaller room that Scott and Kathy had shared so many years before. The backyard still had the fig tree that nestled between the angled cinder block walls of two garages. The trellis that his grandfather had built to support the climbing rose bushes had lost its precise symmetry and lathe strips now hung loose like the ribs of a broken skeleton. Tangled vines hugged the ground instead of climbing the stakes to deliver a crop of fragrant plum tomatoes and the basil plants no longer stretched their sweet scented leaves to the clothesline above. Everything appeared to be the same, only smaller, and he couldn't process the memories fast enough. Scott searched out the minutiae of the apartment like a bloodhound on amphetamines.

"Hey, Mair, check this out." He yelled.

He looked out the window of his parent's former bedroom. The wall of the garage that formed the back border of the tiny yard had mud-balls stuck to its cinder blocks, like a vertical little village of round adobe huts. They had remained there, baked in time, since he, Frankie Falera and Jimmy Scotti packed mushy dirt-like snowballs after a summer downpour, and with all of their six-year old strength, slung them against the garage wall.

"Look at that. After all these years! "We should have patented *that*, Mair."

She walked up to him and put her arms around his waist and tickled his stomach. "Hey, Edison, it's only mud."

"So we'll call it something different."

"Instead," she said, "why don't you start to get creative on your business career. We need the moolah."

One week before Scott started his Wall Street experience, Rosalia and Ed De Feo, Maryanne's mother and father, drove out from Port Washington for their first visit to their daughter's new home to baby-sit for Joseph Michael. With the baby safely entrusted to the grandparents Scott and Maryanne went on a mission to find a business suit for Scott. They boarded the "82 Watsessing" bus from the corner of N. 13th Street and 1st Avenue to downtown Newark. The city still bore the scars of the 1967 race riots, but many businesses remained open, holding staunchly against the changing inner cityscape. On Broad Street, Scott and Maryanne turned into Browning King's Men's Store.

"May I help you, sir?" The well-dressed middle-aged salesman wore a flower in the lapel of his dark tailored suit. He nodded politely to Maryanne and stood back.

"Yeah, thanks – I, uh, need a suit. How much are they?"

The experienced vendor recognized a novice buyer. He turned to Maryanne and answered. "The cloth varies, hmmmm?" She gave him a slight nod of confirmation and an hour later the two of them had settled on a navy blue pinstriped, three- piece Hickey Freeman suit. Up until that moment the salesman and Maryanne did most of the talking.

Scott wanted to hear the bottom line. "How much?" He asked with a hint of anxiety.

"$150.00. Tailored, of course."

"What about untailored?" Scott was serious.

So was the salesman. "$150.00."

"Does that come with an extra pair of pants and a radio?" Scott guffawed at his own wit. Maryanne pulled him aside.

"That's really a beautiful cloth, Scott."

"Oh shit, he's got you saying 'cloth,' too? Mair, that's $25 more than our monthly rent!"

"You can't see potential clients looking like a rag man can you?"

"No, but then I don't want to look like I own Manhattan either, especially when we don't have a pot to piss in."

"They'll never know that if you buy this suit." The salesman realized he had an ally in the young lady and simply stood aside and cleared his throat.

"Yes, we've decided," she said, turning to the waiting salesman, "he'll take it."

The suit was pressed and ready on the day before he started work at Sherman, Hammitt. It looked great.

****

After the first six months in the corporate business world, Scott's one suit wardrobe had expanded to four and so did his family.

"You're what?"

"I'm pregnant"

Scott started to hyperventilate. "Maryanne, your body's going to break down and stuff like that. Don't you think you should plan these things? I mean you only weigh 110 lbs. You can't keep passing 7 lb. objects like that. Sooner or later it's got to take a toll on you."

"Well then, stop mounting me." She smiled.

Scott's eyes spun in his head and he said, "Well, there's got to be a better way."

"Like rubbers?" she queried.

"Aw, God, I hate them and you know it. Can't you take your temperature during the month so we can at least know when you're ovulating...or," he scrambled for words, "or take the pill again like other women do?"

"All other women aren't me, Scott. You know I tried different prescriptions. How did I feel? Do you remember?"

"Lousy."

"So you want me to try it again?"

"No, but..."

"But what?"

"Nothing, I guess. I'm just surprised that you're pregos again."

"Upset or surprised?"

"Surprised."

"Didn't everything turn out fine with Joseph?"

"Yeah – and it's still fine."

"So, what's your concern now?"

Scott sat in one of the two wooden chairs in the kitchen and looked out the lone window and into the gray light of the alleyway. Maryanne's composure helped to level him out and he began to breathe easier. "I really don't have any worries anymore, Mair. What's the worst thing that could happen? Nobody's going to try and blow us up, right?"

"Blow us up? To tell you the truth, that thought never crossed my mind."

Scott was right, there would be no more explosions leveled at him, not literally, anyway. But the wave carrying Scott's deeds in Vietnam and the ghost of Cur'o'ng was building, cresting, rolling and searching to break on America's shore one day, looking to engulf him, and drag him back out to sea.

****

Scott threw himself into his work, and he loved it. Each day that passed helped him bury the Phoenix program deeper and deeper in a submerged mental vault. Vietnam was, again, like the sound of a distant buzz saw – but this time the sound was fading in a reverse Doppler effect. All of his co-workers, with one exception, were never military and had no interest in his military past. This suited him just fine.

He re-connected with his best friend, Chan, who was soon to be discharged from Pearl River Naval Station as a Marine Captain. He had won the bet with his father and became a chopper pilot, spending a tour in 'Nam airlifting dead, dying and wounded Marines from countless fields and hilltops in I Corps. And so, when Scott's phone rang at his desk at Sherman Hammitt, the voice needed no introduction.

"Hey Scotty – don't you have a secretary yet?"

Scott's face lit up. "Chan, hey, come on, I'm still a rookie. I'm still earning my stripes."

"C'mon man, you're a veteran. Doesn't that carry some weight in your company?" The sarcasm was evident to both of them.

"Yeah, right, it carries as much weight as this." He grabbed his crotch. Chan didn't have to see the gesture and laughed at the street taunt. "So what's *happenin'* buddy?"

"I'm flying up north this weekend. Two guys down here need some hours. I'll be giving them flight time. We're taking a fixed wing into McGuire. Can you pick me up?"

"What's in it for me?" Scott busted.

"Two Ranger tickets on the glass for Saturday."

"Ranger games always make me hungry, and thirsty too."

"O.K. O.K., booze and food too. We'll bounce around the City for a night."

"Deal." They both laughed, knowing that Scott would have done it for nothing.

"When do your tires hit the tarmac?"

"Friday sometime. I'll probably submit our flight plan tomorrow."

"O.K. let me know. I'll be there."

The next night the Rangers beat Toronto 3-2. After the game it was time for them to see Manhattan. A blur of taxis and gin mills finally wound down and deposited them at J.P. Cloak's on 56th and 2nd at 1:30 in the morning.

****

"I gotta' take a piss," Chan said.

"I'll hold our spot right here." Scott hugged the heavy wooden bar and tried to broaden himself out in order to secure a spot at the handrail, shoved in against the press of a hard drinking late night crowd. Waldo, the well muscled, forty-something bartender slapped his hand on the bar in front of him. "What'll it be?" He vaguely recognized Scott from past visits.

"Two Pabst."

"No Pabst."

"Two Piels, then."

Chan returned from the men's room. "I'm glad to see certain things don't change around here." Chan spoke through a slight, boozy slur.

"Like what?" Scott burped.

"Those urinals. They haven't changed them in years. If you're under six feet tall you can still stand in them." The huge porcelain receptacles were part of the original building's 1880's construction. Ice cubes were thrown into the bottom of the accommodation in order to wash down the rivers of beer and liquor that drained through them. They didn't flush, but then again they didn't have to. The melting ice worked just fine.

As Chan tried to settle close to his beer he was pushed hard from behind. He turned around and saw the guy who did it. He wore a smirk on his lips and hair that fell below the collar of an

Army fatigue shirt adorned with peace symbols and anti-war slogans.

"Yo, take it easy, man. Relax," Chan smiled.

Scott and Chan both looked back at the bar. An inadvertent nudge in a crowded joint would be understandable if the stranger was only looking to reach for his drink. This wasn't the case, however; he was looking to make a scene.

"Is my friend in your way?" Scott edged closer.

"Short haired fucks like him are always in my way, man."

Chan turned and addressed the guy: "So, you don't like my barber, jerk off?" Even though Chan had on civilian clothes, underneath he wore the mental uniform, attitude, and toughness of a Marine combat pilot. He started to pump.

The bartender overheard the conversation through the chatter of the crowd. Years of experience taught him that a majority of agitated comments between patrons normally resolved themselves amicably, but the tone of this exchange told him this wouldn't be one of those times.

"I don't know your barber, fuck head," the guy said. Conversations around them continued and nobody but Waldo was paying attention.

"Where did you get that shirt, asshole?" Scott asked.

"From a dead soldier who fought an immoral war - somebody that could have been you - right?"

"A dead soldier?" Chan stiffened. They both squared off and braced. Scott didn't see his friend's hand shoot out from

361

his side. It grabbed a clump of the agitator's long hair and slammed his face full force into the edge of the heavy oak bar. Chan repositioned himself and didn't say a word, but before the guy's knees buckled he grabbed his head again and repeated the face slam.

The immediate circle of customers halted their conversation. The rest of the people never even saw what happened. It was over in seconds. The bartender, scrubbing glasses in the three sinks behind the bar, stopped in mid-task and raised up. He pointed.

"YOU! You're out of here. Now. You're cut off. Screw." Scott started to make some feeble apology for his friend. "No, not you, HIM." He pointed to the agitator. "Get that shithead outta' here. Now!" The normally diplomatic bouncer heard Waldo's tone and worked his way through the crowd, grabbed the offender from behind and walked, pushed and finally shoved him towards and out the door. Scott looked over at Chan. His head hung down and he was staring at the floor.

"You guys are military, right?" Waldo asked.

"I was. He still is — pilot—Marines."

"I thought so." He dried his hands on the bar towel and moved to shake Chan's hand. "Waldo Kenny, Marines, 1st of the 5th—Korea."

"Thanks for getting rid of that guy." Scott said.

"No problem." He went back to rinsing the glasses like nothing had happened.

"Are you O.K., Chan.?"

"How do I look?"

"Ugly as ever." Scott slapped him on the neck.

"Wanna' have one and done?" Scott asked.

"No, not here. Let's jump a cab and hit the Landspot for a quiet one. We'll walk over to the Port Authority from there and pick up my car."

Their cab driver, a talkative Irishman from Richmond Hills, Queens, drove his two fares to the corner location of the watering hole.

"Hey, Seamus, park this hack and come on and have a drink with us." Scott implored. At this hour everybody was a friend.

The driver made a half turn to the back seat. "As much as my weak mind says, 'yes,' my sense tells me 'not.' I know in my heart of hearts that I can't have only one potato chip or only one drink. Thanks just the same."

"What a poetic way to say 'no'." Chan said.

"Pay the guy, Chan."

"No, you pay 'em."

"Fuck you, I picked you up at the airport."

"Damn." Chan said and reached into his pocked and pulled out a $20. Scott jumped out of the cab and Chan followed, forgetting to get his change. The driver gave them a big wave as he turned the corner on 11th Avenue and headed east on 46th Street.

"You dunce - you just paid for his kids' school lunches for the next month," Scott needled.

"Damn," Chan said again. "What the hell. We woulda' spent that much on his drinks."

"Get the hell in the bar where you belong. If you're going to blow money like that, at least spend it on me."

They pushed open the vintage wooden door and large smoked glass panel of the Landspot Tavern at the corner of 11th and 46th. The ambient noise level here was much quieter than the cacophony at Cloak's. Strains of Joni Mitchell's "Both Sides Now" drifted over subdued conversations. Couples sat at cozy tables and picked at their late night fare.

Several sturdy bar stools were available as they made their way toward them, and across small white octagonal floor tiles that had been laid decades ago by forgotten craftsmen. At one time a longshoreman's hangout, marks from the workmen's baling hooks were still etched in the pub's wooden bar. Ownership had changed numerous times since those rough and ready days, and now fresh flowers, standing in thin, clear flutes sat next to cut glass salt and peppershakers on delicate linen tablecloths. The dining tables had been placed discreetly apart from where the drinking set lounged.

Customers sipped their beers. A few of them leafed through magazines that had been piled at the door end of the bar. Scanning the crowd, Scott and Chan simultaneously noticed a guy sitting at the corner of the bar near the kitchen, wearing a tan beret and sporting a full dark beard. Snapping open the newspaper in front of him, they could see that he was reading a copy of the *Daily Worker,* a publication that was known to be written and financed by individuals sympathetic to the Communist Party. They grabbed two of the unoccupied stools and sat down.

"Pinko fuck." Chan mumbled, looking down the bar at the guy. Scott clamped hard on Chan's forearm. "Don't even think about it." Each word was pronounced slowly and emphatically. "You're only allowed to bang one head per night, and you've reached your quota. You'll be over your limit with this guy. Now be a nice boy and drink your beer or you won't get any pretzels for dessert." They ordered two Pabst.

"Sorry, no Pabst."

"Jesus what's going on around here?"

"Schaeffer?" the bartender asked.

"Yeah, O.K." they conceded.

"So, what time are you heading back tomorrow?" Scott asked.

"We're scheduled to take off at 2:35. But I want to get there a couple of hours before. I've got to review the flight plan with the young guys and do all the pre-flight shit. Can you drive me down to McGuire?" Chan asked.

"Absolutely, but only if you keep spending your money here."

CHAPTER 40

Sunday morning broke clear and warm for early November, a peaceful prelude to a horrific event that would unfold later that day. Scott carried Joey to the front stoop and looked into a limitless blue sky. "Hey Mair, bring me the stroller and I'll take him with me to get the papers." He sat his son in the seat and trundled around the corner and down 1st Avenue toward Dalandro's bakery to pick up some hot crusty Italian bread.

"What a beautiful day, little man. I bet you wish that you could go flying with your Uncle Chan, huh?"

The baby tried to turn and look back at his father's voice.

"Some day you will. Maybe he'll take us both up there. It'll be a perfect day just like today. We'll go as far as we can, then Uncle Chan will land the plane and we'll just get out and look around. Maybe we'll even have lunch. How does that sound?" Joey clapped his hands together. Scott believed this response wasn't coincidental. "You really do understand me, don't you?

He grabbed the newspaper from the rack and waited in line for bread as the aroma from the hot ovens wafted between the customers, flooding all of them with memories from their childhood kitchens. The walk back home was made at a leisurely pace; the loaf nearly eaten before he returned with the Sunday paper and their son.

"Thanks for saving me some." Maryanne said. She felt the bread and folded the paper bag over the remaining chunk.

"I was only going to rip off the end, and — and then one thing led to another."

She shook her head in resignation. "I don't know who has less self control, you or your son." She placed an egg omelet thick with salami, potatoes and peppers on the kitchen table. Cutting Scott a full section, she handed him the plate, put Joey in the highchair next to her and gave him a piece of bread to gum on. Only then did she serve herself.

"Did I tell you that I'm driving Chan back down to McGuire this afternoon?"

Maryanne looked at him. "You can't, Scott."

"Why not?"

"The hospital needs me 3 to 11 today. You knew that."

"No I didn't. I thought that you told me you were working 11 to 7."

"No, I'm not."

"Now what do I do?" Scott stated.

"Tell Chan you have to baby sit."

"But he's counting on me, Mair."

"So am I."

"I gave him my word. You know how I feel about that."

"First of all, Scott, he's your best friend." She paused. "No. Let me rephrase that. He's like a brother to you isn't he?"

"And how."

"So don't you think that he'll understand?"

Scott didn't answer.

She looked at Joey in the highchair. "*We both* need you today." For the next ten minutes Scott finished his food in silence. When he was done Maryanne slid the plate out from under him and turned around to the sink while Joey played with the wet piece of bread on his tray. Scott sat pensively, elbows on the table, his chin resting in the palm of his hand, until he finally made a decision.

"O.K., I'll call him." He dialed Chan's number on the wall phone in the kitchen.

At Chan's parents' house in West Orange, his mother answered.

"Hi, young lady," Scott said with as much of a mock southern drawl as he could muster. A sweet voice in a youthful South Carolina accent responded. "Why, Scott don't you just have the most complimentary way of saying hello."

"It's sincere," he said, "and you know that."

"Any southern lady would accept such a heartfelt compliment, Scotty."

"Then consider it so." he added.

"You want to speak with Chandler?" she asked.

"Yes, please."

Chan picked up the extension phone in his old bedroom.

"Hey, what's up?" Chan asked.

"Uhhh, Maryanne told me something that I forgot about last night when I told you that I could take you to the airport".

"What's that?" He yawned.

"Well, she's working at St. Mary's and I thought she was working the night shift and, uhh, she was counting on me to watch Joe, and I can't lug him on a 3 ½ hour round trip with us back and forth down there and...and I'm sorry, man, but I can't take you." Scott expelled his breath into the mouthpiece of the telephone in an expression of capitulation to the facts.

"Don't worry about it. It's O.K. I'll find a way to the airport." Chan was both resigned and sad. In that moment they simultaneously realized that their brotherhood would never again be as free wheeling and spontaneous as it had always been. They both recognized, for the first time in their lives, that different commitments were taking them down separate paths. Scott didn't realize how fatally different these paths would be until he got a call the next night.

Maryanne picked up the kitchen phone. Scott was in the bedroom playing with Joey, and thought he heard Maryanne let out a deep-throated moan. She called for him and held the phone out at arms length. "It's Chan's brother, Pete." Blood drained from her face.

"Hey, Pete, how you doin'?"

"Not good, Scott; I have some terrible news about Chan." Without hesitating he continued. "Chan and two other pilots died yesterday." Scott slid down the kitchen wall and squatted in silence.

"Scott? Scott, are you there?" Pete's voice resonated from a hollow, disconnected chamber. Scott took up the receiver and spoke through a dry and knotted throat.

"How?"

"His plane crashed on take- off from McGuire."

"When, Pete?" He asked like the time would matter.

"Yesterday afternoon." For an instant the horror of the message didn't register. Then Chan's blood brother spoke again: "I feel so sorry for you, Scott. I know how close you two were. I'll call again with the details of the funeral."

"Oh Nooooo." Scott let out such a deep and mournful sob that it gave Maryanne goose bumps. He cradled the phone against his chest, slid down onto the floor and leaned into the cast iron radiator, wailing uncontrollably. His mind tumbled in irony and reflected on the tragedy that was out of life's sequence. If Chan was destined to die so young, it should have happened in 'Nam, not Jersey. Marines in uniform don't die back home. He pounded the solid plaster kitchen wall when he thought how he might have prevented his death. Maybe if he *had* driven him to McGuire something would have been different—anything—a flat tire, heavy traffic, a road detour; something to change the schedule of the day and prevent him from flying *that* plane at *that* moment in time.

"Scott, please, please come here." Maryanne wanted to console him but could only watch him pummel the wall. He was out of control and agonized how Chan might have still been alive if he had only done what he'd promised; if he had only kept his word.

****

Several weeks after the funeral Chan's personal belongings were shipped to Picatinny Arsenal in Northwest Jersey. Scott drove there alone where he met Pete and Chan's father in front of a cold, steel gray military warehouse. As they began to sort through Chan's effects, both of them urged Scott to take whatever he thought he could use. But everything he saw and touched had stories and memories oozing from them. Finally, in the last suitcase he found a pair of black alligator loafers and a matching belt that he had never seen.

"I'll take these," he said.

"Scott, take some sport jackets or any of these shirts. Pete and I can't use them, but they'll fit you fine," his father urged.

Scott reached for the pile when he noticed two pictures slipped between neatly pressed cotton shirts. He slid them out and turned to look at them. The first one showed a very attractive woman posing in a colorful ski suit and partially blocking a wooden sign that appeared to read: "Breckinridge." The other one showed Chan and the same young lady, a petite blond with a pixie haircut, on some tropical island. She toasted the camera with a fruity drink as he stood behind her, flashing his trademark smile and reaching around to cup her well tanned bare breasts. For the first time in weeks Scott smiled when he thought about his best friend.

"You snake. So I guess she's back from humping some General in 'Nam. I knew you would get her to sit on your lap sooner or later." He took the pictures and wiggled them into his back pocket.

"What about his skis or golf clubs?" Pete asked.

"No, no, thanks. I think I'll just take these shoes and belt. That's all. They're all I can really use," Scott said again. He really didn't want to look anymore and, aside from finding the photos, the exercise made him feel ghoulish.

"Chan told me the shoes had been hand made for him when he went on R&R in Hong Kong," Pete whispered.

"Thanks. I'll take good care of them. Let's stay in touch." Scott took several steps toward the large metal door of the warehouse and turned around. Sunlight slanted in through a huge opaque window, silhouetting Chan's father and brother as they aimlessly shifted stacks of clothing back and forth, from one pile to another.

CHAPTER 41

Scott continued to avoid elaborating on any events during his time in Ham Thuan, and responded to Maryanne's occasional questioning with brief and sketchy answers. The general public continued to maintain an attitude of disdain for the whole war effort, but Scott's mother maintained a daily ritual of prayer to end the war and for the safe return of other mothers' sons. Despite her supplications, the bloody conflict not only continued, but the tentacles from Phoenix would soon extend back home to New Jersey.

****

Elizabeth Mary Regan was born in June 1971, and her mother said she smiled from the minute she was born. On nights that Maryanne worked, Scott had double duty. At first caring for two kids in diapers seemed like a monumental task, but in fact, just the opposite was true. Joe was so enamored of his little sister that he would stand peering into her crib, and they entertained each other for long stretches of time. This left Scott alone with his thoughts in a solitude that hadn't been available anywhere else in his daily life.

For almost a year and a half he had managed to store every recollection of the Phoenix experience in a safe corner of his mental attic. Now, however, in these new hours of solitude, his mind would inexorably return to the events at his DIOCC in Ham Thuan. The same pictures reappeared, time and again: the M-79 skipping across the dyke, the smell of the ambush, the limp body of Cur'o'ng, Mary's happy little laugh, the partial face of the chopper pilot. He also often thought of how his brief tour of duty had so eerily paralleled that of Willy Payne, and of how close he had come to the same destiny. And then, unexpectedly, as if to add insult to injury, he started to dream again.

He was aware that some emotional level inside him had changed, and he assumed that Chan's death was the trigger, since the dreams always started with a scene from the Official Naval account that described the events of the crash. He would shudder when he thought about what it must have been like as his virtual brother became aware that he had only seconds to live.

The dreams often began with the image of the starkly plummeting T-29 aircraft exploding on impact into a rich technicolor ball of flame, which in turn dissolved into a haunting scene; sometimes he saw Cur'o'ng's gray face slowly regaining consciousness, or Mary, cold and lost and crying out for him, or the image of Clancy Morris' broken, shredded face. Sometimes the ball of fire would just jar him awake with no memory at all except for an aching, empty, hollow feeling in the pit of his stomach and a deep inexplicable depression that settled on him like a damp fog.

CHAPTER 42

For the next two years Scott continued to work hard at developing a book of clients at Sherman, Hammitt. Shelly occasionally praised his efforts, Scott was proud of his accomplishments, and he was starting to make a decent living. He also worked hard to suppress the haunting recollections that still trailed him. Nevertheless, the dreams continued sporadically and, when they did occur, he was as restless and agitated as ever.

Then, one day in early June 1973, a sturdy cardboard trunk arrived. It was deposited on the brick steps of the single family home they'd bought the previous year in Livingston. He parked his new burgundy Mercury Marquis in the short driveway and stared quizzically at the wooden crate that looked as if someone had hastily dropped it off and ran. He tugged at his tie and bounded up the steps to the front door.

"Hey Mair, are you home?" He shouted up to the second floor.

"I'm up here changing the baby." The baby no longer meant Joey. It was now Elizabeth. Lizzie.

"What's with this trunk that's addressed to me?" No answer. He walked back outside, examined the labels slapped on the sides and ran his hands over the solid outline. It was sealed tight and crisscrossed with packing tape. It could be only one thing: his personal belongings from Vietnam that had been collected and stored for him following his quick exit out of country.

"After more than four years? You gotta' be shittin' me."

"Hey Maryanne", he called again. "Did anyone tell you the Army, or somebody else, was going to drop this memory box at our house?"

She walked downstairs holding both freshly washed kids in her arms. "Do I look like someone told me?"

"I'm dragging this thing inside," he said.

"Wait one second," she said. She walked back upstairs and laid both children into their respective beds. Downstairs again, she poked at the sturdy ribbing. "Sealed tighter than a mummy's tomb, Scotty." They lugged it up the brick stairs and into the first floor living room. He cut away the string-reinforced tape that secured the latches and had held the trunk closed tightly during the years of storage and shipment. The contents appeared as if they had been dumped in quickly. Fatigues were rolled in a ball and his boots still held tablespoons of fine clay dirt in them. Family pictures and a half written letter were tossed in haphazardly together with a bundle of military papers. He reached in and pulled out a set of documents immediately recognizing them as the Secret and Confidential intelligence memos he had been given "in country" and remembered having tied them together so they wouldn't scatter into the wrong hands. Apparently whoever had hastily packed his trunk in

Ham Thuan didn't stop to take notice of this sensitive material that should have been destroyed long ago.

Scott turned to Maryanne. "See this?" He held out the papers.

"And?"

"Somebody could get their ass court martialed for letting this information out of Phoenix personnel hands, and also for shipping it out of country. Looks like they couldn't get me, or anything related to me, out of 'Nam fast enough."

"Well, we were all glad they'd gotten you out of there fast."

Scott wanted to say: *"Yeah, but you wouldn't be if you really knew why."* Instead he said nothing. Clutching the papers, he sat down on the living room floor and cut the twine that bound them together. He spread them out on the carpet, fanning documents that were labeled "Secret" in front of him like they were everyday newspapers. *Viet Cong, History, Current Modus Operandi, and Priority of Targets; VC/NVA Tactics and Operations; Interrogation procedures; Targeting and neutralization of the VC infrastructure.*

Maryanne looked down at floor, now almost completely covered with classified military information. "Shouldn't we notify somebody about this?"

"Maryanne," Scott looked up at her, "I don't want to notify anybody about jack shit. I shut that door a long time ago. This material is still classified and very sensitive." He held up a stapled set of papers labeled "Secret."

"See this? This material is downgraded at 3 years intervals. What it means is that in 3 years from the date it was written its classification will be lowered from 'Secret' to 'Confidential.' Then, in another 3 years, it will be downgraded again, but all of these memos will remain 'hot' for 12 years until they are finally declassified. If I drop this stuff off at the Military Intelligence Field Office in Newark, they will have more questions for me than I want to answer."

Maryanne was only half listening. She was, once again, distracted by his persistent reluctance to talk about his time overseas. This was going to be another one of those days, but she still had to softly probe.

"Scott, have you noticed that recently you're becoming a lot more restless in your sleep again?"

"What does that have to do with what we're talking about, Mair?"

"Nothing directly, I guess, but maybe I can have you meet with a doctor that I know from St. Mary's. You could talk to him if you want and then maybe he can give you something to help you sleep better."

"What am I going to talk to him about? Don't bother. I have *no* interest. I'm fine." Maryanne heard him slam the imaginary door again, but this time it sounded like he bolted it. "Now let me just collect this crap off of the floor and put it away. I'll figure what to do with it later."

He gathered the official papers, carefully slipping them into a brown A&P shopping bag but paused a moment, realizing he was handling these transcripts with some unexplainable reverence. He thought he should be looking to burn these papers, not save them. He ignored the notion and continued placing the remaining pages carefully in the bag. He hesitated again when he saw the interrogation guide. He scanned the questions, which were written in both English and Vietnamese.

What is your name?

What is the name of your unit?

Do you have children? What are their names?

What is your rank?

Give me the names of other members of your unit. These were the light, initial interrogatories meant to gauge the sinew of the captive; the really tough questions would follow.

A coldness filled him as he read down the register. He remembered hearing detainees being grilled at his PIOCC in Phan Thiet. He had been allowed to stay at the Provincial Center that particular night in preparation for an early morning intelligence briefing the next day. The interrogation was being conducted in a low, small building separate from the main unit. The ROK's, who were extremely proficient at extracting information from VC suspects, were heading the heated inquiry. The volume of their angry questions and the agonizing screams of their captives rolled up the walls and through the window of his second floor quarters. By the time dawn finally broke, the

South Koreans, together with the assistance of CORDS interrogators, collected every morsel of useful information from the now silent subjects.

He slid the guide into the bag with the rest of the correspondence and folded the top. He walked to the trunk, looked in and spotted his old canvas and leather jungle boots. Reaching down to grab them, he shuffled with the A&P bag to the hall closet, stuck the boots with the classified material in the far rear corner, then walked back to the trunk and slammed the squeaky top shut. He couldn't imagine ever wanting to lift that lid again.

****

Somewhere in the pre-dawn hours the following morning, and through a haze of sleep, he thought he heard Maryanne crying. He turned over on his side and, through heavily lidded eyes, saw her holding her nose and mouth. Blood trickled from between the tips of her fingers. He bolted up. "Mair!"

"Scccccot," she elongated, "you hit me!" He rolled on to his stomach and held her head by both temples. He wiggled his fingers along the sides of her skull and blinked rapidly. He saw Cur'o'ng's face flash- brighten before him and fade.

"Mair, I'm sorry. I mean, I think that I rolled over and hit you by mistake. I must have caught you with an elbow. I think.

Lemme' see." He let go of her head and rolled across the bed and reached for the light on the night table.

"Scott! Look at you. You're dripping wet." She reached across the mattress and touched the back of his t-shirt. He jumped defensively.

"I wasn't…I don't remember dreaming, Mair. I'm O.K. Come here and let me see your face." She moved closer to the light of the single bulb table lamp.

"Jesus, I don't know how this happened." He held her face lightly in his damp hands, turning it from side to side so he could see the full extent of the damage he had done. "But you don't look too bad. I'll get you a washcloth." The wet t-shirt stuck to his chest, drenched as though he had been hosed down. He peeled it off, dropped it on the tiled bathroom floor and grabbed for a hand towel, soaked it in cold tap water, and ran the wet cloth over his neck and arms; staring into the mirror and straining to remember his dream. He couldn't recall a thing, not even a hint of a scene.

"Scott!" Maryanne's voice had that tinge. He was supposed to be getting *her* the washcloth.

"I must be losin' it," he thought. "Sorry, here you go," he said, placing the damp cool towel on her swelling upper lip. She left it on her face and reached to shut the light off.

"Here, I'll get it, Mair. I'll check on the kids and go down to the living room for the rest of the night. I'm sorry for clocking you."

"Alright. Just let me sleep now." She was both annoyed *with* him and concerned *about* him, and he couldn't blame her for either.

On his way downstairs he peeked in on the kids and listened to their soft breathing. He made his way to the living room tinted by the street lights seeping through the front curtains; didn't bother turning on the room lamps, preferring to be in the dark with the thoughts of his nocturnal behavior. He had no concern about his daytime actions. He had them firmly under control. If he occasionally found himself daydreaming he could always shake himself back to the moment. But at night he lost the grip on his will, and a darker force drove his recollections. He reasoned that his best defense against this nocturnal haunting would be to stay awake as long as he could and then succumb to sleep only when he was weighted down with utter exhaustion. He stared at the brightness of the street lamp and folded his hands in his lap. He now felt secure, balanced and awake where no ghost could rise up; just another civilian at home in America with his family and friends. He looked around at the crisp, steady shadows in the room, smiled serenely and settled into the cushion.

CHAPTER 43

The early morning daylight extinguished the mercury-powered street light and turned his closed eyelids translucent. His head was tossed back against the top ridge of the sofa, his mouth, open and dry. At the tale end of a lingering slumber, clarity was slow to arrive, but when it did he felt a sense of relief knowing he had spent several hours in a dreamless state. He pushed himself off the couch and padded, barefoot, into the kitchen. Maryanne was already there and had started to make toast.

"Morning, Mair. Hey, I think I found the solution for my restlessness at night." She had her back towards him and was measuring out scoops of coffee.

"What's that?" She turned to face him and showed the puffed out lip, compliments of his flying elbow. He recoiled at the look but said nothing. Perhaps he could temper the accident and salve her displeasure with news of his latest discovery.

"Well it's a matter of deductive logic," he said with as much cheeriness as he dared. Maryanne, on the other hand, knew he had failed logic in college, and still had the report card to prove it.

"Don't look at me that way." He knew she remembered the "F" grade, but plunged ahead anyway. "Here's what I think:

Number one: I crunched you in the face when I was sleeping, right?"

"Uh, uh." She agreed.

"Number two: I don't do anything like that when I'm awake — right?" Maryanne turned back to the coffee maker.

"So what's the punch line this time, Scotty?"

"Ergo, if I don't sleep, then you don't get an elbow planted in your innocent snoot. Right? Simple."

"No! That's clinically stupid, and you know it."

"Well, it makes sense to me." He was teasing her again.

She used his restless night's sleep as a reason to, once again, knock on his barred door. "Why don't you have the best of two worlds?"

"How's that?"

"Come with me to St. Mary's and have a little sit down with one of the doctors. These guys really are cool. There'll be no pressure. They can work with you and, like I said, they'll probably give you something that will make you sleep more restfully. You won't have to toss and turn, for what*ever* reason, and I won't have to sleep with a thrashing bear. It's a win/win. What do you think about that?"

"Mair, I only go to see doctors when I hurt. Now, do you see anything about me that's either cut or broken?" They both paused.

"Well do you?" he asked again. He needed to regain the upper hand, and had just played his highest trump. He waited.

"It's not always a visible wound that matters, Scott." He knew where she was trying to direct the conversation, and balked. She was closing in on him. He had to concede some ground.

"Look Mair, I was only kidding about not sleeping being the answer. Staying awake doesn't solve shit. I know that because I experienced it." He winced as the image of his last fatigue- induced act flashed for a micro-second on the screen of his mind.

Her eyes squinted, recognizing the crack in the door. "Oh, really? You never told me that. You had always slept like dead weight before you went to Vietnam. When and where did all of this change?" She knew the answer but wanted to hear it from him.

"A few years ago, maybe."

"Really?" she queried.

"Yeah."

"Where?"

"Across the pond."

"Vietnam?" she asked.

"Yeah"

"Why couldn't you sleep there?" Her foot was now firmly in the crack in the door, and she was determined to use this slight advantage to push against it with all her weight. If he ventured an answer here, she might have her break through. He felt her push, knew what she was going for, sidestepped a direct response and reached for the easiest lie.

"No real reason. It didn't last long anyway. There's really nothing to say about the sleep thing. If there were, you know we would have talked about it by now." He was lying through his teeth, but he reasoned it would be the least painful stance to take for both of them.

In spite of the casual dismissal, Maryanne realized he had just pushed back against the door with a lot of weight. Perhaps this was not the time to force the issue. Nevertheless, she had seen a small chink in his defensiveness, and could not pass up the chance for a parting knock.

"I still think that you should see a doctor and get some sleep medication." Her push had lost some steam and Scott raised his voice.

"That's the third time you said that now. Just leave me alone and I'll be O.K. I don't want to take any damn drugs and I don't want to visit a shrink!"

"Did I say shrink, Scott?"

"Well, that's what you're leading up to, isn't it."

"No, I'm not. I meant a GP. A plain old fashioned General Practitioner."

Scott envisioned his door. She was scratching at the frosted glass panel and it was starting to chip, forcing him to come close to his last refuge: open anger.

"No! Sorry, Mair. I'll get through this myself. Don't worry about me hurting you in the middle of the night. That won't happen again, goddamn it! O.K.?"

"That's not my main concern." Her voice cracked.

"Well *it is* mine, and I won't do it again," he yelled. He broke off, turned and left her with an open mouth and trembling coffee mug in her hand.

Scott felt his wife had tried to pressure him into a dark corner that he didn't want to explore. For his part, he knew that he had just made a declaration to her that he had no game plan on how to deploy. He had been banking on Time to heal his wounds, the passing of seasons as the ultimate balm. But she was growing impatient. For her, time was not an ally; it was a ticking wedge between them.

****

In January 1973 the Paris Peace Accords were signed. Among other provisions, a "cease fire in place" became effective on the twenty-eighth day of the same month, resulting in a large North Vietnamese force being left in place in portions of South Vietnam. In addition, in June of that year Congress passed a cut- off of funds for any combat action in Cambodia or Laos. This, coupled with President Richard Nixon's Watergate crisis, had sent a clear message to the Communist Politburo: the American Congress was getting tired of funding the war, and the country's president was hip deep in distractions. As tons of supplies were being transported down the Ho Chi Minh Trail and into South Vietnam, in blatant disregard to the Paris Accords, American military resistance to these breaches were minimal. Congress, U.S. citizens and the media just wanted to end the bloody conflict at any cost.

Scott had no interest in following these events. He was back in the states, raising a family, building a business and trying to homogenize the secrets he carried with him. In order to achieve peace of mind, he had to concentrate on the present and keep an eye on the future. The way he figured it, he could hump this bad stretch of road by staying focused on his family, friends, business, Yankees, Knicks, and Giants. He believed that cramming his waking hours with these diversions would automatically preclude any time for reflection. There would be no time for looking back.

For the next several weeks, Scott's new outlook appeared to be paying dividends. He couldn't remember having any bad dreams, nor did Maryanne complain about his sleep patterns. He was in control until his telephone rang on the Saturday before the Fourth of July.

Maryanne answered. An unfamiliar voice spoke and asked for Scott.

"I'm sorry, *who's* calling?" She didn't volunteer that he was available.

"One moment, please."

Scott was outside in the street talking to a neighbor. "Scott," she called from the front door, "there's an Ed Rheingold on the phone."

Scott turned abruptly. "Rheingold?" he asked in disbelief. He knew only one person with that name. "*Major* Ed Rheingold?"

"He just said Ed."

Scott started for the front stairs as if he were back in uniform and had just received an order from a superior officer. He paused after a few steps, noticing his knee- jerk reaction. He wasn't sure if he wanted to speak to the major at all, but felt a compulsion to do so. As he reached his front door, he looked back at his friend and neighbor. "Don, I've got to grab the phone. I'll see you later." He brushed past Maryanne, who turned to follow him inside.

"How the hell did he find me?" he asked no one. The phone handset rested on the small wooden kitchen table. He stared at it for a second before picking it up.

"Hello?"

"Hello, Scott." The tone was calm, firm and unmistakable. "This is Ed Rheingold."

"Yes, sir. Yes, major." With this brief exchange, the military pecking order was instantly re-established.

"I'm calling you to strongly suggest that we meet as soon as possible."

Scott's mind tumbled with questions. When Maryanne had first announced Rheingold's name, he thought for a fleeting second that the call might be related to investments, but within an instant he had dismissed that possibility. He tensed and turned so that Maryanne couldn't see his face.

"Meet about what, major?"

"I think that we should speak face to face and not discuss anything over the phone."

"Well, I mean...where are you calling from? Where can we get together?"

"Are you familiar with Union, N.J.?" Rheingold asked.

"Yeah, somewhat."

"Then you know where Rt. 22 is?"

"Yes."

"Are you familiar with a joint called the Alibi Lounge?"

"Maybe, I'm not too sure."

"Well call the place and get directions. Meet me there, this Monday at 2130 hours, sharp."

"Major, I don't know if I can make it." Scott groped for a reason.

"No, Scott, we don't have time to dick around with our schedules. Be there."

"Nine thirty," Scott confirmed.

"Yes, see you then."

Scott heard a metallic click as the phone disconnected. Maryanne, standing behind him, asked, "So what's going on Scotty?"

"Oh, that was a buddy of mine from the Army. He, uh, he wants to talk to me about opening an account. He's inherited some money and wants to invest it. He hunted me down. Well, actually he found out that I worked with Sherman Hammitt and he wants to get together next Monday night. Somebody told him I work with a securities firm, so he called me. How do you like that, I'm getting referrals." It was a thin story, but being business related, he thought he could skip by.

"Congratulations. Who referred you?"

"Oh, I don't know yet. He didn't say."

"Does he live in Jersey?"

"Who?"

"The guy who just called."

"I don't know that either. I'll get all the details in a few days."

She continued to look into his eyes until he diverted his glance. She nodded her head slowly. "Interesting. Very interesting, Scott." Maryanne never had any reason to disbelieve her husband, but by now felt unsettled after this curt and cryptic phone call. She sensed that she had just heard a hastily concocted fabrication, and allowed him to believe that she'd bought it.

CHAPTER 44

The Alibi Lounge could not have been more aptly named. Local wise guys dressed in leisure suits and heavy jewelry mixed with hustlers looking for a mark and white-collar businessmen looking to hide from their bosses. Cheaters inevitably found their way to a quiet table before heading out to the plethora of hourly rate motels that lined the East - West highway that started near Newark Airport and ended in Pennsylvania. Either by choice or subconscious design the most often played song on the Sebring juke box was Billy Paul's "Me and Mrs. Jones."

On the night that he was to reunite with his former superior officer Scott pushed the food around on his dinner plate but ate little. "Mair, I'm going to jump in the shower now and get changed. I don't want to be late for this appointment. Do you need me to do anything with the kids?"

"No. I'm just going to wash them and put them to bed. They were both cranky today and I think we all need a break from each other. What time do you think you'll be home?"

Scott had no idea what turns his meeting with Rheingold would take but proffered a guess anyway. "Well maybe sometime after midnight. We're meeting at nine-thirty and I really don't know what he wants to talk about. I do remember, though, that he wasn't one for long winded conversations."

"O.K. then. Just don't wake me up when you get home unless something really important comes up. Otherwise, I'll talk to you in the morning."

Scott agreed and went upstairs to get ready. Within 45 minutes he was easing his Mercury out of the narrow driveway and on to Stoneacre Drive. The jacket to his gray pinstriped suit hung neatly on the back hook. Before accelerating away from the house, he stopped and looked down at his shoes to see if they were shined. This was something he hadn't deliberately done since he left the military, but on this night it seemed like a requisite.

He left his house an hour before the scheduled encounter. A light breeze stirred and lifted the scents of the summer evening through the open windows of his car. Tangerine-colored wisps of clouds settled in the western sky as he drove in silence through Livingston, down South Orange Avenue, into Maplewood and finally into Union where he wove his way to the parking lot and the entrance to the Alibi.

Before locking the car he put his suit jacket on, straightened his tie, and bent to check his reflection in the door window. He noticed his briefcase on the back seat recognizing this business tool wouldn't be needed tonight, but still couldn't figure out why Rheingold had showed up in his life once again, and why he was so anxious to meet with him.

At the front door, he got caught in a gaggle of patrons entering and leaving. The ones coming out, looking rumpled, disoriented, and had clearly overstayed "happy hour." The ones going in were decked out in their club- clothes, and ready to make their night moves.

Scott was fifteen minutes early and decided to go right to the bar. The suggestion of dirty carpet and English Leather cologne wafted over him in various degrees of intensity as he made his way through the changing shift of customers. Plopping his elbows on the stuffed vinyl bar rail, he looked around at the variety of lounge lizards starting to flick their tongues at the entering bevy of female prey. He was sure that, in true chameleon style, they were ready to change their colors and stories to meet any circumstance. Whatever it took to get laid. He didn't see the bartender slide up to him.

"What'll you have?" he smiled beneath a pencil thin mustache that made him look like a condescending David Niven.

Scott wanted to say; *"I'll have a band-aid so I can slap it over that Hollywood hair lip you're sporting."* Instead he asked for a beer. "Pabst."

"Sorry, no Pabst."

"You, too?"

"Me, too, what?" A phony, slick smile was plastered on his face.

"You don't carry Pabst either?"

"Nope. Never have."

"Got gin?" He asked sarcastically.

"Why, yes we do."

"Then give me a White Satin and tonic."

Scott was about to check the time on his watch when he locked eyes with the major, looking exactly as Scott would have pictured him in civilian clothes. He wore a cream- colored oxford button -down shirt, navy blue pants and mahogany colored loafers. The shirt was starched tight and the alignment between the row of buttons and his belt, the "gig line" in military parlance, was perfect. His hair was still short and he didn't look a day older or a pound softer.

He walked over to the former lieutenant and extended his hand. "How are you, Scott?" His handshake was firm, almost warm, and Scott thought for a second that he might really want to know how he was.

"I'm fine, major. I'm O.K., How about you?"

"Good — things are good." They released their grip and turned to face forward. They saw themselves eyeing each other though the mirror behind the bar. Rheingold turned. "Let me grab a drink and we'll sit down and talk."

Rheingold ordered a Glenlivit on the rocks and pointed to a small, round table that was perfect for their conversation. Scott spoke first and dispensed with any pleasantries. "How did you find me, major?" Rheingold was equally direct. "Think about it. Your MOS was 9666, Intelligence Research Officer—counter intelligence agent to us. In addition, you were a combat advisor, in the Phoenix program, with access to classified information about a deliberate Vietcong "neutralization" effort that tens of millions of Americans never even knew existed. With that knowledge, do you think that the U.S. Intelligence community would just let you drift back into civilian life without keeping tabs on you?"

Scott didn't reply, gulped his drink, and sat back in the contoured padded chair. Rheingold shifted his glass to his left hand, reaching into his pants pocket to remove a pack of Camels. He pulled one out with his lips and tossed the pack down next to his drink.

"I didn't know you smoked, sir."

"I started when I came back. I was 31 years old when I started."

"No peer pressure, huh?"

"Nope."

"Great choice, major."

"So when did you get back to the World?" Scott asked.

"September '69. I was rotated out of the field shortly after your replacement reported to our DIOCC. I had already done my 6 months in the bush so this assignment was SOP."

Scott leaned closer. "It didn't have anything to do with me, or Cur'o'ng?"

"No. Nothing was ever mentioned after I filed the report concerning the circumstances surrounding your evacuation." Scott relaxed a little, knew he still hadn't heard the whole story, but getting over this first hurdle mattered.

"So what are you doing now, major?"

"I'm still in."

Scott thought for a second. "Then you gotta' be close to a Light Bird now, right?"

"You're right. I'm a recent Lieutenant Colonel."

"Why didn't you say so? Here I am, still calling you major."

"It doesn't matter here."

"So where you stationed?"

"Belvoir."

"Doing what?"

Rheingold gave Scott a look of dismissal. The intelligence officer in Scott immediately remembered that no one in MI would ever appreciate that question, nor would he answer it, unless there was an absolute need to know. Rheingold lit another cigarette and exhaled slowly. He placed it in the ashtray and reached for his single malt, positioning himself more upright in the naugahyde lounge chair. His steel blue eyes focused on Scott.

"Lieutenant, we may have a problem."

Scott drained whatever gin remained in his glass and he signaled to the waitress for another one. Rheingold had his undivided attention. "Several years ago, August 1970 to be exact, The New York Times published a comprehensive exposé on the Phung Hoang program. Much to the displeasure of the military and civilian intelligence agencies, the report was both accurate and revealing. Did you read it?" Scott shook his head "no." "Well, it didn't tell *us* anything that *we* didn't already know, but it sure laid it out in vivid color to Main St., USA. The official military response was a stone- wall of counter accusations, misinformation, and lies.

"In an attempt to seal any further leaks, the Joint Chiefs of Staff tacitly ordered a review of any past activities within the Phoenix Program that might become fodder for future public exposure. Despite this subtle directive, the intelligence community was slow to conduct an investigation on itself; there were too many ghosts in too many closets. The study limped along until June 1971 when the New York Times started to print the Pentagon Papers. Robert McNamara had ordered the papers when he was Secretary of Defense, as an outline for a documentary history of the involvement of the United States in the Vietnam conflict. These papers ultimately established that the Johnson Administration had methodically lied and obfuscated facts, both to Congress and the citizenry, concerning the depth and breadth of our embroilment in 'Nam. Our Government went ballistic and tried to stop the presses but lost the final Supreme Court decision against a restraint." He stopped and took a sip. Scott listened intently to a seemingly well- rehearsed dissertation, but couldn't understand why he was getting a political history lesson until the Colonel spoke again.

"This is when the investigation involving *us* started picking up steam."

Scott felt his heart pounding and heard himself swallow. "Us? You mean everyone in the Program or you and me specifically?"

"Both."

"Good Christ," Scott mumbled. "So where does everything stand now?"

"Right now it's one big cluster fuck. Everyone is in 'cover your ass' mode. There's been pressure to disclose people's names and events to Congress before the press does it first. The Congressional investigators seem to be satisfied, at this point, to accept a number of token indiscretions for public scrutiny. The military would be more than happy to name names in the hope of avoiding deeper probes."

"So where do we come in?"

"We may be one of the tokens."

"Shit!" Scott spit, "How did you find this out, and yes, I do have a 'need to know'."

"General Larson. You may remember him as Colonel Larson in Japan."

"I remember him well. He said that he had a lot of respect for you and that you were friends."

"We still are. The focus is on us because we represent just the right amount of foul play. Enough to be a scandal, but nothing like a large- scale massacre of civilians. Just one murder of a Viet civilian and a small cover up, conducted with the cooperation, if not outright blessing, of the Phoenix

Program. This way the press can get their pound of flesh and the politicians can work the story to their benefit. We very well could be the perfect sacrificial lambs."

"Christ, maj…Colonel, he was no fuckin' innocent fuckin' civilian. You goddam know he was 100% Cong."

"It doesn't matter what the truth is, Scott; the fact is that on the night you killed him he was still considered an American ally and nothing has ever been proven otherwise."

"Motha' fucker, Rheingold!" Scott's voice rose in volume but was absorbed by the noise of the crowd. "I've got a family, a job and bills to pay. No cock sucker is going to drag me back to account for anything. That shit's over. I'm back home. It's fuckin' over." Scott pushed his chair away from the table, but before he could stand Rheingold barked a command.

"Get back here!"

Scott slid back to the table, but not to his former intimate position. He sat ramrod erect and looked Rheingold coldly in the eyes. "What can we do to make this go away?"

"Move the hell closer so I can talk to you," Rheingold said. Scott leaned in again, elbows on the tabletop but his back still stiff.

"It's my belief that what they're looking for is *proof* of…or any examples of — irregularities, things that can be gleaned from doctored records and eye witness accounts. According to Larson the personnel who have been identified and questioned about your actions that last night in Ham Thuan have almost universally developed permanent amnesia. Others have offered up recollections that were sketchy at best."

"That's tough to believe," Scott said, "you know our techniques can be drop dead effective. I know only a handful of guys who wouldn't roll over on somebody when their balls were squeezed."

"Well, you may now have others you could add to your list. Nobody sees the truths of combat like an enlisted man and, don't forget, the troops laying the commo wire with you that night were also with you during the M-79 incident and the ambush. Maybe they agreed with what you did to Cur'o'ng."

"How do you know they didn't rat me out?"

"I don't know for sure. All I've been told is that the guys they'd recently grilled hadn't told them shit, but the investigation is still ongoing." A waitress in high heels and a mini skirt brought four drinks to the two couples sitting at the next table. Rheingold turned around and tapped her on the thigh.

"Glenlivit on the rocks, when you're ready."

"I'm ready" she smiled. "And you?" she looked at Scott.

"Yeah, sure. Burnett's White Satin and quinine water...you know, tonic." He still somehow managed to joke, "I'm still trying to ward off malaria." The waitress winked like she understood what he was talking about.

The Colonel continued. "There's another part of this inquiry that is of particular concern to me."

"And that is...?" Scott asked. He was starting to feel less agitated. It was probably the Burnett effect.

"You were ushered out of the country with bogus medical reports orchestrated by me. I was looking to cover both of our asses. The m.o. wasn't original. It was probably used numerous times before. Everybody understood the deal, and I met with no resistance and no questions." He paused when Scott signaled the waitress' return. Scott pulled out a ten, deposited it on her tray and waved her off when she began to make change. Rheingold sat back, clutching his fresh drink. He had held his thought until the waitress was out of earshot, but now continued.

"Since we have *both* been identified as potential sacrificial lambs, you should know that you might be called in for a chat. Likewise, I might be ordered to discuss what I remember about you."

Scott interrupted before the officer could continue. "So what are you worried about?"

"I just want to make sure that we're on the same page."

"O.K. Go on."

"A cover up, and the series of lies that follow, are usually more offensive in the eyes of the public than the act itself. You just mentioned how guys could react when their nuts are in a vice and how effective our interrogation techniques are, right?"

"Yeah...still, so what?" Scott prompted.

"In theory, and I'm not saying you would do this, but theoretically you could blow the whistle on me and walk out clean."

"What? And admit that I killed a VC scum bag who was posing as a civilian ally?"

"You don't have to do that."

"What do you mean?"

"You don't have to indict yourself, but you still could indict the Phoenix mission and include me and a group of others."

"Slow down, Colonel. First of all you saved my ass, right?"

"I removed you from the scene, therefore the cover-up."

"I understand that. You got me out to save both of our asses. But to do this, you put your own cheeks on the line, right?"

"I took a calculated risk."

Scott tapped his quickly drained glass. The waitress noticed and walked over. "Yeah, we're ready."

"Two?"

She looked at Rheingold throwing down the last of his second Glenlivit, as he nodded to her, "Yep."

"So when do you think I'll be called in for a talk?" Scott asked.

"Well, that's just it. I don't even know for sure if you will."

"So what the fuck are we doing here?"

"You ought to know by now how we operate, Scott. The heat's on and we're all suspect. General Larson gave me a big heads up. That's all. I wanted to meet with you, like Larson had met with me, and warn you of the possibilities."

"Do you think that I'll...that I would...somehow give you up?"

"Well I never *did* get to know you all that well, so I could never be too sure." Scott's next question caught Rheingold off-guard. "Where did you grow up, Colonel?"

"California, why?"

Without answering, Scott asked "Did you have close friends in your neighborhood?"

"Of course."

"Did you ever, like, squeal on them to the cops or to a teacher or to a rival gang? Anything like that?"

"No. Not that I can remember."

"Not that you can remember? To me, that says *maybe.* Where I come from, *sir*, that's an automatic 'yes or no.'"

"What are you getting at, Scott?"

"What I'm getting at is that you just busted back into my life to tell me that I might need to cover for you, but in the next breath you also tell me that you don't trust me. That's got to make me wonder about *you*, Colonel. We're not playing for chump change here. So the way I see it is that the safest thing we can do is to stick to our story as it existed from the day I got lifted out."

Rheingold didn't like the tone of insubordination in Scott's words, but he also realized that he was dealing with a civilian now, not a junior officer in the Army.

"You're right," Rheingold leaned forward, "and here's what our story is going to be."

****

They talked for 45 minutes more, concluding their four-drink conversation in the Alibi's parking lot. The Colonel was driving a gray, generic brand, four-door rental and dangled the key chain around his index finger twirling the "We Try Harder" slogan.

"So Let's go over this one more time. The original, and most plausible cover reason for your evacuation, was an allergy that severely limited your vision. You had irritated scar tissue in both corners of your eyes from your operation and we had a physical indication that your vision was not normal.

"Precautionary measures were being taken. The VC had hit us during Tet the same time the year before, and there was a push to clear field hospitals for troops that might be injured if another Tet offensive had been launched. So, the fact that you were flown from the 8th Field Hospital to Japan wasn't unusual, considering the relatively minor status of your condition, because bed space in field hospitals needed to be cleared.

410

Let's just stick to that storyline and hope that nobody digs any deeper."

"And what if they do?" Scott asked.

"I don't know what will happen. I guess it depends on how strongly someone wants to fry us and make headlines for himself."

The consequences were left wide open as they stood next to each other in silence. Scott reached for the door handle of his car. Despite Rheingold's intrusion back into his life *again,* he felt this reappearance might now help him to tie down some dangling ends.

"Hey, Colonel," Scott didn't move to open the car door, "do you remember a little girl back there who lived with us?"

"A little girl?"

"Yeah, about 4 years old, an orphan?" Rheingold paused, squinting for recollection.

"Ohhh, yes, yes I do," he finally answered. "Members of your detail that night reported you screamed Cur'o'ng had been responsible for her missing." Scott had no memory of voicing that, but years later, still believed it was true.

"So was he responsible?"

"Scott, that kid was never missing..."

"Mary," Scott interrupted, "Mary was her name."

"O.K., Mary. Mary wasn't missing, and was still in our compound when you attacked your interpreter; you were too mentally strung out to even notice."

411

"Well, what happened to her?"

"Hey, I wasn't running a missing children's bureau over there, but I do remember, shortly after you left, she was found in a DIOCC in Mui Ne."

"Mui Ne? A Lieutenant Buono was stationed there. I met him in Vung Tau and we got friendly real fast."

"You're right. He and his CO told me the same thing when they contacted me after finding the kid carrying a picture of you and a woman standing in a swimming pool. Buono recognized you from Phoenix orientation and was concerned that the little bastard might be showing your face around Viet Cong social circles and telling them anything they could coax from her." Scott smiled when he realized why he had never been able to locate that snapshot and how determined she was, for whatever reason, to get that picture.

"So what happened after that?"

"As far as I know she remained with Buono right up until the night the DIOCC took some heavy shelling and ultimately had its perimeter breached." Rheingold anticipated Scott's next question and continued. "Shortly after the assault I saw Lt. Buono's CO at a CORDS briefing up at Province level. He told me the night that Charlie broke the perimeter, things got really dicey; a lot of close in stuff, I mean, M7's, machetes, shovels, whatever they could grab. Lt. Buono's actions and bravery were instrumental in preventing the compound from being completely overrun. In light of his efforts he was awarded the Silver Star — posthumously."

Scott stood motionless with his hands in his pants pockets, absorbing what he had just heard. He envisioned Rudy's actions and reflected again on his own. Rheingold turned to step toward his car when Scott's next comment made him stop and turn around.

"Colonel, ya' know, I think that if I had to do it again I'd probably do it the same way. I saw Cur'o'ng as a threat to all of us." Rheingold moved toward Scott and placed one hand on his shoulder.

"Listen to me. We were *all* participants in an experimental laboratory in guerilla warfare. None of us really had any meaningful references; it was virtually all new to us and a work in progress. Given the same set of circumstances, I believe a significant number of men would have done the same thing you had done."

Scott wanted to say "thanks" but didn't. "Well, I'm just waiting for the time when I stop thinking about it so much." The Colonel reached out and tapped him slowly on the chest. He paraphrased the same advice he had given the young officer in the aftermath of the ambush.

"It can't happen until you finally digest it and let it out like last night's chow, kid."

CHAPTER 45

The 45-minute ride back to Livingston seemed to take only seconds as he replayed the conversation with Rheingold and rehashed what he would tell Maryanne about the possible investigation. He slapped the steering wheel and then slapped the vinyl armrest.

"Nothing!" he said aloud, "I'm telling her nothing."

The house was dark except for a night- light that cast a soft golden glow in the kitchen. He took off his shoes in the small front hallway and walked barefoot across the rug. Opening the refrigerator door, he squinted into the white light and poked around the shelves. He settled for a large round mozzarella and a stick of pepperoni. He cut a piece of the soft cheese. The knife slid through the soft fresh hunk, milk oozed out and the blade made a squeaky sound as it sliced.

"Now *that's* fresh!" He wrapped the slice of cheese around a chunk of pepperoni and shoved it into his mouth. He was slicing a second piece when he heard Maryanne's footsteps squeak down the stairs. "So how'd it go tonight?" She yawned.

"Can't sleep, Mair?"

"I *was* asleep until I heard the car pull in. So how *did* it go," she asked again.

"Just like I told you. He had heard that I was a stockbroker and called on me for some advice."

"Does he live around here?"

"No, he lives in South Jersey, just outside of Philly."

"Is he still in the Army?"

"Nope. He owns a car dealership now. So, then," he said as he cut another slab of cheese, "how were the kids?" Maryanne felt a visceral uneasiness at Scott's change of topics.

"They were fine," she yawned again.

"Did he open an account with you?"

"Not yet. I've got to get more info from him."

"When do you plan to see him again?"

"Next week."

"Where?"

"He's going to call me."

Maryanne took a deep breath and paused, "Do you think that he will?"

"Maybe."

"Do you have a number where you could call him?"

"Yeah, I might do that if I don't hear from him." Another lie.

She sliced the mozzarella and flipped it on the wooden cutting board without eating it. "I'm going back upstairs to bed."

"O.K. I'll be up in a minute."

She looked at him and smirked.

Scott leaned against the refrigerator door and wondered what the next call from his military past would bring.

****

The neighborhood 4th of July celebration two days later helped to ease his unspoken worry. Beer and softball took his mind off of the looming threat. The neighbors enjoyed spending time together, for a simple cup of coffee or a full-blown block party; it didn't matter. Scott often thought that they couldn't have handpicked a better bunch of people to live around. For the moment, at least, he was comfortably lost in the camaraderie.

"Hey, Pat, go get your Dress Blues." Don O'Patrick called to his buddy Pat Horan, who lived next door to him. Aside from being neighbors, Pat and Don shared the bond of being former Marines who had served their hitches in the relative peacetime between Korea and Vietnam.

The ballgame was done and everyone was heading back to the Horan's backyard, where a barbeque was planned before they all went to see the fireworks later that evening. Don still kept in shape and was always within striking distance of his fighting weight. At 6'3" he still had a chiseled chin that bore a resemblance to a uniformed soldier on a recruiting poster. For every extra pound that Don avoided, Pat seemed to take on two. It had, therefore, become a tradition for Pat to try on his Marine formals each 4th of July, in order to see how much weight he'd put on since the previous year.

Several of the men stood near the iced beer keg in the backyard and made bets. Wes pointed to Pat who was struggling to fit into his jacket. "I say he can't close the front past his tits." Mike, a Newark fireman and a cagey bettor, wouldn't bite. "He couldn't do that last year. Get serious." All speculation was cancelled when Pat failed at the attempt, holding his arms out like the rigid limbs of a scarecrow.

"At least 20 more since last year," Mike noted. Don leaned against a tree in the corner of the yard and laughed. "Hey, Horan, take it off, button it up to the collar and frame it. It's history." Mike helped Pat wrestle free of the tourniquet sleeves, shook it out and handed it to him. "Leave it on the hanger, man. You'll *never* fit into this again." Mike said. Pat huffed, laughed and reached for a handful of potato chips and a beer.

Scott watched the proceedings, amused by the neighborly interactions, but felt strangely distanced from it. Just as he reached for a handful of pretzels, he heard the whumping of helicopter blades and froze in mid-reach. He looked up through the trees and saw the police chopper moving quickly toward the West. Even though he was four years removed from Vietnam, the sound of choppers always drew his attention, and inevitably he would ask himself, as they flew out of sight, what he expected to see.

The activity of the afternoon gave way to the interlude of dusk, introducing a new moon and a raven-colored night sky. The fireworks started on schedule at the grassy oval in front of the high school but the rockets and colorful bursts seemed brighter and closer this year; the explosions louder. Scott flinched and dropped slowly to his knees on the blanket that Maryanne had placed on the thick grass. He reached out for Lizzie, drawing her closer and pulling her down until they both laid flat on their stomachs. She giggled and looked at her father's face. His eyes were closed as he pulled her in tighter, covering her from the noise and light above, and could have sworn he smelled the combination of lubricating oil and burnt powder from the ejection port of an M-16.

CHAPTER 46

The holiday passed and the second week of July began with 90° temperatures and stick-to-your-skin humidity. Scott had not been contacted by Rheingold or anybody else in the Government.

Richard Nixon's Watergate turmoil began to dominate the headlines as John Dean, Counsel to the President, blew the whistle on his boss. In response to this, Nixon refused to testify before The Senate Committee and would not allow public disclosure of Presidential Documents. He drew a line in the sand and struggled to keep the White House team all on the same page. It was a monumental battle with Nixon constantly fighting a rear guard action all the while continuing to loose supporters by the droves.

Scott, like the rest of the nation, followed the political dénouement in the media. On Friday morning, July 13th, he had just completed reading the latest Watergate news in the Newark Star Ledger. Flipping through the back pages, he saw a small article with the headline: "**Fire Destroys Military Records**."

The AP news item described a fire of undetermined origin had raged through the 6th floor of The Records Center in St. Louis. It reported an initial estimate of tens of millions of individual personnel records that had probably been destroyed.

A full damage assessment couldn't yet be made since the inferno was still not under control. Scott dropped the paper, blinked through the kitchen window and stared at their neighbor's house. Maryanne walked into the kitchen and saw his trance. "Mission control to Scott. Hello out there." He unraveled his thoughts and answered. "Hi, Mair. Hey! I'm really late for work. Sorry I gotta' jump."

Throughout the rest of the day, and between business calls, Scott racked his brain to figure out how to get in touch with Rheingold. He called the main number listed for Ft. Belvoir, Virginia, but was told that there was no Lt. Col. Rheingold stationed there. He had a lot of questions about the fire. It could have burnt the altered personnel and medical records that might serve to indict both of them. His only contact for clarification was Rheingold, and the Colonel appeared to be stateside MIA. Either he had lied about working at Belvoir, or somebody had been ordered to lie for him. Either way, Scott was at a dead end.

For the first time since he had come home, Scott felt an overpowering need to spill his guts. He wanted to tell everything, and he needed to get feedback from somebody. Jack Noble was the perfect sounding board. He and Scott were co-workers at Sherman, Hammitt, and good friends. They played racquetball with each other at the Newark "Y" and often frequented The Roost Restaurant around the corner on Fulton Street.

Scott knew Jack had been in Saigon with the 25th Infantry Division during the 1968 Tet offensive and that he was involved in the defense of the Tan Son Nhut airfield. But that's all he knew. No elaborations and nothing more. For his part, Jack knew that Scott had been a combat advisor in 1969 attached to something called "Phoenix," and that's all he knew about Scott's time. Scott walked over to Jack's desk as he was on the phone and pitching a stock called RetroCare.

"I know the principals at the company personally...What? No, I don't guarantee it, but if you'll commit to 500 shares today you'll be thanking me next month. O.K.? Five hundred at the market to buy, O.K."? He hung up and turned to Scott.

"Done."

"That was too easy. You should have pushed for five thousand," Scott said.

"I couldn't."

"Why not?"

"Not enough money there. I know. She's my sister."

"Your sister?" Scott laughed.

"Yeah, I like to practice on her when I'm slow. She's always good for a ticket."

Scott bent down to Jack and in a hushed tone said, "How does the Roost sound after work? I have something that I want to bounce off of you."

Jack looked up. "Sounds serious."

"No —well not really, but maybe. Anyway, I think I could use your opinion."

"No problem."

In a quiet back booth at The Roost that evening Scott talked for an hour, non-stop, and didn't skip a single detail. When he finally concluded, Jack exhaled a long, deep breath.

"So, you think the fire was arson?"

"I think it could be one way to cover up any ongoing Phoenix investigation. It may be that there were guys in the Nixon administration who were compliant in allowing the Program to function as it did. Who knows where those tentacles reached? I do know that Nixon has got his plate full dealing with this Watergate shit, and clearly doesn't need another investigation probing under well hidden rocks."

Although Jack couldn't help him with any answers, just talking to him had allowed Scott to lighten his load of memories.

Days passed, and Scott jumped every time the phone sounded at home. At work when it rang, he held his breath until his secretary, Rita, announced who was calling. He scoured the daily newspapers in an attempt to find an update on the fire but news had so thoroughly vanished it was if it had never happened; until one morning in the middle of an August heat wave.

Scott had showered, dressed and poured himself a large glass of tomato juice before opening the Star Ledger to the "below the fold" headline. It read: **"Eighty percent of military records destroyed."**

Needing details, he perused every sentence of the account. He looked for some bit of information that would at least intimate that the ongoing investigation was now dead in the water. Instead, he discovered just the opposite. Eighty – percent of the documents that had been destroyed belonged to military personnel who had been discharged from active duty between November 1912 and January 1960. His heart dropped when he realized that *his* personnel and medical records might not have been involved in the fire. He folded the newspaper, quickly left the house, and hurried to work. He needed to see Jack Noble.

Jack heard Scott's heavy footsteps thumping across the thin office carpet and looked up from his morning paperwork. He saw that Scott looked worried as he sat down in the single chair next to his desk. Scott laid the paper in front of him.

"Just read that, Jack." When he finished, he looked up at Scott and shook his head. "I can't believe *they* could fuck up like that."

"Maybe it wasn't arson," Jack suggested. "Maybe it *was* just an innocent fire. It *could* have been pure coincidence. From what you've told me these spy- guys play for keeps. If they're looking to destroy evidence they ain't gonna' to do it half-assed. That's my take on it."

"But I can't imagine them developing a better cover story than this fire. It could have been the perfect set up," Scott said.

"Maybe they'll squash the investigation another way. You know, bribe somebody, kill somebody."

"Or, maybe my paperwork was part of the other twenty-per cent that got destroyed," Scott hoped.

"Yeah, maybe, who the shit knows, you can't read too many details into this crap, it just leads to more speculation."

"Yeah, you're right, but if Rheingold and I are to be the sacrificial lambs, then I'll never be able to stop looking over my shoulder; not until the day I *know for sure* that the investigation has been shit-canned."

CHAPTER 47

1980

Scott downshifted his 1979 BMW 320i around the corner and on to Stoneacre Drive. He had had it hand washed and polished while he was at work, and the subtle orange and cream pinstripe now brightly accented the chocolate brown body.

Lizzie saw her father's car swing into the driveway and pumped her bike pedals as fast as her 9 year old legs could push. She dropped the bicycle on the lawn and ran toward him.

"Hi, Daddy," she screamed, as he raised her lithe body up for a kiss.

"Hey, you're getting heavy, what did you eat today?"

"Lentil soup," she said.

"With bread?"

"Yep."

"I can feel it." He tickled at the little nothing of a belly and she giggled in a high- pitched squeal.

"Stop it Daddy, you can't feel the lentils."

"Oh, but I *can* feel the bread," he teased. "Where's Mom?"

"She's with Mike and Maggie in the schoolyard. Let's go!"

Within seconds of his changing into shorts and flip flops, she was leading him through the narrow walkway between the houses that led to the baseball field across the street.

"There they are!" she pointed. Mike was tossing a baseball back and forth with his son, Darrin, and Joey. Lizzie rushed on the field to play but lacked both a glove and ability. Her older brother taunted her.

"Elizabeth," he shouted, "why don't you learn to play another sport. Leave us alone." She bristled. "Joey, why don't you learn to ice skate like me? How about that?" Standing only 4'3", she held her ground pretty well.

"I don't want to get up to skate at 5 o'clock in the morning. That's why." Mike hit a ground ball that skipped through Joey's legs before he had the time to drop his glove and field it.

"Ha-Ha! You don't practice enough." It was her turn to taunt. She continued to heckle him as she ran to the safety of her mother, who was gabbing with her neighbor, Maggie.

Scott waved to Mike, who continued hitting baseballs to Joey and Darrin, and strolled toward the ladies. Within minutes it was obvious that Scott was not interested in joining their conversation and Maryanne made a mental note of his distraction.

"I'm going back to the house," he said. "Why don't you grab Lizzie and come on along." Maryanne concluded her chat with Maggie, called for Joey to end his game and come home to wash up for dinner. Slipping an arm into Scott's, she took

Lizzie by the hand and the three of them started back toward the house. They had walked only a few yards when Joey called for them to wait for him. Scott continued walking with Lizzie, and Maryanne paused for their son. When he ran in front of her she gave him a moment to catch his breath and reached out to hold his hand. He recoiled from the gesture, and his embarrassment was obvious.

"*Mom!* He protested, "I'm almost 11 years old."

"So that means you can't hold your mother's hand anymore?"

"Are you kidding me?" The question was asked in a tone of voice indicating his mother really didn't get the big picture. "If any of my friends see this they'll all bust on me. I can't take that chance." She put her arm around his shoulders and gave him a hug. "Is that O.K. to do?"

"O.K., but make it quick someone might be watching."

"God forbid." A wistful smile crossed her face as she thought of a time not so long ago when he would unashamedly crawl onto her lap and ask her to read "The Cat in the Hat."

Scott and Lizzie were first to arrive on the small stoop that led to the front door. He pushed his Yankee cap back on his head and watched the other half of his family cross Stoneacre and come to the house. Inside, the kids bounded up the stairs and headed for the small bedrooms that they were rapidly outgrowing. Scott stopped Maryanne at the doorway.

"Mair, I've been thinking about something we've discussed, on and off, in the past few months. See if you don't agree with me. We both know that this is a great neighborhood with super neighbors, right?"

The answer was obvious and she didn't reply. He continued. "The only problem is that Lizzie's outgrowing her bedroom and we can't expand it. We don't have an extra bedroom and when your parents visit they have to sleep on the pull out couch. We only have one bathroom and that gets crowded at times. When we have parties it's a good thing the guys don't mind taking a leak in the bushes."

Maryanne was not warming up to this discussion. Scott knew she would balk at the thought of moving away from Livingston, but he had anticipated her objection and had a ready response.

"But Mair, I don't think we would even have to move out of town. We can still stay local. We'll just move to a bigger house. What do you say we call a realtor and take a look around?" Maryanne recognized that a larger house would probably serve her family better, but was reluctant to pull up any roots.

"And what about money?" she asked.

"Well, we have about $23,000 left on the mortgage and the house is worth about $80,000. So we can put down about $55 or $60 thousand on the new one."

"Could we use any of your veteran benefits to help us?"

He waved his hand, dismissing anything that might touch on his active duty time. Deep down, however, he *had* thought about exploring his VA benefits as a means of finally determining what his military records actually said, but had never taken any action that might disturb the status quo. In all the years since his last meeting with Rheingold, he never felt sure that his actions in Ham Thuan would not resurface. Periodically he had the same dream where he would stand at the opening of a large, pitch-black cave and yell into the darkness for something to come out and fight. The demon was still there, still hiding.

"No, Mair, we'll get a conventional loan. I'm sure we'll qualify."

"But it can't hurt to call the VA, can it?"

"No, no. I'd rather just let a sleeping killer lie." She looked confused at the analogy but it was out of his mouth before he could recall it.

"Sooo, then…why don't *you* call a realtor tomorrow and I'll check the papers to see what's for sale," he said.

"Alright, but I don't want to rush into anything, Scott, O.K.? Promise me?" She knew that once he caught on to the energy of an idea, everything had to be done yesterday. For her part, she wasn't about to settle on a new nest without a lot of prodding and poking, touching and feeling, and she wanted to make sure that she would have that luxury.

"O.K. I promise."

****

The next morning Scott put Rita's bagel with cream cheese and her standard coffee, light with extra sugar, on her desk and grabbed the doorknob to his office.

"Handle the calls for an hour." Rita knew which clients to forward to Scott and which ones to service herself.

"Got it, Scotty." She didn't even glance up from her morning paper.

He closed the door behind him and swiveled his chair around to the window that overlooked Military Park and south down Broad Street. "Fuck it" he thought. "I'll call 'em." He dialed information and asked for the number of Veterans Administration Hospital in East Orange. He didn't know where else to start. A young female voice answered.

"Yeah, I want to find out about getting a VA loan for a home purchase. Can you help me out?" He was intentionally brief and hoped to get an answer without having to give his name.

"What you'll have to do is go to a VA location, fill out the required forms and attach a copy of your DD Form 214. Your application will then be reviewed, and you will be notified in 4 to 6 weeks."

"DD Form 214? I really don't remember the last time I saw it. What if I can't find it?"

"Well, you would need the form to complete the paperwork. Without it, you won't be able to take advantage of any VA benefits. If you can't locate it, I would suggest that you contact The Personnel Records Center in St. Louis. They should have it on file." She paused. "Were you discharged *after* 1960?"

"Yes, I was."

"Then your records should not have been destroyed in that fire several years back." She reiterated her suggestion. "Give them a call, if you can't find your Form 214, I'm sure they can help you out."

"You know, I just might do that. Thanks for the help."

He hung up and his mind now raced again with speculation about what his personnel records contained on his time in Vietnam. On occasions in the past when he had been at this point of anxious curiosity, he had stopped and not pressed any further; letting no news be good news. But today, through a pounding heart and dry mouth, he didn't dismiss the ruminations. He now had *two* reasons to find out what his records said, but getting the VA loan was a distant second. He dialed the operator, got the area code for St. Louis, called St. Louis information and asked for the number of the Personnel Records Center. After getting bounced around through several departments, he was finally connected to National Archives.

"Tom Gorman," the voice at the other end of the line said.

"Hi, Tom. My name is Scott Regan. I'd like to know if you could help me out."

"I'll do my best."

"I'm looking to get a VA loan and I don't have my DD Form 214. Is there a way that I can get a copy of it? I was told by my local VA administrator that St. Louis would have all of my records."

"I'll take a look for you, lieutenant. It'll take some time. All our records are stored on paper and in folders. Do you have a number where I can call you?"

"Lieutenant?" Scott thought. *"How the hell did he know I was a lieutenant?"* His suspicions aroused, he decided to play things safe.

"How about I call you back in a few hours?" Scott said. "Would that be enough time to pull my records?"

"Plenty." Gorman answered.

Scott moved around from his desk, opened his office door and, as casually as he could manage, made his way to the coffee machine that was near Jack Noble's office. Jack was shuffling a list of prospects' names he planned to call that day.

Scott pushed up next to his desk. "I just talked to a stranger from the St. Louis Repository who knew I was a lieutenant."

Jack broke from his concentration. "Say again."

"I *said*, I just talked to a guy about getting my DD Form 214 to apply for a VA loan and he knew who I was."

"How?"

"I don't know, man."

"So, what's next?"

"I'm supposed to call him later today. He says it'll take that long for him to pull my records."

"So what are you worried about?"

"You know what I'm worried about, Jack."

"Hey, Scott, too many years went by. Forget about that shit."

"I can't."

"Well then, call the guy and get it over with. They must have buried all of the bad news by now."

"I feel," Scott searched for the word, "*unpatriotic*, realizing that I can't trust some of our own people. I still may be a threat to somebody."

"Fuck trust. If they were really looking to slam you, don't you think that they would have done it already?"

"I don't like the fact that some stranger on the telephone called me by my former rank. I didn't tell him shit, but he knew who *I was* when I only said my *name*."

"Then confess. Get it off your chest and tell everybody what you told me. What's the worst that could happen?"

"Who knows what the worst is? I still don't have my final discharge papers, and because I was in Military Intelligence I won't be finally separated until 1988. They could mess with me for a long time."

"Hey listen, Scott, you're a pretty successful stockbroker now. Go the hell forward and, for Chrissake, don't look back. Alright?"

Scott didn't reply for seconds, shook his head, stood up and slapped Jack on the shoulder. "I probably should have never pissed Captain McGuiness off at the Boston Army Base."

Jack Noble looked to finish the conversation. "Hey, buddy, I ran out of ideas for you."

Scott didn't hear him. "So I'll call Gorman this afternoon."

"Yeah, do that." Jack turned back to his prospect cards.

Instead of returning to his office, however, Scott took the elevator to the ground floor, went to get his gym bag from the trunk of his car and walked one block to the Newark "Y." He needed to discharge some tension before he made that call. After 45 minutes of racquetball and a shower, his hair was still wet when he stopped at Rita's desk before entering his office.

"Any calls?"

"Just one." She tore a single sheet from the note pad, handed it to him and he looked at the name.

"Did he leave a message?"

"Nope, and I couldn't get anything more from him. Not even his telephone number. He said all you would need was his name." She started to sound a little apologetic. "I *told* him you always want me to get a number to make it easier for you to return calls, but he said he was not a business client and you would understand."

He glanced down at the message again. It simply read: "Gorman, Ext. 2443."

"Don't worry about it, Rita. I know this guy and how to get in touch with him." He turned toward his office and started to say something when she interrupted him.

"Yeah, I know. Hold your calls."

He shut the door, moved around behind his desk and stared at his darkened terminal. He absently pushed the letter "T" and hit enter. The Bunker Ramo stock quote machine groaned to life, showing the price for AT&T in an eye- irritating green color. Without waiting to see the quote, he picked up the receiver and dialed the long distance operator for assistance. Within minutes, she had connected him to the switchboard at the Personnel Record Center, and he gave the switchboard operator the extension.

"Gorman." The man answered his phone on the first ring.

"Yes, Tom, this is Scott Regan, I spoke to…"

Tom Gorman cut him short. "I have an answer for you."

Scott was silent.

"Your records show that you have only been credited with time in the Inactive Reserve."

"Inactive Reserve?" Scott parroted. He wasn't sure what he was hearing, "I was assigned to inactive reserve because I was in 'Nam and wasn't required to continue on active reserve after my two years on active duty."

"I'll repeat again, lieutenant. There is no record that you had ever served in Vietnam, nor any record of you ever having served on active duty *anytime, anywhere, whatsoever.*" Scott became even more confused, and was on the edge of sacrificing the cover story so he could finally get a resolution to his decade long ordeal.

Scott wanted to argue with him. He wanted to tell him he had all his original records from Ft. Benning and his orders to Vietnam. He wanted to tell him about the documents he had assigning him to the Phoenix program, and his boots with Vietnam's soil still in them. He wanted to tell him about Clancy Morris's face, and Cu'o'rong's lifeless body. He wanted to say he had his medical records from the 8th Field Hospital in Cam Ranh Bay, and the 249th General Hospital in Japan; he wanted to tell him about his class "A" uniform that was rolled in a ball and thrown in the attic, yet one of the ribbons still pinned above the left breast pocket was the Vietnam Service Ribbon. Instead he asked a question.

"How did you know I was a lieutenant?"

Gorman hesitated.

"Several years ago, the National Archives here in St. Louis received a list of names on microfiche and in alphabetical order. We were instructed to scan this list every time we received an inquiry from a former serviceman about his 201 file, his medical records, or anything else pertaining to his active duty time. If his name was on the list, we were ordered to note that he contacted this department, and then forward it up the chain of command. After countless occasions of scanning the list, the names and rank of those that hadn't been checked off started to stand out. Yours was one of them. I'm surprised it took you so long to call."

"Well I just wanted to find out how I can get a copy of my DD form 214. That's the only reason I'm calling now."

"Uh, uh" Gorman uttered.

Scott continued forward with caution. "So what you're telling me is that I have no veteran benefits because I was never on active duty?"

Tom Gorman didn't directly answer him. "Mr. Regan, I can only tell you what your folder shows. I am not judging the accuracy of its contents. In addition, I have not been privy as to why this list of names was forwarded to this department to begin with, nor do I have any idea who these individuals are and what their names represent." He paused, and Scott thought he was finished speaking. He heard Gorman suck in a deep breath.

"What I *will* tell you, is if a common thread exists between everyone on this list it's this: None of the records show *any* evidence of *anyone* ever having served on active duty." Scott sensed that Gorman knew a lot more than he was telling him.

"But what about all the ribbons and medals and pictures some of these guys have?"

"I'll rephrase it, Mr. Regan." He spoke slowly and deliberately. "None of them have any *official evidence* of ever having served on active duty."

Scott ventured further in order to crystallize this crucial message. "So what you're telling me, is *if* the people on that list are considered to have never been on active duty, then any acts attributed to them while in uniform never could have happened."

"Yes." Gorman confirmed, "that *is* the intended conclusion."

Scott rubbed his head, pushed his padded chair away from the desk and stared up at the ceiling. He finally understood what this messenger was telling him, said goodbye, and hung up.

It was now time to unbolt the door. Scott's muscles started releasing tension he'd never known he'd stored, and he felt a bath washing through him, clear and cool, flushing out years of emotional sediment. He somehow managed to surface through the backside of an ocean wave and turned to see it crash, together with the ghosts, on shore without him. Contained in Gorman's message, also, was the realization that whatever secrets lay hidden in the workings of the Phoenix program would remain eternally sealed. Lieutenant Scott Regan was one of the names selectively scrubbed from the roster of Phoenix operatives, along with any evidence of his active military history. He understood that he would never be able to apply for veteran's benefits, but it seemed like a small price to pay considering the possible alternatives. In the larger scheme of things he had been only a bit player with the Program, but was now infinitely grateful to have been included, with chosen others, under its cloak of self- preservation.

Recollections of what happened in Vietnam, or what might have happened, were now coming closer to conclusion, and his thoughts would no longer be locked in the collective memory bank used only by those veterans who had served there.

He swiveled his chair to face the office window and tried to blend a barrage of emotions. He felt guilt and remorse, his dark companions for years, but also resolution and an emerging outpouring of relief, turning the strength of his muscles to loose twine. Standing, he looked down at the panorama of lush green canopies formed by oak and maple trees that flowered Military Park. With the back of his hand he rubbed his eyes to clear them and re-focus. Saline rivulets slipped off his cheeks, and not since the night he had received the news of Chan's death had he ever reacted like this to anything. Despite a rising, swelling feeling of freedom, the verdant city foliage below slowly blurred into watery, irregular shapes as his digestion finally started, and he stared at them through his tears.

EPILOGUE

1985

"Like I told you, don't you feel like a real man?" It was a natural question expressed by the pool salesman waiting for the last payment. Scott stopped by the diving board and planted his flip-flop on the stanchions supporting the springy outreach.

"Yeah, Al, you were right. It feels great." They both looked down at the blue shimmering ripples bumping against the sides of the ornately tiled wall that hugged the water in a silent embrace.

"What's the balance?" Scott opened his checkbook and the salesman, draped in a summer weight gray jacket and opened collar black silk shirt, whispered the final tally like it was their secret.

"I bet you can't wait until you have your first pool party, huh?" Scott was filling out the check and said nothing.

"If you ever need a caterer...," the salesman explored.

"Al, please, my family can cook for an army."

"Just asking," he shrugged, the light summer jacket hunching up to the middle of his head.

"Thanks for staying on top of the project." Scott pivoted and reached for Al's hand. The salesman glanced at the correct amount, slipped the check into his jacket pocket and reached out to shake.

"It was a pleasure."

"Don't thank me until the check clears, my friend."

Al looked up from the silvery-blue rhythms of the circulating water. "What? You're not a man of your word?" He reached again into his jacket pocket and fingered the edges of the check like it might have been on a string. Scott threw his arm around the man's bandy shoulders. "You did what you promised and completed the construction on time. We're having Maryanne's family next week for our first pool party—just as scheduled."

"So a caterer, then?" He pressed.

"No caterer, but I want you to come to the opening event. Bring your family."

"I'll ask my wife, Helen. She runs our social calendar and my life."

"So ask."

"I'll ask."

****

Maryanne's cousins, their teen-age daughters, uncles and aunts all arrived from Long Island and the Bronx like they were dressed for a Manhattan barbecue. Mascara, slip dresses, hair spray and spiked sandals stared at the suburban Jersey pool like it was a liquid pit waiting to rinse them of their sleek urban look. The males wore designer slacks, tailored silk shirts and circled the pool cautiously, staying safely out of the kids' splash range. Al and his wife, Helen arrived in matching cabana outfits and mingled easily with their new acquaintances.

Uncle Tony and uncle Charlie sat comfortably in the shade of towering pin oaks, as their wives brought them small plates of cheese, pulled crusty bread and sopresata. Rolls of savory smoke billowed from the Weber charcoal grill that cooked hot and sweet sausages until they were ready to be removed and nestled in a giant serving dish of sautéed peppers and onions.

Tony's granddaughter, Tina, bounded toward her grandfather and asked him to tell her a ghost story about the wind and old houses. He smiled proudly, put his plate to the side and picked her up. She sat motionless in his lap, gap-mouthed and wide-eyed as he began the spooky tale.

"Grandpa, don't tell it tooooo scary," she pleaded with feigned fright. He pulled her closer, tickling her lightly under her arm, evoking a screeching giggle.

"O.K. then. How about the vampire, graveyard and coffin story?" He asked with a poor Boris Karloff accent. "Oh, please no, Grandpa. That one always gives me bad dreams!" She secretly wanted to hear it again even though she knew it meant a head- long ghastly dash into her parent's bedroom sometime in the middle of the night. "O.K., O.K.," she changed her mind, "but whisper it so I don't get too scared." Before he started, she spotted Scott standing by the pool and talking with cousin Joe.

Heat from the searing August sun tumbled down in waves as they backed into the shade of a dogwood tree.

"Hey, Scotty, come hold my hand, Grandpa is going to tell me a ghost story," she implored.

He bubbled at her excitement and broke from Joe, moved across the yard and dragged a cooler to sit on. She grabbed his hand and held tightly as her grandfather began his story. She interrupted him just as he was starting to whisper the tale; haunting and ominous, like a disembodied spirit.

"Scott, do you get bad dreams, too?"

He paused before answering and looked around the backyard. Three neighborhood males had spotted the bedecked female teenagers and were chatting with them over the fence; the little ones barreled in and out of the pool, maintaining a constant tempest and he heard his mother-in law call out through the open kitchen window for some potholders. He returned his gaze to Tina as she continued to hold his hand.

"No, I haven't had bad dreams for years now, honey, and you know what?" He continued before she had time to answer, "I really don't think I ever will again."

Printed in the United States
113176LV00006B/65/A

9 781418 450427